WEAK SIDE

BEXLEY U

SJ SYLVIS

Weak Side
Special Edition
Copyright © 2023 S.J. Sylvis

Published: S.J. Sylvis 2023
sjsylvisbooks@gmail.com
Cover Design: Ashes and Vellichor
Editing: Jenn Lockwood Editing
Proofing: On Pointe Digital Services
ISBN: 978-8-9858020-8-5

Lil- This one is for you.

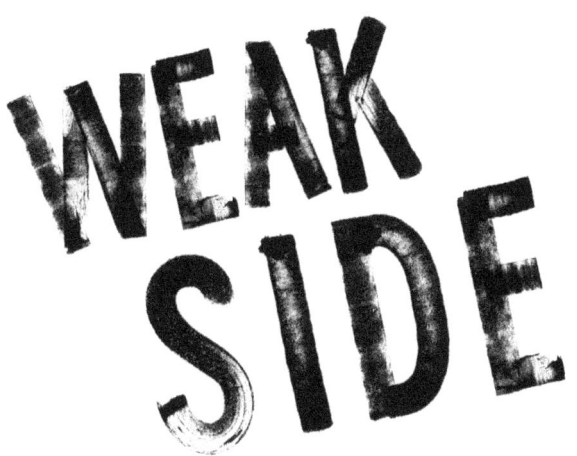

USA TODAY BESTSELLING AUTHOR

S.J. SYLVIS

CLAIRE

HOME.

The scent of pine, fresh air, and crisp autumn leaves swirled around me as I shut my eyes and breathed in the first real breath I'd been able to take in the last several months. Technically, Bexley University wasn't really considered home because it was a temporary placement. It was a four-year college, and I was in my third year. I'd only lived here eight months out of the year for the last three, but still, it felt more like a home to me than the small, run-down apartment my mother and I had shared since I was old enough to remember how to leap from one end of the hall to the other without touching the rug.

I took in another deep breath, relishing in the calmness I felt staring at the athletic dorms as I rested against my old Toyota parked behind me in the student lot. It was packed with cardboard boxes full of dorm-room knick-knacks and some dance gear. I was likely the only junior that was actually looking forward to being back at college with its chaos of midnight study seshes, not enough sleep, frat parties—not that I went to many of those, if Taytum had anything to say about it—and dorm rooms that were only big enough to do a split and nothing else, but not many students at Bexley U grew up the way I did. It was an elite college, and I was never the type of girl who belonged, hence why I was here on a partial scholarship.

As if on cue, my phone pinged, and a message came in, sending my entire spine into a steel lock. I sighed, shutting the door to my Toyota with my foot.

Mom: *Don't forget the electric is due tomorrow.*

I mumbled under my breath. "Oh yes, I could see how I could forget that *your* electric bill is due tomorrow. Thank you for the reminder to pay the electric bill that I will not be using for the next eight months."

"Talkin' to yourself again?" My shoulder got nudged lightly by Taytum as she blew a bubble with her minty gum and popped it in my face. She didn't let me answer as she dove in the backseat of my car to pull out a box of my things. "I wish you would just live with me in the sorority house. This whole living-in-the-athletic-dorms thing is lame-o."

"You know I can't join a sorority, Tay. I tried that my freshman year, and it did not go over well."

Memories of being reprimanded by the other sisters in the sorority as if I were back home with my mom slid into my brain, and I shivered on the spot. Even though I had made it through the *rushing* process, I quickly learned that I wasn't made out to be in a sorority. Between keeping my grades up so I didn't lose my scholarship, dance rehearsals, and auditions, plus working in my free time at The Bex— the local restaurant and bar on campus—so I could afford the other half of my tuition plus help my mom with bills, I just didn't have the time.

So, living in the athletic dorms was my best bet, and I was fine with it. It didn't make any difference to me.

"Yeah, but you're like a top dog now. You can do what you want, and all the littles will do whatever you need them to do. You have seniority now."

"I would never make an underclassman—"

"Sister," she corrected, pushing her adapted sorority language onto me.

I laughed as we climbed the cobblestone steps to my new dormitory. "Whatever. I wouldn't make someone else do something for me. You know that I like to do things myself."

"Oh, yes. I know. Little Miss Independent. I'm surprised you're even letting me carry one of your boxes for you."

"What are you even doing here anyway?" I asked, putting my box down by my feet to pull my phone out again. I sorted through my emails, looking for my room number that had unsurprisingly worn off from the key I was given. Bexley University was one of the oldest schools in New England, and the primeval architecture wasn't the only thing lacking in the 21st century department.

Room 213.

"I came by to snag a schedule for when the auditorium is available for practices. There's a ridiculous number of auditions this semester and one that I know you'll be interested in. If you get it, your tuition will be paid next year."

I already knew of it, and she was right. I was interested.

"I grabbed you and Jaclyn a schedule."

I sighed in relief, grabbing my box from her. "You're the

best. Thank you. Is Jaclyn living over here too? I thought she was living off campus with her boyfriend."

"She dumped him. Oh, what room are you? Maybe you guys are rooming together."

"I'm 213."

Once I got to the stairs to head to the second floor, bypassing one too many underclassmen who had no choice but to live in the athletic dorms, unlike me who chose to, I realized that Tay was no longer beside me.

"What's wrong?" I asked, lifting the box up a little higher. I could hear my pens and pencils rolling around in the bottom.

Taytum's eyebrows folded inward, and her pink lips were suddenly turned downward. "Are you sure you're in room 213?"

"Yeah." My voice dropped as she came closer to me. "Why do you look so concerned?" I started up the stairs, hoping she would follow. "Stop trying to get me to join your sorority. I don't have time for that. Some of us peasants have to work, ya know."

Taytum is one of the lucky ones, as I like to call them. You know, the ones that came from a wealthy family and had a juicy bank account that their parents liked to fill every so often so their children could focus on their academics and extracurriculars. Don't get me wrong, though, she wasn't spoiled. Taytum was smart, driven, and kinder than any friend I'd ever had. It drove her absolutely crazy that I'd never allowed her to pay for my coffee or—even worse—my books for the semester.

College books were expensive, and quite frankly, it wasn't fair. Three hundred dollars for a book that I'd use a handful of times? It was just unethical at that point.

"It's the male floor, though. My brother used to live in this dorm before he got his apartment."

I stopped walking for a split second, freezing at a standstill on the third step from the top of the stairway that led to the hall that reeked of too many different types of colognes. There was a hint of AXE body spray, and I was suddenly transported back to freshman year of high school, after Christmas break, when every boy in my grade seemed to get three gallons of it under their tree.

I hesitated before asking, "Wait, what?"

"Yeah." Taytum stepped beside me, and our eyes met. "This is the male floor. Females on floor one, males on floor two, females on floor three, and males on floor four."

"I thought this was an all-girls dorm." Skepticism began to seep through my pores, as if my skin was deprived of that very thing.

"Not Dorothy Hall. I'm pretty sure some of Emory's friends live on the second floor," Taytum whispered, moving closer to me as a skyscraper of a man jogged down the stairs, eye-fucking her for several long seconds before smirking and continuing on his way.

Heat blasted my cheeks, and I cursed under my breath. "In any other world, I would assume this was a joke, but it's me, and the world has a way of shitting on me every chance it gets."

Taytum stayed quiet as we continued on our way to our final destination, which—*surprise, surprise*—was a hallway full of jocks.

Each set of eyes swung our way, and Taytum—being the total knockout that she was and used to jocks because her older brother, Emory, played on Bexley U's hockey team—straightened her shoulders and put on her best *don't-fuck-*

with-me face as we walked in silence until we stood in front of room 213.

"Check your email again," she said, looking over at me as snickers came in every direction. I was pretty certain I heard a catcall, too, but that may have been my overactive imagination.

Instead of checking my email, I put my key in the keyhole, and sure enough, the door opened right up. Again, our eyes met, and Taytum began laughing hysterically. I, however, did not. "Are you sure you don't want to join my sorority? You get your own room."

I shot her a look of annoyance and let the door shut behind me, glancing at the glow of the lamp on the desk to the right. There were already books stacked on top and a black bag on the floor beside the somewhat lumpy bed. The comforter was navy, and you could tell right away that it was a male's room. Not a single twinkle light was hung, and everything was so *moody*.

"I've had my fair share of roomies," I started, following Taytum as she put my box on the desk opposite of the one on the right. "The emo girl who left her straightener on during our freshman year and almost burnt down the entire building. Then there was the swimmer who made everything smell like chlorine."

"And the girl who Chad hated with a passion because she tried to drag you to frat parties every weekend." Taytum threw her blonde hair into a bun on top of her head. "Oh *wait*, Chad hates everyone that gets close to you."

Taytum wasn't wrong. My boyfriend did hate everyone that got close to me. He was the jealous type, and it was my least favorite thing about him.

"Anyway," I interrupted her, moving past the discussion

of Chad, who Taytum loathed. "I've never had a male roomie, so this has got to be a first."

"And a mistake," Taytum clarified, putting her hands on her hips. "Is that even allowed? I mean, we're all adults here, but I don't think males and females room together at Bex U. Other colleges? Maybe. But at Bex U?

"You need to go talk to admissions before you move any more boxes in here. It had to have been a mistake. Come on." She took the box from my hands and put it on the desk. Then her hands found my shoulders, and she spun me around and pushed me out the door. "I'll go with you in case they try to walk all over your sweet little personality."

"I can be stern when I need to be."

Taytum rolled her eyes. "Mmhm. Let's go. I can be there for moral support if you so deem it appropriate that you handle this yourself like you do every other situation in your life."

She and I walked down the hall, ignoring every male who looked as if they belonged in a locker room instead of a dormitory, half of them glistening in sweat from a practice or workout, and the other half looking like they were ready to go to the club at 2 p.m. on a Tuesday afternoon.

CLAIRE

AFTER GOING through the five stages of grief, acceptance finally made itself known, just like the pit in my stomach.

"You are welcome to live off campus, Claire. But unfortunately, this is something that cannot be fixed right now."

"What do you mean it can't be fixed? She's been going to this school for three years. How do you just randomly screw up her name?"

I scrolled back to my email and held back another defeated laugh as I read the information given.

Name: Bryant Claire (Partial Scholarship - Performing Arts/Dance)
Major: Art of Dance
Minor: English
Dorm: Dorothy Hall, Room 213

"Tay, it is what it is," I said, wiping my sweaty hands on my jeans.

The admissions officer gave me a tired smile, obviously feeling bad. "Is there any way you could live off campus? Or maybe stay with a friend? Just until someone drops out and we have room for you in another dorm?" She eyed Taytum, probably indicating that I should stay with her, which wouldn't be possible, considering she lived in a sorority house.

I shook my head and stood up, pulling on Taytum's arm so she would come with me. Dizziness made the room spin, and sweat started to trickle at my hairline. Panic was starting to creep in, and I didn't have time to deal with it.

"I'm so sorry, Claire. I'll keep looking for an opening, okay?"

I nodded, knowing that the admissions officer was likely too busy with her normal job duties to continue looking to solve *my* problem. The second Taytum and I were out of her office, I breathed in the fresh air and began to compartmentalize the last hour and moved onto the next order of business.

"I've gotta get to work," I said, walking toward my car.

"Whoa. That's it? You're just accepting this?"

"There's nothing I can do about it," I answered simply. "You heard her. There aren't any openings, and you and I both know I cannot afford to live off campus. Everything is taken by now anyway unless I want to rent a room from some creep that wants to peep at me through a hole in the wall. School starts in less than a week. I don't have time for this."

It wasn't like I was out of touch with coping with difficult things in my life or unaccepting of things that made me uncomfortable. It was how I was raised. Nothing came easy to a Bryant—my mother's words, not mine—but they still rang true.

Taytum's mood was agitated at best. Her arms crossed over her chest as she stomped beside me to my car. "This is such bullshit. How do they just fuck up your name and put you in a male's dorm?"

Stealing the extra hair tie off Taytum's wrist, I pulled my hair into a high pony and stripped out of my jacket before throwing on my work t-shirt with the words *The Bex* plastered across my boobs. I reached into my backseat and grabbed another box as Taytum continued to rant and rave before she pulled on my arm at the entrance to the dorms.

"What about Chad?"

"What about him? Why isn't he helping me move my boxes?" I grimaced internally, hating that I had to explain his behavior all the time. "He was supposed to. He isn't answering his phone."

"No, no. Why don't you move in with him? Doesn't he have some fancy apartment over on Bex Street?"

I clenched my teeth together, feeling my cheeks ripen. Even though Taytum had been my friend since freshman year when we were paired together in the yearly performing arts show for the duo contemporary dance, I still felt like the smallest pebble beneath our shoes, making excuses for my four-year boyfriend.

"Oh, we talked about it already."

"And?" Her eyebrows raised as she waited for my answer.

I shrugged. "He said he wanted to focus on his senior project."

"His senior project?" she questioned, making my thoughts spiral right along with hers. "What's it called? *How to create some stupid fucking equation on how to be a douche to your girlfriend?*"

I laughed out loud and shook my head. "Yeah, something like that."

The door opened, and I stepped inside, resting my backside against it. "Look, I've gotta get my shit in here and then head to work. We have a meeting tomorrow for this year's show and auditions, right? I'll see you then?"

"Yes, but this conversation is not over." She backed away slowly before glancing at me one more time and smiling. "I hope your new roomie is hot as fuck so Chad regrets"—she raised her hands and used air quotes—"focusing on his senior project."

I laughed and let the door shut, ignoring the burn that came with just about every interaction with my boyfriend and any conversation about him. *Compartmentalize, Claire.*

"Right, don't have time for this," I said aloud, moving past a group of girls bouncing back and forth from their rooms, showing off their cute girly twinkle lights and comparing their schedules.

The walk to my dorm felt like three million years instead of the thirty seconds it actually took. Every male that was standing aimlessly on the second floor suddenly smelled the aroma of a female. Heads swung and their faces were a mix of smirks and confusion. One even rolled his eyes as the muscles along his temples flickered back and forth, as if I were doing something wrong by unlocking the door to my new dorm.

As soon as I shut the door behind me, I gulped up the air of the small room and shook my shoulders out as I placed another one of my boxes on the floor. *This was a disaster.* I could already feel Chad's jealous rage against my skin, and he didn't even know the situation yet. And yes, I could ask him—yet again—if we could move in together, but what did that say about our relationship if he only agreed because he was jealous that I was living in a room with another male? Pity was something that pricked my skin like a thousand bee stings, and I didn't take it well.

Walking over to the small sink, I splashed water on my face and glanced at my expression in the mirror, seeing the forfeit written all over it. My high cheekbones were flushed with frustration, and little chestnut-colored tendrils hung around my face, showing me just how much of a mess I truly was. My light-blue eyes were defeated, and the dark bags underneath were a reminder that I needed more sleep than I was getting. But with being back at Bexley U, studying, keeping up with my performing arts scholarship—which was something I quite literally couldn't afford to lose—working, and helping my mom pay the bills back home, sleep was about to be one of the last things on my list.

I sighed before turning around and resting against the sink, staring at the opposite side of the room. Like any normal girl in her early twenties, I dreaded the fact that I was about to be living with a male. I'd never lived with a male. My father? Nonexistent. Mom's boyfriends over the years? Never lasted more than a few months. I'd stayed the night with Chad over the years, but Chad wasn't your typical college-aged boy. He was clean, tidy, and *very* type-A. I was on the athletic floor, and if the giant gloves that were airing out on top of his desk that had a distinctive scent to them had anything to say about him, I'd say my new roomie was a hockey player.

Great. A big ol' jock.

To be fair, his side of the room wasn't really messy. That could mean he just got here like the rest of us, or maybe he wasn't as bad as I was making him out to be. His bed was lumpy, the covers laying oddly. But other than that, things were in their rightful place.

Maybe it wouldn't be so bad.

I nodded to myself in acceptance, turned to the mirror, and began messing with my hair before my shift. But just as quickly as I put my back to my new roommate's bed, I jumped at the high-pitched shriek and spun back around.

"Get out!"

Stunned, frozen, and a bit pissed off, I slapped my hands over my eyes, and I took back every rational thought I had in accepting the predicament I had just found myself in.

"What the hell!" I screeched, putting my back to the girl.

Excuse me. The *naked* girl.

"Get out right now, you... You... You...slut!"

Did she just call *me* a slut? I wasn't sure if it was the realization that my life was a joke or if it was because I was so incredibly thrown off by the set of boobs in my face, but all of a sudden, a laugh bubbled up from deep within my stomach, and I continuously laughed until the door to the dorm opened up. The light from the hallway filtered in, illuminating me, along with the Playboy wannabe, to an audience full of smirking guys—one of whom was likely my new roommate.

He wasn't even fully in the room yet, and I was already sweating in my spot. He was tall and had broad shoulders and a jawline that belonged in a magazine. He called over his shoulder, his voice smooth but still lingering with an edge of humor. "Why are you all acting like you want to fuck me?"

The very second he turned the rest of the way into the room, my stomach dipped so swiftly that I couldn't even pretend that it didn't happen. His light-green eyes full of mirth settled on me, and I had to blink past my loss of words. A pocket formed in between his eyebrows a moment later as confusion took over, and silence stretched around us until his gaze shifted over to the naked girl in his bed.

"Out." His strong arms crossed over his damp, gray t-shirt, and he suddenly seemed taller with the air of authority that surrounded him with his single demand—as if he were used to getting his way.

"I was here first!" Naked Barbie pushed her boobs out, trying to gain his attention. Which worked. *Typical.* "And I came prepared." Her voice resembled a whiny child's, but I was pretty sure she was trying to be arousing.

I laughed again before turning away. I silently cursed the luck I seemed to have in every situation I found myself in. "Is this a joke?"

"How did you two get in here?" The jock walked over to the girl and covered her up with his blanket. "Where are your clothes? Get dressed. And get out."

"What?" She pouted. "You want me to get dressed?!"

"I want you..."—he glanced at me, running his gaze down my body quickly, which had me straightening my shoulders, as if I needed to prove something to him—"puck bunnies to get the hell out of my room. How did you even find out where I was rooming? Was it Rusty? I'm going to fucking kill him."

My arms flew down by my sides, and I stepped forward, inserting my refusal to be grouped into the same category as the naked girl in his bed. "I am not a puck bunny!" I shouted.

His green eyes swung back over to me, and he looked at me the same way Chad looked at me when I talked about opening my own dance studio one day—which, by the way, he found completely baffling.

"Then, who are you? And why are you in my room?"

He looked back at Barbie and nearly growled, "Get dressed."

My stern voice grew soft as I tried to lessen the blow that had nearly knocked me down an hour prior when I realized the situation I was in. "I'm Claire. Your new roommate."

[3]

THEO

I COULD HEAR the laughter echoing in the hallway, even with my door shut. My traps ached, and the sweat on my back that had dried from my earlier workout was now beginning to form again as anger gnawed on my nerves.

"I'm Claire. Your new roommate."

My head swung to the tiny but mighty brunette standing off to the side, who was fully dressed and not at all your typical puck bunny. It pleased me that she was so perturbed when I labeled her as such that I kind of wanted to do it again, just to see her tiny nose scrunch and her cheeks blaze with an angry heat, but I was honestly too blinded by the words that had just spewed from her mouth that I couldn't do anything but gape.

"Excuse me?" I said, fully ignoring the huffs and puffs coming from the *actual* puck bunny. She sounded like the fucking wolf from *The Three Little Pigs*.

"This"—Claire waved her hand over to the naked chick —"isn't going to work if I'm going to be rooming with you."

"What the hell are you talking about?"

"I'd like to know the same."

My voice turned to ice as I pointed to the blonde. "Get out. You and the rest of campus knows that you don't get to come into my room unless invited, and I didn't invite you."

Her lips parted, and usually, I'd feel bad at the sign of hurt on a girl's face, or I'd sugarcoat my words, but it seemed she needed a little dose of humility. Thankfully, a moment later, she threw on her clothes and took her lack of self-respect with her when she rushed out the room. Before the door shut again, I heard a couple of guys yelling, "Good choice, Wolf!" which indicated that every guy on the floor saw *both* girls go into my room, and not a single one of them had warned me.

Assholes.

I kept my eyes pinned on Claire, wondering what the mix-up was. Roommate? She was out of her fucking mind if she thought she was my new roommate.

"You obviously have your signals crossed if you think you're my new roommate, babe." I pulled my sweaty shirt over my head and tossed it in the hamper in the corner of my room, putting my back to her. I bent down and pulled out a fresh black tee from my bag and spun around, holding the cotton in my hand. "You're far too tiny to be a male." I slid my attention away from her heartbreaker eyes and landed on her small waist. *Definitely not a penis in those tight jeans.*

When I raised my gaze back to hers, I prepared myself for the punch that would soon follow with it. I wouldn't deny it—she was pretty in the way that most girls weren't. Subtle, delicate features but eyes that made your chest tight. *Not my type, though.* She was the type of girl that hated guys like me. It was obvious in the way she was glaring.

"My signals aren't crossed. Admissions switched my first and last name—instead of Claire Bryant, they have me as Bryant Claire—so they put me in a male dorm, and I've already talked to them. There isn't anything else available, so yeah, I'm your roommate."

"No."

Her arms crossed over her chest, and that was when I read her shirt. *The Bex*. Did she work there? Why hadn't I noticed her before?

"Do you think I'm lying? First, you assume I'm a puck bunny, and now you think I'm lying. Do you think I *want* to room with you?"

I opened my mouth to say something, but her little mumble caught me off guard.

"Typical fucking jock."

"What was that?" I asked, inching closer to her.

"Listen." Her hands flew to her hips, and her cheeks were pinker than before. "I've gotta go to work, so you'll have some time to adjust. I'll be back later if you'd like to insult me some more."

Damn, she's feisty.

I laughed as I finally snapped back to attention and pulled my shirt over my head. Her eyes dipped to my defined stomach before she quickly looked away and grabbed her phone and keys off the desk opposite of mine.

"This will be taken care of by the time you get back from your shift."

She paused with her back to me. "I've already tried to take care of it. There are no more open rooms. It is what it is."

Apparently, she was used to accepting things even if they weren't going her way.

"Not to be arrogant, but I have some pull in this school, Bryant. This will be taken care of."

Her eyes sharpened into diamonds. "My name is Claire, and I know you're used to getting your way, but I'm pretty sure there is nothing you can do to fix this except move into your own place. So, I will see you later."

Then, the door opened, and she left, leaving standing there in surprise because, for the first time in my life, I met a girl who didn't fall over her own feet to talk to me.

⸺

The cool air of the hockey rink always brought out a side of me that I kept hidden until the ice was beneath my skates and my hands were holding onto my hockey stick. Everything else faded away. The only thing I focused on was the little black puck that moved effortlessly against the slick glaze of the rink, and I felt comfortable, even if there were thousands of people's eyes on me.

I broke away from the play and stole the puck from Landon, who was the last man standing between me and Emory, our starting goalie. At the very last second, I slipped to the right before lifting the puck up, glove side, just out of his line of sight. The sound of the puck on the post was like a drug to me. I continued skating, circling behind the net before heading back toward center ice.

"Nice, bro." I tapped gloves with my best friend and teammate, Aasher, as he complimented my goal. "What's all the anger for, though?" he asked. "The puck pretty much had fire on it."

I took my helmet off as Coach blew the whistle, ending

practice. I skated toward the bench beside Aasher to head into the locker room. "I'm not angry. Just annoyed. Found a puck bunny in my bed after conditioning earlier."

"Nice, did you tap that?"

I shot him a glare. "No, I told her to get the fuck out of my room. Now, every puck bunny is gonna know where my room is. I was trying to keep that shit on lockdown this season." This was easily the most important season of my college career. I didn't need any extra drama.

"You need to move into an apartment—one with a security guard."

I shot him another look. Aasher knew why I wasn't living in an apartment off campus. Sure, I was at Bexley U on a full scholarship, and I had basically built the hockey team from my freshman year up until now, but it wasn't like Bexley U paid me a salary for playing. My name was known, but I didn't have a paid scholarship as a college student, and under no circumstances would I *ever* allow my parents to pay for me to live off campus just so I could get away from the girls who were desperate for a way to fame by hanging off my arm or being naked underneath me.

"Or...I don't know. Maybe these girls need to have more self-respect."

He laughed, beginning to remove his pads in the locker room along with the rest of the team. "Can't blame them. You're the Wolf."

"Ow oww." Landon took his towel and slapped my padded ass, and I grabbed it out of his hand and threw it in his face.

"That's not the whole reason I'm annoyed, though. On top of this chick being naked in my bed, there was another girl in my room too."

"I heard. It's all over campus. Not one but *two* puck bunnies in your room on move-in day."

My upper pads were off, and I sat down to remove the snow from the blade with my fabric skate guards before putting them in my stall. "Oh, is that what people are saying?"

"Who was that, anyway? The other girl? The one who walked down the hall and didn't look a single one of us in the eye?" I glanced up to Dax, who stayed a few rooms down from mine. "She didn't seem like a puck bunny. I've never seen her before."

"Was she hot?" Aasher asked.

Dax answered, "She wasn't just hot. She was the type you took home to Ma and Pops."

I interrupted Dax and Aasher's conversation. "She isn't a puck bunny. She said she's my new roommate, which is exactly why I have to go talk to Coach. I guess admissions fucked up and switched her last and first name."

Nearly every one of my teammates laughed. Landon blew a breath out of his mouth before smirking. "I would room with her. Wanna switch roommates? I'm down."

"Down to fuck," Aasher grunted.

"If you saw her, you'd say the same."

Like a rubber band being snapped, I glared at my teammates. "How about this is our senior year, and instead of thinking about fucking girls, you think about winning the championship."

"Wolf!" I turned at the sound of Coach's voice bellowing out my campus nickname. "Let's go. I'm late for dinner, and you know my wife hates it when I'm late."

I finished throwing on my regular clothes, pulled my black beanie down on my head, and walked into Coach's office. "What's the problem, Wolf? Is this about the puck bunnies? I can't do anything about that, and honestly, maybe it would do you some good to let off some steam, son. Not that I don't enjoy you flinging pucks like you have your own personal vendetta against them, but you seemed distracted today."

I shouldn't have been surprised at how quickly the news spread around Bex U. This was my senior year, and it had been like this ever since we won the championship three years ago. But *fuck*, it had only been a few hours.

"No. Well, yes." I flung myself into the chair at the foot of his desk and glanced at the whiteboard behind his head with his messy dry-erase scribbles all over it. "One of them wasn't a puck bunny."

For the second time in the last ten minutes, I explained the situation to Coach, and he immediately called the dean and set up a meeting. Then, he called his wife and made *me* explain the situation so she wouldn't yell at him for being late to dinner.

I understood the logic. Karen loved me and the team like we were her own sons.

"Stop at your room and grab the girl. I want her there for the meeting so we can sort this out."

"I believe she's at The Bex, working."

Coach didn't even look at me as he began pulling on his Bexley U windbreaker. "Well, then go get her. I'll meet you both at the dean's office." Coach was a no-bullshit type of guy. He got the job done when it needed to be done. That was why he was ranked as one of the best coaches in the NCAA hockey division. Before leaving his office with his keys in hand, he turned and looked at me. "We will get this sorted. I have a good angle for this problem. The dean isn't going to let our star hockey player get distracted."

"I don't get distracted that easily," I countered, agitated that he even implied such a thing.

"Let's go, Wolf."

Sighing, I jumped up from the chair, adjusted my beanie, and followed him out the door.

[4]

CLAIRE

BALLET DANCERS WERE USED to being on their feet. I'd been a dancer since I was old enough to walk, and although it wasn't my dream to become a professional ballet dancer or to be on Broadway one day, my mother ran with the idea and pushed me into every dance class the studio offered, even if it did cost us an arm and a leg—and oftentimes, the electric.

Still, my feet were aching in my tennies, and I knew my arm would be sore tomorrow from carrying the trays of food to what seemed like every single student at Bexley U. The Bex was the most popular hangout spot for college students, and the tips were decent, but we had been slammed for most of my shift, and after my day, I was over it. My phone buzzed for the fifth time in the last twenty minutes, and I ignored it, knowing one text was my mother with her reminder of the electric bill being due tomorrow, and the other four were from Chad, wondering why I wasn't answering his messages right away even though he hardly ever responded to mine.

"I'm not gonna lie. I didn't miss the rush of move-in day. Not one bit."

A small laugh left me as I placed table four's food on my tray. My arm was a little shaky, and my pulse was thumping from running back and forth from the dining area to the kitchen. "It's dying down," I said back to my boss. "The tips have been good today, at least." I smiled as I rushed past her, placing the food down on the table to a family of four.

"Thank you, honey." The father of what I assumed to be a freshman smiled at me. "Do you attend Bexley U? Or do you just work here?"

Putting the tray underneath my arm, I glanced at the table to make sure their drinks were full and everything was correct with their orders. "Oh, yes. I attend. This is my third year." I glanced over to the girl who had a healthy amount of admiration on her features as she peered up at me with her innocent eyes. I smiled at her. "Is this your first year?"

She nodded, and I watched as her chest rose with a tight breath. "You're going to love it here," I encouraged, trying to make her feel a little better. College was intimidating to an eighteen-year-old, and if her family was anything like they appeared, she was going to be homesick the moment they left.

"Thanks." Her voice was soft as she grabbed a French fry and dipped it into the small cup of ranch. "Were you nervous your freshman year too?"

Not even a little bit. The thought of being on my own and not having to worry over if our electric was going to be shut off or the water was going to suddenly be ice cold after dance practice was more than pleasing.

"Absolutely," I lied. "We all are. If you ever need anything, I'm Claire. I'm here most weekends, okay?" I winked at her, and the softness in her mother's eyes sent a gust of warmth through me. She mouthed the words, 'Thank you,' as I backed away and headed to the kitchen. I smiled and turned around to take a breather when I suddenly bounced off a hard wall.

"Umph." My hand went to my forehead as my tray slipped from my grasp. Before it fell to the ground and caused the entire establishment to stare at me, someone caught it at the same time their other hand landed on my upper arm.

"For as tiny as you are, you sure do hold your own." His smooth chuckle raked over my heated skin, and my gaze flung to his, freezing my senses for a second.

My mouth opened as he handed back the tray and towered over me like a skyscraper. Before I could say anything, my new roommate glanced around The Bex and nodded to a few people before leaning into my space. "When is your shift over?"

"Why?" My question was blunt and bordered on rude, but I was confused and a little agitated that everyone was staring at us. Typical jock of Bexley U, though. They drew attention everywhere they went.

"We have a meeting with the dean."

And just like that, all the heat in my body vanished, and I was left with a dry mouth and cold, clammy skin. "No." I shook my head after clearing my throat. "I mean, why?"

I did not have an issue with authority. I was a star student throughout grade school and high school, and my dance teachers adored me because I was a rule follower by nature. The thought of disappointing anyone, even my mother, sent me into a straight spiral, but this? Meeting with Dean Chiffon? *This* was an issue.

"Trying to fix our little problem, Bryant."

Too stunned by the recent memory of the last time I had come into contact with the dean, I couldn't even act irritated that he called me Bryant instead of Claire.

"Claire?" Angie, my boss, slowly approached us. "Everything okay?" She eyed my new roommate before shifting her confused gaze to me. "Is something wrong?"

"Oh, um."

"Hi. I'm—"

"Theo." Angie smiled. "Yes, I know who you are. My son is obsessed with you. I'm taking him to your first game this season for his birthday." I stood back and angled my chin up toward my roommate. *Theo. Theo Brooks.* No wonder there was a naked girl in his bed. His name was plastered everywhere at Bexley U. Even *I* knew his name, which was impressive because I stayed far away from anything sports related.

"Oh, really?" Theo's smile caught my eye, and I'll admit, it was a nice one. "If I see you in the stands, I'll try to skate over and give him a puck. Do you think he'd like that?"

Angie's eyes widened. "Do I think he'd like that? It would be the best birthday present ever."

I slowly began to back away from their conversation, knowing I had tables that likely needed my attention. And quite frankly, I wanted to escape from this meeting with the dean. *Maybe if I just slowly disappear, he won't notice.*

"Where are you going?" Theo's hand went around my arm, and he shot me a look. "When do you get off work?"

"I–"

"What's going on? Do you need to get off a little early, Claire?" Angie was prepared to lay out the red carpet for Theo even though I was shooting her a look that said, *Save me.*

"We have a meeting with the dean. They screwed up the dorms, and Claire is apparently my new roommate, so we need to fix the problem."

"What?" Angie snatched the tray out from under my arm. "Claire. Why didn't you tell me? Go ahead. I'll cover the rest of your tables. It's almost time for your shift to be over anyway. You can still keep your tips, don't worry."

"Perfect." Theo looked down at me, seeming pleased with himself.

I mumbled a thank you to Angie and quickly went to the back and grabbed my keys and phone, mentally preparing myself for the awkward meeting.

I was in the middle of relishing in the cool air against my sweaty skin as I came to an abrupt stop. Theo turned around with his keys dangling in his large hand, apparently waiting for me. "Do you need a ride?"

"I really don't think I need to be present for this meeting," I said instead of answering him. This time, my voice held a wealth of conviction in it.

Theo's head tilted slightly as if he were trying to figure me out. "Why is it an issue? If it gets you into a different dorm room, who cares?"

I walked over to my car, leaving Theo standing behind me with his question lingering in the air around us. "Because I've already tried once to change rooms. What's the point in trying again? It's not going to make a difference if I'm there. You're the one who is used to getting their way. Remember? You have *pull* in this school."

Another smooth chuckle left his mouth, and I centered in on his lips before looking away and putting my key into my car door and opening it. The creak of my hinges cut through the tension, and I breathed out through my nose, trying to calm down. Theo said nothing as he watched me climb into my crappy Toyota.

"Are you done with your fit?" he asked, putting one arm on top of my car and his other on the door. He leaned down and raised his eyebrows at me, waiting for my answer.

My car rumbled to life, and I nodded curtly, tucking a loose hair from my ponytail behind my ear. He tapped the top of my car twice before winking. "Good. I'll follow you. You know where the dean's office is, yeah?"

"Mmhm," I said before he shut my door.

I glanced in my mirror and watched as he jogged back to his car, which, surprisingly, wasn't some hot rod. It wasn't nearly as old as my car, but it wasn't anything spectacular either.

Unfurrowing my brows, I pulled out of my parking spot and prepared myself for the absolute and utter embarrassment that would soon follow after walking into Dean Chiffon's office and coming face to face with him again.

5

THEO

Coach's car was already parked off to the side when Claire and I arrived at the administrative center which had Dean Chiffon's name centered on the sign in gold lettering. Claire's door of her rusty Toyota screeched loudly as I shut mine and walked up beside her.

She carried herself well. Her determined chin was pulled up high, showing off the soft curve of her jaw. Her hands were a little shaky as she pushed a couple of loose pieces of hair away, showing off the smallest diamond studs in her ears.

"You nervous or something?" I asked, curious as to why she was so tense. Maybe it was just her personality, but when I watched her at The Bex, she seemed relaxed—and a little mesmerizing, if I were being totally honest.

When I had walked into The Bex, I spotted her before the door even shut behind me. She was talking with one of her tables after placing their food down, and there was a softness that came with her interactions. She smiled as she talked, and then she winked at the woman, and it somehow had my feet moving toward her as if they had their own agenda.

"I'm fine."

Her answer was clipped as I opened the door for her. She walked in first, and I followed closely behind. Coach's gruff laugh snagged my attention, and I suddenly took the lead, letting Claire follow me the rest of the way.

I rapped my knuckles on the dean's open door, and both men turned their attention to me, faces lighting up like a scoreboard. "Theo. Come on in. Coach Lennon just sat down. We were talking about the schedule of games this year."

"Ah, yeah. It's going to be tough, but I'm confident."

The wrinkles along the dean's face deepened as he laughed, but his laugh quickly faded when Claire stepped in behind me. Her chin was tilted down, and her eyes were locked on the shiny floor. I switched my attention back and forth between her and the dean, and my thoughts began spinning.

Did it suddenly just get cold in here?

My question was, who had the vendetta with who and why?

"Claire." The dean nodded to her, and her lips smashed together as her arms crossed over her chest. I took note that she stayed by the door instead of sitting down beside me in the other chair at the foot of his desk.

"So," Coach started, "the reason I called for the meeting is because there has been a little bit of a mix-up."

"A mix-up?" the dean asked, glancing at me for a moment before moving back to Coach.

I leaned forward and took charge. "Admissions messed

up Claire's name, and they have her as my roommate in Dorothy Hall."

"Ah." Dean Chiffon placed his elbows on his tidy desk and steepled his fingers together. "Yes. I am aware of the issue. I hadn't realized it was your room, Theo."

"So, it suddenly makes a difference that it's *his* room? But when I had a problem with it, it didn't matter?"

Claire had a point, but I stayed silent as she stole the room with her sudden surge of confidence.

"You didn't come to me with the problem, Claire." Dean Chiffon placed his hands on his desk and slowly moved his attention to her. "Although, I do understand why you didn't come to me, and I am pleased that you didn't try to use your mother's problem-solving skills."

Claire's face flared with heat, and I could hear her teeth grinding against one another. *Well, this is getting interesting.*

"You can see why this is an issue." Coach's sudden need to get this over with was abrupt. "He can't room with a female—especially one like her."

"'Like *her*'? What does that mean?" she asked, stepping forward and looking Coach directly in the face.

I was wondering the same thing. *Where is he going with this?*

"Well, sweetheart. You'd be quite the distraction, I'm afraid." His eyes raked down her body quickly before averting his gaze.

"Distraction?"

"Coach," I warned.

I turned my attention back to the dean and tried to prevent where the conversation was headed. "Is there anything we can do about this? Are there any rooms available for either of us to change?"

"There aren't any rooms available according to admissions. They brought the issue to me to make sure I was aware, but it's, unfortunately, just one of those things."

Coach leaned forward and looked at Claire. "Why don't you move off campus?"

"Um..." Claire's lip disappeared beneath her teeth as she nibbled on it.

I felt sorry for her. I did. Three sets of eyes were on her, and I could see the apprehension there as she thought over what to say and what was to come.

"She can't afford it." The dean cleared his throat. "Trust me." A rush of anger skimmed over my skin at the way he belittled her. It wasn't necessarily about her, per se, but the fact that he'd look down on someone for not being filthy rich rubbed me the wrong way.

"You know what"—I stood up, feeling agitated with the air in the room—"it's fine."

"The hell it is," Coach said.

"With all due respect," I started, trying to ease into the conversation with my coach, who quite literally held my future in his hands. "I'm a little offended that you think I'd let a female distract me. In the last three years, have I ever been so distracted..."—*by pussy* is what I wanted to say, but I kept that to myself—"over a girl that I made a wrong move on the ice? Or lost a game, for that matter?"

"Well—"

"Please don't force me to move off campus." We all turned to Claire, and although she appeared confident, I saw the way her blue eyes shined with a gloss that wasn't there before. "The dean is right. I can't afford it." Her gaze hardened as she looked over at Coach. "But you're wrong if you think I'll be a distraction. Jocks aren't my type. In fact"—she looked at me for a brief second—"I despise them."

Silence stretched around us, and after a few long seconds, Claire threw her hands up. "If it's really that big of a deal, I'll just live in my freakin' car. Honestly, I'd do just about anything to get out of this conversation."

Her back was turned to all of us as she left the office, and her silent departure thankfully cooled my senses before I said something I regretted. Coach and Dean Chiffon were still trying to brainstorm, wondering if they could somehow find a way to get me my own apartment so I didn't have to room with Claire. It wasn't that big of a deal. Sure, it would be nice to have my own space and room with another hockey player, but they didn't know me at all if they thought I would allow something so minor to cause me to throw away my future.

"You heard her." I stood up, hoping to catch Claire before her junky Toyota sped off in the distance while dispersing a thick aroma of gasoline in the air. "Jocks aren't her type, and to be honest, she isn't my type either." I peered down at Coach and his relaxed posture in the chair next to mine. "And even if she was, do you think I'd let her ruin my future? You know that's not me, Coach. I'll see you tomorrow at practice. Goodnight, Dean."

Fucking asshole, I thought to myself as I left his office. Ridiculing someone because of their economic status was pathetic. I was raised to be non-judgmental, and if the dean would pull his head out of his ass, he'd know that I wasn't in the highest economic group either.

The cool air of the evening came rushing toward me as I pulled the door open. "Claire, hold up," I said, rushing down the cobblestone steps. Her back was to me, and her phone was up to her ear.

I slowed my steps as I approached her car, realizing that she didn't hear me. She was talking a mile a minute, but I turned my head and caught every word leaving her mouth.

"I could die right now." There was a short pause, and I assumed whoever she was talking to had said something, because a clipped laugh left her that lingered with sarcasm. "Of course he brought it up. Leave it to my mother to try and seduce the dean to pay for my tuition. I was so embarrassed." Her voice rose as she gulped in a breath of air. "And somehow, my mom was able to make me feel guilty for not appreciating her selflessness."

Shocked at what I just heard climbing from her mouth, I took a step forward and cursed the loose gravel that crunched underneath my shoe. Claire quickly spun around, and the gloss in her eye from before was now ice, and if she didn't already hate me, she definitely hated me now. It was a little entertaining when she glared at me, though. It riled me up for some reason.

Her phone call ended a second later, and she opened her creaky car door and threw her phone inside, as if it were to blame for the situation we found ourselves in. "Did you find a solution? Or should I go ahead and grab a pillow and blanket and make a bed in the backseat?"

Placing my hands in the pockets of my jeans, I shrugged, holding back a cheeky grin. "That depends."

Her glare narrowed. "On...?"

"On if you snore."

Her small nose wrinkled, and I winked at her. "See ya at home, Bryant."

An exasperated breath caused a cloud of mist to float from her parted lips, and I smiled deviously as I walked back to my car.

6

CLAIRE

I ᴛᴏᴏᴋ the long way to the dorms from Dean Chiffon's office, which only added forty seconds onto my trip, but the need to wind down before being trapped in a small space with Bexley U's most popular hockey player was the most pressing thing at the moment.

My head was throbbing from stress. I rubbed my temples gently as I let the cool air seep into my car from my open door—because every time I used my window, it got stuck, and the last thing I needed was to wake up and have rain or snow covering my seat. I had *just* gotten the smell of mildew out of the carpet from the last time that had happened.

"Why aren't you answering your phone?"

My hand flew to my heart as I jumped in my seat. My seatbelt locked up as I turned and looked at Chad, who had pulled up right beside me in his black BMW. "Gosh, Chad! You scared me."

A short chuckle came from him as he began rolling up

his window. He stepped out of his car a moment later, placing his black-rimmed glasses on the dash before shutting his door, seemingly waiting for me to exit mine.

There was no, *"Hey, baby. How was work?"* Instead, it was a deep scowl and an annoyance flowing from his stance that I could sense the second I met his eyes.

"Where have you been?"

I crossed my arms over my Bex shirt. "I could ask you the same. You were supposed to help me move into the dorms, remember?"

He rolled his eyes, and the feeling of loss caused me to stare at the pavement below our feet. It hadn't always been like this with Chad. I could still taste the tender sweetness of his mouth on mine from years ago, when he was gentle with me and kind. Now, he was only like that when he wanted something from me—like the security of a girlfriend who he knew was selfless.

Standing in front of him, I was reminded of the situation I was in. Every time I felt a brush of his skin against mine, a faint threat came soon after, reminding me of the war zone that I often forgot I was in the middle of. My mom's face flashed before mine, and the thought of ruining everything she worked so hard for was like a shot to my chest.

"Claire." The impatient sound of Chad's tone snapped me out of my stupor. "You know that I'm busy. I told you I might not be able to help you move in." I said nothing as he checked his watch. "Where have you been? Did you just get off work? It's a little late to be working, isn't it?"

A soft laugh left me. "It's only eight, Chad. Some of us have to make money."

He rolled his eyes. "One day, you won't have to worry about money. You'll be living under my roof."

"Actually..." I treaded lightly, feeling unsteady on my feet. I cringed internally because I wasn't as docile as I acted. I was only like this with Chad, and I hated to admit it, but I knew he liked me like this. He enjoyed having the upper hand, and he enjoyed thinking I'd have to rely on him one day. He and his family scoffed at my dreams of having my own career. It honestly didn't get more anti-feminist than that, did it?

The sound of cars pulling into the student parking lot left my ears as the words spewed from my mouth. "There was a mix up at admissions, so they put me on a male floor."

"What? What do you mean?"

I crossed my arms over my chest as a gust of wind surrounded us. I paused before ripping the Band-Aid off. "I mean...my roommate is a guy."

His brow furrowed, and his thick dark eyelashes fluttered as he took in the information. "You're rooming with a guy?"

I nodded. "Yeah. And you know I can't afford to live off campus." *Remember? We already chatted about this, and you turned me down when I suggested we move in together.*

"Definitely not," he agreed. "So...who is it? Do I know him?"

"You probably know of him." I put my back to him and began grabbing a box from my backseat, knowing that I was unfortunately stuck rooming with Theo. Disappointment ran through my veins, but I was so used to the feeling that it was like my blood type. "He is the star hockey player of Bexley U."

Chad rubbed his jaw, seeming impatient. "You know I don't follow sports. They're a waste of time."

The one thing Chad and I had in common? Neither one of us was big on sports. It wasn't that I thought the game was silly or fruitless, because that would make me a hypocrite, thinking someone else's passion wasn't important, like Chad often did with mine. But I'd admit, I had a bitterness for jocks. Between my mother's distasteful whispers in my ear from the moment I could ask about the absence of my father and the popular jocks I had to put up with in high school, I wasn't a fan.

"Right. Well, his name is Theo. He plays hockey. We've already talked to the dean, and there isn't anywhere else open, so I'm kind of stuck."

Unless...

He blew out a breath, trying to figure out a solution. "I'd offer for you to move in, but I can't be distracted with it being my senior y—"

Checking out of the conversation, I moved my gaze past Chad and settled on the doors to my dorm room and froze at the sight of Theo standing against the railing of the stairs with his black hoodie pulled up over his beanie, staring directly at me. His expression was hard to read, but I had a feeling he was trying to figure me out, and I couldn't blame him. He was going to be living with me, and I was pretty certain he had heard part of the phone conversation I'd had with Taytum after the meeting with the dean—you know, the one where I was openly referring to my mother and how she attempted to seduce a married man to pay for my tuition.

My face burned at the thought, and I quickly looked away from Theo and straightened my shoulders as I checked back into the conversation with Chad.

"So, yeah. Anyway, I have to go."

"What?" I asked, confused. "Where are you going?"

"I just told you," he scoffed, acting as if I were stupid, but to his point, I did just completely blank out our conversation. "I have to go get things ready for my classes next week."

I slowly blinked, still confused. "It's a Friday night, though. You have all weekend to get prepared for next week." Shaking my head, I changed directions and faked a smile. "Never mind. I know how you are. Call me later? I guess I'm gonna carry the rest of my boxes in and get settled too."

"Sure, baby." Chad leaned in, not bothering to take the heavy box from my hands, and pecked me on the lips. Before he climbed into his BMW, leaving me standing alone in the student parking lot, he shot me a look that made him identical to his father. "Make sure he knows you're not single."

And there it is.

"No need to be insecure, Chad. You know you can trust me."

His forehead furrowed. "I'm not being insecure. I'll see you later."

I opened my mouth to say something, but he disappeared in his car and slammed the door before speeding away angrily, as if I had done something wrong.

Blowing out a breath, I stepped forward and began walking to the doors, hoping Theo was no longer standing there watching me. My eyes stayed trained to the black pavement beneath my feet, and the second I took the first step, a heavy presence made itself known. The box was nearly jerked out of my hands. Theo's finger brushed over mine, and it stole every bit of my attention.

"So that's why you were so adamant that you wouldn't be a distraction to me."

I pulled the box back from Theo's steady grip and peered up at him. He was even taller, standing on the top step, and I ignored the touch of his hand against mine as he slipped his grip from the box. "What are you referring to?"

Theo leaned back against the railing and crossed his arms over his chest. His Adam's apple bobbed as he angled his chiseled chin to the parking lot behind me. "You have a boyfriend."

I shrugged. "That's not why I said I wouldn't be a distraction." I began climbing the stairs, quickly moving past him. "Jocks really aren't my type."

Theo opened the door, and I walked inside, not bothering to say thank you because it felt like a surrender of some sort. I was generally a nice person, but Theo's presence irritated me. Maybe it was the fact that he was a jock, or maybe it was the fact that he oozed arrogance and turned heads every three seconds. The short walk to the second floor was like we were being followed by paparazzi. There was no doubt in my mind that I would be featured in the school newspaper by tomorrow morning. *The Bex Daily News: Popular hockey star, Theo Brooks, was seen walking with the poor girl whose mother tried seducing the dean for tuition money.*

When Theo and I reached the top of the stairs and began walking down the hall, he tried grabbing the box from my hands again, but I quickly pulled it back. A chuckle rumbled from his chest. "I'm not trying to steal your box, Bryant. I'm just trying to help you."

"I don't need help," I snapped. He stopped walking for a brief second, and I instantly felt guilty for being rude. He *was* my roommate, after all. I softened my tone. "But thanks."

Theo walked ahead of me and opened our door, and I shuffled in after him, feeling the air stiffen with an awkwardness so cold I got a chill. The lamp on his desk was still on, and when I dropped my box to the floor, I turned around to grab the rest of my things but nearly choked at the sight of Theo leaning against his desk casually with his hands in his pockets. He watched me for a second that seemed to drag on for eons before I placed my hands on my hips and asked, "What?"

"Does your boyfriend live on campus?"

I wasn't sure why that mattered, but I shook my head no anyway.

"So, he lives in an apartment?"

"Yeah...so?" I slowly walked to the door, wondering how the hell I was going to live with this guy when just a single look from him made me feel *seen*. I didn't like his attention on me because it wasn't brief by any means. His eyes lingered.

When I peeked over my shoulder at him, he had his hand on his chin, as if he were lost in thought. My blood rushed with his next question. "Why don't you just live with him? It's apparent he doesn't enjoy the idea of you living with me."

"How is that apparent?" Annoyance began to simmer as I turned and faced him.

"I heard what he said to you." He shrugged as he bent down and grabbed his gym bag that was near the foot of his desk. "He wants me to know you're not single." Theo wasn't looking at me as he said the next words, but I knew that he was skeptical. "Just seems weird to me. How long have you two been together?"

I bit my tongue because I didn't want to admit that we'd been together for far too long for him to 1) not want to live together, and 2) say something like I needed to make sure another guy knew I wasn't single. Not once in the last several years had I ever given Chad a reason not to trust me or, better yet, given him a reason to think I'd ever be a distraction to his studies. I knew how important academics were to him. They were to me too.

My hand was on the doorknob when Theo posed another question. "He looks familiar to me. What is his major?"

I knew, without doubt, that he had never seen Chad a day in his life. Chad wouldn't be caught dead near the hockey rink, and there was no way they took any of the same classes.

"I doubt you've ever seen him before. He is in some of the hardest classes that Bexley U offers."

"What is that supposed to mean?"

There was an edge to Theo's voice, and I apparently struck a chord. I peeked over my shoulder again, and his golden-boy looks had been replaced with something much harsher—probably the same expression he wore on the ice.

I knew of his campus nickname. During his games, he wasn't the golden boy who offered to help me carry my boxes up to my dorm. He was known as *the wolf*. He attacked his opponents like they were mere scraps of food.

"It's just—"

"A little judgmental, yeah?"

My lips parted, and he put his back to me. "Not all jocks are stupid, Claire. You should remember that."

A second later, I walked out the door and into the men's hallway and cursed under my breath when I saw that several eyes were set on me. Not only did I have to live with a guy who was beginning to dislike me as much as I made it seem like I disliked him, but I was going to have an audience every single time I left my room.

Great.

7

THEO

THINGS WEREN'T OFF to a good start.

It all started with her snarky little comments and the way the room smelled girlish and soft. Claire and I were on completely different wavelengths. I went to bed early, and she didn't. Each morning, since freshman year, I ran the school quad before coming back, showering, and getting ready for classes and practice. She was the opposite. She stayed up entirely too late, creeping back into our room after midnight with her freshly showered self, and sat at her desk to study or whatever the hell she was doing, and cursed me with her sleepy voice when my alarm would go off at 4:30 a.m.

The sun had just barely begun to peak as I banged my open palm against our door. Sweat trickled down my back, and I knew Claire was going to be irritated with me. Not that it mattered. She was gone most of the time anyway, probably avoiding the awkward situation we found ourselves in. "Bryant," I bellowed. "Open the door."

"Use your key!" she rasped, half-yelling. A few doors had opened down the hall, and each guy glared at me as they shuffled down the hall with their morning wood. A few others were already up and at 'em because the one thing about athletes? We liked our regimen. When we were on, we were on. Athletes were dedicated. Most of us were, at least. Landon wasn't a fan of being up early. Morning conditioning made him grumble under his breath as he chugged an energy drink before crumpling the can and throwing on his skates.

"I forgot my key. Open up." I leaned my head against the door and banged my hand several more times before the door finally flew open, and Claire stood back in not nearly enough clothing with the tiniest little scowl on her face.

"I've had it, Theo! This isn't going to work."

I pushed her aside and shut the door, annoyed that guys were *still* trying to catch a glimpse of her. The rumors were running rampant around campus, and every time I proved the rumor wrong, a puck bunny would pop up like Whack-A-Mole, ready to spread their legs for me. So far, none have snuck back into my room to lie naked in my bed. And to my surprise, Claire hadn't walked in on me getting a favor yet, either. It would probably only make her hate me more.

Because she did hate me.

It seemed like it, anyway. She avoided me, but that was fine.

"This was the first time I've forgotten my key. *Relax*." I pulled my sweaty shirt over my head and wiped my neck with it, sneaking a glance at her.

She quickly averted her eyes from my bare chest and stomped her foot. "Some of us like to sleep!" Her bare legs snagged my attention for a brief second. They were toned and smooth, with the remnants of a summer glow on them. I understood the attention she got from the other guys on the floor. I did. I just wasn't as weak as them. My priorities were straight. Theirs were not.

The question popped up out of nowhere as I ignored her hissy fit. "Why are you in the athletic dorms?" I turned to face her, and her lips were set in a straight line. I didn't hide my attempt to check her out, running my eyes down her slender frame, trying to figure out what sport she played. The only students in Dorothy Hall were athletes. I snapped my fingers, and she looked at me like she was seconds from ripping my head off. "Volleyball?" I took my finger and spun it in the air. "Turn around. Let me see."

A bubble of excitement started to creep up my throat when the apples of her cheeks turned pink. "Excuse me?"

I furrowed my brow. "Volleyball players have a pretty decent ass. Let me see."

Her jaw dropped, and I threw my head back and laughed. "I'm kidding, Bryant. Will you lighten up?" I snapped my fingers again, the relaxation halting for a second. "I've got it. You're a dancer, I bet. And not the cheerleading type of dancer. You're in...ballet?"

The sun began to shine through the window as the words left my mouth, and there was a slight glimmer that put her in the spotlight. Her sleepy eyes narrowed, and I grinned. "I'm right, aren't I? That makes sense."

"Why does that make sense?"

"Because you're so uptight." I smirked before grabbing my towel and body wash. Her eyes followed my every move, and I could tell she wanted to snap a snarky response back to me. "Tell me, does your boyfriend ever do anything other than dismiss you every chance he gets? Like, does he ever get you off? I've always heard dancers are hard to please. Is that true?"

There was a voice deep inside my head that was telling me to retreat, but the look on her face egged me on like no other. Her cheeks flared even brighter, and her perky breasts under her shirt were rising and falling quicker than before. I was blaming it on our lack of conversation during our first full week of rooming together and how we had all this built-up tension from pissing each other off. And admittedly, I enjoyed picking on her. It fed me like I was a starving animal. It was like payback for each night that she woke me up with her feminine body wash and the sound of her even breathing when she finally drifted into a peaceful sleep after sitting at her desk for what seemed like hours.

"Of course he does!" she snarked, looking away at the last second.

My head tilted on its own as I tried to read her. Her arms flew to her chest like armor, and I paused. "Does he, though?"

"It's none of your business. What gives you the right to even ask such a thing? Typical jock." She threw her hands up as she walked over to her dresser and pulled out a pair of leggings. *Oh, she is mad. Did I strike a nerve?*

Her hands went to the hem of her shirt, and she began to pull it up, showing off her toned belly.

"Whoa, what the fuck are you doing?" I asked, stunned. I spun around and put my back to her.

"Well, since I'm up because of you, I'm going to go work on my audition now instead of after work."

So, she *is* a dancer. "If you think your boyfriend is jealous now, wait until he finds out that you're undressing in front of me."

Silence stretched around us, and I knew what was going through her mind. Little Miss Night Owl now knew that I wasn't asleep like she thought I was when her douche of a boyfriend would call her late at night. *What was he even doing up that late anyway?* Was I the only college student that enjoyed sleep? I mean, there was a time and place for staying up late and partying. During the week wasn't one of them—not for athletes anyway. We were tired, man.

The tenseness in the room had lessened after a few seconds of my back being turned to her. I could hear her shuffling around, and a part of me began to feel bad that I had pushed her too far. Despite our rare interactions, I've actually concluded a good bit about my roommate from coincidental eavesdropping. Come on, it wasn't like she was *overly* quiet while on the phone. But Claire didn't enjoy conflict. That much was made apparent. In a battle, I was certain she would be the first to throw the white flag. She did it every time she and her boyfriend were on the phone. I couldn't hear what he had said to her, but my imagination didn't need to work too hard.

The dude was insecure as fuck and pretty damn possessive for a guy that didn't want his girlfriend to live with him.

I slowly turned around and saw that she was fully dressed now—well, as dressed as she was going to get. Her black leggings clung to her ass like a second skin, and the sports bra she had on showed entirely too much of her belly, but she quickly threw on a jacket and began putting her unbrushed, wavy hair into a bun.

"You never answered me, you know."

She sighed loudly, as if I didn't know that she annoyed. "What are you talking about?"

"How long have you and your boyfriend been together?"

I stood by the door with my towel and body wash trapped in my tight grasp as I waited for her answer.

Curiosity got the best of me. I mean, we did live with each other, and I was certain she knew more about me than I did her. I was the center of a lot of conversations. The closer it got to our first game, the more my name was shuffled around campus like I was body-surfing the crowds.

"Four years." Her eyes softened around the edges when she answered me, and I wasn't sure what to make of that.

Four years. Fuck. That was about three years and eleven months longer than any relationship I'd ever been in. I'd never been fully invested in long-term relationships or envious of my friends who had the security of a girl to take to prom or follow throughout college. My priorities were narrower than that—stellar student, loving son, good brother, and model hockey player. My ambitions revolved around the NHL, and that wasn't because I wanted the fame that came with it. My need for hockey went much deeper than that, and if I could make my family proud and support them in the way that they supported me, I would know I had succeeded. But still, I couldn't get her answer out of my head for the rest of the day.

"How's the roomie?" Aasher tapped me on the shoulder with his stick as we skated around the rink, wasting time until practice started.

I flung the puck back and forth as I picked up speed. "Honestly, I don't see her much, so it's been fine."

"What does she sleep in?" I stopped abruptly and glared at Landon.

"I don't know." I began skating faster and harder, clearly agitated. Of course I knew what she slept in. Her bare leg was usually peeking out from the covers each morning when I woke to run, but I didn't see why it mattered.

"I heard she sleeps naked."

My stick was out a moment later to knock him down,

but Landon being Landon, missed it at the last second and threw his head back and laughed. "That's the newest piece of gossip on the floor."

I rolled my eyes. "Explains why every guy was loitering outside my door this morning. She doesn't sleep naked, and even if she did, it's not my business."

"You cannot honestly tell me that you don't find her attractive." Aasher raised his brow, calling me on my bluff.

I shrugged, meeting at center ice for practice as everyone gathered. "Even if I did, it wouldn't matter."

Our helmets were on, and we lingered as we waited for Coach to get on the ice to begin calling drills. There was a grunt from Emory as he joined in on the conversation that just about every one of my teammates was checked into. I was captain, so even if they didn't want to admit it, they all gravitated toward me. "Could you imagine fucking your roomie and then her walking in on the many favors you receive before games? Yikes. You can't live with someone you fuck unless you're together-together. You know?"

A low grumble shot from the back. "She could be the one giving all the favors."

My teeth slammed together at the same time my stick split against the ice. "For fuck's sake. I'm thankful she's my roommate and none of yours. Do any of you know how to keep your head on straight when there is a female involved?"

There was a slap against my shoulder pad. "And this is why you're team captain." Coach shook his head as he stood beside me. "You should take the advice of Wolf. Trust me when I tell you that all it takes is one good woman to bring you to your knees and change the complete direction of your future."

"You say that like it's a bad thing, Coach."

My gaze lingered on Jett and the way his mouth curved. He was a big, burly guy who played defense and had been with his current girlfriend since freshman year of high school. She came to every single game and wore a jersey that had his last name plastered on the backside. There was no doubt that Jett was happy with his decision to settle down so soon with a girl, but it wasn't always that easy, and I'd seen enough heartbreaks to make me shy away from the entire thing.

"Yeah, let's all be like Wolf. He has a line of girls outside the locker room after every practice, willing to *massage* his sore muscles, and then they're on their merry way because they all know that Wolf doesn't date."

Mostly everyone laughed. I didn't deny it because it was true.

Coach blew his whistle. "Alright, alright, boys. Back to work. Line up at the blue line, and let's go."

8

CLAIRE

MY TOES FELT RELIEVED the second I untied my pointe shoes, and it was another reminder that I *really* needed to get some new ones. There was chatter around me, and I caught the eye of Taytum as she landed her *grand jeté*. Our smiles matched, and I quickly forgot about the aches I felt as I rushed over to her and squeezed her tightly in the middle of several applauses.

"That was the best leap I have ever seen you do, Tay."

Her chest was rushing as she caught her breath. "Thanks. I literally practiced all summer."

Regret hit me like a brick wall because I knew that I'd fallen behind this summer. I picked up every shift I could at the coffee shop down the street from the apartment to save so I didn't have to kill myself with work at The Bex this semester, knowing that it was going to be difficult to manage working along with my class schedule. Classical ballet was a mixture of technique and academics and was one of the most vigorous classes within the dance major. And not to mention, if I scored the lead role, I would win a scholarship for next year, which would cover the rest of my tuition, and what a freaking blessing that would be.

"Well, it paid off. That blew Kate out of the water." My tone turned into a whisper as I said Kate's name because she was somehow always listening, even if she wasn't on the stage. Kate was always gunning to be number one, which wasn't necessarily a surprise. Not many people considered ballet a competitive sport, but I would argue that it was more competitive than most. There was only one lead role, and that meant you had to be flawless. There was no relying on your teammates to pick up the slack if you fell behind. It was all on you, and that was pressure like no other.

"Fuck Kate," Taytum mumbled, not really bothering to lower her voice. I smothered a laugh as I rushed over to my bag and continued untying my ballet shoes. I had a shift to get to, but instead of heading to an empty rehearsal room after my shift to perfect my audition, I could go back to my room and catch up on some much-needed sleep.

My mother had dropped a bomb on me two days into the semester, and my seamless plan of saving as much money this summer and taking less shifts than normal at The Bex was completely obliterated as she informed me that our landlord of the last twelve years gave her a notice that if she didn't fix the flooring in the bathroom and stopped the leak from dripping to the first-floor tenant's ceiling, she was going to be evicted.

I knew I couldn't blame Ralph. The leak had been there for far too long, and I was certain he'd given my mother the proper amount of notice to get it fixed. As much as she tried over the years, she was irresponsible with finances, *always* needing a helping hand or a favor, which was exactly how she got her job working for Chad's parents. This was the type of situation where I learned from her mistakes, not from her guidance. She did try, though. I'd give her that.

"I gotta get going." I threw my backpack over my shoulders, cursing myself for my own irresponsibility. "I forgot my jeans for work."

"I bet you'd get more tips if you wore none." Taytum laughed as she shuffled through her bag. "Let me see if I have any in here."

I glanced at my phone and saw that I had just enough time to stop by my room to grab my jeans and head to work. "You're good," I shouted, backing away. "I have time. I'll see you tomorrow morning in class."

"Get there early!" she demanded, pulling her hair out of her bun. "We need a venting sesh."

Venting sesh equaled her demanding I answer the questions about Chad—that I had successfully avoided—*and* Theo. Everyone on campus was interested in what it was like to room with Bexley U's right wing for the number one hockey team in the NCAA. Even some of the other dancers were looking at me a little longer than before. But I didn't really have anything to report about Theo, other than he was completely inconsiderate.

I wasn't a hard person to live with. I was clean, tidy, and I tried to be quiet. I even turned my desk lamp off the other night when I kept hearing him toss and turn in his sleep. *That* was being considerate. Theo, on the other hand, blared his alarm every freaking morning right when I hit my REM cycle, and it seemed like the moment I finally fell back asleep from being brutally awakened, he'd come tromping back in the room, huffing and puffing from his run.

That was why I was so excited to get my shift over. I was going to head to the library to finish my paper and then zip right off to sleep at a normal time for the first time since starting classes.

Just the thought made me smile as I skipped up the stairs to the second floor. A few guys passed me, looking at me a little suspiciously because it still wasn't accepted that I was, in fact, rooming with Theo Brooks. I felt their stares every time I crested the top of the stairs, but I had successfully mastered the skill of shutting out their whispers as I entered my room. It was annoying but nothing high school hadn't prepared me for.

A faint snicker came from the left as I put my key in the door and slowly turned the knob. A tall, mammoth-looking guy with curly blond hair covered his mouth with his hand as he watched me. I wanted to say something, but my gaze shifted to the left as I caught the surprised look of another mass of a human. His eyes widened, and he shifted his gaze to my door, and that was when I rolled my eyes. "You guys are so immature," I mumbled. "Why is this such a big deal? We're adults, for goodness' sake. Just because I don't have a Y chromosome doesn't mean I can't room with someone who does!"

I opened the door and stepped inside my room, hoping Theo wasn't there so I didn't have to deal with another encounter between us. This morning started off rough, and there was an awkwardness that followed me throughout the day when I thought back to my unexplained behavior of undressing in front of him. I wasn't sure if I was trying to irritate him, or if I was trying to subconsciously pay Chad back for the way he'd been treating me lately.

Shaking my head and jumbling up my thoughts of my boyfriend, I headed straight to my bed where my jeans were laying. I wasn't even halfway in the room before I turned my gaze to Theo's side of the room and yelped. It was like a car crash. I couldn't look away even if I wanted to.

I was mortified, embarrassed, and completely shocked. My cheeks flamed, even though I wasn't a prude by any means. I'd had sex. I'd been to frat parties with Taytum where people were openly undressing each other as they flew up the stairs. But this? This stole the words right out of my mouth. There stood Theo with his black joggers pulled down to his ankles, completely shirtless and glistening with sweat as his large hands cupped a girl's waist. She was bent over with her long wavy hair hanging down past her shoulder. Her flushed cheeks matched mine, but hers were for a completely different reason.

"Enjoying the show?" Theo's sharp tone broke me out of my stupor, and I stumbled backward before locking eyes with him. My throat closed when my gaze shot downward for the second time in the last five seconds and saw that he was still actively inside her.

"Oh my God!" I yelled, spinning around and putting my back to him. "What the hell, Theo!"

"How was I supposed to know you'd be coming back to the room right now?"

This wasn't going to work! Nope. Nope. NOPE.

The girl's whimper pierced my ears, and anger rushed to my legs, propelling me forward to snatch my jeans off my bed. I was still in my leo and tights with a long hoodie pulled over, but there was no way in hell I was staying in this room for a second longer to change. I would rather change in the hallway in front of several pairs of ogling eyes than stay in a small space with my roommate fucking his puck bunny.

"Have patience," Theo said under his breath to the moaning female beneath him. My eyes widened, and I flushed even hotter. My pulse flew beneath my skin, and I was hoping I'd take flight soon so I could get out of there faster.

Theo called after me as I flung the door open with force, "I'll put a sock on the door next time."

I stopped for a moment before slamming the door shut and canceling out his dark chuckle. My hair nearly fell from my bun as I whipped my head to the left, glaring at the two guys from before that were snickering at me as I entered the room. "Really?" I snapped. "Fucking warn me next time!"

One clutched his bulky chest and cackled as the other shot me a guilty look. I hoped he was conscience-stricken and choked on his own spit later. While on my way to my car with my jeans thrown over my shoulder, I quickly texted Taytum.

Me: I'm coming over after my shift. I need your help with something.

She texted back as my Toyota revved to life.

Taytum: If it involves you breaking up with Chad, I'm down.

I rolled my eyes at her response, knowing that even if I wanted to break up with Chad, it would be a lot more complicated than she thought.

9

THEO

"No PARTYING until after tomorrow night or—" I checked out of the conversation as soon as the threats began spewing from Coach's mouth, because I knew they weren't directed toward me. Did I like to party? Sometimes. Did I get shit-faced drunk and jeopardize my future? Absolutely not.

Pulling my phone out of my bag, I glanced at my texts, ignoring the one from Jess. She was the only girl I frequented, and the reason for that was because she knew I was never looking for anything more. Every once in a while, though, she'd try to ask to hang out, and she wouldn't add the winky-face emoji, which meant that she actually wanted to spend time together. She knew that wasn't on my agenda—ever. Yet, she still tried. *Probably need to cut ties with that one.*

Mom: Make sure to get an adequate amount of sleep tonight, Theodore. And eat a good breakfast.

I texted my mom back as Coach was stirring up Aasher over his whereabouts last season.

"You just can't let it go, Coach. I said sorry."

"She's my daughter, Aasher."

I flicked my eyes up for a moment after texting my mom. Aasher's face was red, and it wasn't from embarrassment. "I didn't know she was your daughter."

"And you all expect me to believe you didn't know," Coach muttered.

"I didn't even touch her. All I said was hi."

"Yeah, well your version of 'hi' always turns into something else. So don't even look at her tomorrow night."

I suppressed a laugh before turning back to my phone and rolling my eyes at my older brother's text.

Carl: How are those puck bunnies treatin' ya?

I smirked.

Me: How's dad life treatin' ya? Give my favorite niece a hug from Uncle Theo.

Carl wasn't technically my brother, but I called him as such and considered him as such too. No one knew the dynamics of my family or upbringing except Aasher—not even Coach. It wasn't really anyone's business, and the last thing I needed was for the news outlets to unbury my family history and see that my parents weren't my biological parents and open up old wounds that I wasn't sure they had healed from.

"You ready?" Aasher nudged my shoulder. I glanced up and saw everyone leaving the locker room, and Coach was back in his office with his door shut.

"Yeah," I answered, slinging my bag over my shoulder before clicking my phone off. Aasher and I walked in silence through the locker room, and I was already getting in my usual vibe before a game—which was shut-down mode. My thoughts cleared, and I thought of nothing but hockey.

When Aasher and I were farther from the locker room and began walking in the chilly evening air, he immediately scoffed. "I have no idea why Coach keeps yelling at me about his daughter or preaching to the team not to touch her."

I laughed, shaking my head. "He's just being a dad, bro."

"Could you imagine if any of us fucked her? He'd probably kick me off the team."

We approached my car. "You're too good for him to do that, and he knows it. Plus, that girl is definitely a virgin."

He shot me a look before flipping his hair off his forehead. "What do you think he cares about more? His daughter's V-card or the game?"

I paused. He had a point.

"What's this?"

My eyebrows raised. "What's what?"

Aasher rounded the front of my car and pulled something off my windshield.

"Is that a fucking parking ticket?" I asked, instantly irritated. I glanced around and made sure there wasn't a sign that said no parking.

Aasher began laughing hysterically, so I snatched the paper out of his hand, ready to walk over to the dean to make him deal with it but stopped as I caught the neat and whimsical handwriting on a torn piece of paper that had The Bex's logo centered on the bottom edge.

Roommate Rules

Use a fucking quieter alarm. It wakes me up each morning, and I don't have the luxury of going to bed at 9pm like a grandpa.
No more fucking girls in our room.
Or sexual favors. Go do it in your car. Or the locker room. Or in the hallway. I don't care. But not near my stuff.
If you're going to listen to trashy music, use your AirPods.
Don't come on my side of the room.

Is she fucking kidding?

I blinked several times after reading the rules. Half of me wanted to laugh, and the other half of me wanted to rip up the piece of paper with her pretty handwriting on it and scatter it all over her bed.

But instead, I folded the piece of paper nicely as Aasher stood with his back against my car with a shit-eating grin, waiting to see my reaction. When we caught eyes, I shook my head and smirked.

"That look is never good," he chuckled as he pushed off my car. "What do you have planned?"

I ran my tongue over my teeth. "She can have her rules."

Opening my car door, I laughed. Aasher adjusted his bag over his shoulder. "That's not the Theo I know."

I turned around and laughed. "You know what they say about rules, Aash."

He looked leery. "They're meant to be broken?"

"There's a loophole in every single one."

He paused, looking deep in thought, and began nodding on his way over to his car. "There sure is, Wolf. Have fun with your *rules*."

My car came to life, and I smiled the entire way to The Bex, where I knew Claire would be.

———

The Bex's atmosphere was quiet during the day and lively at night, even on a Thursday. Irritation pinched the back of my neck the second I walked inside, knowing that I should have been back in my room, continuing to get in the mindset for tomorrow's game, just as I caught Claire rounding the bar. I smiled, preparing myself for a totally different game.

She was very difficult to read, and that was saying something because I lived with her. There was a soft liveliness that hung around her movements, but there was an edge to her voice at times, too. I usually heard it when she was talking to her boyfriend late at night, when she thought I was asleep. She seemed to linger right in the middle of sweet and edgy. One second, she was gentle, and the next, she was tough. Even watching her now...she handed some drinks off to a table of two, smiling cheerfully, but then the moment she turned around to head back to the bar, her shoulders dropped, and she let out a hefty breath.

I moved a little farther into the restaurant, knowing I wouldn't stay hidden for long. Claire's boss, the one who had a son that was coming to tomorrow's game, went over and gave her a little squeeze. Claire's dull eyes had a little spark go back into them, and she seemed to put on a brave face, nodding her head. I read her lips as she answered whatever her boss had asked. *"I'm good. I'm just tired."*

That made sense. She went to bed late, and I woke her up early...by accident. A nagging thought tried to sneak in that told me it absolutely wasn't by accident, but I pushed it aside as I sought out an empty table, preferably somewhere in the back where I could hide out until her shift was over.

"Hey, Wolf." *Well, that lasted three seconds.*

I cleared my throat as I pulled my beanie off my head. "Hey, man." I nodded at a group of football players who were sharing a pizza. I casually walked over to their table and sat down for a second, keeping my eye on Claire. We needed to have a little meeting that I wasn't going to let her escape from. The piece of paper crinkled as I pulled it out of my hoodie pocket, keeping it in my grasp until she looked my way.

"Want a slice?" I wasn't going to pretend like I knew all the football players' names, but I did know the ones who were often beside mine in the school paper. This guy, though? Wasn't sure of his name.

"Nah." Shaking my head, I sat back a little further in my chair. "I don't prefer to eat something full of grease the night before a game."

"Ah, that's right." Rush, the star player of Bexley U's football team, slapped me on the back. "Your first game is tomorrow night. We should go." He looked at his group of friends, and in between chews, they nodded.

"When's your first game?" I asked, having no fucking clue when they played. I enjoyed watching football, and I had played it when I was younger, but it didn't fill me like hockey did.

"Next Saturday. Our schedule is fucked this year. It's going to be tough."

"Same, bro." I glanced back over to the bar and saw Claire standing back, shifting her light-blue eyes from table to table. My chest stuttered with excitement as she landed on our table, running her gaze over each drink and the pizza in the middle. I sat up a little straighter and put my hands on the table with the piece of paper tucked in between my fingers. Her head tilted to the left as her brows dipped slightly, and when she landed on me, those heartbreaker eyes widened, and her cheeks instantly turned pink.

I raised an eyebrow when our gazes crashed, and she quickly turned around, hiding. *Don't back down now, roomie.*

"You know her?" Beck, the best-of-the-best linebacker, took a swig of his beer. "I've been eyeing her since last year, but I never see her at any of the parties, so I haven't approached her."

"She's taken." I paused at the sound of the irritability in my tone.

"By you?" Every football player stopped eating and stared at me.

Brushing off my testiness, I chuckled. "No. I just know she has a boyfriend. She's actually my roommate."

"What? Your roommate? You two live together?"

"Oh, shit. I thought that was a rumor." There was a loud laugh and a slap on the table. I glanced at the guy wearing a Bexley U football shirt with his hat on backward as he filled in the rest of his teammates on what was like crack to the rumor mill of this school. His sentence faded as Claire slowly approached the table, keeping her stare far from mine.

She commanded attention as she stood at the foot of the slightly wobbly table with her hands on her hips. "How are we doing over here? Do you want another round of beer? Or if you're finished, I can bring the check?"

I didn't let anyone answer as I spread my legs out wide under the table and held the piece of paper in between us. "Hey, Bryant. Care to have a chat about this?"

Her little jaw ticked as she flicked her attention to the piece of paper. "Not really. What is there to chat about?"

Silence stretched around the table and possibly throughout the entire restaurant.

"Plenty."

She pulled her attention from mine and put it on the rest of the guys at the table. "Do you guys want the check?"

Rush cleared his throat from beside me and said, "Sure." Claire forced a small smile onto her lips, and the bun on top of her head bounced as she tried to turn around, but my hand quickly shot out, and I slipped my finger in her belt loop, causing her to fling backward.

A little growl left her as she spun around and glared as she peered down at me. "I'm not discussing this while I'm in the middle of work, Theo. I know you're used to people catering to you, but I'm not one of them."

Someone let out a low whistle, and I laughed at her confidence. *There it is. The tough side of her.*

"That's fine. I can wait."

Defeat covered her features, and she sighed. "I don't get off until ten. Isn't that past your bedtime, Gramps?"

Her attempt at wounding me made me laugh again. I knew we were attracting attention—something I really wasn't looking for tonight—but I couldn't seem to help myself. "Like I said, I'll wait." I winked at her, and her nose crinkled at the sight. She huffed as she spun around and walked away, swaying her hips for every guy to salivate over.

The silence broke at the table when every football player laughed out loud. "That was entertaining."

And it's about to get even more entertaining.

10

CLAIRE

"Hey, you're good to clock out, sweetie."

My shoulders slumped as I pushed away the stray hairs from my half-falling-down bun. I saw Angie peering back at Theo as he sat in the far back booth, hardly visible.

"Are you only letting me off early because you know that Theo is waiting for me?"

She looked as if I had caught her in a lie. She had the whole deer-in-the-headlights look. "Angie!" I hissed. "You're supposed to be on my side here!"

"I didn't know there were sides." She raised an eyebrow.

"If there are sides, I'm on his." I glared at our cook, Jamison. He wiggled his eyebrows as he flicked his attention to Theo.

What was so appealing about jocks? What was *so* appealing about a guy who commanded the room with arrogance and a sly smirk? My mother's tired face and cursing voice skimmed the outer edges of my brain. '*Stay away from jocks, Claire. All they do is break hearts. Look at what your father did to us.'* That was all I knew of him. He was an athlete of some kind and left us for the sport. Whereabouts? Nada.

I stole a quick look at Theo and knew, deep in the hidden part of my body, why he was appealing. He was like a majestic being. He was tall and muscular without looking like all he did was spend his time in the gym and consume juicy steaks for every meal. He was blessed with high cheek-bones and green eyes that sparkled with something wildly inviting. And his smile was nice, too. White, straight teeth. And he showed them often, despite his campus nickname of being called the wolf and obliterating people on the ice.

Maybe if I was a different girl with a different upbringing and future, I could be swept off my feet by a guy like him. But that wasn't possible being who I was and what I was up against.

"He *does* have a game tomorrow. He needs his rest." Angie was messing with the register as she reminded me of what it was like being an athlete. I understood. I needed my rest before a big performance or audition too. But that didn't necessarily make me feel bad. It wasn't like I had asked him to sit over in the corner, watching my every move, until I was off work.

I ran over the rules that Taytum and I implemented last night while I was still fueled by anger over his earlier escapades in our room and noted the faint touch of embar-rassment painting my cheeks. Taytum threw herself onto her bed with laughter every time I scribbled one rule after another, totally egging me on. To say she enjoyed herself and my tantrum was putting it mildly.

Theo glanced at his phone and threw out another sigh before moving his attention to me. My pulse stuttered when he caught me staring, and he waved the piece of paper in front of him, as if he were telling me to hurry.

I turned to glance at my tables, which were all empty. *Damnit.*

"Go," Angie urged, shooting me a half-smile. "He seems pretty persistent to chat with you about something."

I growled one last time and put my ordering book down on the counter. *Fine.*

Walking as slowly as possible—like putting a few more seconds between us was going to make a difference—I finally reached his table. He tipped his sharp jaw in my direction. "Hi, Bryant. Nice of you to finally make your way over here. I don't need a refill. Thanks for asking, though."

His glass of water was empty, and his plate didn't even have a single piece of food left on it, but I was, under no circumstances, being his waitress.

"Sorry." My apology was sarcastic. "I'm off the clock." I slid into the booth in front of him, glancing at my phone with only one text from Taytum. *No surprise that Chad hadn't texted me back once today.*

I clicked it off as a crumb of disappointment settled in the back of my head and pulled myself to the present as Theo's large hands unfolded the piece of paper that I scribbled on the night before.

"Couldn't help but notice that you didn't stay in our room last night."

I pulled my hair down out of my bun and let my brown hair tumble over my shoulders. Some of the strands were still damp from my shower after practice, and it filled the empty space with the smell of my shampoo. His nostrils flared for a second before he tapped the paper that laid in between us.

"Were you busy working on this?"

I shrugged. "I was just waiting for the smell of sex to leave our room before coming back."

He barked out a laugh, and I knew it had gained the attention of the group of girls at the bar. "Has anyone ever told you that you're dramatic, Bryant?"

I wished he would quit using that stupid nickname.

"Nope," I said, lying through my teeth. Chad called me dramatic often. The only difference was that when Chad said it, I wasn't being dramatic.

He pursed his lips and gave me a look that told me he knew I was lying but continued on with the conversation. "This isn't going to work."

I slumped backward and crossed my arms over my Bex shirt. "Us being roommates? I agree! That's why I made the rules."

He shook his head. "No. I'm referring to these." His fingers tapped the paper. "These are completely one-sided."

I bit my bottom lip as I reread what I had written.

Use a fucking quieter alarm. It wakes me up each morning, and I don't have the luxury of going to bed at 9pm like a grandpa.

No more fucking girls in our room.

Or sexual favors. Go do it in your car. Or the locker room. Or in the hallway. I don't care. But not near my stuff.

If you're going to listen to trashy music, use your AirPods.

Don't come on my side of the room.

Okay, fine. He was right. I wasn't going to apologize, though. There was no backing down when it came to guys like him.

"Do you agree?" he prodded, pulling the paper out of

my grasp. I bit the inside of my cheek, refusing to answer him. He squinted as he studied me, and his sigh was so strong I felt his warm breath brush against my skin. "And you're stubborn. Noted."

"I am not," I said, sitting forward. I lowered my voice. "I just don't like the idea of you bringing a ton of girls back to our room and fucking them all over the place. I just picture you fucking them on my bed or something, and it's...gross."

His grin was a warning sign like no other. "Do you picture me fucking often?"

"No!" The word sprung out of my mouth as my cheeks puffed with anger. "I don't have to picture it! I saw you in action yesterday!"

His pink lips rolled together, and he looked away, shoulders shaking with quiet laughter.

He is annoying. I take back what I said earlier. Theo Brooks is not appealing—at all.

I began to scoot out of the booth with annoyance backing my every move, but Theo's voice made me pause for a second. "Oh, come on! You know if you don't discuss this with me now that I'll just corner you in our room later."

There was a flutter in my lower belly that had me questioning my sanity.

"You can't escape me." His fingers tapped against the table. "So, sit down."

I sat down begrudgingly but then smiled deviously as a sudden threat floated from my mouth. "Fine, then be serious, or I will walk over to those girls staring at you and see if they'll switch rooms with me."

Theo's smile disappeared. I nodded before glancing at them. "Mmhm. Do you know how many random girls have tried trading me rooms because they want to room with you?"

The color drained from his face. "Are you serious?"

I nodded. "Yep." The sound of my P had a distinct pop to it. "There's a whole bunch of puck bunnies running around this campus that would die to be your roommate."

"You wouldn't." He sat up a little straighter, showing off his rising chest. He was right, I wouldn't. That was just plain mean because the girls that had approached me would probably rape him in his sleep or something, and considering I was actually a nice person, it would weigh on my conscience.

"Stop fucking girls in our room, and you have my word."

Angry lines formed on his forehead. "That's like telling you that you can't have sex with your fuck-boy boyfriend in *your* living space. How is that fair?"

"He isn't a fuck-boy." My voice wasn't nearly as convincing as it should have been.

Theo half-rolled his eyes as he leaned back and crossed his arms over his chest. "He seems like one, but it's not my business. Just like it isn't your business who I have sex with."

We both blew out an agitated breath at the same time and stared each other down. His jade eyes were hardened around the edges, and I knew he was challenging me. He had a point, but I wasn't willing to give up the control and concede, so instead, I jolted my hand out and snatched the paper back from him. I lifted up from the booth and pulled the pen I used for taking orders out of my back pocket, flipped the paper over, and wrote *Claire and Theo's Roommate Rules* at the top.

"Fine," I sighed. "We can both set the rules."

"That's more like it—"

"But," I interrupted him, "if you break them, I swear to

God I will switch rooms and let a puck bunny room with you. Don't test me, Theo."

He stared at me from across the table, and The Bex began to feel smaller as each second passed. His gaze wandered over my features so slowly I began to feel uncomfortable, but then his cheek lifted, and he grinned. "I was right about you."

"You were?" I asked.

"You are tough, Bryant. Tougher than you make yourself out to be."

I shrugged, watching him pull the paper back across the table. "Only when I need to be." His large hand reached out quickly, and his fingers brushed mine before he stole the pen from my grip.

"You should be that way with your boyfriend," he mumbled under his breath, but before I could question him, he wrote the first rule on the paper and raised his brows, waiting for my response.

1. **Can have sex on own side of the room but must put a nonverbal warning on the doorknob for the other person to see.**

"Fine."

"That goes for you too. If your boyfriend ever decides to actually spend time with you, you're welcome to..."—he paused, glancing away—"do *whatever*...on your side of the room."

"He spends time with me," I snapped, more irritated that he had noticed than irritated that he was right. "And we have sex. What? Did you think I was a virgin or something, because I'm not." *When was the last time we had sex, though?*

"Easy, killer. I never said you were a virgin. I just don't

see your boyfriend—ever. The only thing I've witnessed is him acting jealous that you're rooming with me but never giving you an out." He shrugged again. "It's just weird."

"When did you witness that?" I asked, suddenly feeling nervous. "Are you spying on me?"

"That brings me to rule number two." He wrote something else down, and humiliation came a moment later.

2. **No late-night phone calls after 11**.

My lips parted as I reread the rule three times before looking at him.

"You've been listening to my phone calls?"

He pointed at me nonchalantly. "Not on purpose, so stop looking at me like that."

Ugh.

"So? You good with that one?"

"With Chad? Obviously! He's my boyfriend. Our conversations are none of your business."

He shot me a look that had me wavering. "I meant the rule, Bryant."

My cheeks warmed as I snatched the paper from him and scribbled number three down below.

3. **No blaring your alarm before 7am**.

"Use a quieter alarm." I peeked up and waited for his response. These had started out as my rules, and now, suddenly, they felt like they were his.

"Okay."

Surprise washed over me at his acceptance. *That was easy.* Was I being the difficult one here? I tried to calm my jets as he wrote another rule down before sliding the paper over to me.

4. **No lights on after 11**.

My shoulders slumped. "That's not fair. The library

closes at ten, and I have to get my homework done. It's not my fault you go to bed so early."

"Do your homework earlier?" It wasn't a statement but more so a question. Did he think I chose to do my homework late at night when I was utterly exhausted?

"I don't have the luxury of that. I go to class all day, then I have to practice for my auditions, and soon after, depending if I get the role, rehearsals will start. Then, add in conditioning and stretching, and I can't afford not to work with my mom—" I stopped talking the second I felt the pressure in my chest get tighter. I didn't share my personal problems with anyone, let alone Theo. Chad only knew of my financial situation because my mother was employed by his parents, which was something he enjoyed hanging over my head.

Theo's hand landed on mine as my breaths grew rapid. My gaze jerked to my burning skin, and one second later, he pulled his hand away, and I put mine in my lap. "Chill. I get it. But maybe use a dimmer light?" We both turned to Angie as she approached the table and smiled cheerfully.

"Take your time, but I just locked up. I still have to go through the register and prep for tomorrow."

Theo and I both looked around the restaurant and saw that it was completely empty besides Angie and a few other waitresses going through their tips. Jamison caught my eye through the kitchen window and winked at me.

"Is it ten already?" I asked, glancing at the clock above the bar. The few flat-screen TVs were already turned off, and the large, glow light that read The Bex was next.

"Yes, but take your time, sweetie." She turned toward Theo. "And good luck tomorrow! I'll be there watching!"

He smiled after thanking her, and when she turned around and left, he gave me an apologetic look. "I've gotta go back to the room. This is not the norm for me on the night before a game."

I wanted to laugh, but I didn't. "You are such a grandpa, but fine. I just have one more rule."

He groaned. "I have a feeling you'll add more as time goes on, but by all means, write down the last rule, Bryant."

"Actually, make that *two* rules."

I quickly wrote down my last two rules, and he gaped when he read them.

"Stay out of your underwear drawer?! Really?"

I shrugged, sliding out the booth.

"I'm not a creep. Why would I go into your underwear drawer? Why would I even have the urge to do that?"

I shot him a look. "That goes for your friends too. Their crude comments and lingering stares are plenty to deal with."

He rolled his eyes. "Okay, fine. But wait."

The pen flew over the paper as he crossed out number six.

6. ~~Stop calling me Bryant~~.

"I'm still calling you Bryant because you call me grandpa." He popped up out of the booth a moment later and towered over me. "You going straight home? Do you need a ride?"

My tongue felt heavy in my mouth as I peered up at him. Did we just become...neutral? Were we on the same terms now?

I blinked. "Um, uh...no. I mean..." I cleared my throat. "I'm going to work on my audition for a few, so I'll be late." Why was I acting nervous? "But...I guess I'll try to be quiet when I get in."

He grinned, waving the piece of paper in between us. "This was a good idea, yeah?" Then he winked and headed toward the door where Angie met him to unlock it. They chatted for a few moments, and it wasn't hard to see the appeal. Bexley U's best hockey player was charming in a sense, but a charming guy was a red flag if I ever saw one. Unfortunately, most girls loved red flags.

Not me, though.

[11]

THEO

THE BUZZER SOUNDED, and relief sunk down in my gut. We lifted our sticks in the air in celebration and all met at center ice for a team hug as the crowd roared with excitement.

The first game of the season was always like this. It was the intro of the season. The student section was high on adrenaline and booze, and the girls all tore off their jerseys with our names on the back, waving them above their heads. I saw a whole lotta *"Brooks"* in the crowd, which made sense with this being my last year playing for the Bexley Wolves—I had gained *a lot* of fans over the last three years.

"That's how you fuckin' do it!" Aasher threw his stick on the ice and jumped on my back. I laughed as I skated forward. "You're coming out with us tonight. Don't even say no, Theo."

"I always go to parties after games," I shouted. "No need to beg me."

"No one is begging you," Emory joked, "except every

single puck bunny in the stands right now." He laughed as we all began skating to the bench before taking off toward the locker room, the crowd cheering and banging against the glass.

Silver and black took precedence in the stands as the Westin fans began exiting the rink, defeat making their heads hang low. We played a hell of a game and beat them 3-1. It wasn't bad for our first time playing with a few new players and a new team dynamic. There was room for improvement on our third line, but at least there weren't any major penalties like last year's opening game.

The thing about hockey players? We were hotheads. Every single one of us. It was an instinct I think we were born with. Some of us were testier than others, but none-theless, we could get downright dirty if provoked.

Just as I began taking my pads off, something caught my eye, and I saw the locker room door shut before someone slipped out. Emory snagged my line of sight, and there was a faint shout in the hall, and that could only mean one thing. "For fuck's sake," Emory mumbled, following behind me.

"What the hell is he doing? I'm the fighter on the team." Emory stood beside me as we watched Aasher holding a Westin player up against the tiled wall by his throat.

"Wolf! Who the fuck is out there?" I ignored Coach's question as the locker room door shut behind me.

The Westin player that was talking shit the entire game smirked at Aasher before he saw me coming up behind him. His smile wavered as I popped beside Aasher and glared at the side of his face. "Let him go before the reporters come down here and see you holding him by the throat. What the fuck are you doing? And why the fuck are you even in our hallway?" I directed my last question to the Westin player, knowing that there must have been some shit-talking going on during the game that led to him meeting Aasher here for a sparring.

The Westin player's ungloved hand went to Aasher's wrist as he tried to free himself from the death grip he was trapped in.

"Get the fuck in the locker room!" Coach shouted, opening the locker room door with a beet-red face.

"Aasher," I gritted, seconds from lifting my arm up and giving him a snap elbow. *Snap the fuck out of it.* Emory went on the other side of Aasher and pushed on his chest as he finally let go of the player.

"You deserve a fucking punch for the way you played that game," I seethed. "Go before I let him land one."

The Westin player chuckled as he began walking away. Emory was pushing Aasher back into the locker room, and the very second the hallway disappeared behind the door, I started my rant with Aasher. "What the hell was that? Can we get through one fucking game without there being some conflict? You're lucky we weren't on the ice when you pulled that shit."

"We're hockey players. There is always conflict." That came from someone in the back, and I was pretty sure it was Jack, one of our younger players.

I reared back. "We can't play that way in college. If we were on the ice, he would have gotten a penalty, and that hurts the team."

Aasher was seething, clearly worked up. I nearly put him through a wall as I began getting fired up by the lack of self-control he was posing. "What was that?!" I roared. "You were fine during the game. And we won! Get it together, Aash."

"You better give me a good fucking reason, son. Or your

ass is going to be doing suicides at practice on Monday," Coach said from behind me.

Aasher paused as he looked over my shoulder at Coach. I let go of his jersey and backed away, bending down to finish taking off my gear. "You sure you want to know?" he asked, voice vibrating with anger.

I glanced at my teammates and their wary expressions and wondered where this was going. This wasn't good. Someone from the other side of the locker room said, "I don't think you want the reason, Coach."

"Well, this just got interesting," I said. "What did I miss while I was apparently the only one fucking focused?" The last part of my sentence wasn't necessary, but I was irritated.

Aasher huffed as he placed his hands on his hips angrily. Andrew spoke for him, and it was probably a good thing.

"They were bragging. Saying they were..." Andrew looked at Aasher but kept going. "They were talking about your daughter."

"Excuse me?" Coach's face turned an even brighter red than it was during the game. The one thing you didn't fuck with was the coach's daughter. It was rule number one with any sport you were in—*especially* Coach Lennon's daughter.

"For fuck's sake. This is why I cursed the moment my wife told me I was going to have a baby girl." He threw his hands up and stalked off to his office before slamming the door shut and leaving us all to ourselves.

"What did they say?" I asked, looking over at Aasher, who was sweating more than usual beneath his uniform.

"They were talking about taking her V-card. Said they had heard she wanted a hockey player to take it."

I cringed internally. "Where did they hear that? That sounds made-up and just a way to get someone riled up." *Apparently, that someone was Aasher.*

Someone piped up from the showers. "I say fake news."

"Whatever. I don't want to fucking talk about it anymore. They deserved to have their fucking faces bashed in for even suggesting it." Aasher scoffed before stomping off to the showers.

Berkley tore off his jersey. "They were talking about running a train on her, but honestly, I'm not sure if they were trying to get a rise out of anyone. I think they were discussing it among themselves, and Aasher overheard, and then they saw it was a soft spot, so they ran with it."

A train? Jesus. That was what they were thinking about while we were playing the opening game? That was exactly why we won and they lost—they were too busy thinking of other things instead of making goals.

"Let's hope they don't show up at the party," Emory added, looking at me.

I knew, without a doubt, that I was most definitely going to have to go to the party now. Like I said, hockey players were hotheads, and the last thing we needed was for Aasher to get in trouble with the law for fighting on campus.

———

The hockey players used to have their own hockey house, much like the football house that the party was currently unfolding in. Campus used to call it Puck Bunny Meadow for obvious reasons, but two years ago, there was a huge scandal. A freshman was date-raped, and Coach shut it down the very next day. We lost our privilege of having a campus hangout, but I thought it was better that way. It kept us out of trouble. Though, most of the players lived off campus, unlike me. I got free room and board on campus due to my scholarship, so it was financially smarter for me to live in the dorms—even if I was currently rooming with a female.

The front of the football house was brick and looked like your typical frat house. There was a painted sign on the very top of the porch that read *Wolves* in silver with a makeshift wolf head that someone had obviously painted while intoxicated because I was pretty certain my niece, who was four, could have done a better job.

"No sign of Westin players," I said, nudging Aasher with my shoulder. "Wouldn't want you to lose your shit again."

He said nothing as we walked in. The party was in full swing. Rush was coming down the stairs with a girl trailing him that had no doubt been fucked minutes before by the look of her flushed face and messy hair. "Good game, Brooks!" he said, coming in for a bro handshake. "Beers on the house for you guys." He looked over at Aasher as he scanned the crowd. "And I banned Westin players, bro. I heard about the fight. This is a calm environment. No fighting here. Our team can't afford it, and neither can yours."

"Problem solved," I said, catching a beer in my hand from Emory.

Aasher seemed distracted as he caught his beer. I watched as he scanned the party, apparently looking for someone, but I paused on an overly drunk girl with a random guy that looked familiar.

I squinted but moved through the party with Aasher by my side, questioning him over his slip after the game.

"You got a hard-on for Coach's daughter or something?"

"What? No." He seemed unsure but slugged back his beer, half-shielding his skeptical expression.

"Good, because that would be a hard no."

I moved out of his space a moment later, accepting his lie for what it was because I knew him better than he thought. I stood beside him as he moved his gaze through the crowd once more, landing on the same shitshow that I was staring at.

"Who is that guy over there? With the sloppy chick?" I asked, feeling more eyes on me the longer I stood in the middle of the party. Chaos was erupting around us, and the smell of needy females started to skim my senses as they began to flock to us.

"I don't recognize him," Aasher answered, swigging back more beer. "I know the girl, though. She moves on quickly, apparently." He took another swig of his beer and moved his attention elsewhere.

"Don't get shit-faced," I warned. "Not during the season."

I had a two-drink limit during the season. I didn't mind letting loose, but getting uncontrollably drunk wasn't the smartest decision, and if Coach found out, he'd make us run suicides *with* a hangover, which often ended with vomiting on the ice. We'd all leave cursing our bad decisions, full of regret.

"Good game, Wolf." Jess smiled at me as she walked past, shaking her tight ass a little more than usual. She turned around and began to walk backward as she tipped her head and swallowed a shot. "Was waiting for a text from you but didn't get one."

I squinted my eyes at her and whispered in her direction, "You know I don't have the energy after a game, Jess." *She is becoming very needy.* I shifted my attention from her seductive gaze, and my mood was instantly edged with annoyance.

Too many girls were beginning to loiter around us, and I wasn't lying to Jess. Unless a girl was offering to suck me off to fulfill her own fantasies, it was a no-go. Jess wasn't that type of girl. Our arrangement was just as much for me as it was for her. I always repaid her in the bedroom.

An hour had passed, and after a quick game of beer pong, I was ready to head home. I'd had one too many back pats and cheers for winning the game and too many swift kisses from girls that were whispering in my ear for more. Aasher kept his word. He hadn't gotten drunk, but he did keep his eye on the crowd, looking for someone.

"You ready?" I asked, nodding to the door.

He pulled his gaze from someone that was tucked in the back. "I'm gonna stay."

I got a better look at the girl in the corner and groaned. "Bro, no."

"What?"

"You better stop, dude. It's noticeable as fuck, even with her hiding out in the back."

"What are you talking about?" Aasher said, acting as if I couldn't see Coach's daughter—the meek, nerdy girl that did *not* belong at a party like this.

Landon showed up out of nowhere and leaned in between us. "You eye-fucking the coach's daughter is what he's talking about."

He scoffed. "I'm not eye-fucking her. I'm just making sure she's...safe. Did you hear the way those Westin players were talking about her?"

"But they're not even here, and why do you feel the responsibility to keep her safe?" I cocked an eyebrow. He could deny it all he wanted, but he wasn't telling the truth.

Aasher turned his back to me without answering, and I gave Landon a nod that was a silent agreement between us that he'd keep an eye on the team. I spun around with the confirmation and made my way through the party. The crowd was thinning out as the night went on, but I was stupid to think I could make it to the door without catching Jess's eye again. She nodded to the stairs and raised her brows. I shook my head. *Not tonight.*

Just as I opened the door and the cold air flowed into the stuffy entryway, I turned and glanced at the stairs. I caught the back end of the inebriated girl being pulled by a hand, which wasn't unusual, but when I saw who was pulling her, I did another double-take.

Oh, shit. That was how I knew him. The guy that was flirting with her earlier *was* familiar to me, and it wasn't because we'd had classes together. Claire's face flashed in my brain like a memory I couldn't hide from, and confusion made me pause for far longer than I meant to. *Fuck, this made a lot of sense.*

"Change your mind?" Jess's voice broke me out of my stupor, and there was something that had *almost* made me say yes but not because I wanted to fuck her. More because I wanted to investigate what Claire's boyfriend was doing going upstairs with another girl. I mean, it was kind of obvious, but as far as I knew, they hadn't broken up.

"No," I snapped to Jess before hastily walking out the door and heading straight for the dorms.

12

CLAIRE

THIS WAS the first time I had been in my dorm room without Theo sucking up all the energy inside the small space with his masculinity and overbearing need to make himself known by just breathing.

He was sound asleep by the time I got in last night from practicing my audition, and since I was staying true to our new-and-*improved* rules that hung crookedly on the wall in between our beds, I ended up texting Chad instead of answering his phone call, which made him irrationally angry.

I was still in my left split on the floor in between Theo's and my beds as I skimmed my finger over my screen and reread our texts, feeling a deep pit form in my core.

Chad: Why won't you answer the phone?

Me: My roommate is asleep.

Chad: So?

Me: It's called being considerate. He has a

game tomorrow, so he went to bed early, and we have established some roommate rules that entail being considerate of one another.

Chad: Since when do you care about some jock's game? Is there something going on, Claire?

Me: Like what?

I turned my phone screen off as I stood up from my split and threw it onto my bed. Things with Chad were more tense now that I was back at campus versus over the summer when I was living with my mom in our hometown. It was almost like he was frustrated that I was back, which was confusing.

Compartmentalize, Claire.

Sighing, I cleared my head and climbed onto my bed, trying to find an angle of the room that I could do a split leap without hitting something in the process. The thought of an injury causing me to bow out of fall auditions caused a line of stress to fly down my spine. Now, more than ever, I *needed* to land a role in the spring show. I *had* to be in the running to win the scholarship. Most of my paychecks were about to go to Ralph for the repairs for my mom's bathroom floor, and I was beginning to think I wouldn't be able to afford next semester's books.

There was nothing quite like the fear of being kicked out of school because you couldn't afford it for motivation, now was there? Wiggling my fingers out in front of myself and lengthening my spine as much as I could on top of a mattress, I was mid-leap, fully in mid-air, when the door flung open. Theo stood in the doorway, shocked, as I landed in front of him.

"Jesus Christ, Bryant!" he shouted, bending down and gripping me by my upper arms. "Are you okay?"

A laugh bubbled from my chest as he pulled me to my feet, looking completely alarmed. He dropped his eyes to his hands on my arms, and he quickly tore them off before shutting the door with his foot.

"I'm fine. I was practicing," I said, half-laughing. "Relax, Gramps."

"Practicing what?" His voice neared hysteria as he walked farther into the room and threw his bag on the foot of his bed. "How to attack someone?"

Going back to my side of the room, I shrugged on my cardigan and pulled the scrunchie from my damp hair, letting the wet ends fall over my shoulders. "No"—I went to my bed and grabbed my phone to see if Chad had finally texted me back—"my split leap."

Theo kicked off his shoes before shifting his gaze back and forth in between the space of our beds. When he landed back on me, he raced his eyes down my body and back up again, as if he were sizing me up. "Leaps? In here? Don't you have, like, a studio for that? A dance studio? That's like me practicing hockey in here."

"It's definitely not the same thing. And yes, we have a studio, but when I saw you were gone, I decided to just do my stretching in here, and that then snowballed into"—I wafted my hand out, feeling stupid—"a split leap."

Theo bent down and plugged his phone in, and I knew that was my cue to get ready for bed because he was beginning his nightly routine. He really was like a grandpa—so serious about his routine. Theo was definitely a creature of habit. "Where were you, anyway?" I asked, checking the clock. "It's *way* past your bedtime."

His sarcastic chuckle rubbed over my curiosity, and for

the second time in one minute, I felt stupid with his response. "You might be the only student on campus who is unaware of the hockey schedule." *Oh, that's right.*

Even after recalling there was a game, I mentally rolled my eyes. As if I had the space in my brain to worry about something like Bexley U's hockey games on top of my work schedule, schoolwork, my mother's bills that she just *couldn't* get on top of, and the whereabouts of my boyfriend.

Sensing my discomfort, Theo left the room, and I quickly changed into my sleep shorts and t-shirt and crawled into my bed. I had been ready to go to sleep the second I got off from work, thankful that I had the early shift—which, in my defense, was partly why I'd forgotten it was game night on campus. If I had the late shift, I would have known, without a doubt, that there was a game. Most of the students stopped by and got food at The Bex before heading to the after-parties.

I understood why Taytum wanted me to go out with her now too. The parties on campus were always a little rowdier when there was a home game, and I was certain they had won because the hockey team was *"unstoppable"* per the campus gossip.

Theo walked back into the room a moment later and immediately saw that I was in bed. He was carrying his dirty clothes in one hand and had changed into a gray BU shirt with a pair of workout shorts. We said nothing as he flopped onto his bed, sending a wave of his body wash in my direction, and checked his phone for a second before clicking it off. I leaned over and turned the light off on the small bookcase that sat right beside my bed, and nothing but our even breathing filled the tiny area.

Usually, Theo was fast asleep when I'd get back to the

room. He'd occasionally huff and puff if I was being too loud, but he usually fell back into a slumber when I was finally crawling into bed for the night. But this was the first time we were both actively awake and trying to fall asleep at the same time. A weird sense of discomfort settled in my lower stomach as I tried to listen to anything but his breathing, but I couldn't help but latch onto it. There was an awkward shift in the air, and I heard him turn beneath his blankets, so I did the same before grabbing my phone to do something other than listen to his breathing like some sort of obsessive puck bunny.

My brightness was turned down, but I knew if he was looking at me, he could see the annoyance on my face from Chad not responding to my texts. I shoved the frustrating and pesky thoughts behind a thick wall of denial in the back of my head.

I turned my screen off, laid my phone face down on the shelf, and inhaled a deep breath before blowing it out slowly. My mind was reeling, and just like every night, my worries began to surface the second I tried to fall asleep. Long, antagonizing minutes passed, and I couldn't take it anymore. I continued to listen closely to Theo's breathing, and when I thought he may have been asleep, I threw my covers off, slowly climbed out of my bed, padded my way over to my desk, and sat down in the dark.

I flipped open my *Classical Ballet Technique* book and grabbed a pencil out of my pencil holder slowly so it wouldn't make a noise. After building a barricade around my desk lamp with my other textbooks and tying my chiffon tie-on ballet skirt that I typically wore with my leo around it with a scrunchie, I flipped the light on and hoped it wouldn't be too bright and wake Theo. Technically, I was breaking a roommate rule, but I was still being considerate with trying to make my light dimmer, right?

My hand skimmed the pages of the book as I tried to lose myself in my studies, focusing on classical ballet theories and the comprehension of soloists, seemingly allowing my mind to drift in other directions—like my future.

I didn't want to be a soloist in a famous ballet show one day.

I didn't want to continue down a path of writing papers about famous ballet dancers like Anna Pavlova or Natalia Makarova. But, nonetheless, I saw the importance in gaining an education, and back when I applied to Bexley U and they gave me the partial scholarship, I thought I knew what my future would look like. Now, I wasn't so sure.

My pencil pressed down harder than before as I wrote down several important ballet terms that I knew would be on the quiz next week. The snippets of my mother's unrelenting encouragement to push me to a future that I didn't necessarily want caused the lead of my pencil to snap with heavy force.

I gripped my pencil so tightly I heard the creaking of splintering wood. Theo's bed creaked a second later, and my back straightened. I peeked over my shoulder and jumped in my seat when I saw that he was awake and his head full of messy dark hair was leaning on his hand as he stared at me. I reached for my light and shut it off abruptly. His chuckle made me smash my lips together.

"Did you just try to pretend like you weren't murdering a pencil at your desk by turning the light off? As if we didn't just make eye contact?"

Embarrassment flooded me, and I was thankful I turned the light off, because I instantly felt idiotic.

"I thought you were asleep," I said softly. "Did I wake you up?"

His swallow sounded rough, but his voice was as smooth as ever. "Are you referring to waking me up by building a wall of books around your lamp, or are you referring to the vigorous scratching of your pencil against paper?"

Theo didn't give me a chance to answer his question, which I realized was just his way of poking fun at me, as usual. "I've been awake. I hadn't fallen asleep."

"Oh." That was surprising. "I assumed you'd be super tired from your game that I'm guessing you won?"

His scoff was as cocky as they came. "Of course we won."

There was a pause as I stood up and pushed in my chair, heading back to my bed. I eyed my phone but didn't dare pick it up as I crawled under my covers and stared up at the dark ceiling.

"I can't sleep after games."

My eyes moved to his side of the room, although all I could make out was a large shadow on his bed. "Really? Why?"

"I get too hyped up. I start going over plays in my head to figure out what we can do better for the next game. I usually lie here for hours until my body gives up and I crash."

I wasn't sure why, but I found that both admirable and shocking.

"I figured that you would be out partying and celebrating your win like the rest of campus."

A throaty chuckle came from his side of the room. "I was out, but I never party hard during the season. I usually make the rounds..."

His words trailed off, and I had a big feeling I knew why.

"By 'making the rounds' you mean you meet up with a puck bunny and then you come home." I scoffed.

Years of snarky remarks about jocks from close friends who'd had their heart broken by the star football player or hockey star—or hell, even the top golfer of our school—came back to me as if I were still that same freshman, holding a hostility for jocks because that was how I was raised. It was hard to form your own opinion that wasn't clouded by judgment when you were told something negative from a very young age. I'll never forget the first time I had the courage to ask my mother why I didn't have a father.

"You sound a little jealous. Where's your boyfriend tonight, Claire?"

A hard lump formed in my chest that I tried to massage away. "I'm not jealous. I'm just stating the facts. I'm right, aren't I? Isn't that what you jocks do?" A bitter laugh left me because his question struck a nerve. I had no idea where Chad was, and it stung.

"What is it with you and jocks?" Theo's tone had definitely changed from light and airy to tense and heavy. "Did a jock break your heart or something? Is that why you're with a guy like Chad? You *are* still with him, right?"

I turned and faced him, even though he couldn't see me. I traced the outline of his profile, annoyed that his nose was perfect and straight, even in the dark. "No, a jock didn't break my heart." *But I did have one who abandoned me as a baby.* "I've never dated one because you're all the same."

"I call bullshit," he muttered. I could practically see his eye roll in our pitch-black room.

"Whatever," I muttered back, crossing my arms over my chest.

Silence passed between us, and the room was as tight as the scrunchie around my wrist. I tore it off and threw it to the ground with force when Theo's steady tone filled the tense space. "But seriously. Where's your boyfriend tonight? We've been rooming together for, what? Two weeks? I've seen him once."

My heart leapt in my chest, and those thoughts that I had pushed behind a thick cloud of denial were suddenly very clear in my head. "Are you implying something?"

The vibrating of my phone stopped Theo from whatever he was about to say. I hurriedly reached and grabbed it, hoping it was Chad and I could actually answer Theo and not have to lie about knowing the whereabouts of my boyfriend—which, to be frank, was none of his business.

"Is that him now?" he asked, making me feel even worse when I realized it wasn't.

Sitting up in defeat, I answered my phone while ignoring Theo. "Tay?"

"Claire, I *hate* to do this, but could you...posssssssssibly... come get me and the rest of the dance girls?" The background of whatever party she was at was so loud I felt like I was there with her.

I sighed. "What happened to Ubering?"

"Katelyn got super wassstteed, and they won't let her come. They said they didn't want her to yack in the backseat." I suppressed a laugh at the way she said "yack" and began pushing the covers off my legs.

"Well, I don't want her to throw up in mine either," I said, "but yes, I'll come get you guys. Are you sober enough to send me a pin?"

"I love you so, so, soooo much," she said before hanging up. A moment later, I got a text with her location, and I threw my hair up in a high bun with the scrunchie that I'd thrown onto the floor a minute prior. I annoyingly opened up my dresser and searched in the dark for my joggers and pulled them on over my sleep shorts.

My hand was on the doorknob, and I had no intention of saying another word to Theo, but his light turned on, and his voice stopped me. "You never answered me, Bryant."

Turning around, I raised my eyebrows at him and saw that he was fully sitting up with a determined look in his eye that I felt in parts of my body that should have been asleep.

"Do you know where your boyfriend is tonight?"

I heard my heartbeat in my ears as Theo's temples flickered back and forth, waiting for my answer. *Does he know something I don't?* I felt as small as a seed, standing by the door, looking at him.

I swallowed and stayed silent. The hardness around his green eyes lessened the longer we stared at one another.

"I hate to be the one to say this"—he flew back onto his bed and flipped his light off—"but I'm pretty sure he's cheating on you."

The pounding in my ears intensified to the point that I couldn't hear anything else after his statement. I pulled open the door and slammed it on my way out, compartmentalizing my worries just like I had learned to do over the last few years.

13

THEO

I AVOIDED my room like it was the plague, and people were starting to notice. Believe it or not, I didn't like to be the bearer of bad news, and I felt like a fucking dick after last Friday.

"I would rather not go back to my room tonight." My face depicted exactly how uncomfortable I was feeling. "She drives me crazy."

The nights were getting colder, and a cloud of air flew from my mouth as I referred to Claire. The team and I hustled to the locker room after leaving the bus, and most were heading to bed and talking about the parties they were going to head to tomorrow evening. The celebration parties for away games were held on the day after, and thankfully, we'd won. It was a disadvantage to play at another school's rink, but as always, my worries left the moment the stick was in my hand and the ice was beneath my skates. NHL scouts were rumored to be at Heston U for tonight's game, and if they were, they'd be impressed because I played a damn good game, putting up five points for my team. I could only hope it got word back to Tom Gardini, the man who owned the Blues and the only other man, besides my father, that I strived to impress.

"She'd drive me crazy too." Dax bumped his shoulder into me and wiggled his eyebrows. "It would be hard not to crawl over to her bed in the middle of the night."

I groaned as he snickered and walked off to his locker to put his gear away. The team incessantly teased me about rooming with Claire, and Coach consistently asked if she was becoming a distraction—which she wasn't. Truth be told, it was frustrating that I was even allowing her to make me feel uncomfortable in my own room. She hadn't even made eye contact with me since I told her I thought her boyfriend was cheating on her.

In fact, I was pretty sure she gave our table away at The Bex yesterday because she didn't want to wait on me. Didn't hurt my feelings, but it sure did hurt my teammates' feelings because we had a male waiter instead.

"What exactly is she doing that's driving you crazy? What happened to your rules?" Aasher asked.

I pulled my hoodie over my head and grabbed my bag before heading out to my car. It was late. The Bex was closing soon, so everyone was heading to their beds or trying to catch a puck bunny before crashing. I didn't want to do anything but decompress after the game, but if Claire was in our room, I'd have to figure out a way to block her out.

"Yeah, we did," I said. "But things between my little roomie and I are a little rocky at the moment. I told her I thought her boyfriend was cheating on her."

Aasher paused mid-step. "Bro, what? Why would you tell her that?"

I shrugged. "Because I'm pretty sure he is." I looked

over to gauge his reaction. "Remember that guy that I said looked familiar at the party last Friday?"

The crease between his eyes smoothed out before he shook his head. "Nope." *That's right, you wouldn't remember because you were staring at Coach's daughter all night.*

"Well, I think it was Claire's boyfriend, and she got all weird when I asked about him." I started to climb in my car. "I saw him going up the stairs with some other chick before I left."

Aasher shook his head as he began walking away. "I would stay out of it, dude. It's not like you have a responsibility to her just because she's your roommate. I mean, I live with Efrain, and I haven't told his girlfriend that he beats off to anime porn every chance he gets. Not my business."

An uncomfortable visual came to mind, and Aasher laughed loudly. "Now you get to know that information too. You'll never look at him the same."

I slammed the door and cursed Aasher the entire time I drove to the dorms. The visual of Efrain and his hand around his dick was stuck in my head, even as I rounded the hallway and laid eyes on my door.

I stopped in my tracks as the quietness of the hallway disappeared and then made my way to a giant red flag waiting outside my door. *Fucking shit.*

"No," I snapped, making my way toward my room. Same shit, different year. It was only game two of the season, and the puck bunnies were already starting up? Last year, this occurred later in the season, but color me fucking surprised that they were starting up earlier.

The girl quickly popped to her feet and ran her hands down her tight jeans and crop top that showed off her flat belly. "I didn't ask you anything."

I chuckled, walking slower than normal. "Yeah. You did." I brushed past her and put my key in the door. I peered down at her puppy-dog eyes that were a little glazed. *Liquid courage?* "How did you find out my room number?"

She laughed shyly. "It's not that hard to find out."

I raised an eyebrow at her. "Who told you?"

"It's all over campus, Wolf. It's not like you have security guards outside Dorothy Hall. You just wait for someone to walk in and then slip in behind them. There are only three athletic dorms on campus. Third one's a charm." The way her eyes twinkled after she explained herself made me think that she thought she was charming, but she wasn't. She was desperate and sloppy, and that was only hot when I was too intoxicated to notice.

"Come on." She slowly ran her finger down my arm, and my muscles twitched with annoyance. "I heard you haven't experienced college until you've had a wolf in bed."

"Sorry," I said, wanting her to back up so I could get in my room without her trying to slip in. She seemed like she'd be one to try it. "Not tonight. You're cute and all"—cue me trying to let her down easy—"but showing up to my room after I just played a game isn't the way to my bed, babe."

"But—" Her bottom lip jutted out, and I gritted my teeth, knowing this was going to be impossible to get out of, and the number of times I had to call security last year to remove my posse of...*fans*...from waiting outside my door was unjust. Look, jocks have feelings too, and we like our privacy, okay?

I turned toward her. "Will you please just leave? This is my senior year, and the last thing I need is a bunch of puck bunnies trying to weave themselves into my life through a quick fuck. Because no matter how many times you girls say it, none of you are just trying to fuck. You all get attached, and I don't need that drama, alright? Especially not this year." My unneeded explanation began to spike my blood pressure. "Pass it along to everyone else. I'm not getting mixed up with puck bunnies this year, got it?" I hadn't totally made that decision until this moment, but fuck it.

"But—"

"No," I snapped. *Fuck.* I pulled out my phone, really not wanting to call campus security on this girl, but then the door opened, and Claire's face came in between us. An idea popped in my head, and before I could stop myself, my phone slipped back into my pocket, and a grin spread across my face.

"What is goi—"

"Hey, babe." My sly greeting made Claire pull back in confusion and maybe a little disgust. My arm went around her waist, and I tugged her in close. A swallow got lodged in my throat when I felt her bare skin against my hand, knowing I had accidentally slipped my grip underneath her shirt. She had on a pair of black-rimmed glasses perched on the end of her nose, and a blush spread across her face as quickly as I regained my composure. "Thanks for waiting up for me."

"Wait, isn't she your roommate?" The puck bunny slowly began to back away as defeat crossed her features.

"Yeah." I stepped even closer to my roommate, who no doubt hated me at that moment. Claire began to move away from me the closer I got to her, but I dug my fingers into her side and breathed down into her space. "She's my room-mate...and other things." *Come on, Claire. Play along.*

I stayed turned toward Claire but peeked out of the corner of my eye at the puck bunny. Embarrassment rushed to her face, but it seemed to sober her up. "Oh, I...I didn't know."

"No, that's—" Claire's panicked rebuttal needed to wait at least another five seconds until this girl ran off. I cut off her words by peering down and piercing her with a stare. My arm was a steel brace against her back, and my fingers spread out against her flesh. Her lips snapped shut as she glanced up at me with surprise, and the goosebumps that rushed to her skin beneath mine made me pause for a second before I realized we were suddenly alone in the hall and the puck bunny had disappeared. I pushed Claire inside our room, and the second the door was closed, she flew from my grasp in a wrath of anger.

"What the hell, Theo!" Her hands went to her hips, and the blush on her cheeks grew redder with what I had assumed was anger. "Why did you do that? If that gets around campus, everyone is going to think we're a thing!"

I threw my hands up. *Shit, that's brilliant.* "Yes! That's perfect. Maybe they'll stop showing up here unannounced."

"I have a boyfriend!" Claire's tiny foot stomped against the floor, and that was when I ran my gaze down her body. *How does she look so cute when she looks like a mess?* Her brown hair was in a wild bun on the top of her head with a bunch of loose strands framing her face. She had on glasses that made her look a little nerdy, and she wore baggy, light-pink sweats with a BU Dance logo on the upper thigh and a loose shirt that was sporting her braless chest. "Stop looking at me like that."

I snapped back to reality and met her eye. "Like what?" Surely she had no idea what I was just thinking, because I couldn't even believe what I was thinking.

"Like you can't believe that someone like me has a boyfriend." I caught a few words that she mumbled after her utterance, and they closely resembled what I'd told her last Friday about her boyfriend.

I shook my head and walked farther into the room, trying to put some space between us. My head was swimming, and her response irritated me. "That wasn't what I was thinking, Bryant."

"Yeah, *okay*," she scoffed. "Don't do that again."

"Don't do what? Look at you?" I asked innocently, trying to ease up the tension that was currently collecting on my shoulders.

"Touch me and act like I'm your girlfriend or fuck buddy in front of these girls."

I couldn't help but smile. She was so riled up even her chest was rising, and it was confirmed—she did not have a bra on. "Okay. I won't do it in front of those girls. But does that mean I can do it behind closed doors?"

Her nose scrunched up before she grabbed one of her millions of scrunchies from atop her desk and threw it at me. It hit me right over my heart, and I stared down at the purple hair tie before clutching my chest. "Ow." I suppressed a laugh as her mouth twitched. She spun around, putting her back to me, and I bent down and put the purple scrunchie on my wrist just to irritate her even more.

Claire left a moment later with her shower stuff, and I smiled to myself as the door slammed behind her. There was something about irritating her that entertained me. It was invigorating, and I couldn't help but laugh to myself as I lay in bed, waiting for her to come back to the room. Sure, there was still an air of friction between us, but it was innocently placed and a little bit comical.

At least now she was angry because I had used her to make a puck bunny go away and not angry because I pointed out the obvious with her loser boyfriend who left her alone on yet another Friday night. *He couldn't make it any clearer than that, right?*

When Claire came back into the room with her damp hair and body wash that made my blood warm, I forced myself not to smile at her, even though the mischievous boy that still lived inside of me was clawing to come back out to play with her. *What am I, twelve?*

The lights were out a moment later, and we both lay in silence, and for the first time after a game, I actually felt tired. My breathing was beginning to slow, and my muscles were exhausted. The sound of her smooth breathing was kind of...comforting? Before I fully fell asleep, I turned toward her and tried to make amends.

"Hey, Bryant?"

Her voice was raspy, but I still heard an edge to it as she snapped out, "What?"

"Thanks."

A breathy sigh was all I got, but for some reason, the next morning, when I woke up to run and caught a glimpse of her relaxed face and closed eyes, I turned off my alarm before it could go off, and I went back to sleep, not wanting to wake her up.

14

CLAIRE

"He said what?" I asked, holding my books in a tight grip with my phone pressed up to my ear. The second floor was thankfully less chaotic than the first as I walked to my room, listening to my mother.

Her voice was nearing hysterics, but I brushed it off, knowing she was as dramatic as a thirteen-year-old girl who just hit puberty. "Claire! Aren't you listening? He said I had to pay at least 50% of what the contractor wants by tomorrow morning!"

I leaned against the wall beside my door, unsure if Theo was in our room or not. If he was, I didn't want him to over-hear the conversation, and knowing Theo, he'd listen to every single word. He'd already admitted once to listening to my phone calls, and I was sure he'd do it again.

My cheeks burned at the thought of last weekend where I was forced to act like his girlfriend. I walked around campus for the next several days, bouncing in and out of classes like a pariah, wondering if his worshipping puck bunnies were going to shun me for stealing their number-one guy. But to my surprise, the girl who was a witness to Theo's show either hadn't remembered or was too embarrassed to tell anyone. No one looked at me with distaste, and better yet, nothing had gotten back to Chad, so I put the whole thing behind me, hoping Theo wouldn't do it again. He wondered why girls were constantly showing up to his room unannounced, but maybe it was because every day this week, he'd brought one home.

Technically, he didn't break any of the roommate rules because he did put a "nonverbal warning" on the doorknob to indicate that he was in there with someone, but instead of hanging a sock like a normal guy, he used my freaking scrunchie. *My* purple scrunchie. When I told him that I didn't want my hair accessories associated with his slutty activities, he smirked and began collecting them all. Yesterday, I came home to seven scrunchies tied together, hanging from the doorknob.

"Claire! Are you listening to me?" I jumped as my mother's sharp voice pelted through the phone.

"Ye-yeah." I cleared my throat. "Did you ask Linda if they had any more clients that you could add to your clientele? Maybe make a little more cash in the next couple of weeks?"

Sweat began to hit my hairline as I mentally began counting my shifts and estimating how much in tips I'd make in the coming days. *How am I going to afford my books next semester at this rate?*

"I don't want to ask Linda for more clients. I'd rather them not know that I'm struggling with money again. They don't need another reason to look down on me. Did you tell Chad? Please tell me you didn't tell him."

I swallowed my stress. "No. I didn't tell him." The last

thing I needed was for his parents to give my mother more handouts and put us in an even deeper hole of debt with them. Those handouts were like bullets for Chad. "It's fine, Mom. I'll put some money in your account in just a few. But please, please, *please* make sure you give it to Ralph."

She huffed as I turned my ear toward my door, hearing some type of commotion inside. I glanced down to the doorknob, but there weren't any scrunchies on it.

"What else would I do with it, Claire? I can't be homeless. I told Ralph I'd have it for him in the morning. Look, I gotta go. Mr. Ortiz is coming home any minute, and he likes me to be done with the cleaning by the time he gets home."

"Alright, I'll send a text when I send the mon—"

The line went dead, and I scoffed, pushing my phone in my pocket while mumbling under my breath, "You're welcome, Mom—again."

A sigh began to crawl up my throat just as I began to reach for my key, but I jumped when my door flung open. I was met with a growly Theo, seeming more intense than usual. He towered over me like a dangerous omen, stealing my ability to function as his temples flickered back and forth.

"Go."

What? Theo looked directly over my head, so I looked behind me, but no one was there.

"But I have no pants on—" *Who the hell is that?* I tried to peek inside my room, but Theo, being larger than most, took up the entire doorway.

"There are consequences to your behavior, sweetheart." I watched as he rolled his eyes and nearly shut the door in my face as I stood back in confusion. His large hand stopped it at the last second, and he pulled it open again.

My jaw dropped as a girl came scrambling toward me in nothing but a t-shirt and a pair of underwear. It was like a bull coming straight for a red flag. I quickly moved out of the way and watched her run down the hall, half-naked. A few guys had popped out of their rooms from the rumpus and applauded her as she disappeared down the stairs.

I pushed past Theo and his unusual bout of broodiness before walking toward my desk to drop my books on top. Before the door even shut, I glanced at the room and did a double-take at a pile of girl's clothes thrown all over the floor.

"Really?" I said, rolling my eyes. "What happened to the nonverbal warning?" I kicked the girl's jeans off my side of the room, beginning to feel the pent-up irritation that had been brewing since the moment he used my purple scrunchie on the door. Because Theo didn't warn me of its meaning, I had no idea the scrunchie on my door was his comical "nonverbal warning". So, imagine my surprise when I walked in on his head between a girl's legs. "You've been doing *just* fine with using my scrunchies on the door every single day this week." I picked up the scrunchie from yesterday and held it up in between us.

"I didn't invite this one." The anger Theo had possessed a moment ago lessened as he stared down at the bra that I'd kicked over to his bed. He slowly picked it up by the strap and acted as if it were going to catch on fire at any second. I stared at him as he threw it across the room and smiled as I watched a chill race down his body.

A laugh bubbled in my chest and erupted from my mouth a moment later. Theo whipped his attention over to me. A lock of his dark hair had fallen onto his forehead as he gaped, completely taken aback at my reaction. The more he stared at me with confusion, the more I laughed. My hand flew to my mouth as tears began to gather in my eyes.

"Wh–what?" I asked in between laughs. A few more had escaped me before I was able to regain my composure.

Theo shook his head as he shrugged off his shirt, showing off his bare chest. My laugh had long disappeared, and I tore my gaze from his side of the room and put it on my floor. *He did that on purpose.*

"I've just never heard you laugh that hard."

I shrugged, looking over at my bed. "I just think it's funny that—" I stopped mid-sentence and snapped my neck to look at him. He had on a new shirt, and I was pretty sure he was getting ready for practice. "Theo. Is...is that her underwear on my bed?!" By the time I had finished my sentence, my voice was more of a shriek than anything. Theo's green eyes lit up with something *very* similar to amusement.

"But how—" My gaze shifted to my dresser, and I wanted to throw the entire piece of furniture at him. "Did you...just give your puck bunny my fucking underwear?!"

My hands clamped onto my waist, and I spun around with anger, ready to attack him. Theo threw his hands up with mock innocence, but his chest was tight with laughter. The smirk on his face made me want to punch him. "Theo! You are not supposed to go through my underwear drawer! I *knew* that rule would come in handy!" My words were rushed, and with every single syllable, I grew more heated. "I am going to kill you!" I shouted.

I ran the two feet it took to get over to my bed and grabbed my pencil from my desk on the way. The *used* thong on my bed flew across the room, along with the pencil I had used to pick it up with. They both landed right below Theo's smiling face. "You wonder why all these girls keep showing up to your room! You bring them almost every single day! Our room might as well be a brothel!"

Theo threw his head back, and the room filled with his rowdy laughter. It was annoying because he had a good laugh. It was throaty and masculine but still light. "Correction. I did not go through your underwear drawer." His gaze slowly slid down to my clean basket full of folded clothes that were now rumpled.

"Oh my God! You are unbelievable!" Before I knew what was happening, my feet were taking me over to him, and I tried to hit him on the chest with my fist before he grabbed it at the last second with an even deeper grin on his face.

"Calm down, Bryant! I'll get your panties back for you."

"Ew!" I snatched my hand away from him, irritated that his large hand fully encased my wrist. "I don't want used panties. If she's showing up in our room unannounced, it's hard to tell where her pussy has been!"

Both Theo and I made eye contact with the word that had just come from my mouth. *Did I really–*

"Did you really just say the word pussy?"

An exasperated laugh escaped me, and Theo bent over at the waist, gasping for breath between his laughter. He was laughing so hard that I hardly heard the knock on the door. I forced a sigh from my mouth and stomped across the room, still half-angry. "It's probably her, wanting her thong back!"

Theo quickly began gathering his stuff. "Well, she's not getting them. Do stupid things, get stupid rewards. She can't just show up naked, refuse to leave, and then want her clothes back."

"She has my panties. Which ones did you give her? I bet

they were my favorite ones."

I could see that he was still smirking as he pulled his BU hat backward. I wanted to continue acting irritated with him, but a weird part of me wanted to stay in this moment because, for the first time in weeks, I felt weirdly comfortable around him.

"I'll buy you new ones."

I opened the door with a hidden smile on my face, fully prepared to watch this girl beg for her clothes back, but I choked when I saw that it wasn't a girl at all. Instead, it was Chad.

My smile fell, and it was hard not to notice the way I suddenly felt a change in my attitude. "Chad."

His black-rimmed glasses hid the crease of disappointment that I was certain was grooved in between his eyebrows. The blue of his eyes turned to ice as he watched my cheeks fall. "What? You're not happy to see me?"

I shook my head, a fake smile rushing to my mouth. "Of course I am. I just wasn't expecting you."

My hand fell from the door as Theo pulled it farther open, standing entirely too close to me. "Hey. I'm Theo."

I stepped to the side, away from what felt like a fire brewing, and glanced at my roommate. I was struck by how tense he seemed. All his humor from just a few moments ago was completely gone. He wore a blank expression as he stared at Chad, eyeing him with something I'd never seen before.

Chad looked up at Theo briefly and dismissed him a moment later. "Yeah, I know who you are." His attention was back on me, and I suddenly felt caught in a trap.

Theo's jaw wiggled back and forth, and I caught his quick glance in my direction before he brushed past Chad, letting the door almost slam in his face. Chad put his foot out and began stepping inside my room before we were stopped in the doorway by the sound of Theo's authoritative voice commanding the hallway.

"You know what... I know who you are too," he said, pulling his black bag up on his shoulder a little higher. A guy with broad shoulders stopped a few feet ahead of Theo but kept his back to us all, clearly listening to the conversation. *That isn't obvious at all.*

Chad didn't move from the doorway before he chuckled, "I doubt that."

Theo's white teeth clamped onto his bottom lip, and I gulped. I wasn't sure what was going through his mind, but my entire body tensed from his expression. I was looking at the Theo that was on the ice, no doubt. Self-assured with an edge of a threat backing his words.

Theo's teeth disappeared as he shook his head. "No, no." He squinted. "I'm pretty sure I saw you at a party last Friday. Yeah? Weren't you at Chi Alpha Sigma?"

Chi Alpha Sigma? That was also known as the party house for the football players. I'd gone with Taytum our freshman year. Chad stared at Theo a second too long, and I broke the stand-off. "Chad...at a party with a bunch of jocks?" A laugh left me. *There is no way.*

My boyfriend chuckled as he quickly glanced at me before putting his attention back on Theo. There was zero amusement on Theo's face, though. Chad smirked, agreeing with me. "Yeah, I could definitely find a better way to spend my time than at a frat party with a bunch of you jocks. You must be mistaking me for someone else, man."

The guy that had stopped by Theo turned around and elbowed him. "We're gonna be late."

Theo didn't pull his stare from Chad, though. Instead,

he said, "I hope I am mistaken..."—he glanced at me for a fleeting second—"for her sake."

I kept my expression steady as I stared back at Theo. I could have formed into a statue right there with the look of concern covering his features before he turned around and disappeared down the stairs.

Chad scoffed before pushing me back into my room and shutting the door with force. "That's why I hate jocks. What is it with them and their need to try and act like the bigger man in the room?" He took one look at my room and shuddered. "I do not miss dorm rooms. They're so...small."

I stayed close to the door, hearing Theo's words over and over again in my head to the point that I couldn't hear a single word coming from Chad's. "Is that where you were last Friday?" I asked, ignoring everything that was coming from his mouth.

Chad's eyebrows raised as he took a seat on my bed. "What? No. Of course not. We've been together for how long? You should know that I'd never be caught dead at one of those parties."

It was true. The visual of Chad surrounded by a ton of hunky jocks was almost comical, but the way Theo looked at me was making my stomach twist with unease.

"Where were you, then?" I tried to ask the question without sounding skeptical, but by the look of annoyance on Chad's face, it was obvious that I didn't succeed.

"Are you really going to let some stupid hockey player twist things between us?" My mouth opened, but Chad stood up and crowded my space. "Look at me." His hands gripped my cheeks a little harder than usual. "Don't you trust me?"

"Ye–yeah," I answered, peering up into his gaze that

resembled the boy I fell for in my sophomore year of high school. The only problem? He wasn't that same boy anymore, and the safety and comfort I used to feel with his hands on me had turned to something else entirely, and I wasn't sure how to escape it.

15

THEO

Lena: You owe me.

I quickly texted my older sister back as I pulled my shirt over my head, watching the locker room clear quicker than normal. We had a game tomorrow night, so everyone was ready to head home and catch some z's before our match against Crown Point University. The Hawks were good, but so were we.

Me: Was the package delivered?

Lena: This sounds like a drug deal. Yes, little brother. The pair of women's underwear, size small, was delivered by Maggie. They're on your windshield. Now are you going to explain? Or do I even want to know?

Aasher snorted, and I spun around to see Ford standing on the locker room bench, peering down to look over my shoulder.

"What the fuck are you doing?" I clicked my phone off and glared up at him.

"Women's underwear? What are you up to, Wolf?" Ford's face split in two, and I wanted to punch the smile right off of it.

Aasher pulled his hood up on his head and leaned against the lockers, glancing up to see who was lingering around in the locker room. "I know what this is about. It's about Bryant."

I rolled my eyes and packed my things up, knowing I would have to explain before Ford started to run his mouth and told the team I liked to wear women's underwear the night before a game or some shit. Not that anyone would believe a word that came from Ford's mouth, but I'd like to avoid it altogether if I could.

"Oooh, your roomie? Please, do tell."

Although the other guys in the locker room weren't looking in our direction, they were like a bunch of gossiping girls. I shot Aasher a look, and he smirked, waiting for my explanation.

"You buying your girl underwear now?"

There was a knock in my chest at the thought of someone calling *anyone* my girl. "One," I started, "I don't have a girl." All eyes were on me now, and I knew my team was eager to learn more about Claire, if their longing gazes in her direction every time we were at The Bex said anything about it. Or if they caught a glimpse of her walking into our room for the evening wearing her tight leotard, as if she didn't have pants she could put on over it. To her benefit, though, the girl was perpetually running late. "And two...I accidentally gave one of the puck bunnies a pair of her panties, and she was pissed, so I told her I would buy her a new pair."

Silence filled the locker room until Coach's laughter echoed around us. His bright-red cheeks rounded with humor at my explanation that he was apparently listening to, and it wasn't until he shut the door that the locker room filled with silence again.

It only took two seconds before the rest of the team began chuckling. Ford's mouth hung open as he shook his head. "I've gotta see this."

"See what?" I asked.

"I gotta see her face when you give her these panties. What color are they?"

I groaned. "You guys are so fucking relentless."

I left the team in the locker room as they tried guessing the color of Claire's panties and strode to the parking lot with Aasher and Ford tailing me. I stopped a few feet from my car and spun around, glaring at them both. "What are you two doing?"

"Following you so we can watch you get your ass handed to you by Bryant."

My eye twitched when Ford used the nickname I'd given her.

Aasher chuckled. "Honestly, I kinda wanna see what she says too. I can't see this going over well, and I'm in the mood for entertainment."

I grabbed the bag that was sitting on my windshield, crumpling up the note that was left by my older sister's best friend with her number scribbled on it beside a drawn heart. I peeked inside and saw the black pair of "cheeky" underwear—whatever the fuck that meant—and threw it inside my car before climbing inside. My passenger door opened a moment later, and my resolve fell. "Seriously?" I asked, staring blank-faced at Ford.

His crooked smile was well-known around campus, and

most girls fell for his Southern accent and golden-boy looks. They made me want to punch him most of the time, though. "I've gotta see this."

"Same." Aasher's head popped in between us, and I pulled back.

"When the fuck did you get back there? I asked, hearing his seatbelt click. "We have a game tomorrow. Why don't you two go back to your apartments and get ready?"

"Oh, come on, Dad. Let us watch you get your ass handed to you."

My car came to life, and I shook my head. "I'm not going to get my ass handed to me. I told her I was buying them."

"She wasn't mad that you gave hers away?"

"Of course she was," I scoffed, hiding my grin as I remembered the way her mouth formed a scowl. "That's why I promised I'd buy her new ones."

"Was that before or after you told her you'd get hers back from the puck bunny?"

I eyed Aasher from the rearview. "Remind me to never confide in you again."

Ford gasped in between laughs. "You told her you were gonna get them *back*? You're stupider than I thought. What girl would want *used* panties back from someone, let alone a puck bunny? And where were the puck bunny's panties? I feel like I'm missing parts of the story."

Aasher snorted. "That's because you are. Either way, we need to see this."

"There is nothing to see. I'm going to give her the panties, then chill for the rest of the night, and get a good night's sleep for the game tomorrow." I pumped the brakes at a stop sign and gave them both a look that an unimpressed father would give to their sons. "Something you both should be doing."

"It's six p.m. Where is she? The Bex? Let's go get dinner, and then you can slip her the panties beside her tip." Ford bit his lip to hold back laughter, and I cursed him under my breath.

It was Thursday. That meant she was at rehearsals. Thursdays were her long days. I kept all this information to myself because it would only give Aasher and Ford more ammunition to use against me. Everyone already assumed I had a hard-on for my roommate, and if they were aware that I knew her schedule, they'd run with it. I didn't have a hard-on for her, though. I knew my last roommate's schedule, too, but it just so happened that he was a male, and no one seemed to make a big deal out of that, now did they?

"She's at dance practice. Or rehearsals? I don't know what to call it. She's doing her ballet stuff." I questioned myself, not fully understanding what Bexley U dancers did. I knew, for a fact, that she wasn't a part of the dance team that performed during basketball games, though, because I'd seen up most of their skirts and I'd remember looking up hers.

Ford whistled. "She does ballet?"

"Shut up or I'll make you stay in the car, Ford."

"And miss out on dancers? They're flexible as fuck. Consider me a mute." Aasher laughed under his breath, and before I knew it, we were pulling into the auditorium. The chill in the air cooled my heated skin, and I grabbed onto the bag tightly as Aasher and Ford murmured behind me, following me like two little ducklings.

"I bet you ten bucks that she'll blush."

"I bet you ten bucks she'll slap him."

I spun around before opening the doors and glared at

them both. "I bet you ten bucks I'll slap the shit out of you both if you don't shut up."

Aasher grinned at me before looking over at Ford, who pretended to zip his lips. We were all wearing our black BU Hockey hoodies, and I knew we were going to stand out like three giant billboards the second we walked in there. I wasn't necessarily sure what to expect, but there was an unfamiliar part of me that was excited to see Claire in a different environment.

Could I have waited until later to give the panties to her? Sure. Or I could have just left the bag on her bed because I knew she wouldn't get in until late, and there was zero chance I'd see her tomorrow night unless she came to the party after the game—fat chance of that.

There was loud music coming from the two large doors that were off to the right that was like a beckoning call to the three of us. The bag that Claire's new panties were in suddenly felt heavy in my hand, so I opened it up and grabbed them before stuffing them into the pocket of my joggers.

"That's even better," Aasher said sarcastically from beside me. "Pull them out of your pocket and hand them to her in front of everyone. I'm gonna win this bet."

Ford half-laughed, but I drowned them out as I slowly pulled the door open and snuck inside the back of the audi-torium. The stage was glowing brightly. The lights were centered on the two people in the center. There weren't a ton of dancers running around in tutus and classical music pouring through the speakers like I had half-expected. Instead, I counted four girls and one guy huddled in the corner of the stage, all of them sitting quietly, unaware of the three of us walking in and taking a seat near the back.

The song "Control" by Zoe Wees suddenly began

playing from the speakers, and the moment I saw who was dancing, everything else faded. Claire's brown hair was pulled into a bun on the top of her head, showing off the delicate curves of her cheeks and slender neck. Her skin was glistened with sweat, and although I saw the puffiness of her eyes from lack of sleep, her softness stole the attention of the entire space. She was agile on her feet, and each twist of her body made my heart pound a little harder. I hardly noticed the male dancer that was dancing with her until his hands grabbed her waist, and he lifted her above his head. My hands immediately went to the arms of my seat, and I gripped the plastic with force. I felt Aasher's eyes on me, but I ignored him as I continued watching Claire dance with an absurd amount of talent.

My throat closed as I watched her twirl to the corner of the stage. I watched with bated breath as she took off on light feet and leapt into the guy's hands. The breath escaped my chest, and chills coated my arms when he slowly dragged her down his body, holding her as if she were as light as a feather, and then, just like that, the music stopped, and my heart resumed normal beating.

Fucking Christ.

I pushed myself back into my seat, and for the first time since leaving the locker room, neither Ford nor Aasher made a single remark. The group of dancers that were sitting near the corner of the stage popped up, and they all squealed with excitement. It sounded like a bomb was going off in my head as I was fully snapped out of the complexity of what I had just watched.

Ford quickly stood up, his theater seat screeching in the process, and he began clapping. "Well done, Bryant! *Woo hoo!*"

I pinched the bridge of my nose and wanted to knock

the stupid right out of him, but I couldn't force myself to remove my eyes from Claire and her wildly shocked expression from across the auditorium. Her jaw fell open as her chest continued to heave up and down from the exertion of her dancing.

Everyone turned to stare, and the looks of confusion on their faces only propelled Ford to clap harder. Some would say that Ford loved attention, and they were absolutely correct.

The dancers began dismantling across the stage after saying something to Claire and her dancing partner. Ford coughed under his breath for me to get on with why I was there in the first place.

Right.

Panties. Claire.

On legs that were feeling a little unstable, I smoothed out my expression and fell back into my usual arrogant self as I walked down the long aisle toward her. There were stairs on both ends of the stage, but instead, I placed my hands on the floor of the stage and propelled myself upward and landed on two steadier feet than before. Claire stood in the far back corner with a girl I knew had to be her friend because Claire didn't laugh with people like she was laughing with her. Her smile wavered as she saw me walking toward her with my two idiot friends trailing behind me.

I stopped for a brief second, and as if on cue, Ford ran straight into my back. I spun around and gave him a look that made the amusement on his expression disappear for a moment.

Claire brushed her friend off when I stopped in front of her. Her arms went over her light-gray sweater that she was wearing over her black leotard, and the tights she had on were sheer and made her legs look *that* much smoother.

I opened my mouth, but Ford quickly stepped beside me and threw up a closed fist in her direction. "Knucks, Bryant. That was amazing."

Claire's lip twitched, and she gave him a tiny smile before pounding her small knuckles against his. "Thank you..."

"I'm Ford, and this is Aasher." His gaze switched over to Claire's friend immediately. "Hey, T. Haven't seen you for a while."

Claire's friend, who was also sporting full dance gear, stared at him in disbelief. He turned to Aasher, grinning. "This is Emory's little sister, Taytum."

I huffed before putting my hands in the pockets of my joggers. "Ah, so you're the one who helped Claire come up with the completely one-sided roommate rules?"

Taytum's hip popped out, and her hands flew to them. Ford snickered under his breath and took a step toward her. "Watch how you talk to her, or her big bro will come out of the shadows somewhere."

Ford began to tease Taytum about Emory, and before I knew it, they were in the midst of a full-blown argument where Ford came out on top, smirking wildly. I shifted my eyes back to Claire and dug my hand in my pocket for the panties.

"What are you doing here?" Her brows swooped down with confusion before she scanned the rest of the stage and eyed the few dancers that were waiting around, pretending not to look in our direction.

The quiet conversation between Aasher, Taytum, and Ford stopped abruptly when I pulled out the black panties from my pocket and handed them to Claire. "I told you I'd buy you new ones so...here."

Claire's pink lips opened immediately, and she formed a little circle with her mouth. Her cheeks matched the color of blood, and I swore I saw some steam come from her tiny, flared nostrils. She pounced toward me and stuffed my hand, still gripping the soft silky fabric, back into my pocket. There was a buzz present in my body with the way her nails dug into my skin, which disappeared the second she pulled her hand out of my pants. The soft blue in her eyes as she thanked Ford a few seconds ago was now replaced with a deep navy and burned like ice on hot skin. "What the hell, Theo!"

"What?" I asked innocently. "I told you I'd get you a new pair."

She glanced around nervously and skimmed over my friends, who were smirking so hard I thought their faces might permanently get stuck like that. One of Taytum's brows was cocked as she watched Claire and me, and then there was a faint slap on my chest, hitting me right where my heart was beating wildly.

"People are gonna get the wrong idea! They're gonna think you have my underwear for a completely different reason! I swear, you love to mess with me, don't you?"

I couldn't help it. I smiled, and Claire stomped her foot like a brat. I loved every single second of our interactions. "A little, but come on. I do feel bad for giving your panties away." I dug into my pocket again, and Claire lifted her leg to stomp again, but this time, her ballet slipper landed on my foot instead of the stage, as if it was actually going to hurt.

"Whoa, whoa!" Ford stepped in between us. "That's

our star player. We have a game tomorrow against Crown! Go easy on him, Bryant."

The crease between her eyebrows smoothed out as she took him seriously, and I chuckled, bringing her attention back to me. "Relax. We all know you have a boyfriend and that there isn't anything going on between us."

Taytum exhaled as she grew closer to us. "Oh yes, we wouldn't want your *boyfriend* to get jealous of your roomie, now would we?"

I kept my face even, but I made eye contact with Taytum for a split second, and it was obvious that we both shared a distaste for Chad. *Brownie points for Taytum.*

"Stop," Claire said quietly. Then, she glanced back up at me and rolled her eyes. "Just put them in my drawer when you get back to the room."

I nodded. "Yes, ma'am."

She averted her attention quickly. Did she think a bomb was going to explode if she looked at me for longer than three seconds? I kept my chuckle to myself and ushered Aasher and Ford to the stairs to leave, but as if on cue, Ford had other ideas.

"You girls comin' to the game? Or maybe the after-party?" His eyebrows moved up and down a few times before he looked at Taytum with a sly grin on his face. "Or will big bro Emory throw a fit if you show up?"

Taytum huffed with annoyance and sent Ford a look. She glanced over at Claire, and she shook her head so quickly it was hard to catch the panic lingering.

"Nah," I answered for Claire, just to irritate her again because I simply could not fucking help myself. "Claire has a deep hatred for jocks, and she'd never be caught dead at a party at Chi Alpha Sigma."

Blood rushed to her cheeks, and there was a miniscule

pause in her breathing that I caught right away. Her tight shoulders dropped for a second before she smoothed her expression.

"What? A deep hatred for jocks?! Even us hockey players? Have you ever been to a hockey game?"

"No, she hasn't." Taytum bumped her hip into Claire's and bounced right off because Claire was as stiff as a board.

The voice inside my head was telling me to retreat, but there was a game waiting to be played as I stared at my roommate. I prodded her *just* a little bit more because I couldn't back down from a challenge as enticing as her. "And she definitely doesn't party, right? She'd rather sit in her room on a Friday night and wait for her boyfriend to step out of his science lab to call her." *Science lab or out from between other girls' legs. I swear it was him at the party last weekend.*

Her eyes drove into mine, and if they were knives, I'd be bleeding. I grinned coyly, waiting to see what she'd say. She couldn't argue with me. She knew it was true, and her best friend knew it too.

"That is not true," she forced out, crossing her arms over her gray sweater. A peek of her black strap from her leotard laid still over her shoulder, and I zoomed in on it, waiting for her to back up her statement.

"Then I guess you two will be at the party?" Ford asked, smirking at Taytum. "Don't worry, T. I won't let Emory ruin your fun. We all know you like to have fun, yeah?"

I kept my attention on my roommate, ignoring the rising tension between her best friend and Ford. The little muscles along her cheeks ground back and forth as she shot me a dirty look. Then, she looked over at Ford and smiled, making me do a double-take. "We will be there."

16

CLAIRE

"I smell like food."

"Here." Taytum dug in her bag and pulled out a small bottle of perfume before spraying it in the air. "Now, walk through it." Her hand landed on the small of my back, and she pushed me forward. My palms landed on the charcoal-colored wall of The Bex's bathroom to catch myself, and I spun around to face my best friend in the middle of a coughing fit.

"Really?" I coughed again, grabbing onto my chest.

Taytum laughed as she faced the mirror and painted on bright-pink lipstick that just so happened to match her top. "I cannot believe you are actually going to a party at the football house. I've been trying for almost two years to get you to come out with me again."

"That is not true," I countered, looking at my outfit in the mirror. "I went out with you and the rest of the dancers last year."

Taytum puckered her lips. "An end-of-the-year dinner does not count, Claire. And you know it."

Ignoring her, I pushed my hands in the pockets of my skinny jeans and turned to look at my butt. Nonchalantly, Taytum asked, "Where have you been hiding that outfit?"

I paused. "Huh?"

"Claire." Taytum came up behind me, and we looked into the dirty mirror. "You look *hot*." Her blonde hair fell over my shoulder as she bent forward and ran her hand over the straps of my tight crop top. It was long-sleeved, but that was really the only modest thing about it. It was slightly low cut, dipping in the center between my boobs, and had two thin straps that ran crisscross underneath the hem that just so happened to hit right above my belly button. There was only an inch or so showing off my toned belly (thank you, conditioning) but my jeans were high-waisted so, truly, it wasn't *that* revealing.

"I don't look hot." I brushed her hands away from my shirt and spun around to put my palms on her shoulders. "You just don't see me in anything but a leo and my work shirt with jeans."

Taytum reached up and pulled the claw clip from my hair. My long hair fell swiftly over my shoulders, and she fluffed the strands with her fingers. "When was the last time someone told you that you looked good? Or better yet, when was the last time Chad gave you a compliment?"

"I don't need him to give me compliments." It was true, but my stomach hollowed out because I couldn't remember when he had.

"Come on." She pushed my hair behind my ear and grabbed my hand in hers, giving me a tight squeeze. "I texted a few of the other girls. They're gonna ride with us, and we're gonna have some serious and much-needed fun."

I wasn't so sure about *fun,* and if it weren't for the way Theo had looked at me before leaving my practice yesterday, I would have backed out. But there was a daring glare to his eye. He was challenging me. The bite to his tone when he told his friends that I didn't party drove my nerves wild, and I wasn't sure why, but I felt like I needed to prove something to him. Or maybe just to myself?

The truth was, Theo was right. I sat in my dorm room alone most nights while my friends were out having fun. I was stuck worrying about my mom and figuring out ways to help her, which just so happened to be related to my boyfriend who, admittedly, did not treat me the way that I deserved.

A rush of heat rained over me as Taytum and I climbed into the Uber that had already picked up a few other girls, and I glanced at my phone to see if Chad had responded to my texts. He didn't, and sadly, I wasn't surprised.

Taytum whispered in my ear when she saw me checking my messages. "Did you tell Chad you were going out tonight?"

I shook my head. "No, should I have?"

Taytum snorted. "You don't owe him anything. If he wants to know what you are up to on a Friday night, maybe he should take the time to ask."

My heart ached slightly with disappointment, but I pushed my phone in my back pocket and nodded, knowing she was right.

━━━

The ache in my chest disappeared the moment I walked into the party, arm in arm with Taytum. I'd walked past the football house plenty of times but never during a party and never this late at night. Exhaustion floated right above my sore muscles from yesterday's practice, and my feet ached from my evening shift at The Bex, but I pushed it all behind me as something exciting filled my senses.

It wasn't as if I hadn't been to a party before, but it had been a long time. I suddenly felt alive and invigorated. There was the tiniest pinch of guilt in the back of my head, wondering if Chad was going to be angry with me for going to a party—one filled with a herd of jocks, to make matters worse—but the independence I buried in my chest whispered that I didn't need to get permission from anyone.

So many of my decisions had been based on others—where I went to school, my major, where my money was spent, even my relationship. Something as innocent as going to a college party shouldn't come with a single ounce of guilt.

Rose's voice came in between Taytum and me. "I'm assuming the hockey team won, then?"

An abrupt laugh flew from my mouth as I saw Ford dancing in the middle of a chaotic dance floor that also doubled as a living room. There was a bundle of girls who had formed a circle around him, and I hesitated when I saw that one of them was the puck bunny that Theo gave my underwear to. I dropped my chin to my jeans, knowing I was wearing the new ones that he'd delicately placed in my underwear drawer with a sticky note attached that said, *I didn't go through your drawer, boss. Swear.*

"I'd say so," I answered, feeling the energy of the room flow through my body. *Okay, this isn't as bad as I thought it would be.*

Taytum's hand squeezed mine as Ford spotted her from across the room. He smiled brightly with his flushed face and immediately began heading her way with a flirty twinkle in his eye.

"Come dance with me, T," he said, looking directly at Taytum. I pulled my hand away, and she nervously glanced around the party. "Lookin' for your brother? He's getting his dick sucked somewhere."

"Oh my God, Ford. Shut up." Taytum pushed Ford against his chest, and he captured her by the wrist. "You haven't changed at all since high school."

"You guys went to high school together?" I asked, wondering why Taytum never mentioned anything. Granted, I had never been with her while she hung with any of the jocks because it wasn't my scene.

Ford peeked over at me, and his smile turned from sly to friendly right away. "Yep. T and I go way back." He was still holding onto her hand when he glanced around the party. "Theo is around here somewhere."

I cleared my throat. "I'm not here for him."

"Right." He smirked before turning back to Taytum. "Come on, T. Wanna dance for old time's sake?"

He nodded to the floor, and I gave her a little push at the last second. "You can go dance. I'll be fine over here."

"You sure?"

"Of course." I nodded.

"Wait, you're actually gonna dance with me?" Ford looked surprised, but Taytum threw her head back and laughed while ripping her hand out of his grasp.

"No. But I will find *someone* to dance with."

Ford followed after her a moment later, seeming interested in who she chose to dance with. Rose stayed beside me, but the rest of the girls we rode with had dispersed throughout the party, leaving me feeling a little out of place.

I nodded to the far wall near the stairs, and Rose followed closely behind me.

I put my back against the wall and scanned the sea of undergrads before turning toward Rose. "Did Taytum tell you to stay with me?"

Rose was a year younger than us, so the only time I saw her was onstage. I knew that she was in the same sorority as Taytum, though, which meant that my assumption was probably correct. "Um..." Her eyes darted away, and I sighed.

"It's okay, you don't have to stay with me, Rose."

"She said you'd say that."

My mouth formed a tiny scowl, and I shook my head. Taytum knew me entirely too well, and even though I was annoyed that she thought I needed a babysitter, I was still grateful for her. I didn't have time for many friends. I had plenty of acquaintances, and most of the dancers were nice to me—some of the younger ones even asking my help on certain techniques. And I had my co-workers. But a true friend who I could rely on? It was Taytum.

Rose's lip was pulled into her mouth, and I assured her once again that she could go do what she usually did at parties, but she shook her head. "I'm her little. I'm supposed to do what she says."

"And that's exactly why sororities never worked out for me." I laughed it off before turning all the way toward her. "Well, if you weren't on babysitting duty, what would you be doing?"

She thought for a moment before pulling her shirt down a little and adjusting her hair. "I'd probably go get a drink."

I nodded. "Then let's go get a drink."

She smiled. "Alright, let's go."

The moment we turned to head to the kitchen, my heart jumped straight up to my throat and stayed there for a second too long. Right there in the doorway stood Theo Brooks with a cheeky grin that turned my insides warm. There was a flicker of surprise covering his features, but a moment later came a nod of approval, as if he were proud that I had kept my word and didn't stay holed up in our room on a Friday night.

And for some reason, I liked knowing he was proud of me.

17

THEO

I DIDN'T ADMIT that I was wrong often, but leave it to Claire to cause just that. I whole-heartedly thought she would back out. I gambled back and forth with myself, landing on the assumption that she wouldn't come, even saying as much to Aasher and Ford when we showed up at the party, high on the fumes of conquering the Wildcats. I pushed Claire clear from my head the second I scanned the room and didn't see her or Taytum, but surprise struck me as I turned around to walk out of the kitchen to slip away from some overly accommodating puck bunnies. I choked on my drink as I slipped my gaze down her body.

She looked different, and irritation brushed over my skin at her appearance, because the team was really gonna amp up their remarks after seeing what she looked like outside of her waitressing attire. *Damn it, Bryant.*

Tight jeans and a little black top that showed just the right amount of skin. I'd give it to her—she knew how to fight back. I had pissed her off yesterday, and the moment she accepted the challenge, I should've known she'd show up just to prove a point.

A smirk crawled over my face as I pushed off from the doorframe of the kitchen and headed straight for her. A bob of a swallow worked its way down her slender neck, and she pulled her gaze away from me to talk with one of her friends. I stood, stunned, but only for a split second, as Claire tried to walk past me. I laughed before I gripped her arm and pulled her toward me.

"That's not very nice. You're not even going to say hi to your roommate?"

The sharp sting of her blue eyes was full of annoyance, so I dropped her arm. "Hi," she said, shooting me a fake smile. She started to walk into the kitchen again, but I slipped in front of her.

"That's it? Just a hi? You act like we don't sleep in the same room." I shook my head with obvious disapproval. "What's wrong, Bryant? Fighting with your boyfriend or something?" The sound of her teeth grinding against one another gave me a clue that she was truly angry about something. *What did I do now?* "Don't tell me. You're mad that I put your underwear in your drawer. Didn't you get my note? I swear I didn't go through it." I most definitely wanted to, though.

"Theo," she hissed, bringing her face a little closer to my chest. "Knock it off."

"Knock what off?" I asked, hearing the way my voice skirted very closely to something flirty. *What am I doing?*

"Here ya go!" A drink was placed in between my chest and Claire's face.

"Thanks, Rose." Claire tenderly smelled the brim of her cup, and her nose wrinkled.

She and her friend, Rose, cheered their cups silently,

and something involuntarily forced my hand to snatch Claire's drink before it touched her lips. She huffed and shot me a dirty look, wondering what I was doing. *I'm wondering the same.* I turned to Rose and peered down at her disapprovingly. "Did you pour this? Or did someone hand it to you?"

Rose's cheeks turned a little pink, but I was used to that when talking to a female. They were either too eager for my attention or struggled to get words out. *Except Claire, though.* "I poured it myself."

My hand left Claire's cup swiftly, and I was surprised at my random act of chivalry. It wasn't that I was a bad guy, but ask me if I'd done that to any other girl before. The answer was no. "Okay, carry on."

I stepped away from Claire and her friend and walked toward Aasher and a few other teammates. I was the center of the conversation as I slid up in the middle of their explanation to Rush over the stats of the game.

We were tied 2-2 and down to the last few seconds of the third period until I caught a pass from Aasher, allowing me to tuck the puck under the goalie's leg as he stretched to block the shot. He was a little too slow, though and I gained the point for my team. Moments after the goal horn blared, the buzzer signified the end of the game, and the entire arena rattled with excitement. The adrenaline from those last few moments took a while to wear off, and Aasher's voice grew louder the more he talked.

It didn't take him long to notice my silence, though. I made sure to keep my attention away from Claire and Rose, but I still felt unsettled.

"What's wrong?"

I shrugged, turning my head slightly so no one else

could hear me. "I don't know. I just had an out-of-body experience."

"What?"

I shook my head, not wanting to examine my behavior. I tipped my head back and took a bigger swig of beer than usual and trained my eyes to the left side of the room—the side I knew Claire wasn't on. A puck bunny caught my eye, and she winked at me, and surprisingly, I winked back. *Wait, what am I doing?* I didn't fuck around with girls after a game, and I already swore off puck bunnies for the rest of the season.

Focus. Focus. Focus. That was my mantra. Focus on the game, focus on the after interviews, score a one-on-one with Tom Gardini, and land my dream team in the NHL. I wasn't sure where my head was tonight, but I didn't like that it was skirting in areas it shouldn't have been.

"You gettin' laid tonight?" Emory's gruff voice came out of nowhere, and I shrugged.

"I don't know. Maybe."

"Shit, she *did* come?" I knew who Aasher was referring to, so I didn't even look in the direction he was staring off into.

"Bryant? Yeah, I guess."

There was a rumbly snicker that came from Emory, and I glared over at him, not in the mood for games. "What?"

His brows shot up, and he shook his head innocently. "Oh, nothing."

Why am I acting like this?

I nodded to the blonde who was still staring at me, and she started over in my direction. At the very last second, I turned and skimmed my gaze over to where I had last seen Claire. She was still standing with her friend Rose, and they were chatting about something that clearly was very exciting to Claire because there was a twinkle in her eye. I wasn't sure why I was so concerned with her being here. Maybe I liked her being in a separate part of my mind. She was my roommate, and that was it. I didn't want her to start imposing on other areas of my life, but I wasn't sure why.

"Hey." The blonde slid up beside me, and my breath was heavy as I exhaled. She blocked my view from Claire, and I was thankful. Apparently, I needed a fucking distraction tonight, which—*again*—was very unlike me. "Good game."

"Thanks," I said, pulling her in close. "Were you in the stands?"

The blonde began chatting very frantically about some of the things that had happened in the game, and I would have been impressed with her knowledge of hockey terminology, but instead, I checked out of the conversation and scanned the rest of the party. I half-chuckled as I watched Ford take Taytum away from one of the football players to spin her around to some country song that he undoubtedly put on. Emory rolled his eyes, and when Ford caught his eye, he threw his hands up in innocence. I kept scanning the crowd and paused a moment later when I caught the side angle of a dark-haired guy that made my blood run cold.

"Oh, fuck." The two words came out in slow motion, but Aasher heard the uptick in my tone and stood up straight right beside me.

"What? What's wrong?"

I no longer noticed the blonde as she clung onto my side. My shoulders tensed, and I had lost my beer at some point. I didn't move an inch as I watched Claire's boyfriend make out with some girl with hardly any clothes on in the corner of the room. *Fuck.* I frantically searched the party, knowing that I was right about him cheating on her and that

Claire was about to walk into something that was going to cut deep. I loved to be right but not about this. *Fuck, this was going to be bad.*

"Wolf, what's wrong?" Emory's voice was muffled as my heartbeat thumped in my ears. I felt like I was back on the ice, and everything was fading away except this burning drive in my core. I pushed the blonde away and took a step forward, looking over every single person's head until I landed on those rich, chestnut-colored waves falling over delicate shoulders. I turned back and saw that Chad had no intention of stopping his make-out session with someone who wasn't his girlfriend and brought my attention back over to Claire. I felt panicked, and the expression on Claire's face had my world stopping for the briefest of seconds.

Her pretty lips were parted slightly, and the color had completely drained from her cheeks. The cup of warm beer in her hand slipped from her grip, and Rose grabbed onto her arm, shaking her slightly. It was like watching a tower fall and not being able to stop it. I wanted to protect her from what she was witnessing, but it also wasn't my job to do so. *What is her boyfriend fucking thinking?*

"Shit, is that her boyfriend?"

Aasher's voice broke though the muffled sounds of the party, and my heart was racing so fast I couldn't catch my breath.

Emory answered Aasher, "Yeah, and I guess Taytum was right. He's a fucking douche."

"Ouch," the blonde hissed between her teeth. "Who is that girl? That's awful. I feel so bad for her."

I stared at Claire, unable to move from the chaos that was occurring around me. Some people were unaware of what was going on, but I swore I heard her heart break from clear across the party. The second she tore her gaze from Chad, she landed on me, and I took a step backward from the jolt.

Her eyes were glossy, and the acceptance I saw as she realized that I was right the other night hit me smack dab in the center of my chest. Her wobbling lip was a sucker punch right to my jaw. I moved toward her, but she shook her head and mumbled something to Rose and was out the door a moment later.

"Fuck, that hurt to watch." I met Rush's expression as he clued in to what had just happened. His head tilted, and his eyes squinted. "She mean something to you?"

Does she?

I glared in Chad's direction, watching in disgust as his hands gripped the girl's ass underneath her dress. I was thankful Claire had left the party so she didn't have to see how this was progressing. *Where is she?*

"Just one, Wolf. I'll let it slide this time."

Rush flicked his chin over to Chad, and I shook my head, knowing I needed to leave it alone.

"Just one what?" someone asked.

Before I could stop myself and listen to the rational thought I'd had a second prior, I moved through the party with as much swiftness as I was used to on the ice. I could smell Chad's sleazy cologne, and it angered me that much more. Claire's hurt expression slid into my head at the last second, and I wished it hadn't because it only egged me on further.

I tapped Chad's shoulder roughly, and he tore his mouth away and glared at me out of the corner of his eye. There was a set of glassy, bloodshot eyes set on me from the girl with swollen lips, and I barked, "Move."

She didn't act confused in the slightest. Her eyes

widened, and she backed clear away from Chad and into Aasher's hands. He pushed her behind him and gave me a warning look before I turned back and looked at the dipshit who just hurt my roommate. *Fuck, why do I care so much?*

"You again?" he said, putting his hands on his hips like he actually had the upper hand. "Mind your fucking business, bro."

An angry laugh left me as I shook my head. I turned my back to him for a single second, letting him think that he was superior to someone like me. But newsflash, he wasn't. My knuckles cracked as I formed a fist, and I swung around so quickly you wouldn't have even known I'd clocked him, except the little bitch let out a screech as blood sprayed from his lip.

"One and done, Wolf." Rush's hand landed on my shoulder, and he gave me a squeeze. I shrugged his grip off as Chad smeared the blood across his mouth and glared at me.

"I fucking dare you," I barked, seething between my teeth.

Chad stepped away from me in fear, but I still saw the haughtiness lingering. "She won't believe you." He spit blood onto the floor, and Rush cursed under his breath.

I laughed loudly, drawing attention from the party. I half-expected Taytum to come through to back me up, because it was apparent she didn't like Chad, but I didn't see her or Ford anywhere around. Rose caught my eye, but before I went to look for Claire, I shot Chad a quick smirk.

"She doesn't have to believe me, man. She saw you for herself." His confusion was comical, but I didn't laugh. Instead, I spun around and walked through the party and went on a search for my roommate.

18

CLAIRE

I'M FINE.

A wobbly breath shuffled out of my mouth as I powered my phone down, not wanting to hear his voice through the other line. There was an ever-present ache in between each breath that I forced from my lungs, but I focused on the chill in the air and blamed the trembling of my lip on that instead of the complete and utter disbelief that I was feeling in every hidden part of my body.

I knew I was in self-preservation mode, blocking out the visual of my boyfriend openly cheating on me in the middle of a college party that he swore he'd never go to. The feeling of inadequacy was completely going unnoticed as I hid from the disappointment and feeling of defeat. If anyone were to look into my eyes, they'd see the hurt there, but I was *fine*.

There were a million and ten questions going through my head, all of which were skirting right past the empty feeling in my heart and more so revolving around my mother and our future. Was her job at stake? What about the money we owed? Would they require my mother to pay it back in full if Chad and I weren't together? His warnings were at the forefront of my brain, and even though I tried, I couldn't hide from those—not when they'd been pounded into my skull for over a year.

"Shit." The word was as bleak as I felt.

I wrapped my arms around my midsection, hiding from the cool wind. I wasn't even sure where I was. I refused to turn my phone back on to pull up my map, though, because if I saw Chad's name flash across the screen, I couldn't be sure that I wouldn't throw the device into moving traffic. And let's face it, I couldn't afford a new phone.

The frat houses along the street were partying in full force. The music was blending together, and I was thankful that it was drowning out my thoughts. I stepped down onto the curb to cross the road and stopped at the last second as a car flashed its lights at me. I squinted and blocked the brightness with my hand, but when they pulled up beside me, I felt like I'd swallowed my own tongue.

"Get in."

Honestly, the last person I wanted to see—other than Chad—was Theo. I didn't want to face him—not after I learned that he was right.

"No thanks," I said, stepping back onto the curb and walking along the sidewalk again. I still had no idea where I was going, but it felt right to keep moving forward.

"Claire. Get in my car."

"I would rather walk right now. I n-n-need the fresh air." I was used to the cold, northern air, but I wasn't exactly dressed warmly, and I cursed my dead giveaway that I was freezing.

Theo's car trailed behind me for a few steps until he said, "You know you're going in the wrong direction, right?"

I paused, and next thing I knew, Theo's passenger door was opened, and he was leaning over the center console. The small lights above his head showcased the tiny shadows along his ticking temples, and I sighed in relief at the heat coming from his dashboard. "Just get in my car, Bryant."

I zipped up the emotions that were clogging my eyes and focused on a different type of emotion. Instead of getting into his passenger seat, I moved past the open door and slid into the backseat instead.

"Seriously?" I peeked at Theo as he half-turned around and looked at me sitting in his backseat. "You're that stubborn?" He sighed agitatedly when I didn't answer and leaned over the empty passenger seat and shut the door, closing out the cool air. I sighed in relief, trying to keep my teeth from chattering, but apparently, Theo had noticed, because I watched as his steady fingers adjusted the vents along his dashboard to point in the backseat.

Nothing but the sound of heat blasting from the vents filled the tiny space between us, but to my surprise, it wasn't as uncomfortable as it should have been.

The moment we pulled up to the dorms, I quickly opened my door. His car wasn't even off by the time I unsnapped the seatbelt and started toward the dorms. Apparently, Theo was a freaking magician, though, because when I went to open the door to Dorothy Hall, his large hand was there, and he opened it for me. I went to murmur a thank you but did a double-take at his swollen, bright-red knuckles with the tiniest splatter of blood against them. My cold, shaky hand landed on his wrist, and I examined it before pulling us both inside the warm hall.

"Did you hit Chad?" My voice bordered on terror.

"Yep." Theo looked away, but there was a bite to his answer. "Got a problem with that?" His question felt like a test, as if he wanted me to stand up for Chad just so he could shoot me down.

My slightly gaped mouth snapped shut, and I dropped his hand. "Thanks for the ride." It was a race for me to get back to our room, and I hoped with everything I had left in me that Theo would head back to the party and leave me be.

Knowing that Theo hit Chad made me panic. *Shit.* I began to feel lightheaded as I fumbled with my room key. I let out a quivery breath before I smelled Theo's cologne, and a moment later, his hands gripped my waist. He gently moved me over so he could take charge and unlock our door.

The moment we were inside, I rushed over to my dresser and pulled out some comfortable clothes. When I spun back around with my clothes held tightly in my grip, I spotted Theo leaning against the edge of his desk with his arms crossed over his chest. A second passed in silence before I blurted out the question I didn't want the answer to.

"Is that why you nudged me to go to the party?" I gulped up a mouthful of air, bringing my clothes to my chest as a shield. "You wanted me to see it for myself?"

The angry lines around Theo's mouth lessened. He popped off from the desk and shook his head. "Believe it or not, Bryant, I'm not as bad as you make me out to be. I had no idea he'd be there."

"But you were right." *And I was humiliated.*

The clanking of his teeth confused me. "I didn't want to be right about that." More silence passed, and I dropped my gaze to the floor, feeling worse the longer I stood there, seeming pathetic in front of someone like Theo Brooks. A deep sense of sadness started to move through my body, and my chest grew tight. The floor began to grow blurry, and I bit my tongue to keep myself from breaking. Chad's lips against someone else's was something that was hard to swallow. My face stung like I was being slapped with the visual over and over again.

"I'm going to get ready for bed," I announced, all but running over to the door to head to the bathrooms. It took less than ten minutes for me to get changed and to brush my teeth, because I was afraid Chad would show up to my room and corner me in the hallway.

Theo looked at me abruptly when I stormed in the room and charged over to my bed. We made eye contact for a single second before I climbed under the covers, not bothering to plug my phone in.

My back was to him, and I pulled the blankets up high in a poor attempt to block out the world. I ran through my dance routine in my head, doing eight counts in another poor attempt to keep things locked away, and was immensely thankful when Theo turned off the light.

Thank God.

My breathing was picking up speed as I gripped my blankets tightly, doing everything I possibly could to keep myself together. *I'm fine.* Numbers floated throughout my head like I was back in statistics class as I worked over how my mother and I could pay back Chad's parents if they demanded she pay up front.

His parents were kind to us, but they weren't good people down to their core. It wasn't like Chad's mother baked cookies on Sunday mornings and donated to charities. They weren't warm. They could be ruthless if they wanted, and although Chad was at fault by cheating on me, he was still their son, and unfortunately, our families were tied in more ways than just our relationship.

A single tear fell down my cheek, and I bit my tongue so hard it bled. My throat was tight, and the knot only grew tighter the more I tried to keep my emotions locked away.

I cleared my throat and gripped my blanket harder.

Am I not good enough?

Did I subconsciously become a shitty girlfriend because I knew, deep down, I didn't love Chad like he thought I did? I cared for Chad—I did. There was once a time where his eyes in my direction made my heart jump. But he changed. I changed. And our relationship changed. It became more about how I could please him so he would stop making me feel less worthy, and less about how I could please him because I liked to see him happy.

I knew I was a people-pleaser, and I knew the reason why. There was once someone before Chad that made me feel unfit and less worthy. And sadly, I didn't even know his name. My father's face was a blur in my mind. All I had to go off of were my mother's insults and disapproval of the man who I hadn't even met. *'He didn't want you, Claire.'* And apparently, neither did Chad.

"Claire." Theo's declaration of my first name was a slice in the hold I had on my emotions. A hiccup of hurt crashed through the room, and I quickly tried to cover it up by shifting under the blankets.

Did he hear that?

The tears were an open floodgate, and all my stress, worries, and hurt came out at once, and I couldn't stop them. *Shit. Shit. Shit.* Not only was I humiliated, I was now embarrassed.

"Claire...are you ok?"

My pillow was wet from my tears, and I quickly wiped my face, irritated that I was crying. *I'm fine.* My chest ached, and my lungs burned from trying to hold everything in. I squeezed my eyes shut and tried to breathe through my mouth slowly so I could get it together, but when I felt a dip in my bed, my breathing stopped altogether.

The room was dark, but I opened my eyes, knowing that my vision was completely clear now. My entire body tensed when Theo's heavy arm draped around my waist, and his chest clung to my back.

"What..." I sounded like I hadn't spoken in days by the rasp in my voice. Clearing my throat, I tried again. "What are you doing, Theo? I'm fine."

His chuckle rumbled against my back as his breath tickled my hair. "I have ears, Bryant. I can hear you crying."

"I am *not* crying," I lied. My cheeks blasted with heat from embarrassment.

"You've gotta be the most stubborn person I have ever met."

I wiped at my face again, and Theo's hand gripped my wrist so tightly I couldn't move it if I wanted. His palm against my skin was comforting, and it made my lip wobble. I couldn't remember the last time anyone had ever held me while I cried. I couldn't even remember the last time I cried in front of someone.

"You can cry in front of me, Claire. It's alright." His voice was soft and comforting, and those were two words I had never expected to use while describing someone like him.

Damn it. My shoulders shook, and if Theo wasn't holding me against his chest, my entire body would have shuddered. His fingers around my wrist had lessened when he pulled me in tighter, and I swore I heard him shush me at one point. My tears went on for entirely too long—much longer than I had wanted them to—but being trapped in Theo's arms came with a security that I hadn't expected.

My emotions were all over the place. I hurt in places that I hadn't hurt before but was comforted in ways that I'd never felt before, either. It was like being pulled in two different directions.

Theo's breathing had slowed against my back, and when I was certain he had fallen asleep, I began to pluck the emotions one by one until I settled on anger. I huffed with rage, hating that I allowed myself to crumble from a broken heart—if even just for a few moments. My chest was as tight as a knot as I swiped my cheek one last time before Theo's heavy arm flexed around my waist.

"Moving on to anger now?" his voice rasped against my ear, ruffling my hair. My body stilled, but instead of shying away from him, I latched onto the quietness of the room and our candid moment.

"Yes," I answered, being fully truthful with him for the first time. Since the moment we met, we'd done nothing but dish out quick jabs and tortured each other with roommate antics feigned by irritation. I'd hidden parts of myself from him and the rest of the world, but I was too worked up and feeling too messy to hide what I was feeling.

"Good," he whispered, encouraging me. "You should be angry."

I nodded against his chest, feeling more worked up the longer I lay there.

"So, what are you gonna do about it?" he asked. His arm had moved slightly over the dip in my torso as he turned to his back. Something tingly moved through my body like a slow-rising tidal wave, and there was a pesky little thought in the back of my head that was egging me on to act on my anger in the most deviant way, especially for me.

A shaky breath shuddered from my mouth as I turned onto my side, facing Theo. My quiet voice, with a hint of hoarseness from the inescapable emotions, floated out in front of us. "This isn't me," I admitted, feeling unsure but so incredibly angry and hurt at the same time that I didn't really care.

"What isn't?" Theo asked, turning his head in my direction. I couldn't see his face, but I felt his breath land on my lips, and there was a mysterious push against my back that made me hook my leg over his body. His hand slapped over my thigh, spreading his fingers out wide. "Claire." His breath was heavy. "Don't do this to me."

I froze, unsure of what to do. I began teetering on the force inside my belly that was unfamiliar but too enticing not to follow. I didn't want to think about Chad, or his mouth on someone else, or how unworthy I had felt after seeing him with someone else, or what tomorrow might bring. Even if it was just for a split second. Nothing more than a blink of an eye.

Theo's hand on my leg gripped me even harder, his fingers digging into my skin with a bite that I didn't realize I enjoyed until he quickly pulled it away and placed it on my hip, pulling me on top of him in record speed.

"Is this how you plan to get back at him? Fuck me to make yourself feel better?"

Theo's hands took up the entire fronts of my thighs as he pushed me down. My insides erupted in flames when I felt his hard length between my legs. A gasp suddenly left my lips, and I was quick to admit my truth.

"No," I whispered, letting my hair fall in between us as I leaned down. My heart was flying through my chest, beating so hard that I winced. I was winded, my breathing labored, and I was full of nerves. "Like I said, that isn't me."

"Then what are you doing, Bryant?" Theo's husky voice and flexing shoulders below my hands were like a silent encouragement, but I had no idea what he was thinking or what he would do if I answered differently.

"I just wanted to know what it would feel like to be wanted again." My truth was as shocking as shattered glass. My skin was hot, and I was out of breath, partly from the way I felt with his hands on me and partly from the truth I had just let fly out of my mouth. Theo Brooks was seeing parts of me that I didn't let many people see.

"Every guy on this floor wants you, Bryant. Don't you dare let your cheating boyfriend make you feel less than."

Surprise took hold of me when Theo's hands climbed back to my waist to flip me onto my back. A whoosh of air left my mouth, but he caught it in his when his lips covered mine.

It took my body and mind entirely too long to catch up to one another. I stopped breathing when Theo's talented tongue swept inside, nearly stealing my soul with one flick inside my mouth. My back arched as his hand went underneath it, pulling me closer to him. Butterflies flew around my lower stomach, and I was warm all over. He managed to coax a whimper from me, and although the kiss only lasted a few seconds, Theo Brooks had allowed me to feel more wanted than Chad ever had in the past.

I felt marked. My lips had been touched by someone who knew what they wanted, and for a moment, I let myself believe that it was me, even if I knew, deep down, that it wasn't.

19

THEO

Ah, shit.

I pulled back, and my traitor of a tongue licked her taste off my lips, and I knew that I would never be able to unlive the moment now that it had happened.

It was a minor dip in our platonic relationship—you know, the one where we were roommates and possibly, on some occasions, *friends*—but I had reassured myself moments before falling for her tender voice and sweet scent that I would give her just a hint of what she deserved and nothing more.

The moment my phone pinged, telling me that Aasher was outside our door with the necessities that I'd texted for just an hour prior, I pulled myself back and regained my strength, even though it took much more strength than it should have.

The kiss was hot. It was unpredictably needy, and Claire was much more accepting than I thought she would be. And although I was only supposed to be kissing her to give her some of her confidence back, it was me who suddenly felt deprived of something.

"So, how did it feel?" I asked, wondering if I just needed a slight stroke to my ego so I didn't feel so unrestrained. I had forcefully pulled myself back to gain some control of the situation, and I was thankful that my phone pinged, because I could definitely see myself craving to hear that sweet whimper again.

I couldn't see her face, but I heard her mouth open before her quiet voice blocked out the devious things playing in my head. "How–how...did what feel?"

A chuckle raced from my mouth. "How did it feel to be desired? That's what you wanted, right? Did I succeed?"

As if that was the only thing on my mind.

There was a slight knock on the door, and Claire's entire body tensed beneath mine. My leg was still nestled in between hers, and my teeth dug into my lip like a knife against my throat. It was damn near torture getting off her bed, but I knew I had to slip back into the normalcy of our roommate relationship before I *really* fucked up.

"Yes, you did. Thanks." She cleared her throat and sat up on her bed as I made my way back over to mine. I glanced to the ceiling, putting my back to her as I willed my dick to return to normal before opening the door.

"Good. Now remember that when he comes crawling back to you." I turned and glanced at her over my shoulder as soon as I turned my lamp on. She was sitting upright, peering at me out of the corner of her eye. I dropped my eyes down to her chest and quickly turned away. *Nope.* I knew that the thoughts I was having were a simple reaction to the way her skin felt against my palm and the lingering taste of her mouth on mine, so I quickly got my shit together. "Chin up, roomie. We have a long night ahead of us."

Her hot little gasp filled the room, and I turned around quickly, doing a double-take. Claire's blue eyes were wide, and she looked both intrigued and alarmed. I laughed, hiding my accidental innuendo. "Don't look at me like that, Bryant. That's not how I meant it." I cocked a brow, and her cheeks instantly turned pink. "Up." I took my hand and flipped it palm up, signaling for her to get out of her bed.

"Why?" she asked hesitantly. Her legs swung over the rumpled covers, and instead of looking at her slender body, I kept my attention glued to her face, irritated that I could see the slight puff underneath her eyes from crying.

"Because we have a heart to mend."

I walked over to our door and swung it open far enough for her to see into the hall.

Aasher was standing—rather impatiently—outside the door beside Ford and a worried Taytum. I quickly grabbed the pizza box from his hands and felt Claire's presence beside me a moment later.

"Hey, you," Taytum said, moving past my teammates. "I brought some extra necessities." She held up a bag from the gas station.

Claire huffed out a small laugh. "What's all this?"

Ford stole her attention—along with every other girl in a five-mile radius—with his Southern accent and cocky smirk. "Our ol' captain here is such a good dude, ya know? He texted Aasher and asked him to drop off some pizza and chocolate for you, along with some booze, in case you wanted to get smashed."

Taytum moved in front of Ford, and he glanced down at her briefly. "And I added some other necessities in there that I know you shall appreciate."

I leaned over Claire's shoulder, unable to stop myself from smelling her shampoo again and instantly pulled back after I saw the bright-pink vibrator. I smothered a laugh while simultaneously throwing hands at the hot, little thoughts coursing through my head.

Claire quickly slammed the bag shut and shot Taytum a glare. "Taytum!" she gritted.

"I picked it out." Ford wiggled his eyebrows. "Seven speeds, baby. Makes us men pretty fucking redundant, huh?"

"I like the color," I teased, bumping my shoulder into Claire to lighten the mood and to hopefully get back to normal.

"There's a voodoo doll, too," Taytum added, smirking. "I named him Chad. I say we cut his head off."

Ford looked at her and said, "You're just as crazy as your brother."

Taytum pushed past us and pulled Claire by the arm after taking the bag from her hand and placing it on top of the pizza box in my hand. The door shut a moment later, and surprisingly, I wasn't irritated that I was suddenly locked out of my room.

Ford stole the box of pizza from me and grabbed a slice before handing it back and walking away like nothing had happened. The moment Aasher and I were alone, he dropped his voice and asked, "What the hell was that?"

"What the hell was what?" I asked, wondering if he somehow knew that I'd pushed my roommate onto her bed and kissed her with a passion I'd never felt before.

He proceeded with caution, smoothing out his *what-the-fuck* expression. "I can't remember the last time I saw you punch someone." Shaking his head, he corrected himself.

"Wait, yes, I can. You punched London for fuckin' around on your sister, even though he was twice your age."

"Fuck yeah, I did. I don't like it." My shoulders started to tense again.

"Don't like what?"

"Cheating. It pisses me off. Don't get in a committed relationship if you want to fuck other people. It's just weak. And then this happens." I inched my head to my door. "Girls end up with broken hearts and deny it until they are blue in the face."

"Oh, so that's why you went all ape shit and punched her boyfriend?"

Better be her ex-boyfriend.

"Yeah." My answer lingered for a few seconds. "Why else would I do it?"

Aasher shot me a look, but I interrupted him as I caught movement at the end of the hall. I spotted several of my teammates lingering. "What the hell are they doing?"

Aasher turned around and put his hands in his pockets, sighing. "They're keeping watch."

"Keeping watch?"

"Yeah, they were at the party. They saw you throw a punch. They're here to shoo him away if he comes to make amends to your roomie." He laughed in between his explanation. "Plus, Taytum threatened them all if they didn't keep guard. She has some pull because almost everyone is afraid of Emory."

I was in disbelief. "I'm not that unhinged. I *can* control myself when need be."

"They know that. I honestly think they are here for her more than you."

His eyes flicked behind me, and I turned and stilled

when Claire appeared in the doorway with her swollen eyes and slightly puffy lips. "For me?"

Aasher smiled at her. "They said you're their favorite waitress. You always give them extra fries."

A hint of happiness found itself on her face, and I pulled back in confusion. "You give them extra fries? You've never given me extra fries."

She darted her attention to the pizza in my grasp. Her little hands snatched the box before she shrugged. "They don't use my scrunchies on the door to indicate that they're fucking someone in my room, now do they? Or give my favorite pair of underwear to some puck bunny." *Or kiss the fuck out of you to make you feel better.*

The guys at the end of the hall whistled, and when I shot them a glare, they all turned around and pretended like they weren't listening to our conversation. Claire snickered under her breath as she walked backward into the room. The second she was out of sight to everyone but me, I saw the lingering defeat still covering her features.

The door shut in my face, and I was left standing beside Aasher and Taytum. I peered down at the short blonde, and she sighed. "She said she's fine, but she isn't."

I nodded at her and placed my hand on the doorknob. Claire didn't show much vulnerability, but little did she know, I could see right through her, and so could her best friend.

I was halfway through the door when I heard Aasher say, "I'll see you tomorrow." And to my surprise, instead of going home, he followed Taytum down the hall and sat there with the rest of the team, keeping watch for the fucker that broke my roommate's heart.

I peeked an eye open slowly, irritated that the sun was shining through the small window in my room. My body ached when I moved on my side, and when I fully regained my ability to see through the blinding morning light, confusion swept me off my feet. I was staring at my bed, which meant that I wasn't on it. An empty pizza box and tiny bottle of vodka laid on the floor, and I now had an explanation to why I had slept in *and* why my head had a slight thumping to it.

My eyes shot to the slightly opened door that led to the hallway. I recognized my teammates' laughs, and a sense of relief went through me when I heard Claire's laugh alongside theirs.

I slowly pulled myself up and stretched my arms above my head while cracking my stiff neck. Claire's covers were messy beneath me, and it was warm where she had been lying. My laptop was still propped open on her desk that sat beneath her bed, but either the show we had binged had reached its end as we fell asleep or it had died. Recollections of the night weren't blurry. There wasn't enough alcohol in the small bottle to have gotten us both drunk, but we both took a few swigs to wash down the pizza.

Lifting my shirt over my head, I winced at the smell of her shampoo that lingered. There were very few times in my life that I had slept with a girl—and I meant that literally. There were also very few times in my life that, when I did happen to sleep over with a girl, I was the last one up.

I'd snuck out of girls' rooms plenty of times in my first two years of college, and there were many windows that I'd jumped out of before school had started while I was in high school. But this? This was a first.

Claire and I were strictly platonic after our kiss. We sat together and ate pizza, watched the show she'd requested on her laptop, and took a few swigs of vodka before we both fell asleep on her bed. There was no mention of the kiss, and although every single brush of her skin against mine sent my thoughts into a frenzy, it all ended pretty innocently.

After pulling a new set of clothes on and taking a few swigs of water to wash the vodka out of my mouth, I opened the door to the hall and caught the sight of Claire leaning against the far wall with each of my friends surrounding her, like she was the second coming of Jesus.

Her smile was cheery, as if she wasn't still mending a broken heart from her boyfriend sticking his tongue down another girl's throat last night. *Fuck, was that last night?*

I latched onto her voice, mid-conversation, as I pulled the rest of my shirt down and wondered how she could seem so unbothered. The conceited guy I was down to my core hinted that it was our kiss that had mended her heart, but the righteous man my parents raised told me to keep that arrogant thought to myself.

"He asked for a refund." Claire's cheeks turned pink as her sweet little laugh filled the hallway. "But my boss quickly ran and got the cook from the back, and he escorted him out."

"He asked for a refund?" Dax whistled. "This is why they should ban other teams from ever entering The Bex."

Taytum snorted. "No way. Us girls need choices. We tend to get sick of the same flavor of Bexley U jocks."

Ford acted hurt, but all attention turned to me as I leaned against the door frame and tuned in to their conversation.

"Well, hello, sleepyhead." Dax smirked at me. "Leave it to our girl Bryant to get you to sleep in."

"Your girl?" I questioned before flicking my eyes over to her. She caught my gaze for a split second before pushing off the wall and crossing her arms over her loose t-shirt. She looked down at her bare feet, and it seemed like she was hiding from something. When she brought her attention back up, the apples of her cheeks were redder than before, and it irritated me that she was acting all cheeky and comfortable with my teammates but was suddenly acting shy around me.

"Yeah, our girl." Dax rammed his shoulder into Claire's, pushing her off balance for a second. "We don't keep guard all night long for just anyone."

Claire's hands went to her hips, and her crescent smile was infectious. Every one of my friends grinned at her annoyance with them. "I did not ask you guys to keep guard!" Her eyeroll made everyone chuckle. "And I'm not your girl."

"But we're your guys. You give us extra fries."

Taytum pouted. "You give them extra fries too?"

Claire paused and looked around the small group that had formed around her. She laughed next and shrugged. "You guys tip better when I give you extra fries."

"What?!" Ford squealed like a girl. "You only give us extra fries because we tip well?"

Taytum laughed when Dax put a hand over his heart. "I'm a little wounded. I thought you liked us."

Claire's expression softened as she peered up at Dax. "I do like you."

"Is that so?" I asked, stepping forward and erasing the space between our door and the other side of the hall. I leaned beside her, resting one shoulder against the wall. "I thought you hated jocks."

When our eyes caught, she inhaled a heavy breath. There was a pull in my core that had shifted to my gaze. I quirked a brow, waiting for her to turn away from me, but instead, she seemed to accept that I wasn't going to let her act differently with me just because of last night. "Jocks aren't so bad," she mused. Then, she rolled her eyes, and I felt my lip curving. *There you are.* "I guess."

"She *guesses?*" Ford scoffed, and we all fell into easy conversation again. Dax and I were chatting about grabbing some breakfast and then hitting the gym, and Taytum and Claire were mumbling under their breath, likely about Chad.

Part of me wanted to ask her outright if he had called her yet, but I knew it was none of my business. I was there for her last night, but that didn't mean she and I were the best of friends now. She was still just my roommate...who kissed *very* well.

"Claire."

The sound of restraints snapping was congruent throughout the hallway. *Uh-uh. Nope.* I stepped forward without even meaning to, but Aasher's hand gripped a bundle of my shirt, and I stopped at the last second. Anger split down my spine, but I snapped out of it a moment later when I realized I had actually growled like a caveman.

Well, that's new.

Taytum was the first to step forward, nearly facing off with Chad, who lingered at the end of the hallway like Jack Nicholson in *The Shining*. "Leave, Chad. No one wants you here."

"Tay." I snapped my head over to Claire so quickly I felt a pop in my neck.

Claire moved in front of Taytum, and although I wanted to push her behind me to protect her from him, I didn't. It wasn't my place, and I knew it. That wasn't to say I didn't want to knock him on his ass again or, better yet, stick *my* tongue down her throat—farther than I did last night—

just to see how he liked watching her kiss someone else. *Fuck, why am I so mad?*

Chad crept down the hallway with caution, which meant that he was smarter than I thought. His gaze ran over my teammates and me, even shooting Taytum a wary look before saying, "We need to talk."

"Why?" I asked. My arms went across my chest, and I was literally seconds from pulling Claire closer to piss him off. Instantly, I seemed to find my new hobby. It was no longer irritating Claire with pushing the limits within our roommate rules, or using her scrunchies on the doorknobs to irritate her. Instead, it was pissing off her ex. I wanted to pull her in and taunt him over and over again. I wanted to take the knife out of Claire's back that he'd put there and cut him with it each time I touched her.

Claire peeked over her shoulder at me, and it was a heeded warning. Something silent was there that I wanted to ignore, but instead, I looked away and clenched my jaw in a subtle reminder that this wasn't my problem.

"Come on," I said to my teammates who were all just as bent out of shape as I was. One by one, they walked down the hall, each of them sending Chad a look that should have made at least a tremor of fear run through him. Taytum blew a bubble with her gum and waited until she was right beside Chad to pop it in his direction.

"You sure you don't want me to stay," I whispered, leaning in a little too close to Claire's ear. I skimmed my eyes down to her bare arms and watched as goosebumps broke out along her soft skin. I flicked my attention to Chad and noticed his red ears. *Oh, am I too close to the girl you cheated on? Allow me to step closer.*

My smirk dug even deeper, but a moment later, I stepped away and looked into Claire's eyes, waiting for her answer. She turned away and ran her hands down her arms. "I'm fine. I'll see you...later."

My teeth clanked against each other so hard it felt like I had been sucker-punched. The voice inside my head was telling me to go. But there was something keeping my feet from moving forward.

"Look at me, Bryant."

Chad was approaching, and each step he took closer to her, the tenser she became. Claire's blue eyes were heavy and clouded by something when she finally glanced up at me. "Are you sure you want me to go?"

One second.

Two seconds.

Three seconds.

She finally squared her shoulders and sent me a curt nod. "I'm fine."

I nodded and slowly moved past Chad, sending him a chilling look that I had only ever used on the ice. *Don't fuck with her.*

A gulp moved down his throat, but his expression remained steady and set on Claire. I pulled myself down to the end of the hall where Aasher was waiting for me, and I let him drag me the rest of the way to my car because there was something urgent that was trying to get me to turn around, and I knew that I shouldn't.

20

CLAIRE

WHAT LITTLE RESPECT I had for my boyfriend of four years was long gone as I stared at him from across my room. He stood with his hands on his hips, demanding that I explain why I was surrounded by a bunch of hockey players this morning.

My jaw dropped slightly before I righted myself and pretended there wasn't a sting burning my cheek from the slap. "You actually think you have any right to question me?"

Chad scoffed before running his hands through his hair. I stared at the shiny strands, remembering how the girl from last night had pulled on the ends while he plunged his tongue into her mouth. I dodged the blow to my heart and dug down deep for the anger that I knew I needed to fuel this entire encounter.

"Oh, please. Don't give me that, Claire." Chad kicked the half-empty vodka bottle across the room, and it went underneath Theo's bed. "I'm surprised you even care."

I sucked in my stomach, righting my spine like I was about to take the stage. "You're surprised that I care? I watched you openly cheating on me last night. You're my boyfriend, Chad." *We've been together for nearly four years. Of course I care.*

Chad crossed his arms over his chest and waited for me to say something else. Silly me to think that he'd come crawling back this morning to tell me that he didn't mean it and that he was sorry. *What was I thinking?* "How would you like it if you saw me making out with some guy? Would *you* care?"

The memory of Theo kissing me came the second I closed my mouth, but I quickly disregarded it, knowing that it was nothing but a slip in time. I didn't want Theo to kiss me to rub it in Chad's face. I was just desperate to feel anything except the hurt I was feeling. Chad had a way of making me feel like I wasn't good enough, and for once, I wanted to feel the opposite.

"As if you'd even have time to make out with someone." He laughed it off, as if it would never happen. "You're too busy for anything but dance, school, and work."

I scoffed. "Are you really going to try to blame this on me? You're busy too, Chad. Remember? It's your senior year, and you have this *huge* senior project you have to complete. In fact"—I popped my hip out with an attitude I hadn't used since I was fourteen years old—"I wanted to move in with you this year, and you told me that you were too busy and needed to focus."

Chad opened his mouth, but nothing came out. I raised my eyebrows, waiting for some type of explanation to make the anger and hurt stop circling me like I was open prey to an animal who wanted to do nothing but kill me. I jumped in my spot when his hands flung up in defeat. "Fine," he barked. "I'm sorry..."

"You're sor–"

"But it *is* my senior year, Claire."

Is that supposed to mean something?

Chad began pacing back and forth in my small room, stepping over the box of pizza that Theo and I had shared last night, seemingly more agitated than a few minutes ago. Confusion must have covered my features because Chad stopped in his tracks and scoffed again. "I need to experience this college...stuff."

"Stuff?" I took a step away when he got closer to me. My legs hit the back of Theo's bed, and I just stood there, gaping at him, waiting for him to explain.

Chad shrugged. "We've been together for so long, and you know I plan to marry you." His expression softened, the angry lines around his mouth smoothing out. "I even have the ring."

That made me feel worse.

"But I need to get this stuff out of my system."

Why did he keep saying 'stuff'? As if it was a code to something?

"Oh, come on." Chad was acting impatient, and I was frantically trying to connect the dots. "You know...experience the type of stuff that I can't do with you."

My face stung, and if I weren't standing here, several feet away from him, I would have thought he had slapped me.

"Are you..." I cleared my throat, hating that it sounded as defeated as I felt. "Are you saying you want to...experience things with other girls to get it out of your system before you marry me?" Surely that wasn't what he was saying.

Chad snapped his fingers. "Yes! It's my senior year. I need to do the things you're supposed to do your senior year, you know?"

The blood drained from my face, and my fingers went numb. My voice was shaky as I tried to make sense of what he'd just said. "And you expect me to just...wait around?" Betrayal came in quick, and my hurt was masked by anger.

Chad shrugged. "Do you really have a choice?"

I shut my eyes because the room was beginning to spin. My chest was tight, and the load on my shoulders grew that much heavier. "Of course I have a choice. If you think I'm going to sit around and be your girlfriend while you go out and fuck other girls, you don't know me at all."

"And what about your situation?" My hand fell from the bridge of my nose, and I glared at him from across the room. My fingers were itching by my side, and the urge to slap him should have startled me.

"My situation?" I whispered, seeming apprehensive with my quiet voice and questioning confusion. Knowing Chad, he thought it was because I was being my usual, people-pleasing self and enabling him to get the upper hand, but it was actually because I was trying to keep myself from throwing Theo's lamp at his head.

"Your money situation, Claire. Your mother owes my parents a lot of money, and you can hardly afford school as it is. You end us, and you'll be in a much bigger hole than you are now."

My jaw dropped. "Are you seriously threatening me right now?" My words were sputtering out of my mouth, and I had to take a seat on Theo's bed before I fell over in shock. "You want me to wait around for you, and then when you're done with your whoring-around phase, you expect me to just jump back into your arms and act like nothing happened? And if I don't, you'll what? Screw my mother over? Screw me over?"

Chad sighed heavily, and I didn't even want to breathe the same air as him. I was too blinded by his grand plan bordering very closely to a silent threat to acknowledge the bruise to my self-worth.

"I don't even recognize you anymore, Chad," I whispered, at a complete loss for words.

"You know I love you, Claire. You are my future. I've always told you that."

Does he truly believe that?

"Blackmailing someone to stay with you after you treat them horribly isn't love, Chad."

"I'm not blackmailing you." The groove between his eyebrows grew deeper. *He's right. It was more of a threat than anything.*

"You are," I reminded him. "You're telling me—someone who you claim to love—that you are going to sleep around with other girls to get it out of your system and then come back to marry me when it's all said and done because I have no other choice but to say yes? My mother owes your parents money, and I'm poor, so if I say no, then you'll destroy her job and demand the money back? Sounds like a threat, actually."

Silence surrounded us, and I could see the wheels turning in the back of his head just like I could hear the plans formulating in mine. Chad was out of his mind if he thought I wouldn't do everything in my power to get out from under this. People wondered why I never asked for help or accepted it, and this was why.

"I see what you're saying, Claire." Chad took a step toward me, and if I weren't already sitting on Theo's bed, I would have moved back to get away from him. "Maybe we should just consider this a little break, then?"

My eyebrows raised. "A break?"

His hands went into his pockets as he peered down at me on Theo's bed. "I don't want to regret spending my entire college experience studying my ass off and not doing what guys do, babe. Tell me you understand and that you won't force me into a bad position. Tell me you'll be waiting for me after graduation." My heart was racing through my chest, and if I couldn't feel it ramming against my ribs, I would have thought it had stopped beating altogether. I felt nothing but unwanted and used as I gazed up at someone I used to feel comforted by. I used to feel safe with him. "Tell me, and I won't say anything to my parents. Your mom's job is safe. The money she owes is just that. Owed."

I knew I didn't have much of a choice—not at this moment, at least. But I wasn't going to be the dutiful girl-friend he could keep on a leash while he was out doing his own thing with the safety blanket of knowing I'd be there in the end.

"Fine," I said softly. When his face relaxed and his shoulders dropped, I slowly stood up and put my hand on his chest to push him away. "But if you're on a break, then I am too."

He frowned as I walked past him and grabbed my dance bag. "What does that mean?"

"I won't sit in my room each night, waiting for you to call me after you've been with other girls." I shook my head. "So, if you're on a break, then I am too."

"Are you saying you're gonna go out with guys?" He scoffed as he put his hands on his hips.

I didn't answer him because that wasn't my plan. My plan was to focus solely on school, take as many shifts at

The Bex as I could to save more money, and work my ass off to get the lead part in the spring showcase so I could win the full scholarship for my senior year.

Chad laughed under his breath as I held the door open for him with my dance bag slung over my shoulder. Before he walked past me, his hand wrapped around my waist, and he leaned in close. His breath tickled my ear, but what used to make me feel calm felt like a storm brewing. "You talk a big game, Claire Bear. But you and I both know that isn't you. You don't have time for me, let alone anyone else." The breath in my lungs left with him after he kissed my cheek.

The second the door shut was the second I let my guard fall.

21

THEO

"EXTRA FRIES." Claire dropped a basket of fries in the center of the table, and everyone dove in except me. Her smile was misplaced because it didn't reach her eyes, and the second she turned away, I slipped out of the booth and followed her over to the bar. I caught the eye of her boss, and she gave me a little wave before glancing at her employee who she was obviously worried about.

I wouldn't admit this to anyone, but I was worried too.

Claire had been quieter than normal. I'd hardly seen her since last weekend, when I had spent the night curled around her as she mended a broken heart. I didn't ask her what Chad had said to her after Aasher pulled me away and nearly slapped me for getting so worked up.

Our one-sided exchange worked, and I'd been more focused on our game schedule and practices than usual— throwing myself into my driven, high-focused mindset and thinking of nothing but proving myself to Tom Gardini.

"Ready for the game tomorrow?" Angie came over and

leaned against the bar, right beside Claire as she was putting something into the computer. Claire's eyes sliced to mine for a second, finally spotting me, before she went back to the computer screen. I couldn't help but notice the way the light from the screen enhanced the dark bags underneath her bottom lashes.

"Yeah." I grinned, pulling one side of my mouth up. "I'm not worried. We've had some good practices this week."

Angie nodded. "I'll be there with my son again. He still isn't over the puck you threw him. He sleeps with it."

My chest rumbled with laughter. "Sounds like me at that age."

"Well, I can only hope he turns out like you."

Claire was still standing by the computer, but I knew her attention was on me. I looked up at her for a split second, catching the blue in her eyes, and turned back to Angie. "Is he coming to the winter day camp?"

Angie blew out a breath. "Are you kidding? He'd never forgive me if I didn't sign him up."

I nodded. "Tell him I'll see him there. I'll slip him another puck."

Angie walked past me and patted my shoulder. "You're a good one, Theo. Never lose that part of yourself when you make it big."

"If," I corrected. "If I make it big."

I knew I was destined for the NHL. It had been whispered in my ear since I was young by coaches, other parents, and even other players, but I still liked to remain humble.

Angie laughed me off as she walked away, leaving me and Claire alone at the bar area.

"Not busy on Thursdays, I see."

Claire began stacking cups off to the side. "Not really,

but tomorrow night we will be. Everyone seems to come here after the game, before they hit the parties."

"You work tomorrow night?" I asked.

Claire shook her head, and I watched her closely. She looked both relieved and deterred by that.

"So..." I leaned in close so she was forced to peer up at me. Her cheeks turned pink when I smirked. "That means you're coming to the game, then?"

Her laugh was abrupt. "No."

I slapped the top of the bar and pulled myself away from her space. "Come on, Bryant. What else are you gonna be doing if you're not working? You've been nonexistent this week. I live with you and haven't seen you."

Was this my attempt to dig and figure out what was going on with her and Chad? Yes. Was it a poor attempt? Also, yes.

Claire's shoulders fell. "I'll be catching up on homework, and I'll probably head to the auditorium and practice."

I felt the skepticism in my expression before I allowed it to come out in my voice. "How often do you need to practice? You're already there by the time I wake up to run." I thought I was obsessed with being the best, but damn.

Claire paused as she tucked a stray hair behind her ear. "How do you know that?"

I stilled but recovered quickly. "Because I run past and see your car there every morning."

She didn't need to know that running past the auditorium was not my usual route, but deep down, I knew it. *So what?* I wanted to check on her. There wasn't anything wrong with that.

Claire thought for a moment, but then she brushed me off, walking around the bar to clean off some tables with her wet rag. I followed closely behind her, not allowing her to avoid me any longer. *Is this about us kissing?*

"So, you're coming to the game?" I teased, poking at her a little more.

"What?" she asked, spinning around on light feet. "N–"

Ford leaned out of the booth beside the one she was wiping down. "You're coming to our game?! Are you going with Taytum?"

"You're comin'?" Jett pulled out his phone and began texting. "You can sit with my girl if you want. She comes to every game. I'll let her know."

"And she wears his jersey. She's honestly our biggest cheerleader." Dax rolled his eyes. "If I didn't like Alicia so much, I would be annoyed with your relationship."

"They're in love. It's adorbs." Ford drew a heart in the air with his finger, and everyone chuckled. I watched Claire closely to see how she'd react, but she only laughed at Ford, lighting up the restaurant with her pretty smile.

"There. Done." Ford held his phone up and showed Claire. Her huff came quickly, and I grinned down at the texts between him and Taytum.

Ford: Claire is coming to our game tomorrow. You going with her?

Taytum: What? She is? Are you sure?

Ford: Yes, she said she'd go if you do.

The wet rag that was bundled in her hand shot out and hit Ford in the center of the chest. Everyone at the table laughed, and Claire stomped her foot in a poor attempt at protesting. I heard her phone buzz, and she pulled it out of the back of her jeans and pursed her lips at the text from Taytum.

Tay: Not sure how that happened, but you're not

getting out of going to the game. You need a night out and to stop killing yourself by working and practicing. If Chad is gonna "experience" college and expect you to be with him after, then you're going to as well.

Experience college? What?

"Hmm," I whispered, reading over her shoulder. "I agree."

Claire shut her phone off, and her pointy elbow went straight into my tight stomach. I let out a hiss between my teeth that ruffled the back of her ponytail, making me pull on the strands a moment later. Her head flew back, and she spun around, ready to slap me with the towel, but I dodged the blow and went around to the other side of the booth and slid in beside Jett, stealing a fry from the basket she'd given us.

My smirk was the cherry on top of my triumphant mood. I was a natural-born winner, and even winning this little spar with Claire seemed to feed into that.

━━

I could tell Coach was shouting by the spit flying from his mouth and the vein popping out of his right temple. The crowd was roaring, like it usually was at a home game, and I couldn't help but do a quick search for Claire in a sea of black jerseys. I hadn't spotted her yet, and usually, during a game, everything around me blurred the moment my skates hit the ice. Tonight, though, I kept glancing in the stands, appearing unfocused to my team and, most of all, to Coach.

It wasn't until he had pulled me aside, ripping me by the jersey, to inform me that he'd gotten word that Tom Gardini had sent a few of his most trusted scouts to our game, that I quickly became engrossed. Irritation backed my thoughts of Claire, and I refused to look back in the stands until the game was over.

The first two periods were scoreless, and tension was high. We were out for blood with only three minutes left in the third period. That was when we finally got our chance. Ford, Aasher, and I were on the line together, and when I noticed the game clock rapidly ticking down, I nodded at the pair of them and set the play into action. Ford passed the puck back and forth with Dax, making the forward from Valley skate laps like a feral animal near the blue line. My focus was razor sharp as Ford got the puck and snapped it to me, waiting at the crease, eager to lift it just over the goalie's glove, giving us the W.

My blood ran hot as the team and I skated to center ice to celebrate, silently thanking God that we pulled it together in the end. My breath was escaping like air from a balloon, and it continued all the way to the locker room as I began pulling my gear off. The moment the winning puck made it in the net, the arena was like an anthem roaring through my ears, and I swore I could still hear it. I had an overwhelming rush of satisfaction of not only winning the game but playing the best I had all season—that was, after I had pulled my head out of my ass and stopped worrying about Claire being in the stands.

"And that's why you're going to be able to pick what-ever fucking team you want next year, Wolf." Coach had sweat trailing down his face when he peered up at me. He was a short man, but he could be intimidating as fuck.

I nodded and paired it with a half-shrug. "You told me that Tom Gardini had sent some scouts. I knew I needed to kick it up a notch."

Aasher threw up a fist. "And you fuckin' did."

Ford chimed in after stripping down to his boxers. His

chest was still heaving from the excitement and physical exertion. "I'm surprised the ice hasn't melted, because you were on fucking fire, man."

I chuckled but quickly got changed, knowing there were a few journalists waiting outside of the locker room to ask questions. Coach usually only chose a few of us to head out of the locker room early to answer questions. It was my turn tonight, unfortunately.

"And here I thought you played your best because a certain someone was in the stands." Jett's gruff voice hit the back of my neck as he half-whispered so no one else would hear. Aasher turned to see my expression, but I kept it as level as it should have been. *I was distracted early on in the game, and they knew why.*

"Who?" I asked, not wanting to play their games and feed into my already rising disappointment over my slip in focus. "You mean Claire?"

Jett sent me a questionable look as he waited for me to walk out with him to answer a few questions. Coach was waiting by the door, vividly chatting with the assistant coach about the game.

"Why would I care if she was in the stands?"

Ford snickered. "Well, you *were* the one who invited her to the game."

"No." I pulled on my hat backward and covered my slightly sweaty hair. I glanced at Ford as I fixed my long-sleeve Bexley U Hockey shirt. "I was just trying to irritate her, as usual. You were the one who conned her best friend into dragging her out."

He glanced across the room at Emory before turning away and smirking at me. "You're welcome."

A crease dove between my brows, but Coach yelled my name, and I brushed my friends off and walked out into the mass of journalists who held their notepads tightly and swung cameras my way. I quickly slipped back into the part of myself that I was most comfortable with: Theo Brooks, the wolf on ice. The guy who was driven by the intense need to follow his goals for more humble reasons than most people probably assumed.

22

CLAIRE

I TAKE back everything I said about sports.

In all my years of high school and attending Bexley U, I had never been to any type of sporting event. I never went to the football games, or basketball games, and especially not hockey, but that was one of the best experiences I had ever had. The smell of the ice was crisp and refreshing. There was a wave of egotistical athleticism flowing from every single hockey player, but instead of it turning me off in the way that most jocks did, I was mesmerized by their skill and focus.

"So, what did you think?" Taytum pulled me down the long hall, and the farther we got away from the stands, the clearer my thoughts came.

"Honestly?" My cheeks were beginning to ache from smiling so much. Even my voice came out raspy because I had shouted during the game. *Who even am I?* "That was the most fun I've had in a very long time."

Taytum squealed and clapped. "Finally!" Her hands

landed on my shoulders as we stopped in the middle of a random hallway that seemed like a secret passageway of some sort because not a single person followed us. We were going in the opposite direction of the rest of the crowd. "You"—Taytum's head fell to mine, our foreheads resting against each other's for a second—"deserve to have some fun, Claire. Okay?"

I swallowed as she pulled back. Her blue eyes drove into mine, silently touching on what was really going on with me. With Taytum, I could be myself. She knew my insecurities and what I was up against. I didn't get into all the nitty, gritty details about Chad, but she knew enough. "Thanks for dragging me out." I sighed. "I won't lie. It felt good to just put a pause on everything." I had been totally engrossed in the game, and even though I tried not to watch Theo, it was impossible not to. It was difficult to avoid him, considering he was easily the best player on the ice.

She scoffed as we started down the hall again. I followed after her and watched as she pulled her phone out, reading a text. "I can imagine. You have a lot going on. Rose told me that you've been practicing nonstop too."

I crossed my arms over my Bexley U shirt that I'd received at freshman orientation. Up until tonight, it'd been nothing but a sleep shirt. "How does Rose know?"

Taytum didn't even bat an eye. "Oh, she goes and gets me coffee every morning at Bex Press."

Bex Press was the campus coffee shop that most students went to in the mornings to get their fancy lattes and expensive espressos. It was close to the auditorium, and every morning, as I dragged myself out of bed to practice, my mouth salivated at the thought of one of their delicious muffins that I couldn't afford.

My jaw dropped. "Are you serious? You make her get you coffee every morning? Taytum!"

Taytum laughed me off. "I order her one every morning too—as a way to pay her back for going to get it." Taytum stopped at the end of the hall and turned to the left, going down another hall.

"Where are we going?"

She glanced over at me, tightening her high ponytail on the top of her head with a flirty grin. "You'll see. But for real, how good were the guys? I didn't know hockey could be that fun to watch. We've gotta come to more games. I already invited Rose and Harlow to the next home game. You're coming if you're not working."

I didn't pretend like I was turned off by the idea, because the thought of going to another game was exciting.

Tay slowed her steps as we grew closer to some chatter. We weren't close enough for me to make out what people were saying, but I could feel the uptick in energy.

"Theo's really good."

Taytum peered over at me for a second. "There's a reason his nickname is Wolf." She paused before turning away to mumble out her next few words. "That and his reputation in the bedroom."

I was thankful she didn't glance over and see my expression because I felt the warmth blossom on my cheeks. I was absolutely certain that he lived up to his reputation in the bedroom by the one, meaningless kiss he gave me.

"How is it going with him anyway?"

"What do you mean?" My question was panicky, and Taytum noticed.

She pulled me back by my wrist and stopped me from walking any farther. "Is the whole roommate thing still going okay?"

My lips rolled together as I tried to come up with a way to avoid the conversation altogether. I didn't even allow myself to think about Theo unless it was in an innocent, informal way, and the reason for that was so I didn't get wrapped up in something that wasn't even there.

Were we friends now? I wasn't sure. But he did watch me break in half, kissed me after I nearly embarrassed myself with desperation, and then continued on with life like nothing had happened.

"Claire?" Taytum snapped her fingers in front of my face, and her face quickly came back into focus.

"Yeah, things are fine. He..." I lifted a shoulder, unsure of how I felt about him, especially after last weekend. "I was wrong about him."

Her eyebrow quirked, and I put my hand up.

"Don't get that look. He just isn't what I had expected."

"What did you expect?"

"I expected him to sleep with a new girl every other day and then treat them poorly afterward, like the stereotypical jock. But that's not really true." I rolled my eyes and contradicted myself a moment later. "Well, he does have multiple girls following him around, but he's at least up front with them and doesn't fuck every puck bunny that comes into sight. And he's..." I stumbled over my words, trying to find the right way to describe him. "Respectful. Although, he likes to irritate me too. Shit." I breathed out an exasperated sigh. "Theo is just...Theo. I don't know."

Taytum waited until I was done nervously rambling. It was obvious I was confused about the rooted preconception of jocks that my mother had instilled in me because of my father and his absence. Was I becoming impartial to jocks? To Theo?

"He took care of you."

Although I wanted to deny it in every way, I didn't. I simply nodded at Taytum and agreed, because he did, and she didn't even know the whole story.

"And you let him."

I sighed at the obvious elephant in the room, but the mouth of the hallway Taytum and I were slowly walking down opened up, and my attention was immediately stolen. My gaze went directly to Theo like he was the only one standing there, but he wasn't. A posse of girls—excuse me, puck bunnies—was surrounding him like he was Jesus Christ himself. *Are they going to drop to their knees too?* Ford was leaning against the wall right outside of what I assumed to be the locker room with Jett and Alicia. Alicia was Jett's girlfriend who had disappeared from the stands the very second the game ended, telling us she was going to meet Jett by the locker rooms like she did after every game.

Taytum's phone dinged, and I glanced down at her screen.

Ford: Well, what are you two doing just standing there? You are invited to the VIP area.

Taytum playfully rolled her eyes and put her phone away without texting him back. I kept my attention away from the four girls that were vying for Theo's attention and mumbled under my breath, "Seems like our VIP spots are taken already."

Ford, Jett, and Alicia met us halfway, but I noticed that Theo stayed back with the girls. I held back my eyeroll at the thought of a scrunchie being on my door later. *Maybe I should beat him to it and put my own scrunchie on the door.*

A laugh escaped me, and Taytum nudged my shoulder with hers. "What's funny?"

Without meaning to, I turned my head and locked onto Theo. My voice disappeared when I saw him staring at me instead of the four girls competing for a spot on his roster of girls he'd slept with. His jade eyes weren't bright with amusement like usual when he'd looked at me. Instead, they were intense and piercing. Goosebumps covered my arms, and I briefly heard Ford say, "Oh. I think it's funny, too. No matter how many times he tells them to leave him alone, they just won't stop. Look how annoyed he is."

I couldn't seem to look away. Theo's brow hooked upward, hitting just below the brim of his backward hat. His arms went across his chest, and that damn lip of his curled upward, and before I knew what I was doing, I took a step toward him. *Damn you, Theo.*

"What is she doing?" Ford's confusion hit the back of my head as I headed toward Theo.

Did Theo and I just have a silent agreement?

The closer I got to him, the more my lips ached to curve. The hardness in his gaze softened, and it was obvious he was relieved to see me heading his way. I straightened my shoulders and slowly slithered up beside him, looking all four puck bunnies in the eye.

Theo's arm snaked around my waist, and I sucked in a quick breath. "There you are," he whispered, leaning down into my space. I tilted my head to the side, allowing his warm breath to hit the side of my neck.

"Who...?" The girl with pretty auburn hair scoffed, stopping mid-sentence. "Oh, so you already have plans for tonight?"

"Looks like it." I smiled sweetly and wrapped my arms around Theo's torso, noticing how tight it was. I briefly remembered how chiseled his muscles felt when he was curled against me last weekend. There was a familiar pull in my stomach that I quickly stomped on.

Taytum's laugh echoed down the hall, and Theo's hold on me got tighter, as if he knew that I was about to step away. *"Don't,"* he whispered, letting his lips brush over my cheek. My entire body grew warm, and I raised an eyebrow at the girls staring at us in disbelief, hoping they'd turn around and take off before I orgasmed from my roommate's raspy voice.

Shit. Shit. Shit.

I slowly blew the trapped air out of my mouth as each girl turned around begrudgingly and trudged down the hall, ignoring Ford as he sarcastically waved at them.

The second they were out of sight, I peered up at Theo. "You can let me go now."

The playfulness on his features was back, and his curved jaw caught my eye as he grinned down at me. "Now why would I do that, Bryant?"

I bounced my eyes back and forth between his, and I hated that I couldn't figure out what he was thinking. There was definitely something formulating in the back of his mind, and I was afraid to know what it was.

"Was that planned?!" Ford asked, sliding beside us. Theo eventually dropped his arm from my waist, and I stepped away a little too quickly. Taytum caught my eye, and I purposefully looked away. *What the hell am I doing?* This was Chad's fault. He crawled into my head and burrowed his insults in there, causing me to latch onto something that wasn't even there. It was a type of subconscious revenge.

Theo chuckled as he pulled his hat off and ran a hand through his messy hair. "No, but it's not the first time Claire has stepped in and rescued me."

"Um, what?" Taytum looked at me and pursed her lips. I pretended not to notice her disapproval.

I sighed. "You forced me to do it last time."

Ford stuck his head in between Theo and me. "Forced you? Careful what you say, girl."

I shook my head. "No. I—"

Theo pushed Ford back out of my space. "You know how puck bunnies are. They're relentless."

"Not if you have a long-time girlfriend," Alicia said, grabbing onto Jett's hand. He brought their clasped hands up to his mouth and kissed her knuckles. *Okay, they are cute.* A wave of disappointment flew through me, realizing that Chad and I never, ever had that.

"Exactly." Theo snapped his fingers. "I acted like Claire and I were a thing the other day and scared a puck bunny off. It seems that Claire is the best form of defense when it comes to these leeches."

His shoulder bumped into mine lightly, and he smiled at me, throwing me off balance. "Thanks, roomie."

Roomie.

"Dude, that is brilliant." Ford snapped his fingers just as Aasher walked out of the locker room, looking fresh-faced and ready to go.

"What's brillant?" he asked, sliding up beside Theo. He nodded at me, and I sent him a small smile.

"Claire acting like Theo's girl." Ford slapped Theo on the chest. "That'll be the end of your worries."

My face began to turn red. I knew it because I felt the same way I had in fourth grade when I fell off the stage during one of my recitals.

Aasher threw his hands up. "You're the only fucking dude on this team that would complain about too many puck bunnies wanting your attention."

"They're unwavering in their attempts, and I don't want them around when Tom Gardini is looking to put me on his team. He needs to see that I'm focused. Plus, they show up in our room naked. Unannounced. Ask Claire. She knows."

Who is Tom Gardini? Taytum's elbow made contact with my ribs, and I quickly snapped my head up and made eye contact with Theo. "It's not like you turn them all down," I blurted, seemingly more irritated than I actually was.

Theo's eyebrows climbed upward, and one of his lips disappeared behind his white teeth. "I would if you were my girl."

My heart fell down to the very bottom of my stomach. The way those words made my chest squeeze told me all that I needed to know. Chad had hurt me, even if I pretended I was fine.

"Come on, Bryant." Theo reached his hand out and pulled on the strands of my hair in a teasing way. "I'd be the most faithful fake boyfriend you ever had."

"Wait, what?" Taytum stepped forward and stole the spotlight. "You want to pretend to date her?"

Theo's eyes stayed glued to mine, as if he were waiting for an answer from me, but my voice was gone. If I dared speak, I was sure it would come out more like the croak of a frog.

"Yeah, Claire acts like my girlfriend, for all intents and purposes. That way, the puck bunnies stop hounding me after games, showing up to our room unannounced, waiting for me after practice..." His voice trailed off, and I knew everyone's eyes were on me. "It is a solid plan."

No. No way.

I paused for the briefest of seconds and was irate at the fact that Chad's name appeared in the back of my head.

What would he do if I *did* agree to that? Would he go ballistic? I mean, I did tell him that I wouldn't sit here for the next year and act like his wounded girlfriend on the side if he was going to be out having sex and *experiencing college*. But Chad had a hold on me, whether I wanted to admit that or not. I was worried about the future, and money, and everything in between, but the independence I had yielded since a young age flooded my blood, and I seriously found myself contemplating it.

"And what's in it for her?" Taytum asked.

"Pissing her loser of an ex off, obviously." Ford said it jokingly, but everyone was thinking it—even me.

Taytum turned to me, and her baby blues bounced back and forth between mine, wondering what I was thinking. We were both on the edge, teetering over the idea of this little plan, but I could see that Taytum was ready to push me over. Except, she also knew there was more at stake than just my heart and wounded ego.

My head shook slightly, and I let the panic win. It was obvious I didn't know Chad any longer. He'd proven that to me last weekend when he cheated and then told me he expected me to wait for him to move on from his phase, or else he'd put an end to my mother having any financial stability and potentially ruin my future. It was too risky, right?

"Alright, let's leave Claire alone," Taytum said, pulling me by the arm. "Ready to party?"

"Party?" Ford smirked as he pushed Taytum and me apart, coming in between us. Each of his arms was twisted in ours, and he led us down the hall, calling to the rest of his friends, Theo included. "Let's go show these ladies how hockey players party."

There was tension in my shoulders at the thought of

showing my face at another party after I was humiliated last time, but Taytum was right earlier. I deserved to have fun because, come tomorrow morning, I would be back in the auditorium, going over my solo number and killing myself to come out on top instead of ending up beneath Chad.

23

THEO

WOULD it really be so bad? Being my fake girlfriend? Or at the very least, acting like she was mine for the night while obnoxious puck bunnies popped up like whack-a-moles? I mean, she had already done it twice now. What was another thirty times? Just until the season ended?

I sighed with irritation and pouted like a child. I understood why she was reluctant. She *did* just get her heart broken and was likely staying far away from anyone. It was clear she was keeping herself busy and distracting herself. If she wasn't working, in class, writing some paper, or studying for an exam, she was at the auditorium.

I was surprised she had come out tonight, but Taytum whispered a conundrum in her ear, poking at Chad's whereabouts, and conned her into it. I wasn't complaining. She deserved it. She worked harder than I did, and that was impressive.

There was a cup in her hand that I'd watched Ford hand to her when I walked into the party. Claire and Taytum rode over with Ford and Aasher, and I followed behind in my car, but the moment we walked in, I found her immediately. Her gaze snagged mine from across the room, and her sweet smile made me feel slightly uncomfortable but strangely calm too. Was Claire the first girl I cared about? It agitated me that I was looking for her during my game, but as soon as I pulled myself away and focused on playing, I played better than ever. There was a nagging voice in the back of my head that told me it wasn't only because I knew Tom Gardini's guys were there. I wanted to prove myself to her, to show her what she'd been missing out on by hating all jocks.

She surely didn't look like she hated us now. Her head flew back, and her pretty, soft waves that I rarely ever saw cascaded down her back as she laughed at something Taytum said. A few other girls had formed around them, and by their whispers and awe-struck looks, I assumed they were younger dancers. They had that *I-want-to-be-you* look on their faces that all the freshman hockey players had whenever we'd practice together.

"Whatcha lookin' at?" Emory's voice hit the back of my neck, and I nearly elbowed him in the jaw for catching me.

"Go away," I snarled. "You smell like a whore house."

He sniggered under his breath and came to stand beside me. "Jealous?"

I glared over at him. "Of you fucking a puck bunny? No." I could have had my pick. I just didn't want to.

His lip curled upward as he ran a free hand through his dark hair. The hair on his face had fully grown in, and he already had the look of a pro NHL player. "Nah, I'm talkin' about her."

I didn't follow his gaze across the party because I knew he was referring to Claire. "Jealous of what?"

"Being so close to her but not being able to have her."

"Watch it," I warned. Heat crawled up my neck, and a heavy breath left me. "And I don't want her like that." I shrugged, taking my attention from his squinting gaze. I glanced back at Claire and caught her eye for a brief second before she turned away, pretending like she wasn't watching me. "She's...my roommate. I feel kind of protective over her." My words were coming out a little too quickly, and I felt myself trying to cover up something that wasn't even true. "Plus, you know I don't get involved like that. Not until I've made it big and can afford to settle down a little. She's just my roommate. A friend."

"Brother," Emory patted my chest and I instantly wanted to fling his palm off my body because I was suddenly extremely irritated. "You don't look at friends the way you're lookin' at her."

If she's just my roommate, then why do I want to walk over there just to be beside her?

"Knock it off," I snapped, "or I'll call your mom and tell her you fucked her best friend last season after the championship game before they took you to dinner. Or maybe I'll tell Taytum, and she can tell your mom." He knew I'd never stoop so low, but I was starting to grow angrier the more he fucked with me.

"You punched her boyfriend." The cup in my hand began to crumple when Aasher started in too.

"*Ex*," I corrected. "He's now her ex."

"You gonna punch him again?"

Maybe. I snapped my neck to Emory. "Why would I punch him again?"

The humor that was there moments ago when he was fucking with me was gone. "Because the way she's looking at him while he sweet-talks another girl across the room makes *me* want to punch him."

Someone had gripped me by the throat and cut off all breathing as I whipped my head over to the left and searched for him. *This piece of shit.* The way my blood ran cold was an obvious clue that I was about to lose my mind if I didn't remove myself from the party. My ears grew warm, and my eyes narrowed in his direction, locking onto the way a girl was somehow being swooned right out of her pants from whatever it was he was whispering to her.

"The fucking nerve," I gritted. I handed my cup to Emory, pushing it into his chest, and kept my attention on Chad and his little toy as I strode through the party like I was on a goddamn mission.

And I was.

At the very last second, Chad caught my eye, and the way my lip curled should have clued him in that I was about to fuck with him like he was fucking with her.

I forced Claire's eyes to meet mine as I blocked her view from him. The way her pink lips were tugged into a frown told me that she saw exactly what Chad was doing across the party. Her little nostrils flared with irritation, and her cheeks were painted pink.

"There you are," I said, taking another step toward her. My foot went in between hers, and I tipped her head back with a finger under her chin, letting those brown locks fall down her back again.

"What?" she whispered, voice shaky and not sounding at all like the tone she used with me, which was usually full of irritation, skimming right on top of subtle humor.

"I said..." My hands went to her hips, and she sucked in a breath, straightening her spine and pushing her chest into mine. *Damn.* "There you are." I gave her that same look I'd given her just a couple hours prior when I desperately needed her to rescue me from the girls waiting outside the locker room who wouldn't leave me alone. *Play along, Bryant.*

There was a tiny dip in between her brows, and although everything had basically disappeared for me except her, I still heard Taytum say, "Better do it right. He's looking over here."

The smallest amount of panic flickered across Claire's face, but then her hands landed on my wrists, and my fingers twitched to pull her in even closer. I dipped my gaze to her mouth, and for the second time since meeting her, I had the inclination to kiss her and make her forget his name.

"Hey," she whispered. Her sweet breath flew to my lips, and I gritted my teeth to keep myself from completely obliterating the plan and slamming my mouth on hers right then and there. *Slow it down.*

I dropped my voice low enough so only she would hear me. "I'm gonna spin you around, and you need to lean back on my chest, yeah?"

Claire nodded, and the panic disappeared as she put her game face on. I couldn't have stopped my smirk even if I tried. Claire's ass was pressed to my front a moment later, and my hands rested with ease over her hips. Taytum and Ford played their parts well, keeping the rest of the group around us entertained with a conversation so it looked as if this was nothing out of the ordinary, but it was. We garnered looks from all across the party, and the satisfaction it gave me, knowing that some of my fan girls were pouting and realizing they weren't going to end up in my bed tonight, was enough to make this worth it, even if Chad didn't notice us.

Oh, but he did.

I looked in his direction and pulled Claire even tighter against my front. Her breathing had stopped when Chad paused his sloppy kisses, and my mouth dipped down, my lips a breath away from her ear. "Breathe, Bryant." A little gasp flew from her lungs, and I smiled against her neck. "I'll lead. You follow."

She turned her attention to me, and I knew I was going to kiss her. I hardly doubted she noticed, but my entire body seized for a split second because I'd lost all control, and that didn't happen often. "This is going to make him irate."

I pulled my gaze from the shape of her kissable lips and stared right into her worried blue eyes. "He gets to fuck around on you and expect you to wait around for him as he *'experiences'* college?" The shock of realization only lasted a moment. *Oh yes, I know more than you think, Claire.* "Absolutely not. No roommate of mine is gonna be played like that. I won't have it."

Her warm hand covered mine on her hip as my other one snaked up her neck. I cupped her face, splaying my palm out against her cheek, my fingers disappearing in her hair. "I'm gonna kiss the hell out of you, Bryant, and don't you dare pull away."

For the second time, our mouths sealed, but this time, the kiss was undeniably soul-wrecking, and that was when I knew that Claire Bryant was about to become my weak side.

24

CLAIRE

THE FACT that I was kissing Theo Brooks—*again*—just to prove a point to my ex was a long-forgotten thought. I felt the kiss in my bones. My core burned as bright as a flame when Theo's teeth tugged on my bottom lip, pulling my mouth open a little farther so his tongue could sweep inside and quite literally sweep me off my feet. I couldn't breathe in the air of the party. Instead, I could only breathe in Theo. I was no longer at a party with watchful eyes and an ex who had provoked me into this position. I was lost, and I didn't want to find my way back again.

Theo's other hand left my hip as I turned all the way around, and he cupped both sides of my face. My mouth was his, and the way he coaxed me to kiss him back with passion instead of urgency made me feel something I'd never felt with Chad. My heart was beating wildly with excitement, and my body ached to move a little closer to him, just to feel the hardness of his chest brush against mine.

The smallest groan left him as he pulled away and peered down at me. I darted my tongue out and licked my swollen lips, wondering if they felt as branded as I did. His hands didn't leave my face, and the light and airy green of his eyes was hardened to emerald rocks.

"Now"—his Adam's apple bobbed as he forced down a swallow—"that's how you do it, Bryant."

I swallowed his taste on my tongue and nodded, breathing out a thank you. I wasn't sure what was going to happen next, and I braced myself for the impact of Chad's glare from across the room. Guilt began to drown out the pounding beats of my heart inside my ears, but it had nothing to do with actually kissing Theo, but more so because I didn't regret it for a single second.

"Make sure you look over at him when I step away, because he will be staring over here. Two can play that game, baby. And he doesn't get to make the rules when it comes to you."

Theo's voice was gravelly and daring. The hard and absolute look in his eye never wavered, and he suddenly seemed so much more rugged than usual. My face burned when he winked at me, and the moment he stepped away, I pulled my shoulders straight, flicked my hair off my shoulder and looked Chad right in the eye. Theo was right. Chad was looking right in our direction, but instead of sending me a chilling glare, like I'd assumed, he was standing back against the wall with his arm draped over the shoulder of the girl that I'd watched him kiss just moments before.

Irritation flicked down my spine, all the way to my toes, but Theo provoked me in the best way. *He doesn't get to make the rules when it comes to you.* Almost as if I was putting armor on, I reached down and grabbed onto Theo's hand and intertwined our fingers together. Chad laughed silently, looking across the party at me like I was pathetic, but I refused to let him make me feel anything but powerful in the moment.

Theo's fingers squeezed mine as he pretended not to pay attention. He joined in the conversation with Taytum and Ford, who also acted as if Theo kissing me was nothing out of the ordinary, although just about everyone knew it was. I stayed unmoving as Chad began pulling the auburn-haired, fair-skinned girl by the arm toward the stairs, rolling his eyes in my direction before putting his back to me.

"You make the rules," Theo said.

I inhaled quietly and let the air out before I tugged on his hand, noticing the calluses on his palm rubbing against the softness of mine. Aasher coughed under his breath from behind us as I continued to watch Chad prowl through the party with one of his toys trailing behind him, and he said, *"Does this mean she's rethought his earlier proposition?"*

Theo and I both ignored everyone who was having a quiet conversation behind us and were suddenly on the same team. He crooked an eyebrow when he caught my eye, and the playfulness was back on his face, which all but demanded a smile from mine. There was a challenge surrounding him when he subtly flicked his chin over to the stairs and tugged on my hand. I followed after him willingly, feeling nothing but irresistible as heads turned every few seconds. There was a mix of expressions that surrounded us. Some of the athletes of BU were both in awe and confused, and then there were a few jaw drops from some of the students that I knew were in the same classes as Chad. The puck bunnies' lips jutted outward as they pouted, knowing they wouldn't be scoring with the most popular hockey player tonight, which made me feel prouder than I should have.

When we got to the bottom stair, I peered up and saw Chad touching the auburn-haired girl with an eager intimacy he'd never used on me before.

"He's taunting you," Theo growled, pulling me up the steps, passing by a few other couples. "And I've gotta say...I don't like it."

I stayed silent as we passed behind him, letting Theo lead us, but his voice stopped both of us in our tracks like we'd been caught doing something we shouldn't have been doing.

"That's fine, *Claire Bear*." Chad went back to kissing the girl who was embarrassingly clueless as to what was going on. "You could use the experience."

I forced myself to keep my jaw from falling open with complete and utter disbelief. I knew he wanted a reaction out of me, and he wouldn't get one, but *ouch*. I tugged on Theo's hand, but it was like trying to pull down a building. He didn't budge. I glanced at him, pulling again, but his feet were cemented into the floor of the hallway. A red-hot color began to crawl up his neck from beneath the collar of his t-shirt, and the muscles along his temples flickered back and forth just as quickly as my heart was beating. His eyes narrowed, and his breath hit me in the face as he leaned backward and shot Chad a look that would make anyone shiver.

"You think she's going to go back to you when I'm through with her?" My stomach dipped at the thought of Theo touching me. *Remember, this isn't real, Claire.* "She won't even remember your name after I touch her."

I was too busy trying to put out the fire in my body to even care that Chad's jaw tightened. Theo pulled me the rest of the way down the hall, opened the door on the right, and pushed me inside with a look on his face that I'd never seen before. His cheeks had hollowed out, and his tongue had darted out to lick his bottom lip, making it glisten in the barely lit room. He pushed me to the side, and the locking of the door cut through the thumping inside my ears.

"I could go back out there and throw him down the fucking stairs." Theo's hands went to his hips as he stood back and stared at me from several feet away. He was out of breath, his chest rising and falling so quickly it seemed like he was back on the ice, putting the puck between the defenseman's own feet before taking the shot on the net.

"It's fine." I crossed my arms over my chest and looked away with embarrassment.

Theo erased the space between us with two long strides and gripped me by the waist, pushing me against the door. His breath cascaded down in between us as he stared into my eyes. "It's not fine. Did he blame his cheating on you? Did he say that you weren't experienced enough or something?"

I blinked several times, trying to work through what I was feeling. "I...yes. I mean, no." *I mean, he didn't technically say that.* "Why do you care so much? It's fine, Theo. Seriously, I'm fine." I pulled away when his hands left my waist, and he took a step backward. I knew he was looking at me, and I suddenly wanted to cover myself up. I wasn't wearing anything that was revealing. In fact, I was still in worn jeans and my Bexley U shirt from the game, but I still felt seen. *Too seen.* "I appreciate you... helping me downstairs, though. I won't lie. It kind of felt good to piss him off."

"I owe you. You came to my rescue earlier."

I nodded, still making a conscious effort to keep my attention elsewhere because I was too afraid that I'd look at his lips again and show my cards. I couldn't stop thinking about how it felt when he'd kissed me. It was rejuvenating. Maybe it was because I knew I was pissing Chad off and taking back some of the dignity that he'd stolen from me, or maybe it was just Theo.

"We aren't done, though."

My body stilled as I slowly tore my gaze from the faintly glowing lamp on the dresser and met his determined expression. "What do you mean?"

The anger that Theo was putting off had lessened as he slowly walked over to me. His smirk had too many thoughts racing through my head that I'd done a pretty good job of ignoring until now. "Do you really believe that what I said didn't bother him?"

I thought for a moment before shrugging. "Honestly, I'm not sure."

"I guarantee that he's still lingering in that hallway with that girl, waiting to see if we come out of the room soon. Or better yet, he's probably listening for certain sounds."

Theo's hand appeared in front of my face as he smoothed out the crease in between my eyebrows. "Trust me, Bryant."

I tried to deflect the attention and half-laughed. "There's probably a line of puck bunnies out there too, waiting to get their turn with you."

He shrugged. "Then they'll be waiting a while."

"Why?" Hesitation backed my question, and any bit of confidence that I had left faltered with Theo's dangerous smirk.

"We gotta make them believe it. Especially Chad, because I'd love nothing more than to piss him off even further."

Theo must have seen the pure panic on my features,

because he smoothed his voice and shook his head softly. "We will hang in here for a while, cause some thumping, maybe make a few noises, and they'll believe it, yeah?"

I couldn't help it. A laugh bubbled out of my stomach and hit Theo in the chest. "Cause some thumping and make some noises?" I laughed again. "What?"

Theo's smile was so perfect it hurt my chest. He had one of those smiles that could make you do anything. "Like this." Theo moved toward me with the precision of a lion and gripped my hips again, pushing my butt against the door so forcefully that it shook the hinges. His hand went behind my upper back to shield it as the other stayed gripped on the waist of my jeans. I noticed a few of his fingers had slipped under my shirt and touched my skin, igniting a fire. "Now..." His smile grew wider as surprise took me captive. "I want you to make the same kind of sounds you made with him...and don't be shy."

All humor left me. My smile vanished, and embarrassment was like two hot rods burning my cheeks. Theo's brows went inward, and his head tilted to the side slightly, like he was trying to figure me out. My mouth opened, but nothing came out, so I slammed my lips together and quickly looked at my feet.

"Don't tell me."

I managed a whisper. "Don't tell you what?"

"Has he..." I pulled my chin back up and stared at the side of Theo's profile as he turned his head to the side in disbelief. There was a thin layer of facial hair starting to sprout, and I wondered what it would feel like to have it rub against my skin. When he turned back to me quickly, I jumped, realizing his hand was still placed over the small of my back. "Has he never made you come?"

Not without my help. "Um..." *Lie, Claire.*

Oh my God. I want to die.

"Is that why he said you could use the experience?" Theo's grip grew rougher on my body, and suddenly, his jaw seemed sharper than before. "He's *really* gonna hate me now."

"Why?" My question was breathy, and I watched Theo turn from lethal to devious in a matter of seconds.

"I'll lead." The hand behind my back slowly slid down my spine and around my stomach, landing at the button of my jeans. "And you follow."

[25]

THEO

CROSSING lines never felt so fucking good. My thumb slid against the button of Claire's jeans, and although I tried to take a pause and rethink the situation, her rising chest caught my attention, and I might as well have walked myself right to the sin bin after this.

"What are you doing?" she asked, looking down at my fingers on her jeans.

She's your roommate. You have to live with her.

I swallowed roughly and held myself back as tightly as I could. "Playing the game. Are you in?" I bounced my attention between hers, almost begging her to let me touch her. I knew it wasn't the competitiveness that lived within my bones that was pushing me to slip the button through the hole of her jeans. It was the fact that I was beyond perturbed that someone like Chad could make someone like *her* feel as if they weren't good enough.

He's never made her come? Are you kidding me? I was

going to blow him right the fuck out of the water, and when he heard the noises coming from the girl he gave up to dip his dick in other places, he was going to regret his decision pretty quickly. That I knew for certain.

"Don't overthink it, Bryant," I coaxed, unzipping her pants. Part of me was waiting for the other shoe to drop. Would her hand shoot out and stop me from going further? Or was she in this with me? "It's just me."

"It's *just* you?" she shot back, craning her head back and looking to the ceiling. I took my hand and cradled her waist again, resting my palm over the very top of her panties that were peeking out from her unbuttoned jeans. "You're the most popular guy on campus and—"

"A jock?"

Her chin came back down, and that lip of hers was tucked in between her white teeth. "I was gonna say...my roommate."

I chuckled, unable to keep myself from zeroing in on her mouth. "Even better. He'll think we're fucking every night. It'll drive him wild, and the puck bunnies will stop showing up in our room. We gotta make them believe it, and if you can't do that without my help, then here I am."

Her swallow was loud enough to catch my attention, and when I crept my hands farther underneath her shirt, skirting with the underwire of her bra, her ribcage sucked in, and her blue eyes were instantly hooded and full of need.

"Focus on the game," I said, dragging my hands back down the sides of her torso. "If there's one thing I've learned about you, it's that you are just as driven as I am."

"Fi—fine." Her acceptance was like a rubber band snapping. Usually, I was able to keep some control of myself, even while in the bedroom, but I was already hard from the mere touch of her flushed skin beneath my palms.

I locked onto her eyes as I gripped the sides of her jeans and forcefully pushed them down over the curves of her hips. For a dancer, she wasn't what I had expected. She was on the smaller side, but she still had curves, and she absolutely had an ass to grab onto. I slipped my eyes down past her belly button and stilled at the view of her standing there in a certain pair of panties.

"Did you wear those on purpose?" I asked, caging her in between my arms. Her lip was tucked between her teeth again, and I quickly cupped her chin, taking my finger and pulling her lip out from behind her teeth. "Bryant...?"

She shrugged, leaning back on the door of the bedroom. "I like them."

"You like them because I bought them for you? Or do you just like them?"

Silence filled the space between us, and my smirk was as deep as the pull in my stomach. My heart was racing, and it was unnerving to feel so worked up in this situation. *Shit, am I nervous?* I didn't get nervous when it came to this stuff. My brother was fifteen years older than me, and he taught me what to do for a girl before I was even a legal adult. I knew my way around a female's body, but suddenly, I was nervous in her presence. I was confident, but the stakes were higher with her. I didn't want to be just as big of a disappointment to Claire as Chad was.

"Tell me what you need," I said, moving my hands behind her and gripping her ass. The jolt from my fingertips to my chest was something I'd never felt before. *Damn, that's a handful.*

She gasped as my fingers dug into her, and her lips parted. She glanced away, and I wanted to demand she put her eyes back on me. Determination came in swift, and I was done holding back. The new objective of the game was making Claire forget all about Chad.

"Do you like this?" I whispered against her ear, erasing any space that was left between us. My hand slowly moved to her front, and I gripped the inside of her thigh, spreading her legs a little farther apart. Her hands flew to my biceps, and I flexed beneath her palms, wanting her to touch me everywhere. My grip was rough as I cupped my hand underneath her knee and wrapped her bare leg around my hip, pushing her harder against the door to make it rattle again. Another gasp lingered on her lips, and I surprised myself when I went in for the kill and swallowed it. Our tongues moved against each other in a melody of their own, and when my teeth skimmed over her bottom lip, I pulled back and looked down at my hand creeping below the top of her panties.

"Tell me, Claire. Do you like this?"

She nodded, peering up at me with soft blue eyes that I could see myself getting lost in. *Wait, what?* I gritted my teeth. No. *That's the lust talking.*

"I'm gonna need you to be vocal, sweetheart. Remember, we gotta make them believe it. Chad could be listening right now."

Fuck him, I thought. But I also knew I needed to get my head back in the game and get back to reality. Claire was my roommate. But goddamn, I felt the heat coming from in between her legs, and I knew when I watched her come, I was going to have to keep myself from falling to my knees.

"I like it," she said, more resolute than before. Satisfaction propelled me to continue my way down her front until I found her sweet spot.

"I can tell." I rubbed her wetness between my thumb

and first finger. Her cheeks were redder than mine after a game, so I stopped my hand from moving. "It's not a bad thing. Why do you look embarrassed?"

When her eyes met mine, she hesitated.

"Tell me," I demanded, pulling her flush against my body before I pushed her against the door again, making a thump. A soft whimper left her before she let the truth fly.

"I just didn't get this way with him." She paused for a moment before bringing her hooded eyes back to mine. "Only with myself."

The brief visual of Claire touching herself to this extent and making herself wet was absolutely going to be replayed in the shower later.

"Jesus," I mumbled before snaking my free hand up past her slender neck and wrapping her hair in between my fingers. I pulled her head back and lightly bit onto her neck as I pushed a finger inside of her. She sucked in a breath, moving her head to the side to give me more access to her sensitive skin. My tongue jolted out to lick the spot I bit because it was a surprise to me. My teeth grazed over her earlobe before I pulled on it, pushing my finger in a little farther and working her body into a frenzy. My thumb pushed on her clit, and when her hips jerked toward me, I knew I'd hit the jackpot.

"Tell me," I pleaded, sounding just as desperate as I felt. "Does it feel good?"

"Yes," she rushed out, moving her hips back and forth. I moved her face to mine and couldn't help but kiss her again. I knew that the goal was to make her come so hard she yelled out my name and sent Chad into a complete spiral, but I needed her mouth on mine. Suddenly, I was the one who needed more in this moment. I *wanted* more.

I knew she was getting close as her breathing grew frantic, and her kisses became sloppier and hotter. I kissed her back just as feverishly as she was doing to me, and I was racing to make her come on my hand. The thought of dropping to my knees to replace my fingers with my tongue crossed my mind, but I forced myself to stay upright. I untangled my fingers from her hair and pulled my mouth away, latching onto her neck again. My hand flew down to her ass, and I grabbed it tightly, relishing in the softness of it against my fingers.

"He's out of his goddamn mind for letting you go." I pulled on her ear with my teeth and blew my hot, seedy breath against her neck. "It wasn't that he couldn't make you come, baby. It's just that he didn't want to." A small moan left her, and my eyes shut just as tightly as her cunt did around my fingers. *God, fuck yes.* "I've gotta say...if you were mine, I'd make you come every single second of every single day, because I've never witnessed anything as beautiful as this."

Her walls shattered the instant I flicked my tongue against her neck, and she moaned so loudly that I was forced to pull back to watch her break. The breath had been stolen right out of my lungs as I watched her ride the waves. Her dainty chin was tipped upward, and her long hair gave way to her face as it fell down her back. The red marks that I'd put on her neck were temporary tattoos on her fair skin that I wanted to be permanent.

After I knew she was satisfied, I finally sucked in a breath and let oxygen fill me up again. The black spots in my vision cleared, and the pink color painted on Claire's cheeks made her look even more beautiful than before.

"So, this is what you look like when you're truly relaxed?" I said, surprised that my voice was more of a rasp.

I cleared my throat and finally pulled my finger out of her wet pussy, hating that I had to take a step away.

The goal was achieved. The game was over.

But I wanted to play again.

And again.

Claire's breath was as shaky as her legs. When I finally let her leg fall back to the ground, I bent down and held out her jeans for her, letting our hands skim against each other for a second. Her eyes flew to mine, and I latched onto hers, holding on for as long as she'd let me.

I stood back in silence, watched her slip back into her clothes, and pretended like I wasn't a fucking fool for touching her like that. But I couldn't help it, and there was no way I was going to be able to forget what had just happened even though I knew for a fact that was what she wanted me to do.

"Well..." I crossed my arms over my chest and watched as Claire ran her fingers through her hair that I had messed up.

Her swollen lips smashed together as she waited for me to continue.

"How did I do?" I knew I had done a good job—I didn't need the validation—but a misogynistic part of me wanted to hear her say it.

We stayed staring at each other from across the room, and her lips twitched to curl. The left side of her mouth slowly curved up, and I had to force myself not to smile. "That good, huh?" I asked, rocking back on my heels.

"As if your ego needs any more stroking, Theo." She rolled her eyes.

I couldn't help it. I smiled like a fucking fool and stormed over to her. I held my palm out, and she looked down at it hesitantly before putting her hand in mine. I squeezed it and unlocked the door. "Put your game face on, Bryant."

Her smile shook me to my core, and I pulled her out of the room to flaunt her as my girl, even though we both knew she wasn't mine.

[26]

CLAIRE

"Your boy is here." Angie's voice snuck up behind me as
I punched something into the computer. My finger froze
over the word *chicken* before I played it off and went about
my business.

"Who?"

She snickered. "Oh, stop it. The whole table has been
staring at you since they walked in. They're in your section.
I know you can see them."

I half-rolled my eyes and peeked up at Theo, Aasher,
Dax, and Ford all sitting in the corner booth with their
menus propped up on the table, shielding the bottom half of
their faces. It didn't matter, though. I could still see that
they all were sharing shit-eating grins, per usual.

"They just want extra fries," I joked, spinning around to
pretend like I had no issues seeing Theo after what we did
over the weekend. A slight throb started to beat in between
my legs, and I sighed under my breath. *Damn him.* Things
had seemed to go right back to normal between us, though.

We fell into our same routine, acting as roommates and nothing more, but to be truthful, between running back and forth to classes, studying in the library, my extra shifts at The Bex, and rehearsing every chance I could, we weren't together much. I did, however, listen to his breathing when I finally lay down at night, and the thought of him touching me again like he did at the party always slipped in before I finally fell asleep.

And as for Chad? Silence ensued, and I wasn't sure if that was a good thing or a bad thing. I hadn't had a single call from my mother either, so I assumed that meant Chad was staying true to his word.

"Get your butt over here, Bryant." Ford ducked behind his menu as soon as I looked over at him. Theo was grinning at me, and I sighed wistfully as I walked over to their table, knowing all eyes were on us.

"What can I get you guys?" I asked, pulling out my small notepad that I took orders on.

As if on cue, all four of them slammed their menus down onto the table, and Ford tapped his fingers over the top of it. "For you to be our fake girlfriend, too."

My jaw fell open, and I looked over at Theo. He threw his hands up before showing off his gleaming-white teeth. "I told them you were mine."

I lowered my voice, leaning into his space. "I'm not your fake girlfriend, Theo."

"So, you're my real girlfriend?"

"I could slap you," I mumbled. Straightening my spine, I leveled my shoulders and glanced around the restaurant. The attention we were gaining was obvious, and the puck bunnies weren't even pretending not to stare over at the four girthy hockey players sitting in my section.

"Come on," Ford said, leaning in closer toward me and

Theo. "You guys worked effortlessly together the other night—not once, but *twice*."

Aasher, who was quieter than the rest of the hockey players, decided now was the time that he wanted to put his two cents in. "You should get her a jersey with your name on it." He buried himself back in his phone, and I watched the idea come to life on Theo's face.

"I do not like the look on your face," I said, tapping my pen on the paper.

"Take a look around, Bryant." Theo leaned back in the booth and crossed his arms over his chest. "The puck bunnies are waiting to see what you do." He shook his head, a lock of his rich brown hair falling over his forehead. His hands landed on top of the table, and I watched as his first finger tapped against it slowly. My heart rate climbed, and sweat started to prickle the back of my neck as I remembered all too clearly how talented those fingers were. *He made me come without a clue of what made me tick.*

A rebellious chuckle left his mouth, and my face burned when he cocked an eyebrow at me. I huffed and glared at all four of the guys who were smiling. "That's it! I'm bringing you all salads and water."

"What?!" Ford squealed, and even though I wanted to pretend like I was annoyed with them—especially Theo—I walked off, holding in a laugh. My cheeks ached from holding back my laughter, and when I got back up to the computer, I put in their usual order and caught Angie smiling at me.

"What?" I asked, sneaking a peek at Theo, who was staring at me, still seemingly waiting for me to do something about the girls staring at him throughout the restaurant. Annoyance was quickly replaced with an uncertainty. *What harm could it do?*

"What exactly *is* going on?" Angie asked, crossing her arms over her Bex shirt. "You know..."—Angie looked around for a brief second—"Chad came in here yesterday."

My fingers gripped the cup I was filling with ice. Angie knew that Chad and I were at odds right now, but that was all she knew. "Oh, yeah?" I asked, pretending that it didn't bother me.

"He was with a girl, and he still had the nerve to ask me where you were. He wanted me to seat him in your section."

"What did you tell him?" I gathered all the cups for the guys on a tray and saw that some of the football players had gravitated toward their table.

"I told him it was none of his damn business."

A laugh flew out of my mouth. Rebecca came up behind Angie to punch something into the computer and said nonchalantly, "I almost fake tripped and dropped a plate on his lap, but I didn't want you to get mad at me." She said the last part to Angie, and the loyalty of everyone at The Bex resonated within.

"I love you both." I stepped in between them, wrapped my arms around their waists, and hugged them at the same time. "You don't have to drop anything on Chad's lap. I have my own ways of making him feel like shit."

"Oh, yeah." Rebecca continued to put her order into the computer. "I saw you and Theo at the party."

"What party?"

My face was hot to the touch, thinking about how Theo and I must have appeared from the outside looking in. My ears rang as Rebecca filled Angie in on the *kiss* that everyone saw, and even though I told myself not to do it, I looked over at Theo from across the busy establishment, and the brief longing of feeling desirable came rushing back in. When our eyes caught, he mouthed the word, "Jersey?" at me, and I couldn't find it in me to shake my head. Instead, I turned around and sucked in a deep breath before I grabbed a glass of water and walked over to the man sitting in the corner booth.

"Here you go," I said, placing it down before pulling out my notepad. "What can I get you?"

The man leaned back in the booth and stared up at me, saying absolutely nothing. I couldn't help but wonder who he was, because most of the people that came into The Bex were college students, and occasionally, those college students would bring their parents who were visiting on the weekends or during move-in day.

But the man was alone, and I could tell by the way he was peering up at me from his sitting position that he was studying me. I began to shift on my feet, glancing over to Theo, seeing that Rush and a few of his friends had pulled up chairs to his table. I quickly pulled my attention back and sent the man a hesitant smile before he shook his head and pulled open the menu.

"Uh, what's good here?" He chuckled. "Besides the hockey team."

An abrupt laugh left me. Was he saying that because he caught me looking over at Theo's table full of hockey players? I mean, they *were* in my section, although that wasn't the reason I was glancing at them.

"Well..." I started. "Honestly? Everything is good here. I'm a burger gal myself."

A warm smile flitted across his face, and he shut his menu a moment later. "You know what, surprise me. I like any and everything. Order me what you would order yourself."

I shifted on my feet again, but then I nodded and

grabbed his menu. "I can do that. It'll be right out. Can I get you anything else to drink? Or is water okay?"

"Water is fine," he said before seeming uncomfortable. He glanced away before mumbling, "Thank you, um...?"

"Claire." I smiled as I walked away, feeling strange the entire time I put his order in the computer. It wasn't until I wandered back over to Theo's table that I felt the strange feeling lessen.

"Here you go," I said, putting their drinks in front of them. "Fries are on their way."

"Thanks, Bryant," Dax said. Ford blew me a kiss, and Aasher laughed at him before taking a sip of his water.

As soon as I turned around, I realized I was suddenly trapped behind a group of girls. One was sitting on Rush's lap, and the other three lingered, chewing on their fingernails and batting their eyelashes at anyone who would look.

"Um, excuse me," I mumbled, suddenly annoyed. The girls parted, and I watched as the one on the left, with her hair in a high pony, sighed in relief, setting her eyes on the prize.

Theo.

I took a step forward, my tennis shoes lightly pressing against the sticky floor, but then paused. Irritation landed on my skin like I had been sprayed with little droplets of water, and before I knew it, I was spinning around and putting my hands on my hips to stare at Theo. His eyebrows jumped with surprise. I licked my lips and sighed before I walked over to him and peered down at his pleased expression.

"Take a seat, roomie," he whispered slyly with his arms spread open, motioning to his lap instead of the empty seat beside him.

Silence fell over the table like a plague when I sat down

on his lap, and as if the stars aligned, the door to The Bex opened, and in walked Chad with Iris, one of the girls he had studied with in the past. My heart slowly dropped to my feet when the realization hit me like a ton of bricks.

Did he cheat on me with her too?

Theo must have felt the way my body went rigid, because his hand rested over mine for a brief second, and he squeezed it twice, bringing me back to the present. I pulled myself away from Chad's hand around Iris's back. He was coming in here on purpose. His small smirk in my direction told me he was enjoying this little game he was playing with me, and he thought I'd be his prize when it was all said and done. That was why he wasn't bothered by Theo.

"See you tonight in our room?" Theo asked, tapping the inside of my leg. I looked back at him, and his eyes bounced between mine, like he was trying to read my emotions from seeing Chad. His brows folded in on themselves, and his eyes dipped down to my lips.

"Order up!"

I nodded to Theo and faked a smile. "Yeah," I lied. "Now let me go so I can go get your fries." I spun around and told myself not to look, but sure enough, everyone was watching us, including the lonely man in the corner booth. He eyed me suspiciously, but I didn't focus on that as I moved on to Chad and Iris. The anger rushed in, and I gritted my teeth before standing up and leaning down to kiss Theo on the cheek. I squeezed past Rush and the groupies quickly, all while keeping my face even.

"Shit, man," I heard him say. "I thought you didn't date."

I didn't wait to see what Theo's response was. Instead, I focused on putting on a brave face for the rest of my shift, especially in front of Chad.

The music blared from my phone as I focused on keeping my back engaged and my head up, waiting for the count to start my jeté—a leap I'd been practicing nearly all my life.

I was preparing for two different auditions. My duo with Adam, which was hard to perfect when he didn't put in nearly as much time as I did. I didn't blame him, though. He didn't have as much at stake as I did. And then my solo, which was the number that I was most in tune with.

A ding came from my phone as I landed on the opposite foot, ignoring the slight sting on the outer part of my ankle. I wiped my sweaty forehead on the back of my hand and huffed my way over to my bag, hearing two more dings throughout the melody of "She" by Jake Scott. I paused the song, and silence erupted around me. I was the only one here, which wasn't a surprise, but it did get a little eerie after hours.

Taytum: Emory just texted me and asked where you were. I'm assuming he is asking for your boyfriend.

I texted back quickly.

Me: Theo isn't my boyfriend, and I'm practicing.

Taytum: You're gonna end up killing yourself from exhaustion. It's almost 10. Go back to your room. Or are you avoiding Theo?

The little voice in the back of my head taunted me as I typed.

Me: Why would I be avoiding him?

It wasn't like we were going to be touching or acting like boyfriend and girlfriend while in our room, alone. It was all for show. No one would be watching us. We could just be platonic. *Friends, even.*

I sighed and clicked my phone off, not wanting to read her response. Just as I was about to press play on the song, I got another text and did a double-take at the name.

Theo: Didn't you say you'd see me later in our room?

A drop of sweat fell onto my phone from my forehead, and I quickly wiped it off, rereading the text.

Me: Did you put your number and name in my phone?!

Theo: ...where are you?

Me: When did you steal my phone? How did you even manage that?

Theo: Shouldn't your boyfriend have your phone number?

My stomach dipped so quickly I confused it for butterflies.

Me: You are not my boyfriend, Theo.

Theo: Campus thinks I am. ;)

The next text that came in was a news article from The Bexley University Newspaper with an image of Theo in his hockey gear, storming the ice, from the last home game. I quickly read the contents and exhaled when I realized that I wasn't in there by name. Not that my mother or Chad's parents were even interested in Bexley U's newspaper, but I knew there would be many questions if I was pictured with a hockey player or, even worse, if my name was listed.

Theo texted again, and I quickly closed out the article.

Theo: Where are you? I thought you nodded when I asked if I'd see you in our room later.

Me: I only said that because everyone was listening. Thought it would be a good way to keep the puck bunnies out of your bed for the night.

Theo: Nice play, Bryant.

He texted back just as my finger hovered over the play

button for the song to begin again so I could continue perfecting my jeté.

Theo: Not gonna tell me where you are?

Me: Rehearsing. I'll be here for a while. I'll be quiet when I come in so I don't disrupt your sleep, Grandpa.

I quickly pushed play on the song and put my phone down. I shook out my hands and stretched my neck before taking position in the middle of the stage to run through my number. *Again.*

27

THEO

My hands dug into my hoodie pocket as I jogged up the stairs to the auditorium, frustrated that Claire's beat-up Toyota was out front. I wasn't sure how I felt with her being here, all by herself, after dark. It made me uneasy, which was confusing.

If Aasher were here, he'd make a crack about how I was awfully protective of a girl who wasn't technically mine, but he wasn't here, so I was going to tuck away that thought and save it for a rainy day.

The door was unlocked, and the only thing I could hear was loud music blaring through the two doors that I knew Claire was tucked behind. My heart sped a little faster the closer I got to the music, and when I slipped inside the darkened auditorium, my eyes went directly to her gliding across the stage like a graceful angel. There was a single spotlight shining down, and the strands of her brown hair glistened underneath the lights as it was half falling out of her bun that was held together by one of those damn fuzzy scrunchies.

I took a seat in the back, like a first-class creeper, and watched as she twirled and leapt with determination that made her look supple in every step she took. Her chest was expanding in her pale-purple leotard, and the short, curtain-like wrap around her waist flew up and showed off her soft curves that I very clearly remembered touching.

She was elegant, and soft, and all the things I wasn't used to. My hands dropped to the armrest when the music abruptly stopped, and a ring tone started over the speakers. I followed her defeated steps as she walked over to her phone. She unplugged it hastily, took a gulp of air, and answered it.

Although I was in the back, ready to make myself known, I stopped when I watched the way her shoulders edged up to her ears with stress. Her sweet voice carried throughout the empty space, and I waited.

"Hey, Mom. Why are you calling so late?" Claire's free hand went up to her mouth, and she nibbled on her thumbnail nervously.

I relaxed back in my seat and began to wonder more about her than before. How did she grow up? What was her family like? Where was she from? I knew that she wasn't wealthy, and I also knew that there was some tension with her mother from the first time I had eavesdropped on her...which I was doing again. Though, this time was purely accidental. It wasn't like I was purposefully staying here to gain intel, and it wasn't like I was sitting in the back of the auditorium during her rehearsal just to be a creeper. I didn't want to interrupt her in the middle of the dance, and it would be rude to do it now, yeah?

That's a load of bullshit. But whatever.

"Well, did you use the money I gave you? For the repairs?"

The money she gave her? Was that why Claire worked so much? To give her mom money?

"Well, where did the other half go?" Claire began pacing back and forth, and it was obvious that stress was beginning to propel her steps. Her hand went to her hip, and then it fell abruptly, like she was taking a beating. "Mom, you have to stop relying on them. Please." There was a pause. "Yeah, I know. Bu—" Another pause. "Things with Chad and me are fine."

Huh?

My stomach twisted as she flexed her fist by her side and squeezed her eyes shut. Her back was turned to me next, and she ended the phone call with telling her mom she'd send what she could, and although there was a part of me that understood the hardships that some families who weren't wealthy went through, there was also a part of me that was angered for Claire. Didn't her mother know how much Claire worked? Didn't she know that Claire was beyond exhausted? My parents had never asked me for money, and I knew that when I made it in the NHL and began to indulge in things they wanted and deserved, giving back to them, they'd want to refuse.

I was pulled away from my thoughts as the music started up again, and I decided that I'd show my face after she finished her rehearsal. My hands continued to grip the sides of the chair as I watched her work harder than before. Her movements were no longer fluid and graceful but harsh and rushed. My breath was stuck in my chest as I followed her light run across the stage until she ended up in the corner, preparing for something big. I sat up a little straighter in the chair and fisted my hands as I watched in awe as she did some fancy leap in midair like a professional ballet dancer and landed on one foot, seeming a little off balance. Her dance ended a few seconds later, and I immediately knew she was feeling defeated by the way she sat on the floor with her head hung low.

"What am I going to do?" the sentence was a whisper, but at some point, I stood up unknowingly and gravitated toward her as I watched her become overwhelmed with some type of battle in her head.

"You know, you shouldn't practice when your mind is elsewhere. It usually ends badly."

Claire's eyes flung open, and the glossy blue within them was just as breathtaking as that time I fell through the frozen pond out behind my house while trying to perfect my own version of *The Michigan*. She blinked several times before rolling her right ankle out and evening her face.

"What are you doing here?" she asked, placing her hands on the floor behind her for stability. I slowly bent down beside her and glanced at her foot, wondering if she was hiding some type of injury, because I swore there was a tinge of pain on her features.

"Has anyone ever told you that it's not smart to practice when you're exhausted?" *Or when you have an injury. Or when you're stressed.*

"I'm not exhausted," she argued, exhaling a breath. She rolled her ankle again, and I raised an eyebrow, shooting her a look.

Claire's teeth clamped down hard as she began to stand up on less-than-stable legs. "Whoa," I rushed, flinging my eyes back to hers. "What are you doing?"

"I need to run through that one more time."

Claire was still trying to catch her breath and I noticed how her body was shaking with exhaustion. "No, you don't," I argued, pulling her back down to the stage softly. My eyes bounced back and forth between hers, and when her bottom lip began to tremble, I felt something chip off inside my chest. She looked down to her lap, hiding her tears.

"Hey," I whispered, feeling a little panicked. I slipped my thumb underneath her chin and brought her face up so she would look at me. "What's wrong? Why are you killing yourself up here when you're clearly exhausted?"

Silence. But with her silence came glossier eyes, and I didn't like it.

"I can't—" She blew out a sweet, shaky breath. "I have to get the lead in the spring showcase."

"It's that important to you?" I understood the importance of reaching goals, but her tears contradicted the joy she should have been feeling up on the stage. I compared it to my love for hockey, and it just didn't seem the same to her. Was this infatuation of perfecting her audition a determination to prove herself to someone? To Chad?

"It's..." She sighed, pulling her hair out of her scrunchie and hastily throwing it back up into a bun. With every flick of her wrist and twist of her hair, I saw the panic rising. "I have to get that role." She popped up onto her feet and shook out her arms, preparing herself to do another round on the stage.

"Claire." I stood up alongside her. "You need a break."

Her arms wafted out with exasperation as she slowly walked to the corner of the stage. My gaze shot down to her slow steps. *Was she favoring the right side?* "I can't take a break, Theo! Don't you understand that I *need* the money?! I *need* to get this lead role."

"Wait, what money?" I asked, following closely behind her and trying to make sense of her rambling.

She spun around and rushed through her words. "I'll get a full scholarship for my senior year if I get the lead in the spring showcase. I won't have to figure out how to pay for everything on top of paying for college. I have a partial scholarship, but a full would be better. I don't have a wealthy family. It's just me and my mom, and..." Tendrils of hair fell from her bun as she drifted off into a different direction onstage. I continued to follow her until she was in the very back, nearly up against the wall. "Everyone else just *wants* it...but no one understands that I actually need it. I work so hard and..."

Claire was ready to take off again, but I stopped her, moving directly in front of her and caging her small frame within my arms. Her back hit the wall with a soft thud, and she tilted her chin up and stared into my eyes. Her breaths were rapid missiles flying from her chest, and her entire body was shaking with adrenaline. I didn't even think she noticed that a tear had slipped past her cheek.

"I understand," I said, staring directly into her eyes. Without the realization of how soft the gesture was, I swiped away a stray tear that had fallen against her skin and kept my thumb on her high cheekbone for a second longer than I needed to. Claire's tense shoulders dropped slightly, and her breathing had started to calm. "I know what it's like to need money. Everyone thinks I come from a wealthy family because of my skill on the ice." I forced out a sarcastic chuckle, glancing away for a second. "In fact..." I paused, making sure this was something I actually wanted to say, but with Claire's unwavering and sincere gaze peering up at me, I couldn't stop from giving her a piece of myself I'd never given before. "My parents aren't even my real parents."

Her lips parted slightly before the little crease between her eyebrows formed.

"I'm not sure who my dad is." I dropped my head, but I made sure to keep my hands placed on the wall behind her so she'd stay put. "And my grandparents kicked my mom out when I was young because she was a druggie. They took care of me, and we've always just gone with it when people assumed they were my parents. People just chalked it up to them having me later in life. That's what the media believes, at least." Silence erupted around us, but to me, it sounded like a bomb. "We're pretty certain my mother died a long time ago, although it was never really confirmed." I shrugged, as if the realization didn't bother me. It did, but this wasn't about me. "Anyway, there's a reason I'm telling you this."

Her voice was smooth and sincere. "What is the reason?"

"When you say no one understands, I do." I moved a breath closer to her and noticed how her chest expanded with a held breath. "I, better than anyone, understand determination and hard work. I work hard on the ice to reach my goal of getting into the NHL for my parents. Everyone"—I took a moment to remember how she detested me when she first met me—"including you, thinks I'm just your typical selfish jock who wants to be the best at hockey just to make it to the top. But that's not why. I want to give back to the two people who took me in and saved me. And maybe I want to prove to myself that I'm not that abandoned little kid who only felt safe when they were in control on the ice." I forced out a chuckle. This conversation had gone way deeper than I'd meant, but there was something about the genuineness of Claire that kept pulling the truth out of me.

Claire's shaky hands landed on my hips as I continued

to cage her against the wall. A wicked dose of desire flooded my veins, but I forced my thoughts elsewhere because there was no way I could disguise touching her any more than I already had with our fake-dating scheme because, right now, we were alone. *So very alone.*

"Well, fine."

All thoughts halted with the tug of my lips. I was confused but amused at the same time. "Fine? Fine what?"

"Fine. You...*understand.* I guess you and I are more alike than I thought." There was a pause, and I almost pushed off the wall, putting space between us, but then she continued. "I don't know if my father was a druggie or what, but my mother made sure to call him every name in the book for abandoning us. She's never been able to recover—emotionally or financially." The grip she held on my hips lessened, and she dropped her hands a moment later. "That's why I really need this role. Money isn't easy to come by."

I knew there was more to the situation than she was giving, especially considering the conversation I'd overheard, but instead of getting any more intimate with her, I pushed off the wall and quickly walked over to Claire's bag on the other end of the stage and threw her phone inside after unplugging it from the speakers. Then, I walked back over to her, shrugged off my hoodie, and pulled it over her head. The amount of confusion on her face was almost as comical as it was seeing how small she looked in my sweatshirt. I spun around and bent down, cocking a grin over my shoulder at her.

"Well? Hop on," I announced, waiting for her to refuse.

"Hop on?" she asked, looking around for validation from someone.

"It's either that or I throw you over my shoulder, Bryant. You're tired." *And babying your ankle.* "We're going back to the room and rewatching that episode that we fell asleep watching the night you ate an entire pizza by yourself. If I don't figure out how it ends, I'm going to watch it without you."

I knew she was thinking of a way to get out of going back to our room, and I had a big feeling she'd been actively avoiding being alone with me because something had *definitely* happened between us on more than one occasion, whether it was all a ploy or not.

"You need rest," I reminded her.

She thought for a moment, and I turned around and glowered at her. "Do I need to throw you over my shoulder, because I will," I said, beginning to grow impatient.

She thought about it. The wheels were turning behind her blue eyes, but she eventually gave up, trying to hide that little shy smile of hers. I bit back my own smile and turned around, bending to her level. Her arms wrapped around my neck, and she climbed on like a little spider monkey.

The thought did not escape me that the warmth against my back was from the one layer separating us, but when her soft giggle slid into my ears as I jogged through the auditorium with her wrapped around me, I realized that even if we weren't actively playing the little fake-dating game that we kept finding ourselves in, I enjoyed her presence. Her laugh seeped into my chest, and although I was only getting a small piece of her, I didn't want to let go of it.

28

CLAIRE

The sun was just beginning to rise through the window that separated Theo's and my beds. I squinted my eyes after blinking a few times, realizing that he and I had fallen asleep together at some point through the night —*again*. Each night since he had come to the auditorium and demanded I go back to our room to rest, we'd watch at least one or two episodes of *Supernatural* together, sometimes in complete silence and sometimes chatting in between the serious parts of the show. I found a comfort in Theo that was hard not to read into. Things were easy with him, and I was beginning to look forward to going back to our room each evening after work or practice.

My neck ached from the position I had apparently slept in, and I peered down at his unmoving face. There was a warmth filling my chest as I saw his hand still resting against my ankle. He had no idea that there was a slight twinge in it every time I landed from my jeté, but it was as if his hand had subconsciously gravitated toward it. Heat blasted my cheeks when I focused on the way his skin was touching mine, and I cursed myself for not putting on leggings. But when I'd gotten back from my shift last night, Theo was smirking at me from his bed with his laptop already propped open and ready to commence our nightly ritual.

I stared at his wild smirk before following his cue when he motioned over to my bed.

Lying on top of my covers was a silky, black jersey.

His jersey.

The one he wanted me to wear to his next game to confirm that I truly was his girlfriend—you know, to ward off the puck bunnies.

I acted appalled, but Theo pinned me down playfully and draped it over my head, pulling out several laughs from me as I swam in it. He shook his head and blew a breath out of his mouth. Embarrassment made me shy away, but he quickly pushed me back on my bed and peered down at me. The way he scanned my body and told me not to take it off made me feel things I *knew* weren't real. But still, I kept it on. I shimmied out of my jeans, pulled on some short sleep shorts, and for the rest of the night, I lay on his bed and watched *Supernatural*.

Pulling my hair into a high bun from the scrunchie on my wrist, I started to blow out a shaky breath and told myself to get it together. When I thought about the way he had looked at me last night, while wearing his jersey, I got butterflies. And I was perceptive enough to know that it wasn't a good thing to get butterflies from your fake boyfriend.

I glanced around our room, recognizing how much had changed since the first time I met him. I'd had Theo Brooks pegged to be someone he wasn't. He said something the other night that resonated within me. He said that everyone, including me, thought he was just like the next jock—selfish, self-righteous, and only seeking validation in hockey because they wanted to be the best. But what I was, was judgmental. That wasn't Theo. He wasn't selfish, and he wasn't the type of guy who only wanted to reach the top to get his ego stroked. In fact, I hoped he made it in the NHL, because he deserved it above everyone else. He had drive, and that drive came from a passion that was the furthest thing from selfish.

Moving my gaze past my bed, I peered over at Theo once more. His brown hair was flopped over his forehead in the most adorable, messy way that somehow doubled as sexy. His jaw bone looked as sharp as a knife as his face was angled away from me, showing off his arched cheekbone with the tiniest little scar underneath his eye.

He truly was perfect.

There wasn't a flaw to be had. Not a single one.

My heart caught a flame when I dropped my gaze to his lips, remembering how they had felt against mine. The thumping in my heart began to reach my lungs, and suddenly, I was breathing fast while looking at my roommate who was only using me to fend off the girls who were desperate to kiss him—*like me, currently*. And it wasn't like I wasn't getting anything in return. It felt so good to stand up to Chad, even if I wasn't outright doing so. It felt *too* good.

I slowly pulled my ankle out from his grasp and began to move over him to escape my totally inappropriate thoughts. I thought of Chad's insults to help ward off the feeling of being desired by Theo, because I knew it wasn't real, even if Theo made me feel like it was. Even while asleep, with his arm clamped on my leg, I felt secure and wanted. I was blaming my curiosity of how else my roommate could make me feel—with his skilled hands, hard planes of muscle that flickered each time he moved his arms, and perfect lips—on the lack of physical satisfaction from my four-year boyfriend.

I gritted my teeth as I swung my leg over the side of Theo's lifeless body, hoping the bed didn't make too much of an indent as I slowly lowered my foot to the ground. *Shit, my ankle.* The pressure of the floor hit the bottom of my foot, and a breathy hiss left my mouth, but the pain quickly subsided as two strong hands gripped my hips. Theo's eyes flickered, and he squinted at me before pulling me back down and flipping me to my side. One arm was under my head, and the other was draped over the dip of my torso. My ass was pressed firmly against the front of him, and I swallowed a gulp as his fingers splayed out against my belly, creeping underneath his jersey that he insisted I wear.

"Where do you think you're going, Bryant?"

My heart rammed against my ribcage as I slowly brought my hand down and rested it over his. I suddenly felt like I was caught in a web with his arm pulling me closer, and I absolutely noticed the hard length pressing against my backside. Chills bubbled against my skin with anticipation in my gut, and when his thumb slowly skimmed over my skin, I knew he had noticed.

"We fell asleep," I croaked, staying completely still because if I let myself move against him, I'd be in deep trouble.

"I know," he answered, voice raspy and a little daring. "Boyfriends and girlfriends fall asleep together all the time. No big deal. Go back to sleep."

I wanted to laugh to lighten the mood, but my words came out slow and forced. "We're not boyfriend and girlfriend. Not when no one is watching, and I can't go back to sleep. I have class."

"Skip it." Theo's breath rushed over the sensitive skin against my neck. My sigh was breathy, and when he buried his face in my hair, I licked my lips. *Oh, God.* "I'm comfortable with you right where you are, Bryant. Stay."

"I..." I cleared my throat, suddenly feeling panicked with the way my body was revving up with his hand on my stomach and his breath against my neck. "I can't."

"You can," he protested, shifting behind me. I felt the slight curve of his hips as he tilted them, and I questioned if I was tricking myself with the feel of his length against my short shorts or if he was doing it on purpose.

His hand splayed out over my skin, and I knew he had to feel how quickly I was breathing by the rises and dips of my stomach. I was turned on, and I knew it was wrong on every level, yet for a slight moment in time, I wondered what it would be like to use him for more than just show.

The familiar twist in my lower belly that I'd felt at the party, with Theo slipping my jeans down my legs to help me make Chad jealous, began to curl, and I found myself arching my back and pressing myself into him. His fingers froze for a moment before one dipped under the hem of my shorts and swiped slowly over my skin, caressing me in a way that made me feel irresistible.

What are we doing?

I stayed unmoving but noticed the way heat snaked up my back and curved around my neck, locking me in a chokehold. Theo's hips pressed into me again, and this time, I knew he meant to do it. My gulp was loud, and his breathing was even louder. I pressed back, craving his hard length against my body because it gave me the confidence that Chad had stolen from me.

Theo pushed his hand a little farther under my shorts, and if I didn't have any self-control, I'd take my hand and edge him to the spot that I needed him to touch. I arched my back again, letting myself fall into a trap of desire and longing.

"Damn," he rasped, suddenly inhaling deeply before he ripped his hand out of my shorts and pushed me flat onto my back. He climbed on top of me, his leg going in between mine as he stared down at me with his lustful green eyes and flushed neck.

"What are you doing?" I asked, keeping my hands down by my sides because I felt drunk and completely impulsive.

Theo zeroed in on my lips, and I got tingly all over. My breasts felt heavy, and the quickest thought zipped through that his mouth would feel *really* good on any part of my body.

"I can't be held responsible for what I do with you looking at me like that while wearing my jersey." He was still staring at my lips, and all rational thinking was going out the window the longer he hovered over me. "You look *damn* good in it, Bryant."

"I bet you say that to all the girls who wear it," I tried to joke again, but it came out hoarse.

There was a tight crease in between his brows, and he looked almost offended. "You're the only one who has ever worn my jersey."

"It's just for show, though," I reminded him and maybe even myself. "And no one is watching right now."

Theo dipped his face low, and if I moved even a fraction, our lips would brush. With each breath that escaped his mouth, one of the tightly tied strings that was holding me together was beginning to unravel. "But what if they were?"

I flicked my eyes to his, and it felt like I was being fueled with passion. My lips parted, and the very second I threw caution to the wind, a knock sounded on the door, and I jumped underneath him, startling him at the same time.

"Claire! Let's go. We're gonna be late for class, and I brought you a coffee." Taytum banged on the door, and the shock of what I was just about to do resonated the moment Theo pulled himself from me.

His arms hung down by his sides in the middle of the room as I jumped off his bed. "I'm coming!" I yelled back, half-limping over to my side of the room because of my stupid sore ankle. I quickly tore his jersey over my head and was left in nothing but my cotton bra and tiny sleep shorts. I refused to look back at Theo, though, because I was afraid to see the look in his eyes. So, instead, I pulled a sweater over my head, quickly shoved my shorts down, and pulled on leggings over my cheeky underwear.

I kept my back to him after I shoved my feet in my boots and headed for the door with my phone, books, and beanie in tow. "I'll...um...see you later."

The door was shut a moment later, and although Taytum looked at me with suspicion, I said nothing as I grabbed the hot coffee from her hand and downed it quickly in hopes that I'd burn the desire in my lower belly to ash in the process.

29

THEO

My back rested against the wall with my leg hooked over my right ankle, waiting for Claire. I shoved my phone in my pocket and nodded at a few guys who had walked out of the lecture hall, telling me that Claire's class had ended. A group of chatty girls slipped out next, and each of their steps stuttered when they saw me standing there. Their conversation ceased, but I didn't dare look at a single one in the face. I was waiting for an adorable brunette who I couldn't get off my mind.

I kept my gaze settled on the doorway, purposefully above their high ponytails and messy buns, and when I landed on Claire, organizing her papers in her folder, unknowing that most of Bexley U was watching her every move, I stepped beside her, and we began walking in unison.

"Where are you off to?"

Claire's head popped up so quickly some of her hair fell

out of her scrunchie. "Theo!" she gasped, slapping her folder shut. "What are you doing here?"

"Walking with you," I answered, intentionally keeping my eyes off her mouth. This morning was the center of my thoughts even with several hours and a clear head in between. "Are you done for the day?"

I knew the answer was yes because whether we wanted to admit it or not, we knew each other's schedules.

"Um, yeah—well, with classes." Claire pulled her bag higher on her shoulder after shoving her book inside, glancing around nervously at everyone watching us walk together. I smirked before putting an arm over her shoulder and pulling her in close.

"And no work tonight." I turned my head and made it look like I was whispering in her ear. If she were to ask why I was being so touchy-feely with her, I'd chalk it up to putting on a show in front of campus because, after all, we *were* dating. But the truth was, I just wanted to touch her.

"Right. I'm off tonight..." Claire's steps slowed just before we made it to the doors, and at the very last second, I turned us both and headed down the opposite hallway. "What are you doing?" she asked, halting her steps.

"You'll see."

Surprisingly, Claire continued with me down the hallway without putting up much of a fight. There was a hint of confusion that surrounded the air around us, but I kept my arm around her shoulders as we headed to the rink.

Right before I pushed her through the back door to the arena—thankful it was so close to her lecture hall, considering the way she was keeping the pressure off her right ankle—she peeked over at me. "What are we doing here?"

I sighed heavily as the heat whooshed out of the darkened hallway. When the door slammed behind us, I gave her a look that made her cheeks deepen with the color pink. "How long were you going to hide that injury from me?"

My arms crossed over my chest as I waited for her answer. Claire nervously pulled down the beanie over her head and looked down at her boots. Instead of denying it, like I assumed she would, she slowly raised her chin and locked onto me. There was the smallest crack in her strong-girl façade, and I watched the mask slip just enough to make me feel worthy that she was trusting me. "How did you know?"

"Because I pay attention," I answered truthfully, but what I didn't allude to was the fact that I only paid attention to her.

Claire was surprised by my answer, and I smirked, knowing she was satisfied with it. Without giving any warning, I rushed over to her and swooped her up in my arms, cradling her legs under one of them. Our faces were close, so close I could smell the vanilla latte on her breath when she opened her mouth and barked out a loud laugh.

"Oh my God, Theo. Put me down!"

"No."

We were in the locker room entirely too soon, and I was forced to plop her on the bench, hating that I had to take a step away from her so that Zedd, our personal trainer, could look at her ankle. A raging jealousy simmered as I watched Zedd's fingers gently press on Claire's ankle, which was beyond shocking. I quickly tore my eyes from his grip on her leg and silently slapped myself for the hit on my character.

"Well, I don't think it's sprained." Zedd turned over Claire's slightly swollen ankle and turned it toward him with a creased brow. The locker room was quiet, and although our evening training sessions were starting soon, I knew no one would be here yet.

I was the only one who showed up early.

"I didn't think so. I was leaning toward a strain?" Claire sucked her plump bottom lip into her mouth and peered up at Zedd with soft eyes. She looked so small and innocent as she sat on the bench smack dab in the middle of the locker room, waiting for Zedd to tell her what to do for her injury.

Zedd and I had a close, working relationship that was more like a friendship than anything. We'd been together since my freshman year, and he'd seen the way I'd built this team and had molded my teammates to persevere throughout rough games and even rougher injuries. I knew he'd be willing to meet me this afternoon, and although I left out the part that it was for Claire instead of me, he didn't even bat an eye.

"That's likely. You need to cool it on the..." He looked down at Claire, placing her foot back onto the cushioned bench. "What is it that you do?"

"Dance," I answered for her. "She's a dancer."

"They don't have their own athletic trainer?" he asked, clearly perturbed by that thought.

A soft laugh pulled my attention to Claire's mouth again—something I couldn't stop looking at. "I'm not part of the dance team. I'm in performing arts. We're considered a part of the athletics program but the lowest on the totem pole."

Zedd ran a feeble hand down his face, scratching at his short beard. "That's a shame." He sighed as Claire swung her legs down to the ground. "You need to stay off it for a little while to let it heal. Actually, you should head over to the ice tub. Then continue to ice and rest."

"Stay off of it?" Claire nearly came off the bench. "For how long?"

"At least a week."

Claire's mouth opened with protest, but Zedd put his hand up to stop her while looking over at me. "Tell her what I tell you."

I half-laughed, glancing at Claire who was all but pouting, but respectfully so. "You'll cause more problems if you don't listen to him."

"I can't take a week off."

Zedd snickered as he backed out of the locker room, throwing an ACE bandage at me. "Sounds like someone else I know. Bye, Claire."

Her attention was pulled to him, and she rushed her words out. "Thank you! I appreciate you taking a look."

His eyes slid to me. "No problem."

The moment he was gone, I turned around and bent down to get on Claire's level. "Hop on, roomie," I said over my shoulder.

"Theo. I can walk." Claire laughed softly, pushing at my shoulder. The touch of her palm did things to me that I wouldn't admit aloud because I knew it was our antics clouding my head from earlier.

I couldn't stop thinking about it.

And I couldn't stop staring at her last night when she fell asleep beside me on my bed. I thought about just putting her in her own, but instead, I just lay there, looking up at the ceiling, wondering how I had gotten there.

The truth was, I liked her. I liked being around her. I liked watching her from afar. I liked that she was just as driven as me, and determined, and focused. I liked making her laugh, and I liked lying in my bed with her, watching *Supernatural*. I just liked being with her.

I knew I needed to clear my head and get back to the reality of the situation, but instead of doing that, I was finding reasons to make her laugh and, even worse, finding reasons to touch her.

"Hop on, Bryant. Or I'll put you over my shoulder."

She sniggered under her breath as she stood up to walk, and the sound of her sarcastic laugh fueled me like no other. *She thinks I'm kidding?* I smirked, and she only took one step before I hauled her up over my shoulder and began walking toward the training room.

"Theo!" she squealed, banging her fists on my back. My arm around the back of her thighs tightened, and she wiggled, nearly pushing her ass into my face.

I shoved the ACE bandage in my pocket and turned my head to the left so she could hear my words clearly. "Keep it up and I'll spank you, Bryant."

The humor was there, but barely. It was meant to be a joke, but my hand tingled with the thought of touching that peach of an ass that she had. *Fuck, get it together.*

"You would not," she whispered, letting her arms drop down my back in defeat as I entered the training room. The only light was the glow from the ice bath in the center of the floor, and I stalked toward it with an even deeper smirk planted on my face.

"I would," I bit back. "Wanna test me?"

There was a pause on her end, and I stopped breathing for a moment. *Does she like the thought of that? Because I sure do.*

"No."

I chuckled as I slid her down the front of my body, hooking my hand underneath her knee so she didn't put pressure on her foot. Her hands landed on my chest, and I was certain she could feel the racing of my heart, which was a quick reminder that my little roommate-slash-fake-girlfriend was completely embedding herself into my life, whether it was all a ruse or not.

"Was I that heavy?" She frowned, taking my hand from behind her leg. "Your heart is flying. And here I thought hockey players had good stamina."

"You're not heavy. That's not why my heart is flying, Claire." *Don't say it, Theo. Don't say it. Do no—* "And I have excellent stamina." I paused, trying to make the next part of my sentence sound like I was joking, but deep down, I wasn't. "Want me to show you?"

The look of surprise was followed by her reddened cheeks, and it was obvious she knew that I wasn't joking. She looked down at the ice bath, refusing to meet my eye. "That's not a good idea. Earlier was..." *Great.*

Neither one of us finished her sentence because she was right. It wasn't a good idea. I knew that last night, as I stared down at her lying in my arms while she wore my jersey. There was something about her having my last name on her back that made me wonder if my world could revolve around something other than hockey...like her.

"Get in." My demand was a little harsh, and although I wasn't going to dig into my internal feelings any longer, I knew why I was agitated all of a sudden, and it wasn't her fault. It was mine.

"All the way?" Claire put some space between us and walked closer to the ice bath. She dipped her toe inside before quickly pulling it back. "No!"

I rolled my eyes. "Just your foot, then. It's good for inflammation and will improve recovery."

She hesitated but finally sat down on the floor and put her foot in the ice water, hissing between her perfectly straight teeth. A chill raked through her body, so I ran into the locker room and grabbed my extra hoodie that was in my locker and jogged back to drape it over her shoulders, but when I got back into the training room, I nearly tripped.

"What are you doing?" I asked, drowning in confusion. All I could see was the top of Claire's shoulders and the thin straps of her bra resting along pale skin and her hollow cheeks from the intense chill of ice surrounding her.

Her teeth were chattering when she answered me, so I grew closer to hear her better. "My whole body hurts. I–I–I've been pr-practicing a lot. Maybe I-I-I"—she blew out a shaky breath—"won't be so sore after."

"Jesus," I mumbled. I slowly sank down and sat beside her, putting my knees up so I could rest my forearms over them. "You really are just as driven as I am, Bryant." I shook out my messy brown hair.

"I take–take that as-s a compliment." I caught her cheeky smile, and we sat in silence for the rest of the ten minutes that I allowed her to stay in the ice bath. The second the timer went off, I quickly reached in, grabbed her biceps, and pulled her to her feet in one single motion.

I scanned her wet body and did a triple-take at the way my world stopped spinning for a second. She wore nothing but a simple black bra and those damn panties that showed entirely too much. Water droplets raced down in between her cleavage, and I was confident in saying that it was the first time I'd ever been jealous of a small bead of liquid.

I pulled the hoodie down over her body to dry her off, and the laugh that bubbled out of her mouth confused me. Nothing was funny to me because I was about to lose my mind.

"Is it weird that...I feel good?" She looked over at the ice bath in amazement and then back to me with wide eyes full of mirth and high spirits.

I forced a smile onto my face. "No, it's supposed to do that. Why do you think we do it?"

She laughed again, still shivering as she stood in front of me. "I've never really analyzed the way jocks' brains work—especially not someone like Ford."

I threw my head back for a second and let out a loud laugh. "Come on, let's get you warmed up before you head back to the dorms. My practice starts soon, and you can't be here." I gathered her clothes in my hand and shot her a look so she wouldn't protest as I held out my arms. She quickly jumped into them and wrapped her wet legs around my waist before burying her head into the crook of my neck. Her warm breath coated the side of my neck, and my grip on her wet legs grew harder as I tried to pull myself back to reality—again.

"Flip the light on," I said as we walked into the showers. I placed her on the bench and walked over to them, turning the one in the far back on while keeping my eye on the time. "You get five minutes in lukewarm water. Then, we gotta get you back to the dorms before Coach finds you here."

"Am I not allowed to be here?" she asked, standing up on shaky legs. She pulled my hoodie over her head, and I averted my gaze to the lockers behind her. I'd bite my fist if she wasn't staring at me. I'd do anything to keep myself from thinking the thoughts I was currently having.

"No," I answered. "I'm breaking all my rules for you, Bryant."

I spun around and walked out of the showers so I didn't do what I wanted to do this morning, which was to slip into a fantasy world that smelled of her shampoo and was full of inappropriate thoughts of the girl who was my fake girlfriend.

Before I walked out of the showers, I spun around. "Hey, don't change the temp—"

Fuck. Me.

Her bare back was to me, but her hands paused on the brim of her panties as they were halfway down her hips. I dropped my gaze to the bra that was on the ground next to her feet, and this time, I actually did bite my fist.

The arch of her cheekbone came into sight as she peeked over her shoulder at me, and when our eyes met, I had to physically take a step back and remind myself that I couldn't storm over to her and fuck her like I wanted to.

She's my roommate. She's my fake girlfriend. She's my roommate. She's my fake girlfriend.

I pulled open the door and shut out the sound of the shower as I slammed my back against the wall and bent over at the waist, breathing in and out of my nose until I put the restraints back on. "What the fuck," I mumbled, looking up at the ceiling. "She's not really yours, bro."

I almost texted Aasher to come down to the locker room to be a barrier between Claire and me. Not that I wouldn't walk away if she said no, but I had a big feeling that she was struggling just as much as I was, because when our eyes caught, just a moment ago, I swore the air had crackled around us.

Crossing the line was a bad idea. I agreed with her.

But with bad ideas came new opportunities.

30

CLAIRE

THE LOOK in his eye every time his gaze found me was heart-stopping. It was making it really hard to think clearly. I felt like I was slipping whenever I was alone with Theo. Between his innuendo comments, deep smirks, and casual touches to my body, I felt myself changing and falling for something that wasn't even there.

I was still wounded and hurt, and my self-confidence was skewed from Chad. Just one look from Theo seemed to repair my self-worth, and although I denied his half-joke earlier, I wasn't sure my answer would be the same if he were to ask me again.

I felt dizzy as I put my back to the shower doors, just in case he came in again. Although the water was only luke-warm and not my usual scorching temperature, it felt nice compared to the ice bath that I had been submerged in just moments before. I was completely shocked that Theo had noticed there was something wrong with my ankle, and the fact that he went out of his way to have it checked out for me was *so* genuine. Truthfully, Theo Brooks made it painfully hard not to fall for him.

There was a knock on the door that echoed through the empty showers, and my hand slapped on the nozzle to turn it off.

"Stay where you are, and don't turn around."

My palm stayed put as my head snapped up. My wet hair trailed down my back as water droplets continued to pelt me from overhead. "What?"

"Coach is here. There's nowhere for you to hide, and I'm not about to get chewed out for letting you use our ice bath and showers."

"And you don't think he's going to chew you out for being in the showers *with* me?! Don't you remember how angry he was when he found out I was your roommate?" My heart began to race as I kept my spine straight underneath the stream of the shower. *Oh my God, is he looking at me?* I was completely naked and too afraid to look back to see what he thought of my backside. I knew it didn't matter, but my heart and body were not on the same playing field at the moment.

"He isn't going to know you're in the showers with me." My eyes widened when Theo's breath mixed with the water against my shoulder.

"Theo, what the hell are you doing?" I asked, hyper-aware of every single breath he took. His presence behind me was imperative to how I acted next.

"Hiding you," he whispered, voice suddenly husky and strained. Heat raced down the front of my stomach and landed in the center of my legs. I sucked in a breath and told myself not to turn around, but instead of listening to that wise voice in the back of my head that was trying to shield me from mortification *and* another heartbreak, I slowly peeled around and peered into Theo's hooded gaze.

Water cascaded off the front of his forehead at the same time his jaw flexed. I blinked before romanticizing the situation we were in, pretending that Theo Brooks, the hot hockey jock of Bexley U, actually felt something real for me that wasn't skewed by the perception of a fake relationship.

There was nothing more than a breath of air that stood between us, and when I slowly slipped my gaze down the front of his bare chest and landed on what he was sporting, I gasped loudly and flung my attention back to him.

"Make sure you stay where you are." Theo swallowed, and I swore his jaw grew more angular. "If Coach walks in here, which he will, he won't see you in front of me."

All I could manage was a nod, but there was so much I wanted to say and do, which was a scary thought because there was no way that either of us could blame our behavior on a ruse in front of campus or my ex. Theo and I were alone. Not a single person was watching us. Yet, I wanted him to grip me and tell me pretty lies because the way Theo Brooks made me feel, even while pretending, was something I craved.

"Are you okay?"

I shook the water out of my face and glanced up at his question. He wasn't looking at me, though. All I could see was his strong, defined profile with his straight nose and hollow cheeks. "Yeah, are you?"

I was surprised he could hear me over the stream of the shower, but when his gaze cut to mine, I jumped and ended up closer to him.

"No." The tiny word sent goosebumps flying down my spine until my toes flexed against the tiled floor.

"No?" I dropped my attention to his chest, and it was

moving just as fast as mine. Raising my hand, I put it against his wet skin and quickly gasped. "Theo. It feels like you're having a heart attack. What's wrong?" *Is he nervous that his coach is going to find me here?*

"What's wrong?" A tiny crevice appeared in between his eyebrows, and I followed the small bead of water that trailed over his nose, landing in between us. "*This*. This is what's wrong!" Theo moved closer to me, and I gingerly took a step back, knowing that if he touched me, it was game over. His closed fist banged against the tile behind me, and he leaned in close, careful not to let our bodies touch. "Claire, since the first time I kissed you, I've had a really hard time thinking of anything but your mouth." Theo's admittance stole the last bit of self-control I had. "And your laugh. And..." Theo's free hand suddenly landed on my naked waist, and I stared down at his large palm covering my torso with a stealth I wasn't sure he knew he possessed. *I'm a goner.* "And this body."

"Th–Theo."

"I know it's not a good idea," he repeated my words from earlier, and I wanted nothing more than to take them back. "But I'm not sure I can help myself." Theo's eyes shut, and that was when I took my opportunity and glanced at the dips and valleys of his muscles, relishing in the way my body responded by just looking. Knowing he wanted to touch me and was holding back gave me a newfound sense of confidence. *I wanted him to touch me. Everywhere.*

My hand hovered above him as he gritted out his next words. "Honestly." His head dropped low, and I hoped his eyes were still closed. "I would rather get caught by Coach than stand here any longer because it's fucking painful not to touch you, Claire. *Fuck.*"

I couldn't help but wonder if it was just attraction or if it was something more. I knew it was dangerous to think that way, but I would rather see Chad cheating on me again versus asking Theo that simple question, which was a deadly thought.

Right when Theo went to step away from me, I slapped my hand on his wrist and pulled him in. Our bodies meshed together, and my back was suddenly against the wet tile behind us. His bare chest was racing against mine, and the steely look in his gaze was fierce before his lips captured mine, and he let out a throaty noise. His tongue moved quickly, and I had never felt more desirable as his hands roamed over my naked body, palming me from behind.

Theo pulled back, and his hand went beside my head, resting on the tile. "Fuck, fuck, fuck."

Without thinking too much, I gently placed my hand on his hard length, and his sharp inhale fed me like I was deprived of food. I moved up and down, watching as he grew even harder beneath my small palm. I bit my lip and continued to milk him, even when his hand landed on my chin and he angled my face to look at him instead of his dick. "What am I going to do with you, Bryant?"

"What do you mean?" I whispered, tugging on him harder. He scanned me from my head to my toes, and then stunned me with a look that I felt in between my legs *and* behind my ribs.

His mouth opened, but nothing came out as the door to the showers slammed open. I dropped my hand, freezing like someone had a gun pointing at my head.

"Wolf!" His coach's gruff voice sent a shiver through my body, and I quickly made sure Theo's large frame was hiding every part of mine. "Jesus! I could have gone without seeing your ass this morning."

Theo's face was steady and his voice even smoother. "Well, did you expect that I showered with clothes on?"

Oh shit, my clothes. I hoped Theo had moved them before coming in here so his coach didn't see. The thought of Theo getting in trouble by his coach for helping me didn't sit well.

"What the fuck is this news I'm hearing?"

Coach Lennon's voice was a little more distant, so I hoped he'd turned around to block out the view of Theo's naked backside. I was pretty certain that he couldn't see me in front of Theo, but it wouldn't be hard for him to move slightly to one side and see my legs.

"What news?" Theo asked. The way his eyes were peering down at me felt like I was stuck in a trap.

"The news of you and that girl! Your roommate!" His gaze sliced away at the last second, and I knew that his coach was referring to me, and by the bite in his tone, I felt a little slice to my skin from the disapproval.

"What about her?" I gave props to Theo. He was as nonchalant as they came.

"You're dating? I saw the paper. Do you boys actually think I don't look at it when my players are often the ones talked about?" Coach Lennon mumbled something. "What's up with that? Is that why you've been rushing out of practice this week? In fact, I'm surprised to see you here so early. You usually show up at the last minute nowadays. And I know you haven't been hitting your usual run in the morning before training."

"Coach."

I felt defeated standing there because I knew that, on more than one occasion, Theo had skipped out on his morning run because I was sleeping. In my foggy sleep-deprived state, I'd hear him turn his alarm off and roll back over, and that was definitely a noticeable change because, before, he'd purposefully wake me up by being loud and slamming our door.

"Theo. I've given you the space, and I know you are more determined than most, but I've noticed something has been off." Theo's brows crowded, but he still didn't look at me.

"Nothing has been off, Coach. We're still winning, aren't we? Tom Gardini is still sending scouts to watch me, isn't he? Just because I've missed a couple morning runs doesn't mean I'm distracted."

"I knew this would happen with her being your room-mate!" Theo's coach seemed to be spiraling, and I couldn't help but feel awful, especially since I was standing there completely naked in front of him. "You're going to get all wrapped up in a girl and then blow your chances."

"Coach!" Theo's voice vibrated around us. "She's my fake girlfriend. Our relationship isn't real, so you're incorrect in assuming she's a distraction."

Theo was correct, and his argument was completely validated. It was true. I *was* his fake girlfriend, and our relationship wasn't real. And I was fine with that until I realized that there was a heaviness inside my chest from his admittance.

"What? Fake girlfriend? Why would you need a fake girlfriend?"

Theo slowly brought his eyes to mine, and although they were soft around the edges, his words stung. "To fend off the puck bunnies. They kept coming to my room naked and showing up after the games. If Tom Gardini's scouts showed up, I didn't want him to think I was some washed-up, selfish jock who had a line of half-naked girls waiting for him after the games." There was a quick, jutting shake of Theo's head that caught my attention, but I was too stuck to make any sense of it because the reality was...Theo's words hurt.

And they shouldn't have.

31

THEO

It was hard to force the words out while standing there, looking down at her, and for once, it had nothing to do with the way my blood was pumping with desire. The second I admitted to Coach that Claire and I weren't actually dating, nor was she a distraction, she suddenly seemed fragile. Her chin stayed level, but the color vanished from her flushed cheeks, and I was screaming on the inside for her not to believe what I was saying aloud.

But it was true, right? Our relationship was fake. It was a maneuver of good plays to favor us both in our little game. We had our own reasons, but winning was still the goal.

"Oh." Coach was beginning to believe me, and I wanted nothing more than for him to get the fuck out of the showers so I could grab Claire by the waist and put the color back on her cheeks. "So, she means nothing to you?"

Well, now wait a minute.

Blood rushed through my ears, and I could no longer feel the water from the shower pelting me. In reality, Claire and I had been standing in the shower for maybe five minutes, but it felt like an eternity had passed while I stood there, stunned by the fact that I couldn't say yes. Claire Bryant, my roommate and fake girlfriend, definitely meant something to me, but I had no idea what to do with it. I was suddenly four years old again, holding my hockey stick for the first time, unsure of what to do, even though I knew it felt right.

"Wolf?" Coach Lennon barked my nickname, and I quickly answered, blocking out everything I wanted to say to Claire just to get him out of here faster.

"She means nothing! Now can I please shower in peace?! I'll be on the ice at the start of practice."

There was this voice of reason in the back of my head that told me not to look down at Claire, but I did anyway, and the moment I did, I regretted it. *Hurt.*

"Yeah, yeah," Coach mumbled. "But fair warning, Tom Gardini *himself*—not his scout—is coming to the game, so make sure to tell your pretend girlfriend to be on your side. You're smart. Having those puck bunnies around might make you look sleazy, and if there's one thing I know about Tom, he judges your skill on the ice just as much as your character off of it."

The door slammed, and Claire jumped in front of me before spinning around and turning the nozzle off. The stream of water that separated us disappeared, and all I heard was her low, desolate departure. "I should go."

"Claire, wait." I grabbed her slippery arm and turned her back around. I reached behind her, and the water turned back on. I kicked it up a few temperatures because she had goosebumps over every inch of her skin. "Don't go."

"You have practice." She wouldn't look at me and was trying her hardest to get her arm out of my grasp. "I'll get dressed, and when you are all on the ice, I'll sneak out so your coach doesn't know I'm here."

My hand slipped to her elbow when she tried to turn away from me, and I jerked back softly, crowding her space until her back was against the tile and the stream of water was at my back. "Wait," I rushed.

When her baby blues reached me, I felt them bury themselves in my soul. The soft color of blue was sharpened, and the wall between us was stronger than before. I felt like I'd lost her, and I didn't even have her yet.

"I didn't mean it." I had no control over what was falling from my lips. None at all.

Adrenaline rushed through my veins when her shaky breath hit my chest. Her hand lifted, and she patted the muscle that was beating violently beneath her touch.

"Yes, you did. And that's because it is the truth," she countered, smashing her lips together. The wobbling of her chin didn't go unnoticed, and I panicked to make it right even if I knew that I was going back against everything I thought was sending me down the correct path of my life. But somehow, the NHL didn't seem all that significant while looking down at the hurt on her face.

"No." I shook my head.

Claire's brows lowered, and her eyes grew glossier. "Theo, everything you said was true. We are fake dating, remember? That was your idea to begin with. It just...kinda happened."

A single tear crept out of the corner of her eye, and although she tried to hide it, I still caught it with the side of my thumb. "Tell me why you're crying."

"I'm not crying."

Both of my hands went to the sides of her face, and I bounced my eyes back and forth between hers. "Tell me right now why you are crying." *I need to hear it. I need to know that she is on the same page as me.*

The look of annoyance flashed across her features, but then her vulnerability shone through, and I swore the water cascading down my back turned to ice. "Because your words hurt me, and they shouldn't have."

I brought her forehead to mine and peered down into her eyes. I trapped the wet strands of her dark hair in between my fingers as I cupped her face. "I lied."

Her whisper propelled me to take a step closer, to push our bodies together. "You lied?"

I swallowed the fear that came with telling the truth and basked in feelings I'd never felt before because, to be honest, it was terrifying. For so many years, I'd thought of nothing but hockey and making it to the NHL, but now, with just one wobble of her chin, I'd forgotten all about my dream and was focused on something else entirely. "You mean something to me. I lied so he'd get out of here faster."

"But—"

My lips grazed hers when I repeated myself. "It's not fake for me, Claire. I think about you every second of the day. I wonder where you are, what you're doing, how I can spend more time with you in between your busy schedule and my games..." I gripped her hips, and my knee went in between her slippery legs as my heart began filling with warmth. "And don't even get me started on seeing you in my jersey."

I was slapped in the face with what my future could look like the second I felt her slipping from my fingers, and the realization that I'd fallen for my fake girlfriend was humbling, to say the least.

Claire's mouth opened, but before I devoured it, I

silently begged her to say something, anything to give me the green light.

"I'm afraid." Her mighty chin raised, but her body molded to mine underneath the stream of water, and if I didn't bury myself inside her in the next few minutes, I'd have one hell of a practice.

"Of me?" I feared, staring down into her eyes.

Her shoulder lifted, and I glanced down at the perfect mounds on her chest. My breath quickened with the sight of her pebbled nipples that were obviously made for my mouth. I was captivated by her mind, heart, *and* body—and that was new territory for me.

"My mother warned me of guys like my father. Jocks. And even though you've proved you're not what I thought you were, I don't know if I can take another blow to my heart after Chad."

I'd never.

"If you give me a piece of your heart, I'll keep it safe."

I rubbed my thumb over her plump bottom lip as she contemplated my words. *Please.* I'd never felt so desperate in my life. I'd never had to work so hard either, and I'd never felt like I had so much at stake. The thought of Claire turning me down and running away while giving into her fear—*understandably*—was like a bullet headed straight for me.

But to my surprise, her lips were a mere breath from mine, and her leg with the hurt ankle wrapped around my backside. "Don't make me regret this, Theo."

"Never," I said before swiftly taking her mouth with mine and letting the rest of the world disappear. The only thing I could feel was her smooth skin beneath my calloused hands. The only thing I could taste was her pureness and willingness to let me take her under. The only thing I thought of was making this girl mine.

I slowly put her leg down, even though I wanted to do nothing but ram inside of her. I knew we were limited on time, but I didn't care. "Open your legs," I demanded, stepping back into the stream of water so I could get a good look at her. Claire did exactly as I told her with her round breasts rising and falling with lack of oxygen from our kiss. A sly grin slipped onto my face as I slipped past her belly button and landed on the spot in between her legs.

"We're limited on time." I stalked a step toward her, burning with desire in every part of my body. My dick was harder than it had ever been, and it was painful not to have her on it. "But I'll be damned if you don't come more than once."

Claire's sweet face morphed into confusion, but when I gripped the inside of her thigh, she gasped and threw her head back against the tiles. I clenched my teeth as I sunk a finger inside and watched in awe as her nipples hardened right in front of me.

"God damn," I whispered, stealing a kiss from her willing mouth before putting another finger inside.

"Theo." Claire was quiet but needy. Her hips curved upward, and I watched in awe as her body moved against me, chasing the high and not being shy about it.

"That's it," I encouraged. "Let me see you come, Claire." Her blue eyes flew to mine, but I quickly dipped my head down and took one of her nipples in my mouth, flicking my tongue over the bud. Fire ripped down my spine as I swiped my thumb against her clit, pressing harder the more her hips moved.

"Right ther—" Her moan was louder than it should have been, and I remembered we were in the showers and that the team was going to start getting geared up for practice. I swallowed her echoing whimper, took my fingers out of her pulsing pussy, and hooked her leg over my hip.

"Brace yourself," I said before slipping inside. There was a crack in the earth, and my heart did a double-take. "Holy shit," I mumbled, dropping my head to the crook of her neck. My teeth sunk in, and her entire body shook against mine.

"I—" She gasped again as I started to move, and I wanted to stop to hear what she had to say, but I couldn't. She felt too good, and she pulsed around me so quickly it felt like she was milking me dry. If she kept it up, I was afraid I'd come in ten seconds. "I can't... Theo. W–wow."

Claire's hand flew up to her breast, and she squeezed it just as tightly as her pussy squeezed me, and I pounded in faster and harder at the angle that I knew was getting her twisted. I felt her come around my dick, and the tiles of the showers could have been crumbling around us, and I wouldn't have stopped plunging inside.

"That's it," I coaxed, pushing in deeper. "I could watch you come every second of every day and never get sick of it."

A whimper flew from her mouth, and I licked it up, plunging my tongue in her mouth to give her a bruising kiss that I'd hope she'd always remember as I quickly pulled out and busted a load on the shower wall, pumping my shaft tightly.

My jaw ached from clenching my teeth, but my entire world seemed to soften after I dropped my hand and looked over at her. The color was back on her cheeks, and there was a brightness around her blue eyes that I was proud of because I knew I'd helped put it there.

"You"—I stepped over to her and pulled her in close

with my hands on her lithe waist—"are my weak side, Bryant. Do you hear me?"

She swallowed shyly and stared up at me. "I don't know what that means."

I smirked as I reached over and turned the water off. "It means you're mine."

32

CLAIRE

Number 15 was plastered to my back, and the black jersey was a magnet for every set of eyes in the stands. Not only was everyone chanting his name, but they were all side-eyeing me whenever Theo would do something on the ice. I assumed whatever he had done was a good thing, because they all cheered at the same time, so I went along with it, yelling his name and clapping my hands. My voice was hoarse, and Taytum, along with some of the girls from her sorority, laughed every time I jumped up to watch Theo skate over the ice.

"I need you to tell me more," Taytum urged, whispering in my direction. "I feel like you're leaving out vital parts of the story."

"I'm not giving you all the gory details," I answered, brows crowding as I watched Theo use deft footwork to maneuver around the other player. Although I didn't know much about hockey, it was clear that Theo was skilled. He demanded authority on the ice, and the team simply revolved around him.

"I tell you about my sex life all the time." She pouted for a second but then bumped her shoulder into mine. "Chad's been quiet?"

I nodded but kept quiet. The last several days had been a breath of fresh air without Chad lingering in the background like a possessive shadow, but if I allowed myself to think about it, I felt panicky.

I'd taken a small break in my extra rehearsals and babied my ankle during actual practices—something everyone had noticed, especially my professors. Angie sent me home from work one evening after she overheard Theo tell me I'd cause more harm to myself if I didn't take care of my ankle. She promised I could pick up some extra shifts in between my classes the following week, so I listened and went home with Theo—who had been in our room every chance he could get.

We were more wrapped up in each other behind our door than in front of it, but not because he didn't want to keep up with the charade in front of campus, but mainly because he wanted me all for himself—his words, not mine.

I wasn't complaining, and neither was my body.

In fact, I was giddy just thinking about his hands on my skin, and although that should have scared me, it didn't. Instead, it exhilarated me, just like it did as I watched him on the ice, working with his team to secure the win.

"Yes!" I shouted, raising my hands and jumping up and down. The sports commentator announced through the speaker that Bexley was the winner, and I clapped my hands, feeling my eyes well up from relief.

"Oh my God." Taytum laughed from beside me, and I glanced over, feeling my cheeks ripen. "Who even are you?"

My smile was hard to hide, and I shrugged. "I'm not sure anymore, but I kinda like it."

Taytum grabbed onto my hand, and she nodded. "Me too. You look happy, Claire. Happier than I've ever seen." She paused before asking, "Is that because you're rid of Chad, or is that because you have Theo?"

I nibbled on my lip as I looked down at the jersey I was wearing before taking my attention back to the ice. The rational voice in the back of my head reminded me that I wasn't quite rid of Chad yet, but I still answered Taytum. "Both."

Her head went to my shoulder, and I inhaled, finding number 15 surrounded by his teammates who had ripped their helmets off and all shared the same victorious smile. Ford came up beside Theo and ruffled Theo's sweaty, dark hair. My stomach did a somersault when he searched the stands, and when he landed on me, I smiled brightly and gave him a thumbs up. I was proud of him.

Taytum whistled as Theo pointed at me from the ice, and I swore I saw every head in the stadium turn toward us. My cheeks blazed, and a choked laugh left my throat. *Damn him.* I rolled my eyes, and when he cocked an eyebrow at me, I remembered what I'd promised him I'd do if he won the game. My hand went up to my mouth, and I blew him a quick kiss. He winked in return, and eventually, he and the rest of the team all skated off the ice, and I knew that my next part was about to come to play.

"Okay, wow." Rose's eyebrows went to her hairline, showing off her shimmering makeup. "I just got butterflies for you."

I laughed, and we all rushed out of the stands and headed down the long, darkened hallway that Taytum and I had gone down the first time we'd met the guys after a game.

It was quiet, but the closer we got to the locker room, the better I could hear voices. Jealousy started to creep in as I thought about seeing puck bunnies standing there, trying to get the guys' attention, but I gently pushed that thought away because although I was a little jaded when it came to trust, I knew that puck bunnies were no threat to me.

When I rounded the corner, proudly wearing Theo's jersey, I felt a buzz in my back pocket. I paused for a second, pulling it out, and frowned at the name on the screen.

Chad: So you're wearing his jersey now? Is that how you wanna play this game?

Taytum huffed from beside me. "Tell him the game is over, and he's the loser."

The color drained from my face. "I can't. Not yet."

I still had to figure out what to do to get out from under Chad's thumb. I hadn't heard from my mom since the last time she'd asked for help, but even so, I knew she wouldn't listen to me about not taking money from Chad's parents again. The more she took their money, the more debt she was in, and the more I was dangling out there in the open as some type of ransom to Chad.

It wasn't as if the thought didn't occur to me that I could leave my mother to fend for herself. She was old enough to understand how to budget, and she'd surely been an adult longer than I had, but for as long as I could remember, my mother and I were a team. We were always in survival mode, and if I ruined our relationship, who would I have left?

She was my mother, but when Angela Bryant got betrayed, she didn't let it go. I'd learned that by hearing her talk of my illegitimate father for the last twenty-two years of my life. She'd feel betrayed if she knew I was with someone like Theo, and she would be up in arms if I stopped giving her money and ruined the relationship with Chad and his parents.

"And who is this lovely lady wearing my son's jersey?"

My head popped up, and my hair flew out of my face as I locked onto an older man smiling kindly with a gentle-looking woman walking beside him. She was holding onto her purse strap, but her other arm was draped over his as they continued to head my way.

"Hi," I whispered, clearing my throat. "I'm—"

"You must be Claire." The woman, who I assumed was Theo's mother—or grandmother, but known as his mother—smiled at me, and I felt it bury itself into my belly like I'd just eaten a warm chocolate chip cookie from her kitchen. "Theo said he wanted to introduce us, but he's a little busy."

The older man edged his head behind him, and I peeked back, squinting my eyes as I watched Theo talk with someone wearing a suit that likely cost more than what my mother owed to Chad's parents.

"Who—" *Oh, my God.* It was the man from The Bex. The realization clicked immediately, and I instantly felt guilty for the judgment I'd placed onto him when I saw that he wouldn't stop staring at me.

"That's Tom Gardini."

I pulled my attention away and hoped my cheeks weren't too red from my silent embarrassment. It was no wonder he was staring at me. He was probably trying to figure out what kind of guy Theo was, and considering Theo's eyes were on me that entire evening, he must have wanted to know about me too.

Theo's father boomed with excitement. "It's a pretty big deal, huh?"

"Huge!" I smiled as I moved past the shock and into

excitement. I tried to hide the enthusiasm, but Theo's mother let go of her husband, came toward me, and wrapped me in her arms. I was stunned at first, but when she pulled back, I was pretty certain my face was a mirror of hers. "It's sweet to see you so excited for him. We are too. We really just want him to be happy."

Me too. I smiled again. "He deserves to succeed. He works hard."

Both of his parents nodded at me just as Taytum leaned in and whispered in my ear that she'd see me at the party later. I sent her a soft wave, along with the other girls, and turned around to find Theo's parents staring adoringly at their son.

"We're so proud of him." Theo's mom looked back at me and then sighed wistfully. "I'm sorry. I don't even think we told you our names." She patted her husband on the chest, and he let out a gruff noise before spinning around and putting his hands in his pockets.

"I'm sure Theo hasn't told you much about us," he said, skirting around something that I was certain he thought I didn't know, but I actually did. "I'm Daryl, and this is my wife, Linda."

"It's so nice to meet you, and yes, Theo has told me about you two."

"He has?" Linda's eye twinkled with something that I couldn't quite make out, and I nodded.

"Yes." I paused as my heart took a quick beating of envy. "He's really lucky to have you two as parents." I gave them both my full attention. "And you've raised him right."

Linda laughed out loud, and I caught the quick glimpse that Theo threw us while talking to Tom Gardini. "Well, it's nice to hear that." Linda grabbed onto my hand and gave it a gentle squeeze. "I didn't think he'd ever get a girlfriend."

My cheeks blasted with ripening heat, and I forced a smile. Theo and I hadn't really talked much about the logistics of whatever was going on between us. I mean, for all intents and purposes, I *was* his girlfriend. But it started out as fake, and as crappy as it made me feel, Theo had no idea that there was more to Chad than him just being my ex. He had no idea that Chad was simply putting a pin in our relationship until the end of the year and that he planned to have me by his side afterward. And Theo had no idea that I'd kind of agreed.

"Aw, now come on, Ma." Theo's smooth voice stole our attention, and I instantly relaxed when his arm landed on my shoulders. "I was just waiting for the right girl."

"It only takes one," Daryl said, grinning mischievously, just like Theo.

"Sweet talkers, both of 'em," Linda whispered into my ear, squeezing my hand once more before letting go.

I laughed out loud, and when I peered up at Theo, my heart did a double-take. His bright-green eyes were pleased, and there was an air around him that wasn't there before. Confidence? Happiness? I wasn't sure what it was, but I knew that I liked seeing it.

"So, tell us, son." Daryl leaned in closer as the hallway began to empty. I sent Ford, Emory, and Aasher a little smile as they walked past. Ford winked, Emory flicked his chin at Theo, and Aasher made sure to say a quick hello to Daryl and Linda before Daryl pressed his son to fill us in. "What did Tom say?"

Just then, I turned and looked at Tom Gardini. He was the *highly* successful owner of the NHL team that Theo had his eyes set on, and he was the main source when it came to Theo succeeding in his future. He'd told me all about Tom last night as we feasted on French fries from

The Bex before he began his nightly ritual of prepping for the game.

According to Theo, Tom Gardini was destined for the NHL many years ago but ended up in a crash that destroyed the nerves along his spine. He was wheelchair bound, in rehabilitation facilities, and never fully recouped. He was the epitome of success. News articles floated around of his injury and how his future was destroyed, but instead of falling into a pit of despair, he continued to build an empire by assistant coaching, which propelled him into head coaching, and then eventually owning one of the best NHL teams in the league.

It was an inspirational story, that was for sure.

The end of Theo's explanation to his parents caught my ear. "He pretty much sealed the deal with a tryout offer and mentioned a spot at the team development camp."

"Son, that's great news." I stepped away from Theo so his father could wrap him in a hug, and I couldn't help but notice the height difference between the two. Hockey players were big, and I briefly wondered if Theo got his height from the father he never met.

"I am so proud of you, honey." Linda swiped a tear away, and I smiled at her, wondering what it would feel like to have a mother who was proud of your achievements instead of always wanting more.

Theo's hand fell to mine, and I glanced back over at Tom Gardini once more, and to my surprise, he was staring directly at me. A soft smile touched my lips, and I nodded in my attempt to show that I understood why he showed up at The Bex and seemed interested in me. His strong brow deepened, and the suit he was wearing suddenly seemed fancier than before. I dropped my gaze down to his hand as he held his wooden cane in it, and when I crawled back up to meet his blue eyes, my heart started to beat a little faster.

Tom Gardini was still gazing at me, but instead of nodding or looking away, he stared with a curiosity that was painfully obvious. His head tilted to the side, and although someone was trying to get his attention, he had a hard time pulling his gaze from me.

That is weird.

I chalked it up to him analyzing Theo even further, and that was when I realized that Theo's overall plan of fending off the puck bunnies was probably a good idea in the end. I was certain it looked better for Theo to have a consistent girl by his side versus a line of girls who were, nonetheless, considered gold diggers.

But even as Theo pulled on my hand and headed for the locker rooms, I still got a sense of unease, but maybe that had nothing to do with Theo and everything to do with me.

[33]

THEO

"WHAT ARE WE DOING?" Claire asked, nearly tripping behind me as I dragged her by her hand.

Everyone had long disappeared from the locker room, not wanting to stay hidden any longer than they needed with Tom Gardini out in the hallway. I was high on the fact that my parents were here, I had played the best goddamn game of my life, Tom Gardini had noticed, and best of all, Claire was in the stands, proudly wearing my jersey like she was truly my girlfriend instead of this fake spiel that we had created for reasons that seemed so insignificant now.

"I told you, I forgot something." I winked at her, and the pretty brown strands of her hair framed her face, making her look that much more beautiful.

"Your parents are waiting." I spun around quickly and picked her up, draping her over my shoulder. "Theo!" she squealed, slapping my back through a fit of laughter. "What are you doing? Your parents—"

"Are meeting us at The Bex," I finished for her, grinning

wildly with a thrill that woke the second I saw her up in the stands. Her smile was the only thing I could focus on in between plays. It was troubling that I had such a hard time staying on task, but still, I played a damn good game, and it very well could have been because I knew she was there, watching me. I had always thought being focused and canceling out everything outside of the rink was the key to dominating on the ice, but I may have been wrong. Claire balanced me, and she didn't even know it.

"Theo!" Claire huffed out another laugh as I plopped her down onto the cushioned bench in the middle of the locker room. We were surrounded by silver lockers with the letters BU painted on the front in black. The only eyes on us were from the wolf logo in the middle of the wall, and that wolf was about to get an eyeful.

"How is your ankle?" I asked, bending down and taking her foot in my grasp. My fingers splayed over the inside of her leg, and I flicked my eyes up to hers the instant our skin touched. She inhaled sharply, dropping her smile a moment later.

"It's fine." Her tone was playful, but her eyes were telling me that she was curious as to what I was doing. "I have the main audition next week. I'm starting off on light feet tomorrow, so I won't injure it further, but it feels a lot better."

"That's good." I nodded, placing her foot back onto the ground slowly. I was still crouched down on one knee, seeming relaxed, but on the inside, I was burning up. "My parents like you," I said, running my hand up the inside of her leg. At first, when I saw her in these tight jeans, I loved them. But now I was irritated because they were a barrier that I desperately needed to remove.

Claire's swallow cut through the pounding in my ears

for a split second. "I like them too. And..."

I dragged my gaze from the button of her jeans and met her face.

"They're waiting for us. What do you think you're doing?" she asked.

A deep, throaty chuckle rasped from my mouth as my hand got to the inside of her thigh. "Did you truly think I could resist you after seeing you cheer for me during the game?"

Her sarcastic laugh cut through the air. "Oh, stop it. You're too tired after games. Isn't that what you used to tell the puck bunnies?"

"Do you know where my head kept going while I was talking to the one guy who I've looked up to my entire life?" My finger laid over the button of her jeans, and like the needy girl she was, Claire moved back a sliver, and it was the silent green light I'd been waiting for.

"No," she answered hesitantly.

"You." It was something I never thought I'd admit aloud, but here I was, bending for a girl who was never supposed to be mine. "And how much I fucking loved seeing you in my jersey, and how effortless you looked talking to my parents, winning my mother over in a split second. And after every single play I made, I could hear you yelling my name."

Claire glanced away with embarrassment, but I hurriedly turned her chin with my hand and pulled her attention back to me. "Don't be embarrassed. I want you at every single game from here on out."

"You do?" she whispered, almost seeming nervous that I wasn't telling the truth, which made sense. Over the last few days, I'd thought long and hard about her and *this*. She'd been burnt, badly, by her ex. And what was brewing between us had started out as a ruse. Our relationship had been a sham until, suddenly, our attraction and feelings weren't. Each moment I spent with her was another moment stolen, and I was tired of feeling like a thief.

"Yes." I hoped my words conveyed exactly what I was feeling. "Every"—I flicked the button through its rightful hole—"single"—Claire inhaled sharply—"game."

Our eyes crashed, and desire flew through my veins. "Up," I demanded, pulling her jeans down her ass and taking them off in a single whoosh. "Now open."

Claire obeyed every command I gave her, and I was ready to devour her by just the single fact that she was still wearing my jersey.

"This is all I've thought about," I admitted, leaning in close and licking my lips. My hands gripped the insides of her thighs, and she jumped, stealing my attention to her face for a split second. Her pretty pink lip was tugged in between her teeth, but she suddenly seemed hesitant, so I paused. "What's wrong?"

"Nothing." Claire's chest was moving up and down, and I knew by the color creeping up her neck that she was turned on, but there was a sense of caution lingering.

"Tell me." I shook my head before tapping the inside of her thigh, nearly salivating. "You know you can trust me, right?"

Her jaw worked back and forth, and she nodded quickly. "It's just..." She looked down at her panties that were already sporting a wet spot. My tongue tingled, but I forced myself to wait. *Doesn't she know I am starving for her?* "You've never done this to me before."

"I'm well aware." *Please don't make me wait any longer.*

She swallowed nervously, and jealousy flickered within the deep parts of my brain. "What did he do to you that makes you think I don't want this?"

Her mouth opened in shock and then closed abruptly. "I'm beginning to know you very well, Claire. So, tell me. Now." My finger slowly crept over to her panties, and I slipped the moist fabric over, feeling my chest constrict with something that I wasn't able to control.

"He just didn't like to do this often. Not unless I had showered or...shaved."

I could kill him. I'd like to put him in the middle of the ice rink and blast ice pucks at his head all fucking day.

"So, you're self-conscious? You're afraid that I'm not going to like this?" I didn't wait for her to answer. Instead, I hooked my fingers in the sides of her panties, ripped them down her legs and spread her wide. "Watch me," I snapped, licking her from the front all the way to the back. The taste of her against my tongue was something I'd never forget for the rest of my life. Something filled my veins, and I began to ravish her like I was famished. The nickname *Wolf* resonated even more than before as I devoured every single inch of her.

"God, Theo." I hardly recognized her voice as I continued to lick, flick, and plunge my tongue inside her. Her taste was sweet, and I never wanted to go without it.

"My parents are waiting," I teased. "Gonna come on my mouth?"

Her entire body bucked on the bench, and I eyed her white knuckles as she gripped the sides, spreading her legs even wider.

"Mmm," I coaxed, replacing my tongue with my finger as I sucked on her clit. *Fuck.* Claire's whimper was music to my ears, and it truly blew my mind that her ex could ever act like she wasn't good enough. I sucked harder as she climaxed, and the very second she coated my finger, I clenched my eyes and licked every possible piece of her that I could.

She was out of breath when I pulled out of her and wiped my mouth on the back of my hand. I smirked as her mouth dropped open, and her eyes grew hooded with even more lust. The blue was burning brighter than I'd ever seen, and her smooth cheeks were flushed. I said nothing as I slowly pulled her panties back up her legs, and then her jeans came next. I stood up, held my hand out for her, and brought her to stand on wobbly legs.

"Did I prove to you how much I liked that?" I asked, bringing her in closer to my body and brushing my lips over her mouth. Claire's arms went around my waist, and she angled her chin up to me, nodding softly. "I'm nothing like him, so whatever he did or said to you, forget about it." My teeth ground together, and I was beginning to feel something potent when I thought about Claire and her ex. He made her feel insignificant and self-conscious, and the irritation it brought me was clearly significant for this late in our little game. *But is it still a game?*

For the first time since this all started, Claire didn't wait for me to kiss her. Instead, she lifted up on her tiptoes, put her mouth on mine, and silently answered my question.

"Better stop." I pulled back and peered down at her. That tongue of hers that was just roaming around my mouth jolted out, and she licked her bottom lip with a shy smile. "Or my parents will start to worry."

The sudden realization that jolted across her features made my entire night. I threw my head back and laughed.

"Oh my God. I forgot!" she admitted. "We gotta go meet them!"

She took a step back, and this time, instead of me pulling her, it was the opposite. And like the lovesick puppy that I was, I followed after her.

34

CLAIRE

I wasn't sure if it was a good thing that my ankle was wrapped so tightly it was numb, but I supposed it was better than it potentially twisting under the pressure of an injury. Today was my audition for the solo that I'd been focused on since the beginning of the semester, and although this was much more than just your regular audition, my heart felt strangely steady in my chest.

My fingers opened and closed, and I bent my neck to the left and right, trying to warm myself up. I began clearing my head, closing my eyes to block out the curtain in front of me. I'd practiced all week, going over my audition and making sure I could maneuver in the way I needed to without truly hurting myself.

The good thing about Theo and me was that we were both cut from the same cloth. Determination and drive fueled us—although within different parts of our life. We both understood each other, and he hadn't been anything but supportive, which was a breath of fresh air. He left me to practice alone but was always quick to ask me how it went and if he could help with my stretching. I didn't focus on what we were, but I did realize how easy it was to forget about Chad. I'd hardly noticed him lurking in the background and flaunting girls in front of me while I worked, which was something he'd made note of in the unanswered texts I had received from him.

He was still laying low when it came to our parents, though. My mother hadn't said a single peep about Chad. The only thing she'd called me about was the repairs at the apartment, and she'd briefly asked how my classes were.

That was the thing about my mother. She was equal parts selfish and selfless. Her priorities weren't always straight, but she truly did want the best for me. I'd never doubted her longing that I'd have a better life than she did. It was why she had pushed me into dance and we worked so hard to get the partial scholarship. She saw an opportunity for me to succeed in ways she never did and pushed me toward it.

"You ready?" Taytum came up behind me and lightly massaged my shoulders. I glanced down at my pale-purple leo, smoothing out the sheer skirt, making sure it was tied properly around my waist. Taytum made sure my bun was pinned tightly without a single stray hair out of place.

"I am," I answered. For the first time all semester, I felt good. *Confident.* And that most definitely had something to do with the support I had versus the degradement I was used to.

"You have a fan club in the stands."

I spun around on my deft feet. "Excuse me? What?"

We both rushed over to the curtain where most of the other dancers were spectating from. "Back row."

"I'm gonna kill him," I whispered, trying to fight the smile that was creeping along my face.

"Oh, please." Taytum's shoulder bumped into mine. "You love it."

I did. I watched as Theo leaned back to say something to Aasher, who sat beside him proudly, along with most of the hockey team. There were guys sitting in the seats that I didn't recognize but knew they were there because of him.

"They have a game in five hours. Shouldn't they be, like, resting?" I asked, shutting out Theo's wide smile as Ford leaned forward and said something to him. The curtain closed, and I nibbled on my lip as Taytum eyed me suspiciously.

"You have stuff to tell me." She raised an eyebrow and began walking over to her partner, Jaylyn. They were paired together for a duo, just as I was with Adam. But my solo was the important one because not everyone had the chance to score it, and it came with monetary benefits. It was an honor to even be considered, but honor didn't give me what I needed. "But first, get out there and kill it. We can talk after."

I nodded because, in all honesty, this dance kind of determined a lot of what I had to tell. If I didn't come out on top of this audition, I wasn't sure what my next steps were, and although I didn't want to face it, it might be the end of the fantasy world that I was allowing myself to live in with Theo.

I sighed and shook my hands out once more as I heard the growing applause from the judges, one of them being my professor, and focused on the end goal. Get out there, clear your head, and dance your heart out. Because suddenly, there was a lot more at stake.

―――

I kept my head down as the stage grew dark. I wiggled my toes in my ballet slippers, and although it was only a few seconds before the spotlights turned on and the music started, I replayed my entire youth and every lesson I'd learned thus far.

For most of my life, I'd danced for someone other than myself. I proved my worth and skill to my dance teachers, to the other dance moms who abhorred me because of my family situation, and most of all, to my mother. I'd even admit that I danced for a father I never knew and a boyfriend who was as disapproving as they came. But it wasn't until this moment that I decided to dance for myself.

I didn't need anyone's approval. The second I took a step away from Chad—even if it was he who forced it, making me fight with fire to survive as the girl I strove to be—was the second I realized that there was more to life than pleasing others. I no longer wanted to prove something to Chad, or my mother, or a father that was an absence I felt every time my mother and I struggled. I wasn't trying to be the best so I could feel a sense of achievement by gaining their approval. Instead, I was dancing for the taste of freedom that I felt while looking at Theo. I was dancing for a purpose. I was dancing for me so I could get what *I* wanted.

Being selfless didn't mean you couldn't be selfish too. It didn't mean you were self-obsessed or inconsiderate. It just meant that you valued yourself, and I hated to admit that it took a big, hunky jock to prove it to me. I wanted to see the value in myself that he seemed to see.

Theo's face was the first thing I saw when the piano started, and it sent a shower of warmth against my skin.

Before I even started dancing, he smiled proudly, and just like that, I was off.

The music took me, and I was leaping and softly spinning across the floor with a deep-rooted passion, and by the time the chorus came, I felt nothing but love and support. I knew even before the end of the song that I had danced my very best, and it was because, for the first time in my life, I felt grounded and safe. I snuck another glance at Theo as I geared up for my final leap, the hardest one thus far, and allowed him to guide me with energy I couldn't match elsewhere. But at the very last second, I halted. I snagged another pair of eyes in the back, staring me down like I was about to be ruined.

Chad stood with his shoulders straight and his taut chin tipped in my direction. I quickly tore my eyes away in order to save myself, but my resolve slipped. It may have only been a split second, but I heard the rip in my focus, and before I took off for my jeté, there was a knock to my confidence, and I rushed it.

Chad threw me off. It was probably his plan all along. He wasn't dense. He was smart, and he probably realized that I was more into Theo than he thought. He felt the pressure of losing me, and he was right to feel that way.

Chad had lost me, and it wasn't until mid-leap that I realized I might just lose Theo.

35

THEO

SHE WAS MEANT to have eyes on her. The way she danced with elegance and beauty was something that only someone who was as determined as Claire could possess. She was everything I craved and everything I wanted for my future. I was captivated, and by the silence in the row the hockey team and I sat in, I was pretty sure they were just as breathless as I was.

Her leaps were just as poised and strict as my first impression of her, but her spins were as soft and light, like the air around her when we were alone. My heart rammed against my ribs as I continued to watch her trail across the stage, and I was pretty certain that I wanted this for her as much as she wanted it for herself.

My fist clenched as I lost myself in her dance, wanting more. I could spend the rest of my life in this seat, watching her reach her goals, and be perfectly content with it.

"Damn, bro. She's something else." I hardly heard Ford's whisper, but my head tilted with irritation with his next statement. "What are you going to do when your little fake relationship is over?"

I wanted to tell him that it wasn't fake and that there was no end in the future, but all thoughts seized as Claire's eyes skimmed over our row. Instead of her latching onto me for long, she looked behind me, and I instantly knew something was wrong. Call it intuition or maybe I knew her so well that even the tiniest squint of her eye told me more than she ever could with words. I sat up straighter as I watched her take off from the corner and knew it wasn't going to end well.

I quickly spun around, and when my eyes landed on Chad, I had to force myself to turn away to watch the end of her dance before I killed him.

"Oh fuck."

My eyes widened the moment she landed. Her strained ankle bent, and instead of her catching herself like she had in practice this week, she toppled over, and her head hit the hard stage. The sound vibrated against my skull, even through the music, and instead of hauling myself over the back of my seat to strangle Chad, who I knew was the reason she stumbled, I jumped up and rushed down the aisle of the auditorium and met Claire's professor, along with a few dancers.

"Bryant," I demanded, pulling her into my lap. Her body was limp, and her head lollygagged to the left before I cupped the side of her face, caressing it lightly. "Claire, wake up."

"Call 911," someone said in the background, but I ignored them as Claire's eyelashes began to flutter open.

My chest quivered to see her blue eyes, and everything faded when she finally opened them and landed on me.

"Hey," I rushed out, hearing the fear in my voice. "You okay?"

Claire blinked once and then twice before gasping. Her hand tightened around my bicep, but it was a faint grip. Her eyes shut tightly, and there was next to nothing for color along her face.

"Claire, sweetie." Her professor hovered above us. Claire's eyes opened, and I brushed my thumb over the arch of her cheek, ignoring the rising nausea in my stomach. It was like watching my world crumble, just knowing that she was hurt. I panicked. "How many fingers am I holding up?"

Her head shook against my palm, and she tried to sit up. "No, stay where you are," I whispered. "Answer her question. How many fingers?"

Claire looked again. "I..." her voice cracked. "I can't tell. Three?" Her eyes blinked again. "I'm not sure. It's a little blurry, and I...I have a headache."

Goddamnit. My arms went under her legs, and I stood up, careful to keep her steady. "Don't fall asleep," I demanded. "And keep your eyes open."

Aasher opened the door and said, "I have the car ready. Let's go."

I nodded and held on tighter to Claire, not even bothering to see if Chad was still lingering. I'd deal with him later. Right now, Claire was the priority, and I was quickly realizing that she was always going to be the priority.

———

I hadn't been in a hospital since the time I slipped on the ice without my helmet on and busted my head, needing stitches. My mother was livid, but my father only shrugged and asked her what she expected from Rachel's son—

Rachel being my real mother, the one we never brought up. It was a loss that the entire family mourned and continued to mourn to this day.

"What are they saying?" Ford's voice was distant on the phone, and I was pretty sure I was on speaker.

"They did a CT, making sure she doesn't have a brain bleed. I haven't been back in the room. I'm not family, so I can't go in, which is fucking ridiculous because they let Taytum in."

"Well, I hate to admit it, but she's prettier than you."

"You're not funny." I rolled my eyes as I leaned against the wall in the emergency room waiting area. There were only a few people here, but their eyes were moving to me every few minutes, probably because I was wearing my jersey but wasn't at the game.

"Um, I hate to ask but...when you gettin' here, Wolf?" There was some jumbling on the phone, and I knew that Ford had taken me off speaker. "I can only stall Coach for so long. He's gonna start throwing shit soon."

I dangled Aasher's keys in my hand, spinning them back and forth several times to calm my nerves. "When I know Claire is okay."

Ford stayed silent, and I ignored the throbbing in the back of my skull as I angled my head up to the ceiling. "I'll be there before the whistle blows."

"You know Tom is still here, right?"

Fuck.

"I know."

"Where the fuck is Theo?" I cringed at Coach's gruff voice in the background and quickly hung up and began pacing back and forth, holding my phone with a death grip.

The door swung open, and I stopped in my tracks, landing on Taytum.

"How is she?" I asked.

I loved hockey. I breathed hockey. My future was hockey. But nothing seemed important in this moment except for Claire, and I would be fucking damned if I made her feel as insignificant as she had in the past. I wouldn't leave this hospital until I knew she was okay and she knew that I was out here waiting.

"She's tired. A little dizzy. She has a concussion, but they don't think it's anything more serious than that. Still waiting for the results, though."

"Does she know I'm out here?"

Before Taytum could answer, the air in the waiting room turned to ice, and she began to glare. I spun around, and suddenly, I was back on the ice, ready to tear down my opponent.

"Leave."

Chad's shoulders straightened, and he leveled me with a scowl not even close to as intimidating as the one on my face. I was seething. My chest was beginning to fill with hot rage, and if I didn't feel the presence of the security off to the left, I would have pummeled the shit out of this fuck-boy.

"Do you feel good about what you did?" I took a step forward and shook my head, getting straight to the point. "Why do you keep fucking showing up? Every time I turn around, you're there, fucking something up for Claire. I don't understand."

Chad cleared his throat. "You wanna know why I keep showing up?"

Taytum stepped forward. "Chad, just leave. Nothing good can come from you being here right now." Taytum turned toward me. "And you have a game to get to. You need to go too."

"I'm not going anywhere until I see her."

Chad laughed, and I snapped my attention over to him. *Is he purposely egging me on?* "I think I can take it from here, bud."

I tilted my head and the step toward him was menacing at best. "You think you can take it from here? You couldn't even take care of her when she was yours."

"*Was?*"

I knew that Chad thought that he was above a guy like me, someone who was using their physical strength and skill to progress in their future versus someone who was using their prestigious last name and Daddy's money, but I wasn't as stupid as he thought I was.

"Yes, *was*. She isn't yours anymore. Trust me."

His grin pissed me off, and if I was the type of guy who couldn't control his emotions, I might have actually wound my fist back and punched him, despite the security guard getting closer to us.

"She hasn't told you." Chad threw his head back and laughed. "She's still mine, Wolf. But it's pretty typical of Claire not to tell you. She has a hard time relying on anyone but herself. Why do you think she was nearly killing herself onstage? She and her mother need the money so she doesn't have to rely on me."

What?

"Chad!" Taytum's hands landed on his chest, and she pushed him back. He went willingly, winking at me as he backed away to the doors.

"Enjoy her while you have her."

What the fuck does that mean?

My heart was pounding, and my blood was rushing like Niagara Falls, but everything faded when the door to the ER opened, and a doctor popped his head out, looking for the family of Claire Bryant. I spun around and walked ahead of Taytum as she was pushing Chad out the doors with the security guard creeping toward them.

"I'm her brother," I lied. "How is she?"

The doctor's brows furrowed, and he looked over at the receptionist behind the glass window who had told me I couldn't go back with Claire just hours prior. She looked at me, then to Chad and to Taytum, obviously aware of the whole conversation. To my surprise, she nodded at the doctor, and he shrugged, ushering me to follow him.

I mouthed a thank-you to the receptionist, and the old lady winked at me. I followed the white coat and listened intently as he told me that Claire's CT came back okay but that it was confirmed that she had a concussion, and he wanted to keep her a little longer to make sure the dizziness subsided and she didn't get worse.

I nodded before he pointed to her room. "She's a little woozy but is awake. You can go on in."

I sidestepped him, pulled the curtain aside, and watched as she breathed in and out of her mouth with her eyes closed.

"Hey, you," I said, stepping farther into the room. Claire sat up quickly and immediately winced before lying back onto the pillow. "Whoa, take it easy, Bryant."

"Theo." Her brows furrowed, and I noticed that she had taken her hair out of her bun at some point. I watched from across the room as her shoulders dropped in disappointment. "I can't believe I fell."

"We all fall sometimes," I said, absolutely aware that there was a double meaning behind my words.

"I've never seen you fall," she countered, blowing a breath out of her mouth again.

"On the ice? All the time." I chuckled, trying to lighten

the mood a little. I sat down on the edge of her bed, careful not to put too much pressure on it. I lifted my hair up and showed her the tiny scar on the very top of my forehead. "Four stitches. And you've been to my games. You know I fall."

The softest laugh left her, but she quickly stopped and dropped her jaw. "Oh my God. What are you doing here?"

I pulled back. "What do you mean? Why wouldn't I be here?"

"You have a game, Theo! What time is it?"

"Hey." I stood up, hovered over her, and pushed her back onto her pillow. "Rest."

"Theo, what are you doing here?!" She lay back, but panic still backed every one of her words.

Without even meaning to, I crowded her space and stared down into her eyes. "I'm here to make sure you're okay. Game or no game, I wasn't leaving until I knew."

The color was back on her face, and the satisfaction it gave me was indescribable. *Now I could play with a steady head.* "Well, I'm fine! Go to your game right now, Theo Brooks! Whatever happened to *'hockey is the most important thing in your life'*?"

She seemed exasperated, and it was kind of cute how stressed out she was, but before I caused any more unnecessary stress for her, I leaned down and kissed her forehead before whispering, "It's important, but I'm beginning to realize it may not be the most important thing anymore."

Because after all, what was a future without her in it?

36

THEO

Coach's disapproving insults left my head the second I stepped foot in the rink, three minutes before the whistle blew. I didn't have time to warm up with the team, and though I was captain and would have been frustrated if any of the other guys had pulled this stunt, my teammates understood, and each of them patted me on the back after asking how Claire was.

The game was close, but the moment the last puck slid into the net, courtesy of Landon, I threw my stick down and ripped my helmet off. The buzzer rang, and we skated over to him, patting him on the back as the arena roared. Don't think I didn't notice that Claire's voice wasn't screaming my name, though. I missed seeing her in the stands with my jersey, and I thought about her within every empty space my brain could hold between plays.

I hurriedly undressed and threw on my sweats all while getting bitched at by Coach once more. He didn't buy my excuses about why I was late and kept poking me to tell him the truth, threatening back-to-back suicides, all of which I agreed to do.

"I don't blame you for punishing me, Coach. I'll do whatever it is you want me to do. I deserve it."

"Goddamn it, Wolf!" he yelled, pulling the attention from every player still in the locker room. "Quit being so accepting. It's only making me angrier."

"It would suck to be your daughter. Can't please you," someone mumbled in the back of the locker room.

The attention was pulled from me as Coach's face turned a shade of purple I'd never seen before. *Thank fuck.* I pulled my phone out of my locker and grinned at the photo of Claire and Taytum both resting in the hospital bed that was attached to her text.

Claire: Did you win?

Just as I was about to text back, there was a hush that traveled throughout the locker room like a tidal wave, and silence erupted. I spun around with my phone still in my hand and landed on the hockey god himself: Tom Gardini.

I knew he would be here. He told me he would, which was why Coach was even angrier than usual at me for being late. The phrases *'fucking up your future'* and *'making yourself look lazy and irresponsible'* were thrown around a few times before my skates hit the ice.

"Can we use your office, Coach Lennon?" Tom, dressed in his black Armani suit, pulled his stare from me and landed on my coach.

"Sure," Coach said before going back to hurling insults at whatever dipshit made a comment about his daughter.

Tom inched his head to the office, and I followed after him, shoving my phone in my pocket and preparing to defend myself and my character. Coach Lennon said that Tom Gardini didn't allow players on his team that weren't of good nature, so I hoped that he could see my side of things.

The moment the door shut, my nerves squeezed together just as tightly as my fists were bundled in my lap. I rested my back against the chair at the foot of Coach's messy desk and spread my sore legs out in front of me.

"You were late." Tom got right to the point. He didn't skirt around the topic or make small talk, which I appreciated.

"I was," I answered, looking him right in the eye. Tom was a clean-shaven man in his fancy suit, holding his expensive cane. His face was clear of scruff, his brown hair was gelled to the side, and despite him being old enough to be my father, he didn't seem weathered.

Tom kept his mouth shut and continued to stare at me. I glanced away and rolled my lips together before leaning forward and steepling my hands together to try and dig myself out of a hole.

"Listen," I started. "Hockey is important to me. I think that point has been made obvious over the years." I flicked my gaze to his and saw he was listening intently without a flicker of irritation on his features. Coach, on the other hand, would be red-faced with steam coming from his ears. "And I have never in my life been late to a practice or game in the last four years of being at Bexley U."

"I'm aware," Tom said, nodding with a tight jaw.

"There was an emergency."

"I'm also aware."

Okay, then. I leaned back and eyed him cautiously before getting right to the point. "Correct me if I'm wrong, but you don't seem all that upset. Should I be digging myself out of a hole, giving up my first-born to still be considered an option, or..."

"How is she?"

Wait, what?

"Uh..." I was more confused at this moment than I was when I had woken up drunk on top of the Zamboni the morning after our high school championship game. "You mean—"

"Claire," he finished for me, leaning on top of Coach's desk. Tom's eyes hardened, but within them, I saw a vulner-ability that was all too familiar. "How is Claire?"

How does he know her?

"She's...she's okay. She has a concussion."

He breathed out a sigh, and I couldn't stop myself from questioning him.

"I'm sorry, but how—"

I stopped mid-sentence as I tried sorting through the confusion, but that was when I saw it. The flicker of fear ran across his features. When he opened his mouth, he paused before looking away. "Well, Theo...she's my daughter."

I blinked. That was the only thing I could do at that moment. My brain was blank besides the conversation that Claire and I'd had about her father, which was on replay.

"That can't be." My jaw was hinged tightly, molded with anger and confusion. "Because the Tom Gardini that I've looked up to since I was ten years old was painted as a decent man with righteous morals. I've been told you only allow players on your team that are of good character, but what kind of man abandons their daughter and never looks back?"

Claire and her mother had struggled from the begin-ning. She told me her mother had never been able to recover emotionally or financially since he left them. Claire had been *killing* herself this semester by working, attending classes, and dancing to win the scholarship because of the financial strain, and to think that this man, who was wealthier than most of America, was the reason?

It hit too close to home for me, and some would say that this was an insert-foot-into-mouth kind of moment, but sometimes, the truth hurt, and by the look on Tom's face, it stung.

"What did you just say?"

"I said, what kind of man abandons their daughter?" An angered breath left me, and I wasn't sure if I was ruining my chances at a career in the NHL or just my chances with him, but defending Claire felt like the right move, and I wasn't going to back down. "And please don't tell me that you're only interested in me because of her."

"That is *not* true." Tom was angry, but so was I.

"Which part?" I snapped back to him. "The part where you abandoned her or the part that you're not interested in me because of her. I should have known better. What kind of NHL team owner scouts his own players?"

Tom and I were in a complete stare-down. His blue eyes were laser focused on mine, and my chest was ripped wide open with unshed anger and disappointment. Not only was I disappointed about learning that he wasn't as righteous of a man as I had painted him to be, but also because it felt as if all my hard work was a joke that had erupted in laughter the moment he pulled me in here to talk about Claire instead of me joining his team.

Not to mention, seeing a man this successful sit in front of me to ask about his daughter, whom he'd allegedly left as a baby, felt all too familiar to my own scars. Didn't he know that Claire struggled with money? Didn't he know that her mother relied on her to pay for things back home while she was working tirelessly at The Bex and dancing to win a scholarship so she didn't have to figure out how to balance everything? And don't even get me fucking started on what Chad had said about Claire relying on him for money.

Tom finally spoke, splitting the ice around the room. "None of that is true. I didn't seek you out because of her. I have had my eye on you since your sophomore year because of sheer talent and your drive to succeed. You remind me a lot of myself at that age, and I'll admit, if you had been late for any reason other than making sure my daughter was okay, I might have reamed you just as hard as your coach. But how can I be angry with someone who has a piece of my soul in their best interest?" My mouth opened, but I stopped myself so he could continue. "And I give you props for defending her, even to me, but you have it wrong. I didn't abandon her. *They* abandoned me."

"Wh–what?" I asked, bending forward to place my elbows on my knees.

"Sit back," he demanded. "Because we have a lot to discuss."

37

CLAIRE

I spun around in the mirror and dipped my gaze down to my tanned leg sticking out from the black dress that Rose lent to me. At least the leg that had slipped out from the split in the thin black fabric wasn't the one sporting the nasty blue bruise from my fall onstage.

My face burned at the memory of my fall, and although it was just two days ago, I still felt the sting of embarrassment like it was an hour prior. I had a meeting with Professor Petit on Monday, and I wasn't sure what to expect. I was sure they'd given the lead role to someone else, which made sense, but *shit*. I needed it. I really, really needed it.

"Here." Taytum popped beside me in the mirror and handed me a black mask with feathers and small bright gems outlining the sides. I took it hesitantly, still unsure I wanted to be at her sorority party after such a wonky weekend. I'd hardly spoken to Theo since he left me in the hospital on Friday evening. He got in from his game late, having had a lengthy conversation with his coach and Tom Gardini. I was exhausted from my concussion, and the doctor recommended resting as much as possible for at least twenty-four hours, and Theo had taken the concussion protocol very seriously, along with the rest of his team.

They had dropped off an eye mask, an extra-comfy pillow, an entire case of water, and headphones to block out any noise. I made the joke that they just wanted their favorite waitress back at The Bex for extra fries, but instead of laughing, they each wrapped me in a light hug and demanded I text them if I needed something while Theo was slaving away in the rink at their coach's demand.

I felt terrible about that.

Theo didn't let on that he was in trouble for being late to his game, but considering he was hardly in our dorm all weekend, and when he did come back, he was covered in sweat, it was obvious he was trying to make it up to the team.

He told me not to worry and checked on me every few hours in the middle of the night to make sure I was okay, but I still felt like something was off. We hadn't chatted about *why* I'd taken a fall during my rehearsal, and to be honest, I hadn't wanted to think about it. The doctor said to rest my brain, and thinking too much about Chad, my mother, or the future would have been the complete opposite of resting.

And even though going to a masquerade party at Alpha Chi Omega, Taytum's sorority, just a few days later, wasn't my idea of fun, what was I if not a good friend to the girl who had stayed in the hospital with me the entire evening, missing her own audition?

"You look hot."

I flipped my hair over my shoulder. "I look hot in Rose's old prom dress? That's a compliment I'll take, I guess."

Taytum laughed as Rose entered the room, along with one of her friends who eyed Taytum and me nervously.

"No surprise that you look better in that dress than I did." Rose huffed as she pulled her red mask over her face, applying lipstick a moment later. Taytum did the same, and I was next, noticing how blue my eyes looked against the black mask surrounding them.

"So, is Ford your hot date?" I asked, peeking over at Taytum, who was strapping her heels on. I opted for flat sandals, although my feet were going to be freezing if I decided to go outside in the chilly, near-winter air, but heels weren't the best option for someone who was still sporting an ankle injury.

"Emory would lose his shit, and plus, I don't have dates for these sorts of parties."

Rose's silent friend spoke up. "I thought having a date was a rule."

"I don't follow rules." Taytum smiled deviously, and I laughed under my breath.

"And Theo is your date?" the girl asked quietly, taking her eyes from me as soon as I looked over.

"Um, yeah," I answered, rolling my lips together. This was something Theo and I had planned to go to weeks prior when we were still in our era of fake dating. I wasn't sure what we were now, but it wasn't fake. "I haven't talked with him much, but he should be here. He's been on the ice almost all weekend." I sighed. "Which was my fault."

"How so?" Taytum asked, opening the door to her room. The noise from the foyer floated up the stairs, and butterflies overtook my belly at the thought of Theo seeing me dressed up.

"He's getting punished for being late to the game on Friday."

"Oh, right." Taytum darted her eyes away, and the blush on her cheeks looked a little darker than before.

"What?" I asked, eyeing her suspiciously. It wasn't like her to hide something from me, but the telling look in her eyes was even more obvious with a mask on.

Rose and her friend left Taytum and me alone, and the very second they were down the stairs, she pulled me in close. "Has Chad texted you?"

I shrugged. "I don't think so. I haven't really had my phone. The doctor told me I needed to stay away from electronics for a couple of days. Why?"

"He showed up at the hospital."

That was a swift blow to my mood. "The nerve," I gritted, crossing my arms over my chest. "He's the reason I fell. He was glaring at me from the back, just behind Theo and the rest of the guys." Tom Gardini was there too, but I kept that to myself.

"I know. I saw him as we were leaving, and then he showed up at the hospital, and I thought Theo was going to go to jail by the mere look on his face."

Panic rushed to my heart. "What? Did he say something to him?"

"Not in so many words, but..." Taytum sighed. "You need to tell Theo what's really going on if you two are more than what you say you are."

We are. We are more than what we say we are. Right?

"I don't know what to say." I peered down the length of the black shimmery dress. "I don't know what to do, Tay. Chad has me in a chokehold—and not in a good way."

"You need to tell him to fuck off."

"My mom does not have the money to pay his parents

back all that she owes, and not to mention, my mom's entire income is held by a string that his parents can untie in a single second. Then what? She'll be homeless because she can't afford her rent? I will have to drop out of school before my senior year and pay—"

Taytum's hands wrapped around my upper arms. "No, Claire." Her blonde waves bounced as she shook her head. "Your mother's financial situation is not your burden. What do you think she'd say if she knew that Chad had cheated on you and then pretty much blackmailed you into staying in some sort of fucked-up relationship with him just to save her job? That's ridiculous, and if your mother is deserving of all that you've given her, she'd never ever stand for that kind of disrespect. Are you willing to give up what you feel for Theo for her?"

"She'd feel betrayed by me if she knew that I blatantly picked Theo over her. Because that's what I would be doing. That's why I'm trying so hard to—"

"To what? Have your cake and eat it too? Because no matter how I see it, Chad is going to try to destroy you and your mother if you don't do what he says. He's a narcissist, and he's using your selflessness to trap you in a future that you will regret for the rest of your life, and to be honest, Theo deserves to know what's going on because that hunky jock has fallen hard for you."

The door opened downstairs, and my gaze drifted over the banister and into the foyer. Several broad-shouldered guys walked in, each of them wearing black suits and black masks, stealing everyone's breath. I knew which one was Theo just by the air that surrounded him. My stomach dipped the moment he peered up the steps. Our eyes snagged right away, and I burned when his soft lips parted and curled on one side.

"See?" Taytum whispered. "And don't you dare tell me that you haven't fallen for him. I hardly recognize you when you look at him—and that isn't a bad thing."

I let out a soft breath and smiled down at him.

I'd ruin the world for Theo Brooks, and it was about time I told him.

38

THEO

She was devastating.

I was stuck in the entryway with an entire party occurring around me as I watched her descend down the stairs after her best friend. The only thing I could see was her toned leg slipping out from behind her dress and those icy eyes set on me like I was the only guy in the room.

The universe was aligned when she entered the world, and I would be a damn fool if I ever let her out of my grasp. I'd already proven to myself that I'd fallen for her, but I still felt like I needed to prove it to her. The only thing stopping me was a recent truth that was spitting fire in the back of my head every time I thought of her.

After learning what Tom had told me, I could hardly look Claire in the face without spilling every last detail, but I knew that a few hours after getting a concussion wasn't the best time, so instead, I held onto the truth and avoided her.

And now, here I was, holding my hand out to her in the middle of a fucking sorority party, wanting to do nothing but live in the moment and see her smile instead of watch her world get flipped on its side by a man who had the power to grant me my future but potentially break all of the trust Claire and I had formed together.

Either way I looked at it, I had been put in a shitty position—tell Claire what I'd learned or wait until Tom showed up and we'd tell her together. I had no idea what to do, but all I wanted to do right now was pull her in close and press my lips to hers.

Her soft hand fell to mine, and still, it felt like it was just the two of us in the room. There was chatter around us, and everyone was staring, but the only thing I focused on was her.

"Hey," she whispered, taking a step closer to me.

I tugged her in closer and wrapped my hand around her waist. "Hey," I breathed down into her space. *Damn, she was like a fucking drug.* "I miss you."

Her mouth opened slightly from the truth spilling from mine. "You do?"

I nodded, moving my hand from her waist and cupping the side of her face. "Can I kiss you?"

"Since when do you ask?" She grinned, but I didn't have it in me to smile. Instead, I bounced my eyes back and forth between hers and dipped down, pressing a soft kiss against her mouth. Since the beginning, our touches and kisses had been to fool other people and were fueled by none other than desire and lust. But this moment was different.

This was intimate, and she felt it. She pulled back and paused for a split second before grabbing onto my hand and dragging me toward the stairs.

"Where are we going?" I asked.

"Upstairs."

We were all but running by the end, and I almost

stopped so I could pick her up because I knew that her ankle was still bruised from her fall. I lifted the covers this morning while she was sleeping and cursed at the blue bruise before I ran to the rink to continue the extra conditioning ordered by Coach.

"Bryant, slow it down," I said, out of breath. Not from physical exertion, though, more so because that was just what she did to me.

Her devilish grin peered over her shoulder, and if I wasn't already a goner, I would be by the look in her eye. The door slammed behind me, and although the only light throughout the random bedroom was from the moon shining a glow through the window, I could see every last inch of her.

I leaned against the door as she stood in front of me. Time seemed to slow as silence settled around us, and I hesitantly reached my hands out in front of me. My fingers slipped underneath the black disguise, and I pulled it up and over her head, dropping it to the floor beside us. My heart did a triple-take, and a swallow got lodged in my throat.

Claire did the same to me, slipping her delicate fingers underneath the mask and reaching up on her tiptoes to pull the rest of it over my head. She dropped it right beside hers, and I pulled her in close, gripping her tightly because I was afraid that, sooner or later, she'd slip right through my fingers.

"What are you doing?" I pressed, half afraid to know the answer.

Her light and airy tone calmed me almost instantly. "Showing you how I really feel about you."

My heart came to life at the sight of her timid smile. It could have been the end of the world, and I would have been perfectly content, standing here with her body in my hands.

Claire took a step back from me, and silence came between us, but that was what was special about the two of us. We didn't need words. All it took was one look.

Her hand moved to her shoulder, and the thin strap that held the dress up slipped down her arm, and I gulped, watching her undress. "Claire," I croaked. *Fuck. Fuck. Fuck.* "Wait."

"No." A deep breath left her. "I know we need to talk, Theo. But let's just live in the now. We can talk after."

I clenched my teeth and fell for her pretty words because I'd rather die than deprive her of what she wanted.

My hands fell to the pockets of my suit pants, and I tipped my chin, watching her accept my silence for what it was. The tiniest smile caught my eye, but I quickly moved to her hand as she reached over and delicately shoved the other strap of her dress off her shoulder, showing off the top of her bare chest.

Temptation is a bitch.

"Spin," I demanded, pushing myself off the door and eyeing the zipper on the back of her dress. The sound fueled my desire like gasoline on a fire. I let my finger trail down her spine as I unzipped the dress, letting it fall to her hips. I took a step back, and rested against the door again, placing my hands back in my pockets. *Fuck.*

She spun back around, pushing her hair over her shoulder and giving me a full view of her naked chest. My mouth watered, and although I wanted to stand there and watch her undress, I had to do something with my hands or I was going to lose all control. So, just as she was tugging the dress past her hips, I shrugged off my suit jacket and kept my eyes trained to hers as I slowly began unbuttoning my white shirt.

Claire stood in front of me with nothing on but a pair of panties, and I fought the urge to pounce on her. Instead, I shoved my white shirt off my shoulders and let it fall to the ground behind me before moving my hands to my belt. Claire's nipples tightened at the clanking sound, and before I knew it, she had shoved my hands away and finished the job, pushing my pants down and then my boxers.

She gasped when she saw that I was already hard, and I threw my head back when her hand gripped me tightly. It felt good. It felt better than most, and that was simply because it was *her*.

I palmed her waist and picked her up, carrying her over to the bed. Instead of throwing her on it and ravishing her body like I wanted, I slowly sat down with her straddling me and peered up at her sweet face as her brown locks surrounded us like a veil.

I wanted to say *I love you*, but I didn't because it didn't feel right after knowing what I knew and hiding it from her. So instead, I would show her.

"You're perfect," I whispered, peeling her panties down her legs as she lifted up. We were skin on skin. Bare. Just the way I wanted it.

"So are you." Claire sat back down on my lap, and my blood ran hot. Her mouth fell to mine, and the kiss was soft and slow with meaning behind it that I couldn't put into words.

Neither one of us said anything else.

Our mouths moved against each other like it was the most natural thing in the world. My tongue dipped inside, and hers did too. I kissed the side of her neck as she hovered over me, and when she sunk down, I swore I touched heaven.

We were in a slow frenzy. Havoc was occurring on the inside, but we weren't chaotic or rushed. There was no uncertainty or confusion. We both knew that we were in the right place, tangled in one another while putting a pause on everything else.

"Theo," Claire buried her head into the crook of my sweaty neck, and my hand fell to her lower back before I spun her around and laid her down flat. I pushed farther inside of her, my movements slow and steady as I stared down at the euphoric glaze in her eyes. They fluttered closed, and I looked down, watching how perfectly we fit together.

I pulled out of her, slick with her wetness, before plunging back into her and catching her gasps with my mouth. "God," I whispered, moving quicker as I felt her winding up against me. She met me halfway. "The feeling you give me is addicting." The second I hit her sweet spot, she threw her head back and set my world on its side as she came all over my dick.

God. Damn.

I pulled out a moment later and came on her stomach, capturing the hottest visual of my life and saving it for the end of time. I could be ninety years old and still get hard picturing her fully fucked with red cheeks and my come all over her stomach.

"Are you thinking what I'm thinking?" I asked after cleaning her up and catching our breath. I began to slip the dress back over the curves of her body, wanting nothing more than to palm her ass again.

Claire peered up at me with her gentle smile. The party was in full swing. It wasn't loud or frenzied like the parties at the football house, but I would rather be anywhere than where we were now. "It depends. What are you thinking?"

I burned with hope, and it was the strangest feeling not being as confident with Claire as I had been when we first met. There was an inkling that I was going to lose her at some point, and I wasn't sure I'd survive the loss. Maybe it was because the entire premise of our relationship was fake. Regardless, the fear of letting her slip right through my fingers was damn near paralyzing.

"I'm thinking your concussion is giving you a headache." I winked. "And I must take you back to the dorms immediately."

An instant smile split across her face, and I latched onto her bright teeth and swollen lips. I cocked an eyebrow, silently asking if she agreed.

Claire nodded slowly. "The dorm with you sounds like a way better place to be."

Damn straight, baby.

As we crept down the stairs, I kept my eye on the door and nowhere else. I didn't want to see Aasher or Ford and their suggestive faces. I didn't want Taytum rushing over to pull Claire away. All I wanted was to take my girl back to the dorms and be with her for the rest of the night.

I'd been avoiding her, and I wasn't lying when I said I missed her.

And I knew we needed to talk. We *really* needed to talk, especially after what just happened upstairs because that, my friends, *wasn't* just a fuck.

"And where are you two going?" Taytum slipped right in front of the door as my hand reached out to open it. *Damnit.*

"Um..." Claire nibbled on her lip, and I quickly swiped

my thumb over it. The plopping noise went straight to my dick despite that it was just inside of her.

"Claire has a headache," I said, lying straight through my teeth. Taytum half-rolled her eyes, but I saw the hint of a smile.

"Oh, I'm sure she does," she joked, pulling Claire in for a swift hug. I didn't let go of her hand, though, because I was beginning to see that I was selfish when it came to her. I squinted when I watched Taytum whisper something into Claire's ear, causing her to nod sharply.

"Ready?" I asked, tipping my chin in a lazy goodbye to the rest of the hockey players. I skimmed the party for a quick moment, and I stopped with one foot out the door as I landed on someone who was leaning against the far wall with a red cup in their hand.

There was a girl draped against his side like some cheap, drunken date, but his sight was on me, and then it moved down to my hand in Claire's.

"Theo?" Claire looked up at me and then over to where I was unmistakably glaring. Her hand tightened in mine, but to my surprise, she pulled me out the door and put her back to Chad.

I poked her with a question that I wasn't sure I wanted the answer to but needed to hear directly from the source. "We're no longer making him jealous?" I asked, opening the door to my car and ushering her inside. There was a slight worry embedded in between her eyebrows, but her eyes were as stern and true as ever when she shook her head.

"No, and it was never about that to begin with." Her door shut, and I knew that when we got back to our room, we were going to have to talk.

39

CLAIRE

THE NERVES WERE EATING me up inside. The high I'd felt from kissing Theo had been slowly slipping away since the moment I saw Chad staring at us inside the Alpha Chi Omega house. He was beginning to show his face everywhere I was, and that could only mean one thing: he was starting to realize that he was the only one playing the little game he started between us.

"Fuck, it's cold." Theo opened the door to the dorms, and we both rushed inside. Goosebumps covered my arms, but Theo quickly draped his black suit jacket over my shoulders and picked me up like he was carrying a bride to their honeymoon.

"Theo!" I couldn't control my laughter. "I can walk. Again, for the hundredth time."

"I know you can." He held on tighter. "I just like holding you."

A gush of warmth left me as I smiled, wrapping my hands around his neck.

"And how can I not touch you in that dress? It's almost as good as seeing you in my jersey."

My heart grew, and I held onto the feeling as we rounded the hallway and headed to our rooms. I knew that, when we got inside, I was going to have to put some space between us and tell him what was really going on with Chad.

I wasn't necessarily afraid to tell him. I trusted Theo with my secrets and worries, which was definitely a step in the right direction. But I was worried there wouldn't be a good outcome, and that was something I *was* afraid of.

Theo paused at the end of the hall, and I glanced up at him when his arms grew tighter around me. "What's wrong?" I asked, watching as his jaw turned to stone. I followed his gaze, fearful that somehow Chad had beaten us here, but I quickly moved to be placed on my feet when I saw that it wasn't Chad, but instead, it was Tom Gardini.

"What is he doing here?" I half-whispered, peering up at Theo again. "And why do you look so angry?"

Tom leaned on his cane and pushed up from resting against our dorm door as Theo slowed our steps. "Theo," I whispered again, jerking on his hand to give me some inclination of what was going on and why his spine was suddenly tense.

When he looked down at me, my heart skipped a beat. There was no longer anger. Instead, there was fear, and if I could have, I would have moved in front of him to take the bullet. What bullet? I wasn't sure, but I'd block it if I could.

"Um, hi," I said, looking back and forth between Tom and Theo. Tom surveyed our joined hands, and confusion trickled down my spine. *What the hell is going on?*

Tom cleared his throat after pulling his attention from

Theo's hand in mine. He didn't seem haughty and poised like the last time I saw him. Instead, he looked... vulnerable.

Did he promise Theo something and went back on his word?

"Hi, Claire." Tom's knuckles turned white as he gripped the top of his cane tightly.

"Tom..." Theo warned.

"Okay," I blurted. "What is going on?"

Theo and Tom both looked at me with fear, and I took a step back, dropping Theo's hand in the process. My arms crossed over my chest as I waited for an explanation.

"Theo? Did something happen?" I slowly looked over at Tom and noticed the wrinkled edges to his eyes as the air grew stiffer around us. I dropped my voice slightly. "Isn't this...the owner of the team you want to play on?"

Tom's laugh was abrupt. "I'm sorry, but... You don't know the name of the team I own?"

"Why would she?" Theo stepped forward, and the only thing he was missing was shining armor and a sword. He didn't necessarily seem angry, but he was acting awfully protective over me.

"Theo?" I questioned. "What is going on?"

"So, you didn't tell her?" Tom asked Theo, both of them ignoring me.

Theo's shoulders fell slightly, and although he looked defeated, his words came out sharp. "I don't want to do your dirty work. No matter the truth, and definitely not because I want to wear a Blues jersey."

Just then, my heart began to race, and my head started to thump. Only, this time, I knew it wasn't from the concussion. There was a definite regret slicing away at Theo's poised features, and the trust I had found within him suddenly felt unstable.

Tom sighed. "Maybe we should sit."

"No."

Tom and Theo both appeared startled at my sharp answer, but Theo's nod in my direction propelled me to look over at his former idol. "What's going on? Did you find out that Theo and I are fake dating or something? Because I can tell you that it's not fake anymore, and if you don't give him a chance to be on your team because you think he is of bad character for lying or you think he'll be distracted by puck bunnies in the NHL, then you're going to be losing out—"

"Claire, um..." Tom stepped forward, but he stopped before taking another deep breath. It was bizarre to see someone so confident lose their footing. "There's really no easy way to say this..." His hand gripped his cane tighter, and I braced myself for the impact. "I'm your father."

My heart completely descended to my feet, and my lungs burned for oxygen. It took entirely too long for me to suck in a sharp breath, and when I did, it felt like a punch to my lower stomach. My hand immediately went to it, and I wanted to double over, but instead, I spoke with conviction.

"No, you're not," I argued, looking him up and down and spying his fancy leather shoes and nicely pressed suit. Even his cane looked expensive, and it was a slap to the face. With every hardship my mother and I had faced, every late bill or red notice taped to our door, I blamed him. And to see this man, standing in front of me, with his expensive taste and eyes set on Theo, I refused to believe it.

"I am," he whispered gently.

"He is, Claire."

Although Theo's agreement was smooth and steady, it

still made me jump. My eyes were beginning to gloss over as I stared at him with confusion.

My voice broke in all the wrong spots as surprise pulled me into the deep end. "You knew?"

I suddenly understood what real betrayal felt like.

It didn't feel this potent when Chad had cheated on me. It didn't feel this potent when Chad had threatened me, either. It didn't even feel this potent when my mother had used the money I'd given her for something other than her bills.

This is what real heartbreak feels like.

"So, what?" I asked, my question teetering between anger and pain. Theo took a step toward me, but I stepped one back. "Is that how you got on a spot on his team? Was I some kind of trade or something? Lead him to me, and you get your dream?" I turned to Tom. "What do you even want from me? To come crawling back like my mother and I didn't suffer from your departure?"

"Wait, what?" I'd never heard panic like I'd just heard come from Theo's mouth. "You were not some kind of trade, Claire. I'd give up every last one of my dreams for you."

Emotions were flooding me, and I would have been lying if I said I was adapted to deal with them. I hid from the hard stuff. I compartmentalized problems and feelings like they had no real ties to one another, but standing here, looking at two sets of eyes who were waiting for me to say something, I learned that I had two very serious problems on my hands and a few more waiting for me on the other side.

My fingers dug into my temples, and I cursed. "Ugh!" I pushed past both men and held my hand out to Theo. "Give me the dorm key."

Theo reached into his pocket and handed me the key,

staying in the exact spot that I'd left him. I rushed inside the room and slammed the door behind me. I was only in there for thirty seconds, and when I came back out, both men were glowering down the hall, apparently on the same playing field, and neither one of them looked over at me.

"Please move," I said, trying my hardest to keep it together until I was alone. Tom scooted over, just far enough that I could slip between him and Theo, but again, he didn't look over at me.

Theo did, though.

I felt him without even looking. I was overflowing with hurt and confusion, and if I thought I could stand there and look over at him as he stood beside a man who was apparently as shallow as they came, I would, but I knew the second I caught his eye, I'd feel the cut.

So, instead, I brushed past and ignored my name falling from his lips. I headed straight to the end of the hall with my car keys digging into the palm of my hand, helping me focus on the physical pain instead of the way my heart was slipping away.

"Claire, please. Just wait!"

"Oh now, come on. It was never supposed to last, Wolf." My neck snapped at the sound of Chad's voice, and I slammed on the brakes before I crashed head on. "Are you done messing around with him and ready to stop playing the game?"

My blood pressure shot through the roof, and I glossed over the thought of jamming my keys into Chad's glasses to shatter them.

"You know what?" I said, surprised at how level my voice was. Chad's eyebrows hitched upward at the bitterness coming from my mouth. He was still sporting the suit I saw him in at the masquerade party minus the girl hanging off his arm like an ornament. "I am done with the game."

Chad's smirk was as haughty as they came, and the power I felt while looking at the relief on his features was enough to leave a trail of fire behind as I left. But that power turned to something else entirely as I looked over my shoulder and saw Theo standing there, looking as tormented as they came. The smile that I watched for on the ice when he'd search the crowd for me had disappeared, and instead, his lips were flattened with the tiniest frown lines edged along his smooth face. His square jaw was slack, and his hands were down by his sides, and even though it felt like I'd reached inside my chest and pulled out my own heart, I allowed the hurt and betrayal of all three men in the hallway to back my next words.

"I'm done with all the games." I made sure to stare right at Theo with my next sentiment. "We were never supposed to last anyway, right?" I briefly moved over to Tom, who was part of the reason why Theo and I even started our stupid fake relationship.

A moment later, I brushed past Chad, unable to care about his threat and blackmailing scheme. I suddenly didn't care about anything anymore.

His hand landed on my arm at the last second, and I all but bared my teeth. My palm that had the tiniest drop of blood on it from my keys digging against my skin slapped over his wrist.

"Hands off." I paused at the sound of Tom's voice that vibrated with anger. "Now."

Chad pulled back in confusion. He had no idea who Tom was to me. *Was he truly my father?* Regardless, Chad didn't remove his hand. In fact, his grip got tighter.

"I will break your arm in half." Theo was closer now,

and the way goosebumps rushed to my skin didn't go unnoticed by Chad. His eyes snapped to mine, and it was obvious he wasn't happy, but before anything else could happen, I slipped my thumb underneath his fingers and peeled them back one by one.

Then, I descended down the stairs of Dorothy Hall and didn't look back.

[40]

CLAIRE

I SCANNED the parking lot like I was looking for the police after committing a crime. I saw plenty of students rushing to and from classes, even recognizing some of the dancers from my Dance Theory class that I had skipped out on this morning. Instead, I opted to study for my finals inside my car behind The Bex, hoping no one would know I was there before I could rush off to my meeting with Professor Petit regarding my audition on Friday with the dreaded fall.

My phone had been off. The strength it took to shut it down and not turn it back on was something I possessed like a sixth sense. Avoidance apparently ran in my DNA, if it was true that Tom Gardini was actually my father.

I stepped out of my car, cursing at the creaking of the door, as if Theo or Chad were hiding in the bushes, ready to pop out at the sound of it. I crinkled my nose before pulling my light-blue beanie down on my head, angling my face away from the harsh wind. Fall had turned to winter in the last couple of months, but I hadn't noticed until now.

My hand shook slightly as I peeled open the door to the auditorium and walked farther inside. I pushed down the top of my book and glanced at my ankle. It was still bruised. I could have really used that ice bath, but I would rather chop off my ankle than face Theo at the moment.

"You need to ice it."

My keys fell, and the sound clattering against the floor sounded like a thousand bricks falling around us. I removed my gaze from the floor and slowly latched onto the voice from across the expansive, open room.

I wasn't sure how I would feel seeing Tom again, but it didn't surprise me that it was anger that fell from my lips. "A little too late for advice, don't you think?"

I swiftly bent down, swiped up my keys, and backed away from the man claiming to be my father. I had given up a long time ago wondering if he'd ever come back. I was a baby when he left, so it wasn't that I missed the tender presence of my father after all these years—I didn't even know him. Instead, I felt the sharp sting of disappointment and betrayal, and I was on a warpath for destruction.

"That's fair," he said, pulling himself to stand with his cane. I thought back to the story that Theo had told me about Tom before his claim had come to light, and I wondered how much of it was true. "Well..." Tom stopped my thoughts from progressing any further. "It would be fair if what you knew of me was the truth."

"Excuse me?" I wanted my words to come out as fierce as I was claiming to be, but instead, they were weak and brimmed with confusion.

"Do you know how long I've searched for you?"

My stomach twisted, but my chin raised as a defense mechanism.

"And do you know how many times I've been lied to in

my life? Trust is a fleeting thing as of late, Tom." Trust. I wasn't sure I'd ever trust anyone again.

Tom slowly sat back down, placing his cane beside him. I stood several feet away, and he made no move to ask me to sit. Instead, he jumped right into what he had to say with this no-bullshit attitude that somehow doubled as cautious.

"I guess that man does know you." Tom stared at me from across the shiny floor, and I swallowed, refusing to ask what he was talking about. "Theo said that I ruined the trust between you two, and for that, I'm truly sorry."

Tom wanted to get right to it? Well, so did I. "Is it true?"

"Which part?"

All of it. "Did you seek him out to get closer to me? Did he know you were my father?" I paused. "Are you even sure you're my father? Is that why you came to my audition? Catching up on all that you missed out on when you left?"

There was a hint of a smile on Tom's face, and it was soft and warm instead of smug or all-knowing. "Would you like to sit? There's a lot I need to tell you, Claire."

I hesitated at first, but before I knew it, I had taken a seat—three down from him, just out of spite, but at least I was sitting. *Just hear him out.*

"Firstly, no. Theo did not know until he showed up late to the hockey game, and I pulled him aside afterward." I saw him glance at me from my peripheral vision. "He thought I had pulled him into his coach's office to yell at him, but you know what? The second he heard me say that I was your father, he went into total defensive mode. And I'll admit, I wouldn't stand to be talked to like that by any of my players—or anyone in the industry, for that matter—but the fact that he was potentially throwing his career away to stand up for you was okay by me."

What?

My mouth opened, but I closed it a second later. There was a rush of guilt that went through me, thinking Theo was throwing away his career for me. Then, came the undeniable fear that I was going to lose the one person who was on my side no matter what.

"He went off—respectfully. He was poised as he dished out all that you had told him about your nonexistent father and the financial hardships you have gone through with your mother. He was quick to put everything on the line for you." Tom's sigh was an exact replica of mine, and I sucked up my tears as he continued to talk. "That's when I realized that the story you've been told isn't true, Claire."

I looked over at him immediately. "What are you talking about?"

He caught my eye, and it was like he knew something I didn't. His face was merciful, and truth was in his eyes, burning as brightly as a blue flame. "I didn't abandon you. I didn't even get a chance to meet you."

Each word plucked a stitch from a wound that I wasn't aware was there.

"That's not what I was told." My voice was shaky, and I glanced at the auditorium door, knowing my meeting was approaching.

"I've gathered as much. I'm not sure how much you know of me—"

I interrupted him. "Brilliant hockey player. You were destined for the NHL but got into a car accident and destroyed the nerves along your spine, and it ruined your career on ice, but you worked up into the position you are in now being one of the most idolized men in hockey."

Tom's eyebrows flew up, and he smiled. "Wow, Google search?"

I bit the inside of my cheek to keep myself from mirroring his smile because there was nothing to smile about in the moment, but for some reason, I felt the teeniest, tiniest blip of something warm.

"Theo."

"Ah." Tom nodded. "I see." He looked over at me once more. "That's all true, but you're missing what happened after the crash." He rubbed a hand over his face in apparent exhaustion. "I'm not sure how to say this without being insensitive or seeming angry because I've been angry for the last twenty years of my life. The anger has been fleeting, but seeing you sitting here looking at me like I left you makes it hard to ignore." He pinched the bridge of his nose before dropping his hand to his lap. "Your mother left me." I stared at the little crinkles of age around his eyes. "Right after the crash, while I was in the hospital. She was seven months pregnant with you."

"That doesn't make any sense. Why would she do that?" The number of times I'd had to untangle a mess of words that flew from her mouth that resulted in her cursing my father for pushing her into single parenting and how she had to raise me herself made zero sense if she was the one who was responsible.

I looked up at Tom again after trying to find an explanation. "Did you cheat on her? Did you abuse her? Did you…" I ran every route, and each time I threw out a variation of a potential truth, he winced.

"What? No. Of course not!" He glanced at me briefly.

"I'm sorry." I shrugged, throwing my arms over my chest again. "Then I don't understand."

"She was concerned that she wouldn't be able to take care of a…cripple…and a baby all on her own, and at first, I understood. I wasn't in a good place after the crash, and I thought her concerns were valid."

Wait, what?

"Are you telling me that my mother—who has told me time and time again that you left us because you didn't love us—lied?"

"Yes." He threw his hand out in frustration but lowered it quickly, as if he were hiding his anger. "The way it played out wasn't how it was supposed to go. When Angela addressed her concerns, I told her I understood and that I didn't blame her for wanting what was best for you. I did too. Before she left that evening, we'd talked things through. I told her she didn't have to take care of me and that I understood where she was coming from. She was right. I didn't have much to offer either of you as I was lying in a hospital bed with my future completely obliterated. But I *never* would have let her walk out that door if I knew she'd take off the next day. She changed her last name and moved into a town that I didn't even know existed. I didn't realize she was going to cut me out of your life completely." Tom took a breath. "I'm sorry it took me so long to pull together the resources to find you."

I placed my head in my hands, trying to process the information. Anger roared in the back of my mind at my mother's stupidity. I tore my face from my palms and looked over Tom, who was peeking at me curiously. "She has *no* idea where you ended up."

Tom's forehead furrowed, and I prodded forward.

"Otherwise, I wouldn't have grown up the way I did."

I stood up with rising resentment. I wasn't sure if I should have been understanding, or angry, or both. There was no way in hell that my mother would have stayed away from my father this long if she knew that he was as successful as he was. She wasn't as shallow as it seemed, but money was the biggest obstacle in our life—always. Things could have been so different if she had stayed, or at the very least, stayed in touch. He was my father after all.

Tom stood, holding onto his cane with a strong hand and an even stronger brow line. "How did you grow up?"

"Poor."

His face fell, and I began to back away from him.

"I have to go to my meeting," I explained. "And then I need to go home to talk to my mother." I needed confirmation. I needed to understand my mother's decisions.

Tom nodded as he watched me head toward the auditorium doors, seeming to give me space. There was a hint of fear there, as if he was afraid he'd never see me again.

"Here." I quickly walked over to the empty reception area in the lobby and tore off a piece of the sign-in paper. I scribbled my number on it and rushed back to hand it to him, knowing I was late to my meeting, but somehow, it seemed so trivial of me to worry about being the lead soloist in the show at this point. "That's my number."

Tom held the piece of paper in his free hand and looked at it as if it were a piece of gold, but I said nothing else as I propelled around and headed for the doors.

"Claire, wait."

I peered over my shoulder as he stared at the ripped paper. "Theo is refusing to come to the team tryouts unless I fix what I broke between you two." His eyes flew to mine in panic. "I'm not telling you this so he will join my team. That doesn't matter to me as much as it probably means to him. I'm telling you this because it's obvious that he loves you, and love is hard to come by in a world like this."

My eyes welled up, but I only nodded at him before turning my back and heading into my meeting to think of nothing regarding dance and everything regarding my mother, Tom, and the guy who literally threatened to give up his dream for me.

41

THEO

My EFFORT TO fix everything was unavailing, and every day felt futile in the sense that not much mattered when you couldn't adapt to the bitter void in your life. The feeling felt familiar but not in the way that a hug from your elderly grandmother felt after not seeing her for several years. It felt familiar like a bad dream that you've been in before, waking with the same paralyzing feeling of fear.

Claire hadn't answered any of my texts or calls, and although I was trying not to seem obsessive and compulsive when it came to seeing her, I looked for her each time I crossed the campus with my backpack draped over my shoulder. I scanned the auditorium parking lot during my morning run, and every time I opened my dorm door, my stomach would fill with uneasy nerves, wondering if she was inside, ready to spar with me over everything that had happened.

Her last words to me felt as jarring to me as my helmet did slamming against the ice during practice. "Ah, fuck." I winced, rolling onto my back. I stared at the bright lights above and cursed under my breath as Coach threw a hissy fit from across the rink.

"Wolf! What the fuck are you doing?" Then he mumbled something as I pulled myself to a sitting position and tore my gloves off, wincing at my sore muscles. "Practice is over!"

Most of the team skated off and disappeared, but ice flung up as Aasher skated over to me quickly. "Nice fall."

I didn't have the energy to lash out a response.

"You better not play like this at the game tomorrow night, or you can toss that try-out spot out the window, bro. No blue jersey for you."

Aasher had no idea what had really gone down between Claire and me, and Coach had no idea that I'd all but told Tom Gardini to suck my dick if he thought I would play on his team after he came into my life and took away the one thing that made me do a double-take.

Was it all Tom's fault that the trust between Claire and me had been ruined? Not necessarily, but he had put me in a shitty position—something he admitted himself. I'd give him props. He was a decent man with seemingly sensible morals, but how could I play for a man who was at the core of Claire's suffering? The look of shock on her face after the party was something I felt down to my bones. It cut me like a knife against my throat when her face paled at the thought that I'd bargained her for a spot on Tom's team.

She didn't know me well enough if she thought I'd do something like that to her.

Ignoring Aasher's reminder of playing like shit, I got up and snatched up my gloves and hockey stick and skated away before saying, "I'll play fine tomorrow."

"Even without Claire in the stands?"

I snapped a lethal glare in his direction, and he rolled his eyes. "So, it *is* about her. I don't want to say I told you so, but..."

"Aasher," I warned.

"Come on. What did you expect?" Aasher pulled me back by my jersey, and I had no fight left in me to rear back my elbow and clock him, although the thought did cross my mind. "You two were fake dating to begin with. It was never real."

Aasher sounded a lot like Claire when she turned to me at the end of the hall while her smug ex was standing there looking as triumphant as I did after winning a hockey game. *"We were never supposed to last anyway, right?"*

I pushed Aasher away and mentally prepared for a lashing from Coach followed by suspicious looks from the team over my performance. I needed to get my shit together for tomorrow's game. After all, I was going to have to start playing to impress the other scouts because I refused to be on Tom Gardini's team.

"Thank fuck you got your shit together." Ford threw his fist up, and I bumped my knuckles against his, forcing out a smile. "I was afraid you'd go out on the ice still mending that broken heart you're pretending you don't have."

"Ford," Emory warned. "Don't poke fun. One day you'll get your heart broken by a girl, and knowing you, you'll cry."

Ford shrugged. "Your sister is the only one who can break my heart."

The locker room broke out in laughter as Emory stood

up with anger. Ford laughed loudly as he dodged out of the way at the last minute, pissing Emory off even more.

Ford wasn't wrong in his assumption. I was mending some fucked-up shit inside my chest, but if there was one constant about me, it was that I was able to throw my emotions onto the ice instead of allowing them to pull me under. I'd been like that since I was a young child with memories that feasted on my sleep, causing wicked nightmares.

I'd admit, though, it felt a lot better to win, knowing that Claire was in the stands, rooting for me.

"Have you seen Claire at all? She still hasn't been back to the room?" Aasher had bent down low, trying to shield the conversation from everyone who wasn't paying attention to Ford running around the locker room from Emory. I shook my head, avoiding eye contact.

"And she hasn't answered your calls?"

"Nope." My answer was backed with anger, so I brushed past everyone with my shit still half out of my hockey bag, pulled my hood up high as I slipped out Coach's back door that he refused to let anyone use, and headed straight for my car.

The night was cold, and a fog of breath left my mouth as I sighed with frustration. I opened my car door, hopped inside, and opted to go straight to my room instead of to a party. But instead of taking a right at the stop sign to head to Dorothy Hall, I found myself turning left and driving past the auditorium first and The Bex next.

My foot slammed on the brake when I saw her old Toyota parked in the parking lot for the first time all week. Someone honked at me from behind, seeming to restart my heart, and I jumped into action and pulled into the spot beside hers. *Fuck, now what?*

Did I go inside and make a grand gesture? Did I get on one knee and spill my heart to her? Or did I play it cool and have her come to me? Would she even come to me? Her parting the other night definitely sounded as final as a good-bye, but surely she had more to say after she'd cooled down and figured some things out, right?

I shook my head and shoved my hoodie back, running my hands through my hair. I climbed out of my car and began walking to the door to The Bex, still having no idea what I was going to do when I saw her. My pulse rammed behind my skin as I watched the few waitresses that often worked alongside Claire hustle back and forth from the counter to the seating area, and the smell of fried food and beer filled my senses as I walked through the door. There was clapping and hollering over our win when everyone saw it was me, but I ignored them all as I searched for her.

Where are you, Bryant?

I caught a quick glimpse of Angie's face when she saw me, and in that quick moment, I watched the sharp switch of emotions move from relief to panic. When I landed on the booth in the back corner, I stumbled backward, seeming to lose my footing.

My face stayed steady, but every one of my sore muscles screamed in agony as my body stiffened. Claire's pretty pink lips were parted as she placed her hands on top of the table, and when I saw Chad look over his shoulder at me, I wanted to burn The Bex to ashes.

There was chaos around me. Fans came up and patted me on the shoulder, telling me, *"Good game,"* and asking me about the next one, but not a single word left me. I stood in the same spot and stared at Claire as she snapped my heart in two. I didn't think it was possible to feel your heart breaking, but it was. I felt every last snap with every blink of her eye, but instead of going over and ripping her worthless ex out of the booth, I knew I was a better man than that. So, I turned around, got in my car, and went back to our dorm room, hoping she didn't come home.

42

CLAIRE

"WELL, THAT WAS DRAMATIC," Chad said, pushing himself into the back of the booth. I wanted to take my drink and pour it on his lap for the third time in ten minutes.

Seeing the look on Theo's face made me want to run after him, but instead, I stayed unmoving across the table from Chad and continued on with what I came here to do. In true Chad fashion, he wasn't taking no for an answer, but what he didn't realize was that he didn't have power over me any longer.

No one did.

I was growing impatient, even more so with Theo ripping out of the parking lot with thoughts going through his head that weren't accurate at all. I cleared my throat and raised my eyebrows at my ex.

"You were saying that your parents called."

Chad took his glasses off and slipped them into the front

pocket of his polo. I grabbed my glass of soda and took a mouthful, preparing myself for what was to come.

"They told me that your mother resigned."

"I am aware," I countered.

His eyebrows edged upward in surprise. "Did you have something to do with it?"

I shook my head because I didn't have anything to do with it—not necessarily. "I didn't tell her to quit, but I did inform her of our situation."

Chad glanced away nervously. "Our situation?"

My mother surprised me. When I showed up at home, she was just getting in from cleaning Mr. Yates's estate. Her hair was in a messy bundle on top of her head, and her cheeks were shimmering with dried sweat. She paused in the doorway and dropped her cleaning supplies before pulling me in for a familiar hug, only to drop her arms a few seconds later when she realized something was wrong.

I'd started off with Chad, explaining everything that had happened at the start of the semester. Part of me was fearful she'd tell me to suck it up because it was obvious that my mother wanted a life of wealth for me, but instead, she was appalled, and it didn't take longer than a second for her to snatch her phone, call Chad's mother, and immediately tell her that her son was a misogynistic, unfaithful asshole and that her daughter deserved better. She also informed her that she would no longer be cleaning their house, and she was more than welcome to spread rumors to her wealthy friends and ruin my mother's complete clientele. I couldn't contain my laughter when she added in the part where she told her that Chad must have learned such repulsive behavior from her husband, considering she had found used condoms in their guest house that he often frequented.

My mother tossed her phone to the side, and we both laughed for several minutes, but the laughter slowly faded when I eased into the next conversation, knowing it was something that wasn't even remotely funny. I wasn't sure what I expected to come out of her mouth when I told her that Tom had found me, but what I had hoped for, though, was that there was a more logical reason for her decision to completely cut him out of my life. I needed there to be a reason that wasn't vindictive or unforgiving.

And thankfully, there was. My mother wasn't a saint, and she was well aware of the hurt that she likely caused my father by taking me, but her reasoning wasn't all that hard to understand. Her eyes welled up when she walked me through her decision of leaving, and it was the first time in my entire life that I heard her speak of my father with regret instead of anger. It all came down to self-preservation. She said he was understanding of her concerns that she wouldn't be able to provide and take care of the both of us, and so when he accepted her decision, she knew that if she didn't completely remove herself from his life, she wouldn't have the willpower to give me all that I deserved—a roof over my head, food in my stomach, and the possibility to have a semi-normal life with an even better future.

Things were wonky right now, but they were at least out in the open.

"Claire," Chad snapped, pulling me back to reality. "What do you mean, '*our situation*'?"

"Chad…" I grabbed a hold of his hand and gave it the smallest squeeze, even though I didn't necessarily want to touch him. "I don't love you."

At first, I saw the anger, but then I saw the fear. His hand quickly came out from below mine, and he put both of his on top, caging my palm against the table. "Yes, you do, and I love you. Look, I'm sorry for..." He sighed. "I'm sorry for cheating on you. And I'm sorry for everything after. Seeing you with him made me realize what you must have felt when you saw me, and I hate myself for it."

I shook my head in denial because Chad was wrong. Was it a knock to my confidence when I found him cheating? Absolutely. Was I drowning in betrayal and doubting nearly every person I came into contact with because of his actions? Of course. But that wasn't love. What Chad had felt for me wasn't love, and my heart didn't break in the way that it did when I saw the look of hurt on Theo's face last weekend when I told him we were never supposed to last.

"You don't love me."

Chad began to panic as he leaned in closer to me and dropped his voice to argue. "Yes, I do."

"Love isn't forcing someone to give up their wants and dreams for your own, and love isn't trying to change someone to be what you want. Love isn't blackmailing either."

"Okay, fine. I won't try to change you. I like you the way you are."

I stood up in annoyance and peered down at him. I didn't have to sit here and listen to him. I didn't have to worry about my mother and her bills because, for the first time in her life, she opted to grow up.

"Chad, one day you'll find someone that you won't want to change. You'll find someone that you're willing to give up every last dream and hope for, even when they tell you not to." I tapped the top of his hand. "That's love, Chad. Not this."

He said my name a few times before I made it to the door to The Bex, but I kept heading to my car, fumbling with my keys to get to the dorm to be with the one person who taught me that sacrificing your hopes and dreams only meant something when no one expected it.

———

I slipped past the first floor and ran up the stairs, determined to tell Theo that what he just saw at The Bex wasn't at all what he thought it was. The last thing I said to Theo was that he and I were never supposed to last, but I realized pretty quickly that what we shared had nothing to do with how it started and only how it ended.

I ran my hands down the front of my jeans and wiped the sweat off, noticing how eerily quiet the hallway was. No one was loitering around, and everyone's doors were shut. It was quiet. So quiet I could hear my labored breathing and thrumming pulse.

As soon as my hand reached out to our door handle, though, I felt my heart slip to the floor. There was a lump the size of a boulder sitting in my throat, cutting off my breathing at the sight of my favorite light-purple scrunchie hanging loosely on the doorknob. I blinked back the tears, but instead of turning around and running like I usually did when a problem presented itself, I pulled the scrunchie off and flew inside the door, preparing myself for the sight.

"Are you serio—" I stopped in my tracks as Theo flew up from the floor with nothing but a pair of black athletic shorts on. His muscular chest glistened with sweat, and his brown hair stuck to his forehead before he wiped it with the back of his hand, showing off his splotchy cheeks and furrowed brow.

"Claire?"

I stood in the doorway and flung my attention to every corner of the room, looking for whatever girl he'd brought home. When I came up empty handed, I let my shoulders deflate, and we both looked down at the scrunchie in my hand before I let it fall to the floor.

"I put it on there so you wouldn't come in here."

I hated the sound of his voice because it sounded so discouraging, and I noticed the way he kept pulling away, like he couldn't stand to look at me. My lip trembled, but I clenched my teeth and took a step farther inside our room, keeping the door open in case I needed to bolt.

"Why?" I asked.

Theo stayed in the exact spot I found him in, and my hand stayed on the doorknob, my grip tightening with dread. "I wasn't sure I could take seeing you after you were with him. Why do you think I'm in here, doing push-ups, after already tiring out my body on the ice?"

I managed to force a swallow through my tight throat as Theo took a step toward me, finally keeping his sights set on me.

"I wanted to rip you out of the booth so fucking bad I couldn't see straight. I wanted to take you back to our room and kiss you until you fully understood how I felt about you, but instead, I got inside my car and forced myself to drive away so I didn't turn back around and pummel his smug face because goddamnit, Claire. He doesn't deserve you! You deserve better."

A tear slipped down my cheek, and I quickly moved to brush it away, but Theo erased the rest of the space between us and beat me to it, keeping his hand on my face.

"Can't you see your worth? He sure can't. You deserve someone who will do anything to make you happy. Not someone who likes to watch you hurt for their own sick games. You need someone who—"

I stopped him mid-sentence. "Someone who refuses to

join their dream team in the NHL because he thinks the owner of the team hurt his fake girlfriend?"

Theo didn't linger long on what I'd said, because he continued to rant with his hand tightening on my cheek like he was afraid to let me go. "You have never just been my fake girlfriend, and you know it."

"You're not giving up your dream for me, Theo. That's ludicrous."

He scoffed, his hand shaking against my face. "You don't know me at all if you think I'm going to play for someone who hurt you."

I shook my head. "Stop." My heart began to pulse something hot through my body, and the thought of letting him stand here, thinking that I didn't care for him in the way he cared for me, made me want to double over.

"No, I'm not gonna stop," he urged. "You don't have to be mine, but I'm yours, and you're just gonna have to deal with it. My dreams and goals mean absolutely *nothing* if you leave this room thinking I wouldn't give up every last one to show you your worth."

A tight sob climbed up my throat, and my shoulders caved as I stood, peering up at the absolute purest, most worthy person I had ever known.

"Please don't cry. You don't understand what it does to me." His face was a mix of worry and confusion.

I shook my head before letting a breath fly from my mouth. "Am I included in your future?"

Theo's other hand cupped my cheek, and he had me in a hold so tight I couldn't move even if I had wanted to. "Haven't I proven that? I'd do anything for you, and I'd do anything to get you to stop crying, even if that means letting you walk out that door and into someone else's arms. If you're happier with him, go."

"No."

"What?"

"I was sitting at The Bex with Chad to tell him that whatever he thought he felt for me wasn't love. It wasn't love when I stayed with him to secure my mother's job, and it wasn't love when he threatened me into allowing him to go off with other girls until the end of the school year because of the money my mom owed his family. But I'm so thankful he did, because now I know what love is."

Theo's eyes shifted back and forth between mine before he dropped his hand to my hips and pulled me farther into the room. The door almost shut behind me, but Theo bent down at the last second and swiped the purple scrunchie off the floor with a quick jab of his hand and hung it on the doorknob before turning around and sending me a fiery look that promised a future with him that I never expected.

"Tell me you're mine, Bryant. Tell me you trust me, and tell me that you can feel how much I love you just from the way I look at you."

"I'm yours, Theo. I always was."

Theo swooped me up and threw me onto his bed before pinning my arms above my head. "And by the way"—he brushed his lips over mine—"we were always meant to last, Bryant."

EPILOGUE

CLAIRE

I HAD the best seats in the Blues' home arena. Well, techni-cally, I didn't, but that was only because I refused to take any more of Tom's money—considering he offered to pay my senior year tuition so I could focus on studying—and sit in the most luxurious spot available, designed specifically for family and friends of the players. Not to mention, I wanted to be in the middle of the crowd, right smack dab in the midst of all the energy.

"It's been a very long time since I've been to a hockey game." My mom sighed from beside me, but I could tell by the way she leaned forward, with her eyes set on the ice, that she was totally immersed.

I scanned the ice for my favorite guy: *number 15*. It wasn't his first game playing in the NHL, but it was the first game that I had dragged my mother to and only the second game I had been able to attend. My senior year wasn't nearly as trying as my first three years in college because for the first time in a long time, I wasn't immersed in dance. After Tom had offered to pay for my tuition, I called off the second audition that Professor Petit had graciously given me after my fall last year and simply danced for fun instead of killing myself to be the best.

I was partially thankful that Theo's parents weren't able to attend this game because they were on babysitting duty—something they thoroughly enjoyed—but only because I knew this would be difficult for my mom. I was certain they were watching the game, though. Probably while wearing their Blues jerseys with Theo's name on the back. I bet his niece was cheering right along with them in her Blues-themed pajamas that Theo bought her.

I lingered on my mom's bright cheeks and noticed the happy color on them that I hadn't seen in a while. Even though she was honest about what had happened with Tom, it didn't mean things were okay. There was a lot of guilt that she carried with her over the years that seemed to only come out when she was halfway through a bottle of the cheapest Barefoot wine.

Thankfully, she still had most of her clients after the fallout between Chad and his parents. His mother may have connected mine with the rich folk of our hometown, but she wasn't so quick to destroy those working relationships—something I made a mental note of. I had no idea what had happened after I left Chad sitting at the booth at The Bex, or what had happened with his parents after my mom hastily quit being their housekeeper and spilled the secrets of Chad's father, but it seemed that Chad's mother wasn't as shallow as the men in her family, especially because she wiped the slate clean and told my mother the money owed to them was no longer a concern.

I gained the courage to pull my eyes from the ice again

and put my them back on my mom. "Did you watch...um...
Tom often? Before his accident?" *Before you left.*

It was all true. The rumors about Tom Gardini being
this almighty hockey player. And it was clearly obvious that
he was a man of good morals—something my mother never
dismissed after learning that he had come back for me after
all these years.

The first time they saw each other again, after twenty-
two years of being separated, was nothing less than uncomfortable. I was present for their conversation for no more
than five minutes before I excused myself and allowed them
to talk in private. There was a lot of apologizing, probably
some unshed anger, and a whole lotta awkwardness that I
wasn't sure what to make of. They made sure to remind me
that, although I was at the center of their world, their decisions weren't my fault, and I took that for what it was and
let them hash their problems out without the interference of
my feelings being present.

Tom was a good man. He'd asked me to bring my
mother to one of Theo's games, and I wasn't sure if it was
because he was still trying to create a stable relationship
between us, or if it was because he was giving my mother an
olive branch.

Either way, she was here, sitting beside me. Tom was up
in his special box as the team owner, and Theo had just
skated onto the ice with an ease that just about every other
hockey player envied. Butterflies filled me up to the brink,
and I smiled at the sight of the number 15 on the back of his
jersey.

"Yes," my mom finally answered my question, and I
knew her well enough to hear the resolute sadness that
followed the simple word. "I went to every single home
game."

I laughed, hardly able to picture her, at my age, sitting in the stands while watching a hockey game. For as long as I could remember, she *hated* sports, but now I understood why she stayed away. It would have been a painful reminder of the broken heart she was trying to mend while taking care of me. I couldn't imagine having to force myself to leave Theo, and sometimes the only emotion you could latch onto, to protect yourself, was anger.

"What?" My mom snapped her neck over to me. "Why is that funny?"

"It's just hard to picture you, at my age, watching a hockey game. It's hard to wrap my head around."

She rolled her eyes and shifted her body back toward the ice. "Well, just look in a mirror, baby. I looked *just* like you, sitting in a random seat in the arena with the tiniest little spark in my eye while watching the boy I loved play the sport he loved."

"You know," I started, easing my words out with caution, "Tom may have loved hockey, but to my knowledge, he loved you too."

Her laugh was sarcastic as she shifted in her seat, wearing the Blues shirt that Theo bought her. He may have gone a little crazy with the Blues attire for the entire family, but that was what I loved about him. His intentions were always so good. "That was many, many years ago."

I shrugged, watching Theo and his team get hyped up for the game. He skated over to the other team, and I knew exactly what player he was heading for. Emory was the goalie for the opposing team. They briefly tapped gloves and nodded at one another before Theo headed in the other direction, back over to his team.

The lights began to get brighter, and I knew the game was going to begin soon. My heart did a flip, and my stomach filled with nerves. It was as if I were the one playing the game instead of Theo, but I was so connected with my boyfriend that I felt what he felt. When he was nervous, I was nervous. When he was happy, I was happy.

Everything began to fade away as I watched each navy-blue jersey skate into a horizontal line, gearing up for the sports announcers' opening words and the national anthem. The white ice grew blurry, and everything else faded as I unknowingly stood. Theo pulled off his helmet and held it between his elbow and side, freeing his hand to run it through his unkempt brown hair. Excitement surged up my throat, and my smile was wide when we locked eyes. His grin was at the center of my core, and when he winked at me from the ice, my cheeks burned. *God, I loved him.* And I knew he loved me too. There was never a doubt in my mind that Theo Brooks, the best hockey player in college hockey now destined to be the best player in the NHL, loved me. Hockey used to be his one true love, but he made damn sure to show me every single day that it was me instead. Don't get it wrong, though. He still loved hockey. And even though my father was the owner of the team he now played on, he took practice, conditioning, and each game seriously, not wanting anyone to think that he didn't deserve to have that jersey on his back.

My gasp was subtle when Theo tipped his chin, still grinning wickedly at me from the ice, and pointed his free hand in my direction. I glanced at the Jumbotron behind him and saw that the camera was zooming in on Theo's face. His lips mouthed the silent words, *"I love you,"* and then it quickly switched over to me and my parted lips and pink cheeks.

I smiled almost instantly, taking my attention from the Jumbotron and putting it back on Theo. I mouthed the words back, and the entire arena roared—even the other team's fans.

My mom whispered from beside me just before the game started, and I couldn't help but latch onto her advice.

"Your father was right. One of the first things he said to me after twenty-two years of being apart was, *'Theo Brooks loves our daughter.'*" Her hand fell on top of mine, and she gave it a squeeze. "Don't make the same mistake we did. Keep that boy's hand tucked in yours, no matter what."

I squeezed back and nodded, knowing I would never let it go.

The End

AFTERWORD

Stay tuned for more Bexley U books by SJ Sylvis! Head to **sjsylvis.com** for information on upcoming releases!

ABOUT THE AUTHOR

S.J. Sylvis is an Amazon top 50 and USA Today bestselling author who is best known for her angsty new adult romances. She currently resides in Arizona with her husband, two small kiddos, and dog. She is obsessed with coffee, becomes easily attached to fictional characters, and spends most of her evenings buried in a book!

sjsylvis.com

ACKNOWLEDGMENTS

Per usual, I will list my family here first because they're the reason I wake up each day and laugh until I go to sleep at night. I love you and all of our time together—even if it's just playing a board game on a Sunday morning. <3

Lil, you're going next here because, without you, this book wouldn't have happened. You are the best alpha there is and I'm so thankful for you! You taught me all about hockey and you make me laugh every single time we talk (which is usually daily, LOL).

To my close author friends (you know who you are)— thank you for your unwavering support and loyal friendship. I love you all so much! (& *shout out to S. Massery and Veronica Eden for letting me use their hockey teams in my book!!!*)

Emma & Erica—I LOVE YOU BOTH so much and all of your feedback on Weak Side. Not only do you both help strengthen my work but you're my biggest cheerleaders!!

To my fabulous editor, proofreader/pa, and publicist— thank you beyond belief for everything you do for my books/career! I am not sure where I would be with you 3!

Last but not least—thank you to all the readers, PR companies, bloggers, etc., who helped spread the word about Weak Side (and my other books!!). I enjoy every single one of your posts, messages, and reviews and truly adore all of you!